Decolonial Animal Ethics in Linda Hogan's Poetry and Prose

Decolonial Animal Ethics in Linda Hogan's Poetry and Prose is a plea for an urgent redefinition of human-animal relations on the basis of a nonanthropocentric animal ethic embraced by premodern Indigenous communities but depreciated by coloniality. Without decolonial revisions of animal subjectivity and personhood, the animal genocide can never truly stop. It is also a close reading of Linda Hogan's poetry and prose in search of the coordinates of a decolonized animal ethic which would foster interspecies becoming. Having defined the recurring tropes, motifs, and attitudes that underpin Hogan's treatment of nonhuman animals, the book moves on to trace the way she depicts the human-animal bond, especially in the face of the destructive anthropogenic impact. The major questions guiding the analysis of Hogan's *oevre* are as follows: who are the animals we share our earthly lives with; what can they teach us about ourselves; how can animals guide us toward more sustainable futures; and what are the conditions of possibility of an interspecies, human-animal thriving. This book will be of interest to scholars and students of Indigenous Studies, Decolonial Studies, Animal Studies, Ecocriticism, Anthropocene Studies, as well as readers of Linda Hogan's literary works.

Małgorzata Poks is Assistant Professor at the Institute of Literary Studies, Faculty of Humanities, at the University of Silesia in Katowice, Poland. She received her PhD in Literary Studies from Maria Curie-Skłodowska University in Lublin, Poland. She is the author of *Thomas Merton and Latin America: A Consonance of Voices* (Winner of the International Thomas Merton Award) and *Kobieta, która czuwa nad światem* (2021), a translation of Linda Hogan's *A Woman Who Watches Over the World*.

Routledge Studies in World Literatures and the Environment
Series Editors: Scott Slovic and Swarnalatha Rangarajan

D. H. Lawrence, Ecofeminism and Nature
Terry Gifford

Religion, Narrative, and the Environmental Humanities
Bridging the Rhetoric Gap
Matthew Newcomb

Nuclear Cultures
Irradiated Subjects, Aesthetics and Planetary Precarity
Pramod K. Nayar

Contagion Narratives
The Society, Culture and Ecology of the Global South
Edited by R. Sreejith Varma and Ajanta Sircar

Women and Water in Global Fiction
Edited by Emma Staniland

Oil and Modern World Dramas
From Petro-Mania to Petro-Melancholia
Alireza Fakhrkonandeh

Reading Contemporary Environmental Justice
Narratives from Kerala
R. Sreejith Varma

(Eco)Anxiety in Nuclear Holocaust Fiction and Climate Fiction
Doomsday Clock Narratives
Dominika Oramus

Decolonial Animal Ethics in Linda Hogan's Poetry and Prose
Toward Interspecies Thriving
Małgorzata Poks

For more information about this series, please visit: https://www.routledge
.com/Routledge-Studies-in-World-Literatures-and-the-Environment/book
-series/ASHER4038

Decolonial Animal Ethics in Linda Hogan's Poetry and Prose

Toward Interspecies Thriving

Małgorzata Poks

Routledge
Taylor & Francis Group

NEW YORK AND LONDON

First published 2024
by Routledge
605 Third Avenue, New York, NY 10158

and by Routledge
4 Park Square, Milton Park, Abingdon, Oxon, OX14 4RN

Routledge is an imprint of the Taylor & Francis Group, an informa business

© 2024 Małgorzata Poks

ISBN: 978-1-032-42779-9 (hbk)
ISBN: 978-1-032-42780-5 (pbk)
ISBN: 978-1-003-36425-2 (ebk)

DOI: 10.4324/9781003364252

Typeset in Sabon
by Deanta Global Publishing Services, Chennai, India

Contents

Preface   *vii*

Introduction   1

PART 1
The Radiant Lives with Animals: The Poetry of Linda Hogan   35

1   1970s: *Calling Myself Home*   37

2   1980s: Birth of an Ecofeminist   48

3   1990s: Wildness   66

4   2000s: *Rounding The Human Corners*   85

5   2010s: "I Want Mercy In This World"   102

PART 2
Reclaiming Animality, Revisioning Humanity: The Novels
of Linda Hogan   125

6   *Mean Spirit*: Decolonizing Nonhuman Animals   127

7   *Solar Storms*: Reclaiming Wild, Becoming Human   143

8   Of *Power* and Sacrifice: Rethinking Carnivora,
    Expanding Sociality   156

9   *People of the Whale*: Transformational Beings and
the Future of Humanity   171

Conclusions: Implications for Interspecies Thriving in the
Literary Works of Linda Hogan   183

Bibliography   187
Index   196

Preface

The moral covenant of reciprocity calls us to honor our responsibilities for all we have been given, for all that we have taken. It's our turn now, long overdue. … Whatever our gift, we are called to give it and to dance for the renewal of the world.

(Robin Wall Kimmerer, *Braiding Sweetgrass* 384)

This project is a response to Robin Wall Kimmerer's challenge. This is my dance for the renewal of the world, my love song to all my relations, in humble recognition of and gratitude for the overabundance of gifts received. While my training determines the book's academic format, the content and choice of methodologies are informed by a decades long practice of listening to the land and a passionate sense of kinship with the more-than-human worlds. Out of this listening grew a deepening realization that Westernized stories about the land and its inhabitants are profoundly wrong. The missing link in our cultural setup is a willingness to engage in a dialog, to hear the other-than-human side of the story and to re-adjust the lenses accordingly. Unless we re-learn, under the guidance of traditional knowledge keepers, what Kimmerer calls "the grammar of animacy" (48–59), there will be no end to the ongoing devastation of the planet, with all its life forms on it, including humans—the younger brothers and sisters who have been entrusted with the task of caring for all creation.

Still, we linger, letting Windigo sneak up on us and freeze our hearts instead. Windigo—the monster of insatiable consumption from traditional Algonquian lore—has "trick[ed] us into believing that belongings will fill our hunger, when it is belonging that we crave," as Kimmerer puts it. There is only one cure for the Windigo psychosis, continues the botanist and member of the Citizen Potawatomi Nation: gratitude. When we acknowledge with gratitude the gifts of the natural world, they will be enough to sustain and feed all. "No one goes hungry" (Kimmerer 378).

Although I am a white European woman with academic training, I come to traditional Indigenous knowledges as a student eager to learn. I recognize their wisdom and the healing power of stories. I too am indigenous to the place where I live, where I have lived all my life—a small community at the edge of a forest, where my Dad took me berry-picking and mushrooming, and my Grandma taught me about herbs. I am deeply grateful for this.

This book is dedicated to my parents, Bronisława and Gerard Poks, and my maternal grandparents, Waleska and Paweł Nowak. Thank you for all the love you gave me. This dance is for you, too.

I also wish to acknowledge the abundant love I have received from the four-legged friends who share my life: Tosia, Aisha, Agatka, Misiek, and Reks, as well as those who are no longer with me but who will live forever in my heart. The list would be too long to compose, but I need to acknowledge Kajtek, my first dog. I was too young to know that love entailed responsibilities and I am so sorry I was not able to love you as you deserved to be loved. But you taught me some important steps of this dance and I will always keep you in my heart.

My very special thanks go to my colleague David Shauffler for his invaluable help with proofing the manuscript's first draft.

Every effort has been made to trace the copyright holders and obtain permission to reproduce quoted material.

Introduction

Contrary to commonly held beliefs, our attitude to nonhuman animals is not solely, or even mainly, a question of ethics. At the threshold of the third millennium's third decade we can no longer deny that it is a political issue *par excellence*. The way we treat other animals results from our construction and subsequent naturalization of the ontological difference between humans, as the supposed crown of creation, and animals—the abjected Other whose lives have purely instrumental value. Giving us dominion over the more-than-human world, this "most different difference" (Wolf 23) provides the matrix for the operation of all power, as Foucauldian scholars have demonstrated.[1]

As a discursive category, the human comes into being in opposition to and through subjugation of the nonhuman other. It would follow that an effort to imagine an interspecies cosmopolis based on equality and justice for all must start with the questioning of human supremacy and the subsequent dismantling of the ontological difference. As I will argue in the course of this chapter, this must be done in dialog with traditional tribal cultures that have lived in intimate relation with more-than-human worlds for thousands of years.

In Search of an Interspecies Cosmopolis: From Westernized to Indigenous Perspectives

Interspecies cosmopolitanism—understood, after Eduardo Mendieta, as an effort to build a pluriversal, nonhierarchical world in which multiple forms of life can coexist—is all the more urgent in a world of already entangled biosystems, multispecies contact zones, and human/more-than-human interfaces. Epistemologically, as Mendieta explains, cosmopolitanism questions the monopoly of one worldview while, in the moral-ethical perspective, it implies cohabitation and coexistence. "To act and to know the world from a cosmopolitan standpoint is to ask oneself about the conditions and duties of co-existing and cohabitating" (Mendieta 276). Before pursuing the question of possibility of a nonviolent coexistence between humans and other animals in a hypothetical cosmopolis of the future, we

DOI: 10.4324/9781003364252-1

should ask why, in spite of more than a century of welfarist campaigns, interspecies relationships in the Westernized world are still marked by violence.

The operation of the "most different difference" can be seen most clearly in times of life-threatening epidemics: while people infected with contagious diseases are rushed to hospitals despite the health hazards such patients pose to the medics in attendance, nonhuman animals are routinely put to death. When cases of bird flu, mad cow disease, or African swine fever are identified, so-called 'preventive culling' takes place. What this technical phrase means is that entire flocks or herds are 'stamped out,' with no attempt being made to isolate and save uninfected individuals. Obviously, while human lives matter, the lives of farmed animals matter only in the context of food production and food security. It is estimated that in the 1990s, when mad cow disease reached epidemic proportions, in the United Kingdom alone ca. 4.5 million cattle were 'preventively culled,' of which only 200,000 proved to have been infected ("Co wiemy").

More telling evidence of the operation of the ontological difference is the imbalance in the statistics available. While information on the human death toll of contemporary zoonotic pandemics is updated every day, the unimaginable numbers of animals put to death in an effort to contain the spread of these diseases are hard to find. Animal 'culling' happens off-screen, the animals' deaths invisible and purposefully ignored as a sort of collateral mortality. This has been the case with chickens and wild boars killed as 'preventive measures' to stop the spread of avian flu and African swine fever, respectively. As for the latter, although in all probability the disease is transmitted mainly in pig breeding facilities rather than by animals living in the wild, in some countries a ruthless boar depopulation campaign has been launched, instigated by farmers and breeders who were frequently themselves to blame for the pandemic, as they had failed to maintain appropriate biosecurity measures in their facilities. In Poland, where the wild boar extermination campaign has reached devastating proportions, the Supreme Chamber of Control revealed in January 2018 that 74% of pig farms had insufficient biosecurity measures (Jurszo 32). Yet the Ministry of Agriculture has waged a total war on boars, lifting the closed season and allowing culling in protected areas like national parks, with piglets and pregnant sows no longer excepted, in order to reach the planned wild boar population density of one specimen per ten square kilometers (32,000 specimens in total)—five times lower than the European norm. Zoologist Andrzej Elżanowski estimates that an animal whose life expectancy in the wild may reach 14–15 years and who, due to human persecution, often survives a bare year-and-a-half, will live even shorter now (Elżanowski 26).

The concept of animal genocide has been used, among others, by Jacques Derrida, ecofeminist Carol J. Adams, radical animal rights activists like Steve Best, veganarchists, and a number of thinkers and activists inspired by decolonial theories. Animal genocide is a daily occurrence on factory farms, and in slaughterhouses, research laboratories, and areas where invasive species live and proliferate. The terrifying reality of an ongoing animal genocide allows Dinesh Wadiwel, author of *The War Against Animals*, to conclude that humanity is at war with other animals. We eat, hunt, capture, and kill them because they are the spoils of war, he argues.

Wadiwel understands politics in the spirit of Michel Foucault, as "war pursued by other means" (Wadiwel 19). Following in Foucault's footsteps, he begins to theorize war from von Clausewitz's classical definition,[2] with the reservation that in liberal societies the power of the sword has been replaced by biopower, that is, power over life itself. In modern nation states, enmity and aggression have been sublimated through governmentality—the management of populations by means of appropriate policies. Thus, in the socio-political space life is now either fostered or else disallowed "to the point of death" (Foucault, qtd. in Wadiwel 24). Applying these considerations to the concept of human sovereignty, the war against animals theorized by Wadiwel can be seen as biopolitical, with the so-called welfare being nothing short of a "violence that claims to care" (Wadiwel 112).

Historically considered, the welfare movement was launched in England in 1824 with the founding of the Society for the Prevention of Cruelty to Animals. The budding struggle for animal rights required the creation of a consenting legal subject. Postcolonial critic Leela Gandhi's book chapter "Meat: A Short History of Animal Welfare at the Fin-de-Siècle" supplements Wadiwel's reflections with an element of intersectionality when she asserts that

> the history of late-nineteenth-century animal welfare gets caught up in the utilitarian project of producing a disciplinary society, one whose force is felt at home by the indigenous working class (incidentally through the evolution of legislative animal reform), and abroad by the colonized races.
>
> (*Affective Communities* 97)

She is quick to point out that governmentality, along with colonialism as its corollary, is a civilizing mission aimed at the creation of a civilized, enlightened society. In the name of this mission, the noncivilized Other (human and nonhuman) must be improved and refined, supposedly for their own good. However, it is the state and not the noncivilized Other him-/herself that defines what lies in his or her best interests. At this point

Gandhi corroborates Wadiwel's theorizing of welfare as violence disguised as care. Contrary to Foucault's conceptualization of pastoral power, the myth of the good shepherd is one of camouflaged brutality.

As Foucault argued in his 1977–1978 lectures delivered at the Collège de France, the origin of governmentality is to be found in pastoral power, which he understands as the opposite of sovereign power. Invoking the Judeo–Christian tradition, Foucault sees the shepherd as representing the essence of care—the shepherd loves his sheep and lays down his life for them (Clausewitz, *Security* 135–162). Wadiwel, however, faults Foucault for ignoring the perspective of the animal who is entangled in the dynamics of pastoral care. True, the shepherd watches his flock day and night; he feeds it, protects it, and saves it from predators, carries the disabled sheep in his arms, and knows each one by name. What Foucault overlooks, though, is the end result of all this care: healthy, happy, and safe sheep will produce more milk, wool, and meat, and this means that they will bring a larger profit. All in all, the shepherd's power over the life of his sheep is so refined that we call it benevolent. This is why Wadiwel believes that the hidden foundation of biopower is the *tension* between care and violence—contra Foucault, who saw opposition here. Ultimately, the author of *War Against Animals* believes that pastoral power is a certain modality of sovereign power. Both meet and merge in the concept of governmentality understood as the management of violence disguised as care.

Thus, care for industrially farmed 'livestock' may take the form of providing them with regular access to food and fresh water, maintaining appropriate lighting in their enclosures, keeping them clean and well ventilated, and controlling their reproduction through the process of artificial insemination of breeding stock with carefully selected genetic material and sterilization of the remaining stock. Subjugation, objectification, and commodification—such are the dark sides of care, the ultimate objective of which is not the good of animals but human profit and the pleasure derived from consuming animal products or using nonhuman animals for sport and recreation. The flourishing practice of Concentrated Animal Feeding Operations (CAFOs) is perhaps the best illustration of the oxymoronic expression 'animal welfare.' According to the US Department of Agriculture, CAFOs are agricultural enterprises where more than 1,000 'animal units'[3] are kept and raised in confinement for more than 45 days during the year ("Animal Feeding Operations").

Confinement in a closed space is a strategy of war, notes Wadiwel. The analogy between animal factory farms and human concentration camps is a trope well-known in the field of Animal Studies. In this respect Wadiwel's theorizing is indebted to Giorgio Agamben and his conceptualization of the concentration camp as a space which naturalizes the state of exception. Reduced to purely biological life, inmates of a concentration camp can be disposed of summarily, without recourse to standard legal procedures. The camp is the space of biopolitics *par excellence*, with every aspect of life—diet, work, sleep, movement, reproduction—subject to rigorous control. The same biopolitical mechanisms are at work in animal feeding operations, which makes them the epitome of this state of exception. Confined in CAFOs, farm animals have no rights save the enigmatic right to life. For them survival means a few months of pitiful existence in crowded, dark feedlots. For this reason Wadiwel calls the interconnected spaces of farms, research laboratories, and slaughterhouses an animal Gulag Archipelago (24). A death camp is not amenable to reform; it can only be demolished.

The violence inscribed in the operational structure of a Gulag Archipelago is consolidated and naturalized on the level of epistemology. It is the construction of the nonhuman animal as a lesser, utilitarian being that drives the war against animals, a war understood as a form of legitimate human sovereignty. The hierarchization of difference, contends Wadiwel, entails the absolutization of human dominance (Wadiwel 36). The token concessions we are willing to grant to animals in the name of welfare can in no way infringe on human sovereignty, as evidenced by such diabolical concepts as 'unnecessary suffering' or 'humane slaughter.' To drive the point home, it bears repeating that from the welfaristic perspective the killing of animals is not unethical. What is thought to matter is how the animals are put to death, not the very fact that this is done. Thus, rather than eliminating violence toward animals, welfarist reforms merely blunt its blade by making it legitimate. In conclusion, efforts to enhance animal welfare not only fail to undermine our structural dominance over the nonhuman other, but plainly enable it. We care for those we have subjugated and whom we profit from, argues Wadiwel.

The issue is further complicated by the fact that pro-animal campaigns tend to focus on negative rights, like the right to be free from pain. It is here that Canadian philosophers Sue Donaldson and Will Kymlicka locate the roots of the impasse confronting the animal welfare movement. In their *Zoopolis*, published in 2013, they advance a vision of a human-animal commonwealth built on positive rights and mutual respect. Instead of addressing the confusing assemblage of highly heterogeneous creatures we call animals as a single kind of legal subject, Donaldson and Kymlicka propose to ascribe a different legal status to three major groups of animals—domestic, liminal, and wild—in keeping with their different relationship to the human polis. According to the authors, the fullness of rights should be given to animals who accompany humans in our everyday lives, while species living in the wild should be completely free from human intervention and enjoy rights comparable to those granted to traditional Indigenous peoples. As for the third category, liminal or invasive species should qualify as benefactors of the same limited rights as those vested in denizens.

Although this proposal seems innovative and radical, it still operates within the liberal discourse of human supremacy, which sees war as an aberration rather than a permanent state of affairs. For this reason, Donaldson and Kymlicka's zoopolitical project has no value for the more radical endeavor of ending the war against animals altogether. Rights are a form of war reparations granted by victors to defeated populations, argue decolonial critics of *Zoopolis*.[4] The legalist approach advocated by Donaldson and Kymlicka merely naturalizes human dominance, claim its opponents. In this approach it is humans, anxious to maintain their supremacy, who decide what rights to grant and what rights to deny to the nonhuman other. Ultimately, *Zoopolis* consolidates the existing hierarchy of species and, by the same token, ensures the survivability of the existing mechanism of exclusions.

Wadiwel believes that to find viable solutions to the problem of animal suffering—solutions transcending the master-slave dynamic—we need to abandon liberal philosophy and look for inspiration in critical theory. Inspired by the Frankfurt School and the writings of Michel Foucault, some critical theorists hold that 'truth' is a political construct. The power elites within each society create an ideological worldview (called 'truth') to legitimate their domination over subjugated others. Remaining within his book's dominant metaphor, Wadiwel asks whether soldiers who question the 'truth' of war have any choice on the battlefield. Foucault sees desertion as a legitimate choice, a form of liberating counter-conduct, and in the context of the war against animals, desertion, Wadiwel believes, might mean the adoption of veg(etari)anism.[5] Unfortunately, even though abstention from consuming meat and other animal products dismantles the narrative of human difference, thereby successfully questioning the epistemic violence of the ruling legal order, it has practically no chance of becoming the diet of choice for the majority of humans.[6]

Another possible form of counter-conduct is truce. In contrast to the legalistic language of a peace treaty, which implies respect for laws imposed by the winners, a truce is fragile and temporary. In view of the undecided result of an armed conflict, a ceasefire opens a democratic space of equality in which a new political project can be devised. Such a project may take the form of a revised conceptualization of humanity.[7] Transcending biopolitics, such new conceptualizations of interspecies interaction would have to be based on mutual respect and encourage an interpenetration of the conflicted human-nonhuman worlds. According to Wadiwel, what can be glimpsed in the space of a truce is our common animality, which lies at the intersection of the human and the nonhuman animal. In other words, when the din of war subsides and the smoke of ideas clears for a while, we may finally realize that the animal is the future of the human.

Since welfare, understood as violence that cares, is expressive of bio-power and rooted in the idea of human dominance, the project of a democratic interspecies coexistence to be devised in the space of a truce could perhaps be inspired by premodern cultures, uncontaminated by modern binaries and based on respect for, and reciprocity with, nonhuman animal persons. The ceasefire imagined by Wadiwel may give the Westernized world a chance to reclaim some alternative political models that have been depreciated by modernity/coloniality. Treating more-than-human beings—animals, plants, earth, water, rocks—as agents and actors on the political stage, contemporary Indigenous movements advance an ontological pluralization of politics (Blaser 4; De la Cadena). The etymology of the word *tatanka*—the Lakota name for bison, meaning, literally, "He Who Owns Us"—clearly reverses the Western conception of human supremacy, along with our anthropocentric paradigm of managing nature's resources.

In contrast to modern constructions of human independence of, and power over, the natural world, traditional peoples believe themselves to be part of a never-ending network of mutuality, dependent on nonhuman others, whom they treat with due respect. Far from being reduced to a mere 'possession,' earth in this older conceptualization is a living, life-giving mother, permeated by the spirit, as are all other earth beings. As children of this mother, human beings belong to the world of nature and are dependent on it for their survival. In her publication *Interspecies Ethics* (2014), philosopher Cynthia Willett reminds us that Paleolithic, small-scale hunting communities coevolved with other species with whom they shared a habitat. Indigenous hunting-gathering communities maintained complex biosocial norms of solidarity across species. "This Paleolithic-era ethics has cosmopolitan consequences" (74), believes Willett, as coevolved, multispecies communities can perhaps inspire us with alternative social imaginaries where social carnivores are friends rather than foes. In the modern world's surviving pockets of traditional cultures, the good life (whether called *buen vivir*, *minobimaatisiiwin*, or something else) consists in a harmonious coexistence with the natural world. In the unpredictable world of nature, inhabited by a multitude of agential beings, the concept of human dominance would be ridiculous. Indigenous cosmologies can thus offer useful tools for theorizing a viable non-speciesist, anti-colonial (human-) animal ethics.

As a matter of fact, anthropologists working with Indigenous peoples have been among the first to signal a need to incorporate premodern ontologies into Westernized conceptualizations of reality. The ontological turn in social sciences has called for the recognition of the multiplicity of coexisting worlds and realities, each involving a different version of cosmopolitics. "The newer cosmopolitics," specify Shaffner and Wardle in their introduction to a collection of papers of the Open Anthropology

Cooperative, "is all about rethinking inter-entity relationships" (11). Defining ontology in terms of Deleuzian "becoming" (Kohn 312), the new ontologists argue against a singular knowable world and a singular humanity, welcoming each "cosmos" on a nonhierarchical basis. It is in this context that Eduardo Viveiros de Castro calls anthropology "the practice of the permanent decolonization of thought" (*Cannibal Metaphysics* 40). For the Amazonia natives among whom he conducted fieldwork, it is consciousness—or soul—that is common to all persons, human and non-human, while natures are multiple, each associated with the interpretive world of a particular embodied being. In other words, within a particular Indigenous culture each species sees and experiences a different world. It is not representations but the world that changes when different species look at reality.

In "Anthropology of Ontologies," Eduardo Kohn specifies that in view of the human-nonhuman entanglements, "ethical and political problems can no longer be treated as exclusively human problems." In the Anthropocene, he asserts, "new conceptual tools" (311) are necessary. The conceptual tools proposed by the new ontologists have allowed the growing interdisciplinary recognition of Indigenous eco-agency in Western academia and inspired the recent shift to multispecies ethnography. At the very least—apart from the already referenced *Cannibal Metaphysics* by Viveiros de Castro—such recent works deserve credit for their valuable contribution to the field as *How Forests Think: Toward an Anthropology Beyond the Human* by Eduardo Kohn or *Earth Beings: Ecologies of Practice Across Andean Worlds* by Marisol de la Cadena.

In parallel to anthropology's ontological turn, the humanities have registered the decolonial turn, with its call to epistemic delinking[8] (Mignolo) from Western modernity/coloniality and the corollary epistemic reconstruction of knowledges relegated to the margins of the Western episteme. From the perspective of aboriginal inhabitants of modern settler states, however, epistemic delinking is an empty gesture unless uncoupled from legitimizing of usurper states, founded as they are on the dispossession of tribal lands and the subsequent erasure of native worldviews and lifeways. To Indigenous scholar-activists the return of stolen land is a condition *sine qua non* of decolonization, understood as theory leading to action and vice versa. The stakes involved have been summed up by Azeezah Kanji in the following words: "neither nonhuman nor human colonial subjects can be 'recognized' into liberation by the settler state constituted through their subjugation."

Despite—or more correctly because of—the close association between racial discourses and the construction of animality as a category of social exclusion, the intersection between decoloniality and animal studies is a very recent research perspective. One of the first worldwide events that helped to put this new field on the map was a conference organized in 2016 at the University of Alberta, Canada. In the call for papers Chloë Taylor and Kelly Struthers Montford wrote: "Single-issue animal activist campaigns have often functioned to justify racism, xenophobia and exclusion, with, to adapt Gayatri Spivak's phrase, white humans saving animals from brown humans."[9] The list of conference participants was a "who's who" in the newly developing research area. These were, among others: Billy-Ray Belcourt, Kim TallBear, Maneesha Deckha, and Dinesh Wadiwel.[10] In 2019, on the other side of the globe—in Christchurch, New Zealand—a conference entitled "Decolonizing Animals" gathered scholars and activists from five continents, which further testifies to the urgency of the questions posed. Some book-length contributions to the growing body of scholarship in decolonial/Indigenous animal studies include: Susan McHugh and Wendy Woodward (eds), *Indigenous Creatures, Native Knowledges, and the Arts: Animal Studies in Modern Worlds* (2017), Aph Ko and Syl Ko, *Aphro-ism: Essays on Pop Culture, Feminism, and Black Veganism from Two Sisters* (2017), Alexis Pauline Grumbs, *Undrowned: Black Feminist Lessons from Marine Mammals* (2020), Zakkiyah Iman Jackson, *Becoming Human: Matter and Meaning in an Antiblack World* (2020), Amit R. Baishya and Suvadip Sinha (eds.), *Postcolonial Animalities* (2021). The work of Zoe Todd in the self-established field of Critical Indigenous Fish Philosophy[11] also needs to be highlighted.

To the best of my knowledge, an attempt to formulate the conceptual framework for an Indigenous/decolonial animal ethics has been initiated by Cree poet, scholar, and activist Billy-Ray Belcourt. In his pioneering article "Animal Bodies, Colonial Subjects" (2015) Belcourt advocates the dismantling of the settler state, with its underpinning ideology of white power, as a prerequisite for thinking about animal liberation. As demonstrated by Indigenous critics of Donaldson and Kymlicka's zoopolis, the very terminology used in debating the legal status of nonhuman animals (citizenship, sovereignty, rights, etc.) is steeped in a colonial genealogy. A professor of anthropology and American Indian Studies, Paul Nadasdy, in his polemical article "First Nations, Citizenship and Animals, or Why Northern Indigenous People Might Not Want to Live in Zoopolis," argues the necessity of changing—or decolonizing—the terms of the conversation about interspecies relations. To Indigenous peoples, animals have agency and subjectivity; they make their own, autonomous decisions and cannot be mastered. As should be evident in this brief overview of the field, the liberal discourse of zoopolis is doomed to recreate colonial relations and structures of power, subjugating Indigenous cosmologies to non-traditional interpretations of animal interests and animal welfare.[12] Belcourt further asserts that settler colonialism naturalized speciesism in order to erase the radicality of human-animal relations and their decolonial potential (9).

What should be stressed, however, is that despite centuries of destructive assimilationist policies, many traditional peoples of North America have resisted adopting economies based on large-scale animal exploitation. To Indigenous cultures food is sacred and ensouled. Rather than 'harvested,' it must be acquired respectfully, with observance of ancient pacts entered into at the dawn of time by the human and nonhuman ancestors. Obeying those ancient rules, native hunters will not willingly endanger ecological balance by overhunting and they are supposed to act respectfully toward the prey they hunt in order to obtain their favor. Many tribal origin stories hold animals to be the first people and co-creators of the world. Taking pity on the newly emerged, ignorant humans, they taught us how to live. In the beginning, when everything was in a state of transformation, there was no clear distinction between humans and other-than-human beings: animals could become humans and humans animals; everyone lived in peace and spoke one language, bound by ties of kinship and ceremonial treaties. Traditional societies still honor these treaties, respecting the ties of kinship with all life. But modern societies have broken the ancient pacts, betrayed the trust, and transformed the common lifeworld into a deathworld.

Decolonizing human-animal relations—or, as Belcourt puts it, recognizing animals as active agents of anti-colonial resurgence (9)—would, above all, entail the dismantling of the myth of (white) hu/man supremacy and the subsequent recovery of our common animality. Obviously, for Westernized people this would result in a Copernican revolution of sorts. One consequence of decolonizing human-animal relations, for instance, would be the need to accept the right to hunt for food, a move that would apparently reverse the painfully won achievements of animal rights campaigns. Even though the practice has been condemned by welfarist circles for its apparent cruelty, it has to be remembered that survival hunting may be the only means of obtaining food for inhabitants of subarctic regions and other wastelands, inhabited predominantly by colonized peoples. Controversial Inuit folk singer Tanya Tagaq, a tireless advocate for Indigenous rights, criticizes the hypocrisy of Westerners who condemn survival hunting but have no intimate knowledge of premodern cultures and the importance of ritual for survival. "Hunting is not evil, like a wolf is not evil when it hunts a caribou," said Tagaq in an interview. "Big corporations digging oil out and flying up tofu, that's pretty evil," she pointed out. For societies living in harmony with the world of untamed nature, there is no contradiction in loving animals and "surviv[ing] on them at the same time" (MacNeill).[13] What is evil is rather the consumption of neatly packaged 'meat' which—displayed on supermarket shelves—loses its connection to the embodied life and death of an animal. Hunting, on the other hand, is a natural activity for all predators. What is evil and unnatural are megacorporations, Tagaq believes, disrespectfully digging the entrails of mother earth and utilizing oil-consuming planes to transport meat-like substitutes over long distances to cater to the needs of city dwellers who are alienated from the world of nature (Frank).

The decolonial framework has yielded many valuable insights into the state of human-animal relationships, which help us to re-think and redefine such crucial terms as 'human,' 'animal,' and 'race' through the prism of social ontology. As noted by Afro-American activist and philosopher Syl Ko, the 'human' as a Eurocentric, colonial construction was placed at the opposite end from the 'animal' on a scale of beings whose ontological position was determined by their proximity to the 'ideal' human: white, European, rational, heterosexual, Christian, and male. By marking human others as 'less than,' the colonial conceptual apparatus transferred them to "the liminal space, the space of being-not-quite-human" (Ko and Ko, 75), together with other sub-humans and nonhumans, and reduced them all to the status of objects to whom no rights are due, ultimately making the sub-human "a cultural agent of violence" (Deckha).

To disrupt the intimately intertwined violence of racism and speciesism, argues black activist and philosopher Syl Ko, racialized peoples must reclaim the inner animal and "thereby refuse to accept that there is a morally relevant conceptual difference between category 'human' and category 'animal'" (*Aphro-ism* 69). In other words, speaking from the midst of a historically animalized group, activists of decolonial sensibility like the Ko sisters, authors of *Aphro-ism*, argue that the way to liberation leads neither through inclusion and humanization of the animalized (the liberal discourse) nor through the animalization of the human (posthumanism and critical theory), but through decolonization of both terms. In conclusion, as Syl Ko repeats after Nelson Maldonado-Torres, inclusion "is just another form of coloniality" (*Aphro-ism* 108). Only by liberating humans and animals from the human-animal binary can a genuine liberation of both be initiated. In opposition to radical posthumanists, who postulate the elimination of the 'human' altogether, decolonial critics believe the 'human' must be re-valued, re-signified, and re-enchanted (Ko and Ko 116).

The same process must be at work with the 'animal' as the other of the human-animal binary. Adopting the anti-colonial lens and looking at the world from "the underside of modernity/coloniality," we may be suddenly hit with a realization that has been staring us in the face all along, the realization that we

> have never *thought* about animals—whether to what extent they are our moral conspecifics, or who they are in general. We have only thought about them in this literal, "biological," matter-of-fact way under the impression that this will give us clues or even answers about our obligation to them. In fact, their situation and who they are is tied to the larger, grander narrative that establishes who is human and

innately valuable and who is not—a story that is *not* and never *has been* based on biology or biological facts. What will their situation be and who *will* they be when we find the courage to transcend the West's monopoly on storytelling and begin to tell a new story about and for ourselves?

(Ko and Ko 118–119)

As traditional peoples have known all along, human and nonhuman animals exist in relation, never in separation. Among the new stories we can begin to tell once "the West's monopoly on storytelling" is transcended there may, indeed must, be stories about 'humanimal bond' and 'humanimal survivance.'

Such is the hope of critical Indigeneity scholars, contributors to the special issue of *Humanimalia* entitled "Decolonizing Animal Studies" (2019). A political theorist of Blackfeet (Amskapi Piikani) descent, Robert Geroux, writes in the editor's Introduction: "Animals and ancestors (the two terms overlap) force us to challenge not only the North American liberal consensus, but also the 'progressive'-left discourse of respect within a civil rights framework" (Geroux 1). The work of decolonizing, continues Geroux, requires "powerfully subversive" readings of "humanimal survivance" (2) as well as revision of the Eurocentric concept of sovereignty through the lens of Indigeneity to repolarize the flow of power. Believed to have been founded by animal ancestors, Indigenous cultures deploy the concept of *counter-sovereignty* in this respect. Since animal agents grant survival skills to humans and thereby lift humanity out of "the originary condition of vulnerability" (Geroux 2), they meet the Western criteria of the sovereign. As evidenced by contributors to the special issue of *Humanimalia*, the process of decolonization starts "with the awareness that non-human animals are kin, co-founders of communities and revolutionary agents" (Geroux 4).

Much hope in spreading this awareness is tied to Traditional Ecological Knowledge departments within research universities as places where such knowledge archives may be deployed outside of Indigenous communities. This hope, however, is qualified and depends on Western scholars' openness to collaboration rather than appropriation of knowledges. Traditional ecological knowledges (TEK) should be a collaborative project, a field that not only troubles the existing power relations in the academy, but replaces the Western world's obsession with knowing the universe with "know[ing] ourselves well enough so we can act morally in the universe" (Whyte et al., qtd. in Fix 130). Fix, Burnam, and Gutteriez suggest that TEK understood as an egalitarian collaborative project should be committed to "interspecies thinking"—an analytic paradigm rooted in Indigenous cosmologies, capable of both decentering the human and disrupting the existing power relations between Western and Indigenous science (130–131). One way or another, animal studies scholarship is no longer thinkable without the contribution of Indigenous articulations of human-animal relations.

Placing Linda Hogan within the Work of Re-minding and Re-story-ation

In a recent book of essays, *The Radiant Lives of Animals*, Linda Hogan grieves the loss of species that is unfolding on a grand scale right before her eyes. The ongoing sixth mass extinction and human cruelty to animals make her "re-minded." Re-minded, she explains, is

> [e]xactly what so many of us need to be. We need to have changed minds, to look at new ways of thinking about our shared world. We need revised neural pathways, synapses connecting new understand-ings of where we stand within the whole of creation.
>
> (*Radiant* 7)

Hogan wrote these words while living with rescued animals in a wildlife cor-ridor in the Rocky Mountains where among her daily activities are watching, listening, and walking the land to get to know it in an intimate way, like her Indigenous ancestors did. Sometimes she spots a mountain lion, discovers a fox's den, or sees a rare wildflower which she wants to keep safe from wild burros. In winter, wolves may approach the house at night or an elk may wan-der into a walkway leading to the barn. The animals whose paths crisscross the area "are simply a people," Hogan writes, "nations of their own kind with lives as sacred as any of ours. I learn their ways, all different, all unlike human ways, yet all together we are one life, one breath, all part of the same shared earth" (*Radiant* 6–7). Walking the land, watching the animals, and listening to the landscape is how she learns. Her knowledge is experiential, relational, localized, intimate. And she is acutely aware that the future of our planet depends on re-learning this kind of knowing, on being reminded of the more ancient perspectives and ways of looking at the world—ultimately, our shared future depends on reclaiming knowledges rooted in the land.

In her advocacy Hogan joins a growing chorus of voices urging a re-turn to Indigenous ecological knowledges as vital for the survival of the planet, with its multitude of species, the human included. To ensure a future for all the endangered plants, animals, landscapes, and human communities, all of which are entangled in networks of reciprocity, we need to take seri-ously the teachings of tribal peoples who spent millennia on a close obser-vation of the natural world, living with it in respectful, intimate relations. We need to be reminded of the ontological primacy of relationships and recover the ancient attitude of respect and gratitude.

Re-minding is not easy, as Hogan admits. "Learning an ecosystem is like learning another language" (*Radiant* 8). Rarely do we realize how intricate the web of kinship is:

> trees, underground organisms, air currents, animal lives with their numerous pathways crossing one another on their earth journeys, all living and breathing the same air, all the same heartbeat. This relationship takes in the foods and medicines that grow from rich earth, carefully tended.
>
> (*Radiant* 8)

All lives entangled, interconnected, depending on each other for survival; whatever happens to one element in this intricate web of kinship has reverberations upon the whole. Western-style environmental science has difficulty grasping this enormous complexity, the long dominant managerial model of nature conservation routinely upsetting the delicate balance of ecosystems rather than preserving it, to say nothing of the ruthless exploitation of nature's resources in the name of civilized progress and human greed. Only now are we beginning to understand how, for instance, widespread predator control programs contribute to the degradation of natural environments or how bees and other pollinators are vital to a healthy ecosystem as a whole. Tribal nations, who observed their ecosystems over long stretches of time, knew how to live in a balanced relationship with them. They understood sustainability before there was a word for it. The Seneca, for example, knew how to plant the three sisters (corn, beans, and squash) in a way that created a perfect nitrogen balance in the soil—something scientists were unable to achieve until recently. Unlike the advanced scientific technology of the latter, the Indigenous method of planting was based on "the right relationship of support between humans, the plants, and their environment" (Burkhart 268).

In 1987, a United Nations Report entitled *Our Common Future* recognized tribal communities as "the repositories of vast accumulations of traditional knowledge and experience that link humanity with its ancient origins." The authors mourned the disappearance of those knowledges as "a loss for the larger society, which could learn a great deal from their traditional skills in sustainably managing very complex ecological systems" (The World Commission). The United Nations Earth Summit, held in Rio de Janeiro in 1992 to discuss the issue of the environmental crisis, also recognized the critical importance of TEK to humanity's search for a sustainable future. But Indigenous perspectives were not an easy fit within the field of environmental science, with its deeply entrenched anthropocentrism. It was only when posthumanism questioned the premise of human exceptionalism—and revealed our entanglements with, and co-dependence on, animals and machines—that a new environmental paradigm, multidisciplinary and inclusive of non-Western viewpoints, started to come into existence. Ecological humanities, also sometimes called ecoposthumanities (Domańska 14), is a potential game changer in the field. It strives to overcome the nature-culture binary by adopting nonanthropocentric, relational approaches inspired by systems theory, vindicates intuitive, experiential forms of knowledge, appeals to concepts of respect, interspecies cooperation and solidarity, rehabilitates localized knowledges, and incorporates Eastern and tribal knowledges in working toward sustainable futures for all. Still, posthumanities-inspired ecologies, which largely drive ecological humanities, are framed differently than traditional Indigenous knowledges and problems of translation may easily arise. As demonstrated by Brian Burkhart in his book *Indigenizing Philosophy through the Land* (2019), the core problem concerns the conceptualization of nonanthropocentric ethics within Western epistemic frameworks.

Surveying the traditional moral theories of the Western world, Burkhart demonstrates that they are all value-based. An agreed-upon hierarchy of values regulates human behavior and makes moral choices possible. On the whole, however, it is human life that is recognized as valuable in itself. We ascribe intrinsic value to it and protect it against harm, but more-than-human life has purely instrumental value. Still, recent revolutions in science—like research in the human microbiome or in intelligence of animals and plants—question not only the idea of human exceptionality (which allows us to occupy the top position in a value hierarchy), but the idea of the human itself. Since we are in fact human-animal hybrids, not so dramatically different from our evolutionary cousins, attempts have been made to extend intrinsic value to at least some nonhuman life forms in order to offer them legal protection from abuse. In the most radical perspectives of such movements as Deep Ecology, all life is recognized as intrinsically valuable and humans are considered to be just one element among many within an ecosystem in which everything is interconnected and valuable. A radical extension of intrinsic value to everything that exists, on the basis of the sanctity of all life, can be self-defeating, though, because such a radically nonanthropocentric viewpoint removes the principle of differentiation and makes all moral choices impossible, warns Burkhart. On the practical side, then, unless humans devised a way to subsist on solar energy alone (since the consumption of animals, including insects, and even plants would be immoral under such conditions), we would soon die of starvation. It is interesting to realize that nonhuman animals would continue to eat and be food for one another irrespective of the human opt-out, which only betrays the human-centeredness of this supposedly nonanthropological ethical perspective. The above problem, however, arises only when entities become reified, abstracted from the wider context, delocalized. Indigenous morality, on the other hand, arises from the land and is a function of the land. "Value theory in the context of locality," claims Burkhart, "can allow for a nonpolarizing, nonanthropocentric moral point of view" (Burkhart 212–213).

In contrast to the intrinsic/instrumental value binary, Indigeneity knows only relational values. Conceptualized as dynamic and unfinished, reality is an interplay of forces which cannot be separated into the discreet entities Western substance metaphysics is comfortable with. The Indigenous world is continually being created, things are continually emerging, and every person's experience is "a moment in the unfolding of the world" (Burkhart 197). In this dynamic web of ever shifting relationships,

> a great deal of care is required at each step not to unbalance or undo the delicate interrelations, and it is with great care that one must attempt to rebalance what one has unbalanced or reestablish or make new the interrelations.
>
> (Burkhart 193–194)

Ultimately, this is how Burkhart understands localized, value-based ethics:

> Morality arises from my reflection regarding what are the right things for me to do. It is, of course, then from my perspective as a human being in locality that I must decide what to do, to figure out what is right and what is wrong. [...] Simply being required to figure out what is the right path for me to follow in relation to my reciprocal relationships cannot be what is meant by anthropocentrism. In other words, one cannot be charged with anthropocentrism when one is simply as oneself in locality reflecting on what is right to do—what is my right road to walk through my life.
>
> (Burkhart 216)

Indigenous ethics is nonprescriptive; it provides no ready-made answers to moral questions, but obliges individuals and communities to constantly re-negotiate their mutual duties and obligations within the context of shifting relationships. Importantly, truth itself is never fixed once and for all. Like reality, truth is ever-evolving and ever becoming (Burkhart 246).

Kinship established within the context of locality must be responsive to an always already changing world. Indigenous morality is thus always practical, it consists in acting "in a good way" (Burkhart 286), respectfully towards an other, although the course of action may differ from case to case. Inappropriate action is not only harmful and morally wrong, but offensive as well. The offended party may retaliate. It is an Indigenous belief that if plants or animals are treated in a wrong way, they may withdraw their presence from humans (who depend on them for food) and thus bring about starvation.

What is the significance of these considerations for the Anthropocene, and how do they connect with the extinction of species grieved by Linda Hogan? What insights does Indigenous ethics offer to activists and decision makers in this respect? "It seems useful," writes Burkhart,

> to think of the leaving of plant and animal entities as a result of our disrespectful attitudes toward them. Even if one cannot see beyond the literalness of plants and animals being offended by our disrespect and going away, one surely can see that the root problems that cause extinctions brought about by humans is in the attitudes we take and in particular the lack of respect in our attitudes toward our relatives.
> (303)

The Western managerial model of subduing nature and exploiting it as "resources" has failed. It is high time that the mind wired for conquest and profit be replaced by one which is new and ancient simultaneously—a mind attuned to respectful kin-centricity. Storytellers and creative writers have an invaluable role to play in making humanity "re-minded" thus, in offering us stories that re-member the dis-membered world, stories that once again make us participants in land democracy, even perhaps, as Hogan envisages it, "a part of the wilderness congress" (*Radiant* 14). A member of Potawatomi Nation, ethnobotanist Robin Wall Kimmerer, calls this process "re-story-ation" (9). In *Braiding Sweetgrass: Indigenous Wisdom, Scientific Knowledge and the Teaching of Plants*, a book that interweaves tribal ecological wisdom with scientific knowledge, Kimmerer creates "a pharmacopoeia of healing stories that allow us to imagine a different [non-abusive] relationship [to the natural world], in which people and land are good medicine for each other" (x). As I will demonstrate in the ensuing chapters, Linda Hogan's writings belong to the same category of stories.

The broader academic field in which Kimmerer works is called ethno-science. Studying perspectives based on native perceptions, ethnoscience emerged from anthropology in the 1960s, but the growing recognition of the importance of Indigenous knowledges for environmental studies is a recent phenomenon (Berkes 2).[14] One pioneer in the field of reconciling Indigenous- and Western-style science, Tewa author Gregory Cajete, defines Native knowledge (also called traditional knowledge) as "the collective heritage of human experience with the natural world; in its most essential form [...] it is a map of natural reality" (*Native Science* 3). The fact that Linda Hogan lists Native science among her major interests ("Hogan, Linda 1947–") suggests a deeper inquiry into its basic premises should be made before an adequate appraisal of her work can be undertaken.

In his essay "Philosophy of Native Science," published in 2004, Cajete helpfully establishes a point of reference for Western-educated readers in Edmund Husserl's concept of the "lifeworld" or lived experience of the world. Perceptual phenomenology is also the foundation of Native American science, rooted as it is in direct, subjective, ever-evolving human experience. However, apart from being context-sensitive (different for different cultures and places), the way we experience our lifeworlds is also conditioned by cosmology, or what we believe about the world's origin and essential nature. Since origins are conjectural and can only be grasped metaphorically, the stories we tell about origins are a matter of belief rather than hard evidence. Still, it is these stories that determine how we conceptualize humanity and what hypotheses we build to explain our place within the cosmic order. "Science in every form is a story of the world," writes Cajete ("Philosophy" 50).

Native American stories of origin present humans emerging from the elements, vulnerable and dependent on plants and animals. For this reason Native science stories the natural world as an egalitarian community of life forms, with humans as members of the land's community rather than its masters (Cajete, "Philosophy" 47), creatively participating with other entities in the ongoing unfolding of the universe. Far from static, to an Indigenous mind nature is "a dynamic, ever-evolving river of creation inseparable from our own perceptions, the creative center from which we and everything else have come and to which we always return" (Cajete, "Philosophy" 48).

In this conceptualization Cajete identifies another important confluence between Native and Western science. With a nod to the ontological concepts introduced by physicist David Bohm, Cajete elucidates that in quantum theory, much like in Indigenous worldviews, the world available to our sense experiences (called by Bohm the "explicate order") is an unstable and semi-autonomous manifestation of a deeper and more fundamental matrix of reality (the "implicate order") with which it remains intimately connected at all times. Far from fully created, the universe is still evolving, its generative forces being chaos and creativity. From the perspective of chaos theory, nature appears every bit as creative and unstable as it is in Indigenous worldviews, making "new forms and structures out of the potential of the great void." "Chaos theory," continues Cajete, "represents the unpredictability and relative randomness of the creative process, appearing in mythology throughout the world in stories of the trickster—the sacred fool whose antics remind us of the essential role of disorder in the creation of order" ("Philosophy" 48).

This is so because order—ever fragile and impermanent (not unlike the truce theorized by Wadiwel)—emerges out of the ongoing "dance of chaos" (Cajete, "Philosophy" 49), in which all entities creatively participate. With everything in flux and perpetual emergence, there can be no fixed notion of 'truth.' Native knowledge—and increasingly the new Western science as well—sees truth as "an ever-evolving point of balance, perpetually created and perpetually new" (Cajete, "Philosophy" 48). For the same reason, in a whole consisting of intimately interrelated parts, even the most imperceptible influences, most minute adaptations, or seemingly futile fluctuations of energy will eventually affect the whole system, bringing about changes, so that, for instance, "a rain dance done properly, with one mind, can bring rain" (Cajete, "Philosophy" 49). Ultimately, as "a new world philosophy of science, designed to meet the environmental challenges of the future [...] will require a totally different way of living in nature," the belated dialog between Western and Native science inspires hope for the prospect of a livable, truly sustainable planet. As if responding to Linda Hogan's concerns expressed in the opening paragraphs of this chapter, Cajete believes that "the ideas and processes of Native science are conceptual wellsprings for helping to bring about the integration of science and spirit, that marriage of 'truth,' the ideal goal of science, with 'meaning,' the ideal goal of spiritual practice" ("Philosophy" 56). Such an integration cannot but result in what has been called "two-eyed seeing" (Albert Marshall, qtd. in Reid et al. 1).

Attempts to correct the one-sided vision of reality caused by one-eyed seeing are in progress in many academic fields. Trying to liberate itself from the straitjacket of Cartesian dualism which forms the backbone of Western modernity, the academic world is seriously exploring the belief, long held by traditional and Indigenous peoples, that consciousness or sentience is not the sole property of humans but belongs to all animate life, possibly including inanimate objects too. The famous Lakota prayer for "all my relations" (*Mitakuye Oyasin*), human and other-than-human, has inspired a new approach to animism—already being called new or ontological animism.[15] In the words of Graham Harvey, professor of Religious Studies at the Open University in London, new animism is "the understanding that the world is a *community of persons*, most of whom are not human, but all of whom are related, and all of whom deserve respect" ("Animism and Ecology," 80).

New animism is a topic of considerable academic dispute, the participants in which differ even in how exactly to define the term, as evidenced by *The Handbook of Contemporary Animism*, a 581-page-long, interdisciplinary project involving a range of scholars from a number of academic disciplines. In the introduction, the editor, Graham Harvey, provides a succinct overview of the evolution of the term, beginning with Edward Taylor's classic definition, formulated in his 1871 publication *Primitive Culture*, which equated animism with a "belief in spirits." While every religion believes in 'spirits'—entities whose existence cannot be proven scientifically (in Christianity these would be God, angels, devils, and the souls of the dead)—the term soon started to be applied, against Taylor's intentions, almost exclusively to 'primitive,' 'less developed' religions.

Although still in use, Taylor's metaphysical animism is being replaced by the 'new,' ontological animism as defined above. Rather than continue the colonialist project of assuming that "we [moderns] know" and "they [pre-moderns] believe" ("Introduction" 4), Harvey stresses the need to question the commonsensical understanding of 'spirits' included in the classical definition of animism. "Spirits," he speculates,

> might just be a way in which some people try to convey an idea about their personal relationship with trees, animals, rivers or ancestors that others consider inanimate and inert. Claimed beliefs about spirits can be thought of as addressing questions of what enlivens beings. What is it about persons that makes them "alive" rather than "inanimate"? Do people possess a spirit or a soul? If they do, are there other beings that are similarly animated by souls or spirits?
>
> ("Introduction" 4)

In short, there appears to be nothing inherently 'otherworldly' about spirits. When traditional peoples talk about the spirit of trees, valleys, mountains, plants, or animals, they are, more often than not, making an ontological statement, which implies an intimate, personal way of relating to earth beings. These beings thus acquire the attributes of personhood or agency.[16]

One of the first anthropologists to understand personhood in this broad way was Irving Hallowell, an anthropologist working with Ojibwe society, who coined the term "other than human persons." As observed by Hallowell, Algonquian languages (such as Ojibwe) divide the world into inanimate entities and animate ones, the latter including human and non-human persons, such as land, animals, and birds, but also rocks, valleys, and mountains. Inspired by Hallowell's research and reclaiming some of the Indigenous wisdom verified by millennia-old close observations of nature, new animism provides an ontological alternative to the dominant Western worldview (which separates people from 'nature'). As a way of life that foregrounds relationships, ontological animism makes an important ethical statement. "The beginning of animism," writes Harvey in an article published in 2019, "is the celebration and negotiation of plurality, particularity, immediacy—in short of *relations*" in order to accommodate the often contradictory "needs of all beings as they seek to make the world ever more habitable for themselves and their close kin" ("Animism and Ecology" 83). Recognizing that animism and ecology are strategic allies in our urgent struggle against ecological devastation, Harvey puts forward the notion of "animist ecology."

Invited to contribute to Harvey's *Handbook of Contemporary Animism* to represent the Indigenous people's perspective, Linda Hogan voiced a qualified acceptance of the new label, commenting on the bitter irony that the academic world, which once denigrated traditional knowledges, now turns to them for help and instruction to forestall the ecological catastrophe brought about by the very modernity which was to supplant the old 'superstitions.' Although her first reaction was to distance herself from the academic label—"For tribal peoples, our relationships and kinship with the alive world is simply called *tradition*" ("We Call It Tradition" 20)—she nonetheless feels "grateful for the new animism" (23) as a strategic partner. "If what we call tradition is animism," she admits,

> what could be better than to renew a care for the land that we have always loved, with our old knowledge of a region's every plant. Animism is a field that has no choice but to recognize our relationship with the trees that has existed for so many years is an intimate one.

Ultimately, then, "the new, returned animism" qualifies as "a fresh perspective and a way of knowing, grasping at last that we are all of a piece" (Hogan, "We Call It Tradition" 24). Regardless of the name by which we chose to call it—whether animism or tradition—the crucial thing is that the relational approach helps us live respectfully with the world, with all the human and other-than-human persons surrounding us.

The academic world has also begun to incorporate insights provided by Indigenous people to address the challenges of anthropogenic climate change. Most recently, a world-wide, multidisciplinary, and cross-cultural project has been launched by Joni Adamson, professor of Environmental Humanities at Arizona State University, which seeks to "integrate knowledge and forge new constellations of practice"[17] in working toward sustainability and environmental justice. In the book *Humanities for the Environment*, which has resulted from the discussion between scholars and activists participating in the project, Potawatomi author Kyle Whyte introduces aspects of Indigenous Climate Change Studies, which address the colonial specter of the Anthropocene. Although tribal societies have contributed the least to human-caused climate change, they are among the most severely afflicted by its consequences, argues Whyte. Forced for centuries to adapt to the devastating effects of displacement, loss of game, or landscape degradation caused by colonial practices, they experience anthropogenic devastation in terms of a "colonial déjà vu" ("Is it Colonial Déjà Vu?")

As a participant in the project, Hogan discusses the sustainable potential of such Indigenous conceptions as *punyu*[18] (Ngarinman), *tish* (Chicaza), and *hozho* (Navajo). All of them refer to the idea of balance and harmonious coexistence between humans and the rest of creation. Had these notions become part of the colonizers' vocabulary, the Anthropocene may never have happened. Sadly, she argues, the Anthropocene started to take shape in the early 18th century, with the creation of the "Mississippi Bubble."[19] Understood as "a situation in which asset prices appear to be based on implausible or inconsistent views about the future" (Krugman), the idea of the economic bubble surprisingly well describes the predatory, colonial patterns of deforestation, species extinction, and human-animal slavery imposed around that time on Hogan's ancestors, the Chicaza. The author provides a long list of corporate imperialist projects which continue to dev-astate Indigenous lives and landscapes for exorbitant profit, drawing this sobering conclusion: "Those who deny truth are largely the ones whose incomes increase with contamination and violations of nature" (Hogan, "Backbone" 30).

Having examined the roots of the Anthropocene from an Indigenous point of view, Hogan investigates possible solutions to this human-induced problem. A descendant of tribal peoples and a writer herself, she believes in the power of stories in creating change; to be more exact, she advocates a re-story-ation (to use Kimmerer's coinage)—an adoption of alternative stories that would create a corresponding shift in human values and atti-tudes. As she rightly notes, Western cultures, functioning on a linear time-line, are entropic, oriented toward some inevitable cataclysmic event, and as such offer no hopeful vision of earthly futures. The Anthropocene, with the idea of tipping point, is "a closed container" ("Backbone" 29), argues Hogan. Traditional peoples, on the other hand, embrace cyclical notions of time, which enables them to remain hopeful, believe in renewal, and work toward survivability. Rather than futile discussions of the human-centered template, we urgently need to change the story and focus on reversing the change, offers Hogan. "We can't afford apathy" (31). Her words offer a message of hope:

> [R]estoration is taking place everywhere. The returns are numerous. Plants are reintroduced that will save certain necessary pollinators or butterflies. Others will be nitrogen-fixing for planting food in the future. Serious work is being undertaken by people who have learned their ecosystems intimately and are able to participate with the healthy interactions and connections.
>
> ("Backbone" 31)

Punyu, *tish*, *hozho* may still return. "Hope lives deeper in my heart than faith," admits Hogan in another essay ("Ancient Root").

This hope thrives on having the right story to tell. Given the destruction caused by modern overconsumption, salvation may very literally depend on re-story-ing the colonized world. Historian Shawn Smallman explicitly identifies capitalism and corporate consumerism with the Windigo, a humanoid monster with the heart of ice of the spiritual tradition of the Algonquian-speaking peoples. Originating in the depth of wintertime starvation, the myth of the cannibalistic monster who feeds on human flesh and turns his victims into copies of himself is a warning against egoism, lack of self-control, and the consequent exclusion from the web of reciprocity. In *Braiding Sweetgrass* Kimmerer elaborates on "Windigo economics"—or overconsumption gone wild—as opposed to the economy of the gift, which she also calls "the economy of the commons" to capture its similarity with traditional peoples' understanding of earth as accessible to all, as "a commons, to be tended with respect and reciprocity for the benefit of all" (*Braiding* 376). Even though Windigo keeps coming back, he can be defeated, hopes Kimmerer, by "the practice of gratitude" (377), a collective awareness that what we have is enough. Reclaiming this awareness, being re-minded of it, is the anchor of Hogan's hope in the return of *punyu, tish, hozho.*

Still, Hogan knows that re-minding takes time. It is a long and laborious process—given the extent of destruction of Indigenous cultures, with treaties between humans and nonhumans broken, origin stories forgotten or reviled, generations of Indigenous children stolen and forcefully assimilated into white culture, their minds colonized by Euro-American education and poisoned by greed. Changing the stories humanity lives by will not be possible without the tireless work of concerned activists attempting to save the planet for the next seven generations into the future. A writer has unique opportunities to shape the minds and hearts of people across cultures, delineate the contours of environmental disaster, and bring readers to a felt sense of responsibility for our common home. For Hogan writing is largely an activist platform, her poetry and creative fiction being an extension of her speaking and teaching agenda (which should not be surprising, given that in Indigenous cultures everything is connected with everything else). Most importantly, however, her belief in the power of stories has been verified by her growing international reputation. To date, her work has been translated into the world's major languages and she is in constant demand as a speaker. Interestingly, this daughter of two incompatible worlds—of the colonized and of the colonizer—attributes her return to ancestor traditions to "the inhumanity of the Western world" she witnessed as a young woman "to the places—both inside and out—where that culture's knowledge and language don't go, and the despair, even desperation, it has spawned" ("First People" 10). There is irony in the fact that the West is turning back to the same Indigenous stories it once discredited as the childlike expressions of superstitious minds. "The old stories," Hogan notes, "have turned out to be a key to a new understanding by science" (First People" 14).

Intriguingly, tribal origin stories have much more in common with the scientific narrative of evolution than the Christian Book of Genesis does. According to the biblical narrative of creation, the first humans, unlike animals, were made in the image of God himself. As a natural corollary of their god-like status, male humans were given dominion over the rest of creation. Thus, a hu/man-animal binary lies at the very heart of Western cosmology. In Indigenous creation narratives, on the other hand, it is plant and animal people who play an important role in bringing humans—their younger and more vulnerable siblings—to the world. In the origin of time, as Native Americans believe, boundaries between species were fluid and shapeshifting was a common phenomenon. Hogan comments:

> As we know from recent science, this is still the case. We all consist of the same spirit of creation, [...] we contain the same atomic matter as the rest of life, the same DNA as all life forms. Our lives are a fluid interchange with other lives.
>
> ("First People" 8)

Although Hogan has done much reading and research in the field of animal science (for 18 years she was involved with an initiative called Native Science Dialogue[20]), her deep knowledge and understanding of animals is rooted in personal experience. First, as a child on her paternal grandparents' farm in Oklahoma, she listened to tribal stories of creation, saw her Turtle Clan grandmother speak with the totem animals and stayed with her cowboy and rodeo riding grandfather and uncles when they tended horses and cattle. A love for horses has stayed with her for the rest of her life.

In adulthood, she volunteered her time at a raptor rehabilitation center, first in Minneapolis, then in Colorado. For eight years she was "a disciple of birds" (Hogan, *Dwellings* 148), caring for injured eagles, owls, and hawks, cleaning their cages, feeding them, and in many other ways attending to their needs. "The most difficult task the birds demand," she confessed later, "is that we learn to be equal with them. To feel our way into an intelligence that is different from our own" (*Dwellings* 150). It was there that she experienced a sense of communication beyond words, "a language spoken from and to the body," a language which "enters skin, stomach, heart" ("First People" 6). That experience made her think of the mythical times when humans and animals were said to have lived together within a network of family relationships and communicate in one language. At the wildlife rehabilitation foundation, Hogan would instinctively call a golden eagle "grandmother," like many Indigenous people had done before her. Her collection of essays entitled *Dwellings* starts with this dedication: "For my grandmothers, and for grandmother, the golden eagle" (5).

In the male-dominated scientific community of the latter part of the 20th century, an involved, emotion-based approach to the study of animals was still deprecated as bad science, yet a number of women scientists working in the field were undermining the Cartesian paradigm, opening science to such 'feminine' values as care and empathy, changing the story in the process. Most famously, Birute Galdikas, Jane Goodall, and Dian Fossey, who studied primates in their natural habitat, established intimate bonds with their animal friends and were always ready to help them in need, even though this was considered 'unwarranted interference' with nature. Hogan said in an interview: "the women who studied primates were picked by Leakey because of their ability to be empathic and quiet [...]. We should make all our choices like that, pick compassionate people to do the important work" (Stein 118).

Then there was zoologist and musician Katy Payne, whose work influenced the way we now think about animal intelligence. She discovered that whales use rhythms in their songs, varying them depending on the situation, and that elephants communicate by means of long-distance infrasonic calls. Also, ethologist Cynthia Moss, who devoted her life to the study and conservation of African elephants, proved that matriarchal elephant societies have a highly organized structure, much more complex than some people were ready to accept. In the "Introduction" to the collection of essays *Intimate Nature: The Bond Between Women and Animals*, Hogan and her collaborators on the volume, Brenda Peterson and Deena Metzger, pay tribute to these and many other women pioneers who infused science with compassion. Their work was a hopeful sign of an impending paradigm shift toward "what was encoded in our blood, in our DNA, in centuries past," namely, "that everything is alive, that all matter is resonant with energy" ("Introduction" xii).[21] "To honor intimacy across the seeming boundaries of species is to return the sacred to the world" ("Introduction" xiv), assert the editors.

Extending the new story, the new scientific paradigm, back to Rachel Carson and her game changing *Silent Spring* (1962), Hogan and her coauthors speculate in the "Introduction" about an "intimate bond" women have with the nonhuman world:

> Perhaps these women have been transformative because our approach to relationships has been different from that of men. What women have brought into the equation is a respect for feeling and empathy as tools to create intimate bonds of connection. Perhaps it is our own bodies that remind us that we, too, are animal, kin to those we work with, live with, love, and swallow. Perhaps it is because, like animals, we have so often been cherished at the same time we had been hated. Historically we have been identified with animals [...].
>
> (xii)

Avoiding the trap of essentialism, the authors enumerate not only bio-logical but also sociohistorical factors which have gendered human percep-tions of reality. Believing in the power of stories to adjust our perceptions and, ultimately, to transform the real world, Hogan and her fellow edi-tors solicited contributions from an impressive range of famous women, including the celebrities mentioned above. "The women in this anthology are describing a new creation [...] that takes us to new ways of being human in our shared world," they write (xv).

In a world understood as a network of interdependencies—a worldview corroborated by physics beyond the Standard Model—a change in one element leads to readjustments of the entire system. From this perspective it is clear that a renewed attitude of respect for the nonhuman world, one that makes people "re-minded," may ultimately transform humanity into a different, evolved species, potentially even reversing the Anthropocene. After all, evolution is still in progress.

Structure of the Book

In what follows I will attempt a decolonial reading of the human-animal relationship in the literary works of Linda Hogan, one of the most interest-ing contemporary writers of Indigenous US America and a dedicated pro-animal activist. Lacking any Indigenous background myself, I nevertheless feel invited into the intimate space of Linda Hogan's literary and activ-ist explorations of Indigeneity by her poetic encouragement: "Walk your bones along/with mine, in any way you can" (*Dark. Sweet* 310). I accept Hogan's invitation with a sense of responsibility. Rather than appropriat-ing, I wish to 'think with,' to explore possibilities of human-animal thriv-ing from culturally diverse perspectives and hopefully make a contribution to the advancement of interspecies decolonial resurgence. May all the four-footed, two-footed, winged, webbed, and no-footed thrive together. Above all, however, my ambition in this, as well as in many other endeavors, is to learn to "know myself well enough to be able to act morally in the uni-verse" (Whyte et al., qtd. in Fix 130)

Linda Hogan's novels and poetry have been the subject of close critical attention for over 40 years now. Winner of numerous literary awards, in 2007 Hogan was inducted into the Chickasaw Nation Hall of Fame for her contributions to Indigenous literatures. Strangely enough, there has been no single-author monograph, at least in the English language, devoted exclusively to this prolific and remarkably important Indigenous author. What is even more puzzling, given her passionate interest in nonhuman animals and a strong and constant animal presence in her works, there has been no sustained endeavor to explore their deployment in the totality of Hogan's *oeuvre*.

Along with isolated articles scattered in a variety of scholarly magazines, to date there have been only two book-length English-language studies of Hogan's prose and poetry: a multi-authored collection of essays entitled *From the Center of Tradition* (2003) and a comparative study written by Peter I-min Huang *Linda Hogan and Contemporary Taiwanese Writers: An Ecocritical Study of Indigeneities and Environment* (2015). The former book includes ten essays, an interview, and a bibliography of primary and secondary sources. The contributing scholars discuss Hogan's prose and poetry from such critical perspectives as ecocriticism, ecofeminism, post-colonialism, American Indian studies, and narrative theory. The latter project uses the comparative lens to explore Hogan's environmental writings in relation to Indigenous authors from across the Pacific. Out of the book's six chapters, only one, with its focus on the novel *Power*, taps into animal studies perspectives. The chapter begins with the following observation:

> The bond between humans and animals is a subject that leaps out at the reader of Linda Hogan's poetry and prose. The subject has not been given the attention it deserves, and it is inseparable from the eco-critical arguments that Hogan's work makes.
>
> (Huang 96)

While Huang usefully recognizes the issue as seriously understudied, his own contribution is anchored predominantly in ecocritical and postmodernist theories, as well as the rights-based discourse on animal studies. My monograph attempts to bring the analytic tools of decoloniality and critical Indigeneity to the study of human-animal relations in the literary works of Hogan, who is of Chickasaw descent on the paternal side of her family, and who explicitly identifies with traditional Indigenous knowledge and traditions.

Since Hogan claims poetry as her first language ("Hogan, Linda 1947–"), I will devote the first part of this book to a chronological analysis of the animal-centered poems she published between 1978 and 2020. Beginning with her first poetry collection, nonhuman animals have been a constant presence in Hogan's literary work, which spans half-a-century and has yielded eight important volumes of poetry so far. In a 1988 interview, ten years after publishing her first book of poems, entitled *Calling Myself Home*, she said:

> In my whole life I have been a spokesperson for the animals. In my own sense of things I feel that our whole life depends on other creatures on the planet, and I love them, pay them respect, and try to help them.
>
> (Schöler 113)

As I hope will be seen in the following pages, over three decades later these words are still an apt mission statement of Hogan's literary and personal activism.

To highlight the correspondence between the writer's life and her evolving political commitments on the one hand, and the way nonhuman animals function in her poems on the other, I have decided to analyze her poetic output on a decade-by-decade basis, hoping to reveal developments, continuities, correspondences, and shifts in emphases, as well as better illustrate her early prophetic attunement to issues recently theorized under the rubric of the Anthropocene. Each of the five chapters in part one of this book will be focused on one decade in her poetic career. To discipline my research and maintain clarity, I have limited my study to the human-animal bond, excluding a large network of relationships between humans and other nonhuman agents, equally constitutive of traditional cultures' sense of balance and wholeness of life. Even though it is not explored in detail, I have nevertheless tried not to lose sight of this larger, encompassing context while discussing individual poems.

My analysis will be based on a collection of Hogan's poetry *Dark. Sweet* (2014), a volume which gives a chronological overview of the author's most important environmental verse from volumes published between 1978 and 2012, and including a section containing new poems, not previously published in book form, and entitled "Dark. Sweet." On one occasion, when discussing Hogan's verse of the 1980s, I will use the volume *Eclipse* (1983) in its entirety to present a broader outline of her evolving concern with animals, which poems included in the "Eclipse" section of *Dark. Sweet* cannot provide.

Thus, Chapter 1 of my book will focus on the 1970s and will provide a close reading of Hogan's poems inspired by animals from her first volume of poetry, *Calling Myself Home* (1978). I will argue that recollections of the larger-than-human community of the future poet's Oklahoma childhood, in combination with the politically intense climate of the decade, were instrumental in turning her back to tradition.

With Chapter 2 we will move to the 1980s, which saw the publication of three collections of poems: *Eclipse* (1983), *Seeing through the Sun* (1985), and *Savings* (1988). Sensitive registers of the decade's growing ecofeminist attitudes, these poems mature towards a position Val Plumwood has called ecological animalism.

In the 1990s Hogan brought out what is probably her most famous volume of poetry, *The Book of Medicines* (1993), which solidified her position on the poetic scene. Chapter 3 will explore the importance of wildness for the author's revisioning of human-animal relationships.

After the caesura of a near-fatal riding accident, Hogan published *Rounding the Human Corners* (2008), which represents her poetry of the

2000s. It conveys a renewed fascination with the miracle of life, embodiment, and the life of the senses, as well as an appreciation of the smallest, most fragile life forms. Perceptual reciprocity with the nonhuman world emerges as a major theme of the writer-activist's work and it will organize the fourth chapter of this book.

The 2010s brought two important collections of poetry. In 2014 appeared the retrospective volume of Hogan's poetic *oeuvre*, *Dark. Sweet*, with a section containing over 60 new poems ("Dark. Sweet"). Four years later, at the close of the decade, Hogan published *A History of Kindness* (2020). Both volumes foreground mercy, kindness, and compassion as marks of genuine humanity and coordinates of normative interspecies ethics, as I will argue in Chapter 5.

Having identified Hogan's signature poetic voice and established the major animal-related themes, images, and tropes in her poetry, I will then move on to the analysis of the human-animal bond in Hogan's novels. Part 2 of this book consists of four chapters, each of which will focus on one of the four novels the author has published so far: *Mean Spirit* (1990), *Solar Storms* (1995), *Power* (1998), and *People of the Whale* (2008).

Already an important poetic voice of her generation, in 1990 Hogan made a breakthrough as a novelist with *Mean Spirit*, a finalist for the Pulitzer Prize and winner of an Oklahoma Book Award. In turning to the form of the novel she was attracted to the spaciousness of the medium and its activist potential. "Stories have the capacity to make change in ways that other forms of activism don't," she said in 2013, in an interview for *Superstition Review* (Regan). In recognizing the political potential of the novel, Hogan joined a host of other American women writers of color who, beginning in the 1980s, were disrupting "the historic connection between the novel and the nation" in an attempt to "reimagine alternative communities and definitions of freedom" (Romero 12–13). With their focus on agency, relationality, orality, and traditional expressions of spirituality, these women were redefining the novel as an activist arena, one that can help build multidimensional, interracial coalitions to combat oppressions (Romero 1–23). In her 2012 book *Activism and the American Novel* Channette Romero provides the following characteristics of this phenomenon:

> Contemporary fiction by women of color is invested in worldviews and identities demanding individual and communal responsibility, and requiring active, critical interpretation. The novels seek to redefine and re-create a more inclusive public sphere [...]. In doing so they attempt to construct communities, identities and freedoms yet unrealized in the Americas.
>
> (Romero 52)

Critics were slow in catching up with these developments. Their continued reliance on prescriptive critical categories, combined with academic criticism's latent gender bias, often led to charges of historical inaccuracies and the brandishing of the magical realist label, incorrectly identifying the new writing with a Eurocentric, mostly male, genre. Hogan's novel was not an exception. Amidst complimentary reviews of *Mean Spirit*, her first novel, there were also charges of irresponsible use of historical materials and misrepresentations of the Osage people.[22] Defending imaginative literature's license to rewrite history, critic Betty Louise Bell wrote in the Introduction to a 1994 special issue of *Studies in American Indian Literatures* dedicated to Hogan:

> Hogan has been criticized for her deviation from some historical *facts* in *Mean Spirit*. This assumes that there is a sole and accurate historical narrative to every event and that truth resides only in that narrative. In fact, to the advantage of all peoples once absent from History, the privileged voice of History has long been reduced to its narrative form and content. It is just another way of telling a story. As a Native American woman, Hogan knows the dangers of complicity with History; as a writer, she insists on the primacy of the imagination.
>
> (5)

Reclaiming stories silenced by history is part of the re-minding/decolonizing process, toward which Hogan's entire career gravitates. In keeping with Indigenous storytelling traditions, re-minding allows the use of imagination to access the deeper truths mere facts can never reveal. Just as creativity has proved crucial to surviving settler colonial forms of oppression, Hogan's novels creatively rewrite history to highlight such values as flexibility and survivance—of tribal cultures and whole land communities—in the constructions of decolonized futures. Believing in fiction's potential to move readers and convert them to the cause of decolonial justice, she builds pan-tribal, interracial, interspecies coalitions in an effort to heal the wounds of the past and open the future. All the four novels she has written so far are anchored in Indigenous Americans' traumatic past and their often bleak present; still, Hogan's focus is on healing and survival. Summer Harrison asserts: "For Hogan, writing historical novels [...] is a deeply political act designed to make historical events resonate affectively with readers" (Harrison 5). She continues:

> Hogan creates a multivocal ceremonial form of storytelling modeled on healing and mourning rituals designed to reintegrate the individual into a more-than-human living community and to redistribute responsibility for ethical trauma responses among a wider alliance public.
>
> (Harrison 1)

The four novels to be analyzed are historical, activist novels that rewrite history from the underside of modernity and give voice to the silenced. Chapter 6 of this book, "*Mean Spirit*: Decolonizing Nonhuman Animals," will focus on the human-animal bond in Hogan's first novel, a narrative that deals with the 1920s Reign of Terror, which followed the discovery of rich oil deposits in Osage Indian Territory. At least 24 Osage were murdered (May), while many others became victims of land grabs and violence.

Chapter 7, "*Solar Storms*: Re-claiming Wild, Becoming Human," will explore the decolonial potential of nonanthropocentric ethics in Hogan's *Solar Storms*, a novel which follows the tragedy of the Cree and Inuit communities heavily impacted by the 1970s construction of several mega dams in the James Bay area of Ontario and Quebec. Flooded villages and hunting grounds, the deaths of caribou herds and countless other nonhuman beings, loss of local livelihoods, forced resettlements, and a succession of broken promises—Hogan foregrounds the effects of another colonial project built at the cost of life considered to be 'less than' and therefore disposable.

Chapter 8, "Of *Power* and Sacrifice: Rethinking Carnivora, Expanding Sociality," will discuss Hogan's third novel. Once again inspired by authentic events, *Power* focuses on the fraught relationship between the protection of endangered species and tribal hunting rights. The killing of a Florida panther on tribal territory exposes unsolvable conflicts of rights and interests between ecologists, liberal defenders of Indigenous rights, and the fictional Taiga tribe, which is riven by internal splits.

A similar conflict drives Hogan's fourth novel, *People of the Whale*, which is analyzed in Chapter 9, subtitled "Transformational Beings and the Future of Humanity." The book's plot is based on the 1997 resumption of the whale hunt by the Makah tribe of the American Northwest. Action is set in a liminal area where tradition and sovereign rights clash with big business deals, the protection of endangered species, and a fundamental impulse of compassion for a majestic and suffering creature. In all these novels, respecting human obligations to animal ancestors is seen as a condition *sine qua non* of Indigenous survival.

The book will end with conclusions, where I will try to address the question concerning the possibility of interspecies cosmopolis as envisaged in the pages of Linda Hogan's work.

A Note on Language

When referring to animals I follow the practice of using the pronouns 'he,' 'she' rather than 'it,' and 'who' instead of 'which.' I capitalize the word 'Indigenous' when referring to sovereign communities and use the lower case for the common noun (i.e., a person born in a given place). Inverted commas will be used around concepts objectifying and commodifying non-human life (like 'livestock,' 'preventive culling,' etc.).

Notes

1 Nicole Shulkin's *Animal Capital: Rendering Life in Biopolitical Times* (2009). Mel Y. Chen's *Animacies: Biopolitics, Racial Mattering, and Queer Affect* (2012) or Neel Ahuja's *Biosecurities: Disease Interventions, Empire, and the Government of the Species* (2016) immediately come to mind.

2 "War [...] is an act of violence intended to compel our opponent to fulfill our will" (Clausewitz, *On War* 75).

3 An animal unit is defined as "an animal equivalent of 1000 pounds live weight and equates to 1000 head of beef cattle, 700 dairy cows, 2500 swine weighing more than 55 lbs, 125 thousand broiler chickens, or 82 thousand laying hens or pullets" ("Animal Feeding Operations").

4 A thorough critique of the politics of recognition has been undertaken by Glen Coulthard in *Red Skins, White Masks*. The author's theorizing of the Canadian government's recognition of the rights of First Nations can, *mutatis mutandis*, be applied to interspecies relationships.

5 Even though Wadiwel does not explicitly refer to veganism as a most radical form of counter-conduct, his deployment of vegetarianism allows for the accommodation of dietary options which minimize or eliminate altogether a purely utilitarian approach to animal products.

6 It bears stressing that veganism can—and often does—create hierarchies of its own. Coopted by the market, it becomes a profit-generating lifestyle for the rich, which frequently contributes to the loss of animal habitats in regions like Indonesia.

7 Matthew Calarco, author of *Zoographies: The Question of the Animal from Heidegger to Derrida*, extensively argues that the question of the animal challenges liberal humanism and the metaphysical anthropocentrism on which it rests. Mendieta follows the same line of argumentation in his "Interspecies Cosmopolitanism."

8 Zoe Todd, Métis anthropologist and scholar, most famous for her work on decolonizing anthropology and studying human-fish relationships in settler colonial societies, calls ontology "just another word for colonialism."

9 https://www.ualberta.ca/womens-gender-studies/about-us/news/2015/november/callforpapersfordecolonizingcriticalanimalstudiescrippingcriticalanimalstudiesconference.html.

10 The aftermath of the event was the publication of a collection of essays *Colonialism and Animality: Anti-Colonial Perspectives in Critical Animal Studies*, edited by Chloë Taylor and Kelly Struthers Montford (Routledge 2021).

11 https://fishphilosophy.org/about/.

12 In this respect see also Kanji. Donaldson and Kymlicka respond to decolonial critiques of their *Zoopolis* in "Animal Rights, Aboriginal Rights," pp. 157–186.

13 A rising number of Indigenous scholars and activists believe veg(etari)anism can be reconciled with ancient human-animal protocols. One of the most vocal proponents of aboriginal veganism, Margaret Robinson credits her Mi'kmaq roots with the realization that in the contemporary world animals should be absolved from their originary pledge to provide for their human brothers and sisters,

who no longer go hungry or naked without animal products. For activists like Robinson veganism is a way to honor their Indigenous teachings on reciprocity and mutual respect, provided that healthy and sustainable choices are available.

14 The importance of this field is underscored by the essays collected in *The Routledge Handbook of Indigenous Environmental Knowledge*, ed. by Thomas F. Thornton and Shonil A. Bhagwat (2020).

15 New approaches by Philippe Descola, Tim Ingold, and Eduardo Kohn suggest that animism contains the potential for a serious alternative to the ideological foundations of modern science and economy.

16 Caring about, and talking to, cherished objects—like cars, rifles, and dolls, not to mention animate beings like pets—is after all a near universal experience, independent of one's professed religion.

17 This is the subtitle of the book edited by Joni Adamson, as referenced in the next sentence.

18 "Punyu" is discussed by Deborah Bird Rose in her contribution to the same volume that includes Hogan's essay ("Country and the Gift," pp. 32–44).

19 The Mississippi Bubble was a French financial scheme tied to land development in French colonies in North America. The scheme triggered a speculative frenzy that led to financial collapse.

20 In an autobiographical essay she writes: "By some act of fortune, I was invited, around 1993, before my [riding] accident, to participate in the Native Science dialogues in Canada, a group of indigenous and Western thinkers that was started by physicist David Bohm. This was another life-changing event for me, sitting in a room with others who understood, understand, the absolute intelligence of those who came before us, our ancestors, their knowledge, from astronomy to agriculture to mathematics. I realized more than ever that my work was to give Indian people and characters dignity, to reveal the intelligence of our people, and to honor this world we first people inhabited" ("Hogan, Linda 1947–").

21 The Introduction is signed by the three editors, but the style and imagery are uniquely Hogan's.

22 Such a charge was formulated by an Osage critic, Robert Allen Warrior (qtd. in Anderson 57).

Part 1

The Radiant Lives with Animals

The Poetry of Linda Hogan

1 1970s

Calling Myself Home

Emerging from her people's long history of silence, Linda Hogan was a morbidly silent child. "The pain of having to speak was too great for me," she writes in her memoir (*Woman* 101). Without words we cannot know, let alone heal, ourselves. "Words," claims Hogan:

> are the defining shape of a human spirit. Without them we fall. Without them, there is no accounting for the human place in the world. Language is an intimacy not only with others, but even with the self. It creates a person. Without it, in the dawn, in the dark of night, there is no way to know who or what we are.
> One day the words came. I was an adult. I went to school after work. I read. I wrote. Words came, anchored to the earth, to matter, to the wholeness of nature. There was, in this, [...] a light-bearing, soul-saving presence that illuminated my heart and mind and altered my destiny.
>
> (*Woman* 56–57)

This silent, suicidal child grew up to become an eloquent poet, a lover of the world who shapes language as if it is the plastic clay of creation. Words helped the future poet to name and work through her traumas and the traumas of her people's history. To this day poetry, her first language, remains her most intimate, most authentic means of communication—a language that taps into Hogan's innermost self, that expresses something impossible to express otherwise.

If not for copyright, Hogan's first poetic attempts could well be called "lunch poems."[1] She was working with orthopedically handicapped children and had no academic education at that time, but had just discovered Kenneth Rexroth and felt an urge to start writing herself. The only available time slot in which she could write was the lunch break. *Calling Myself Home*, her first published collection of poetry, came out in 1978, the year she graduated from the University of Boulder, Colorado, with an MA in Creative Writing.[2]

DOI: 10.4324/9781003364252-3

Not surprisingly, this volume, which launched her career, plays out the "homing" theme identified as the cornerstone of Native American narratives (Bevis). In the 1970s Hogan revisited, both physically, with her father, and metaphorically, through her writing, the Oklahoma of her childhood—"the place of my heart, my inner world, the place where I lived before I was born" (*Woman* 116)—to celebrate her bond with that storied land. It was here, in the former Indian Territory, that the Chickasaws settled in 1837 after journeying the traumatic Trail of Tears from their ancestral lands in the Southeast. It was also here that Hogan had spent with her paternal grandparents the happiest time of her childhood. More than place, however, the home evoked in the volume's title is also language itself. With her first poems, the woman whose ancestors bequeathed to her "the secret of never having a home" (Hogan, *Dark* 19), finally found her dwelling place, a house made of words. "I live in a house words built" (*Woman* 58), she confesses in her memoir.

The Oklahoma of her memory is a hard land—dry, scorched by the sun, demanding—but also sacred and beautiful in its own way. Hogan recollects its animals and trees, her family and her ancestors, everyday work and the moments of leisure. There, the past is still alive, superimposed on the present, and time can flow forward or backward with the same ease. The boundaries of things are fluid, the hard edges of reality soften, as they do in memories and dreams, reality perpetually realigning itself.

Calling Myself Home was, in Hogan's own words, "one of the first contemporary books of poems by many mixed-blood writers to follow" and she was little prepared for the stir it would cause. When she decided to write about her tribal people she did not know any other contemporary Indigenous writers, because their "books were obscure and in anthropology sections of bookstores, instead of with the other literature" (Hogan, Linda, 1947–). But the phenomenon that critic Kenneth Lincoln called a Native American Renaissance was just gathering momentum. Unwittingly, Hogan was becoming part of an important literary and cultural movement.[3]

In her tribal memoir first released in 2001, she pays tribute to 19th-century Santee Sioux physician Charles Eastman, also known as Ohiyesa. According to his own testimony, a giant turtle once scratched on the door of his house, as if wanting to urge this Boston University graduate to return to the world of nature (*Woman* 61). Hogan's experience was not unlike that of Eastman-Ohiyesa. In the opening poem of her collection, the speaker declares "I'm dreaming the old turtle back" (*Dark*, "Turtle" 3), thereby orienting the volume's ontological map. Indigenous people attach great significance to dreams; this is how ancestors communicate with the living, how problems are solved and mysteries revealed; this is how hunters locate their game. Dreams open communication with another dimension of reality, a path between worlds. Now, "dreamed back," a turtle emerges out of an Oklahoma pond, with his wet shell shining in the sun. But the speaker's attention rests on the water he has left, instead of the animal himself, as if to underline the interdependence of background and foreground, while at the same time signaling to the readers the need to readjust their perceptual routine. In Native eyes every entity is an organic part of a much larger whole and cannot be adequately understood without it, as the poem's second stanza suggests:

> In water
> the world is breathing,
> in the silt.
> There are fish
> and their blood changes easy
> warm to cold.
>
> (3)

The turtle has come out of an aquatic world rich in life that is invisible to the naked eye: patient, resilient, capable of surviving extremes of temperature, adaptable. This submerged world, silently "breathing," perhaps sleeping, at the pond's muddy bottom, subliminally evokes the mute mimicry of Hogan's ancestors, who were forced to adapt to ever changing colonial policies, to keep a low profile in order to survive, but who refused to give up hope of renewal.

With their blood changing easily from "warm to cold," fish and turtles can adjust to conditions beyond their control. Even though they belong to different classes of animals, they share the same environment, contributing to its health together. Turtles, however, not having gills, cannot breathe under water and need the land to survive—which, in turn, is a deadly environment for fish. With this stanza's emphasis on difference amidst sameness, as well as fluidity, adaptability, and change, Hogan shifts the poem's focus from one particular animal to interdependence and transformation. The conjunction "and," with which the next line begins, is a reminder that every act of perception is likewise entangled in an endless web of simultaneity, cultural expectations, associations, private recollections, and extrapolations:

> And the turtle,
> small yellow bones of animals inside
> are walking
> to shine out of his eyes.
> Wake up the locusts whose dry skins
> Are still sleeping on the trees.
>
> (3)

Hogan does not state the obvious, like the turtle's size or external appearance, but looks beyond the visible into the center of his body, observing how even the life killed for food continues to undergo further stages of transformation, broken down into simpler elements to be distributed ("walking") to all the organs and cells of the predator's body, nourishing them, the turtle's shining eyes suggesting perfect health. The turtle is truly back—healthy and strong. With him, the whole ancestral world, known as Turtle Island, is coming back, waking up from sleep, like the locusts freshly freed from their nymph stage, who leave the skin they have just shed clinging to the bark of the tree. The world re-emerges from ancient sleep.

Images of waking up hint at the speaker's desire to make her vision a reality, to let her dream in, as it were, through a gap between worlds. Like a tribal dreamer, the speaker now starts to meditate on how to bring the desired change about:

> We should open his soft parts,
> Pull his shells apart
> And wear them on our backs
> Like old women who can see the years
> Back through his eyes.
>
> Something is breathing in there.
> Wake up, we are women.
> The shells are on our backs.
> We are amber,
> the small animals
> are gold inside us.

(3–4)

The speaker is now part of a collective "we," a group of women who cultivate ancient traditions and honor the old treaties with animals. Putting turtle shells on their backs, they become the animal they impersonate, like tribal dancers do, and they can see the ancient world as the old turtle saw it. When time is a loop, the past does not vanish. It remains, albeit in a dormant state, and can be revisited, perhaps even reenacted. The past is never dead—"something is breathing in there," like the fish breathing under water, invisible from the shore. The women in their ceremonial dresses try to awaken this hibernating ancient life, to let it know it is time to come back. "Wake up," they cry on behalf of the whole human, animal, plant, and mineral world. The shells worn on their backs and the animal food circulating in their bodies make them part of the animal world, while amber and gold, suggestive of ceremonial ornaments but also referring to tribal women's beauty, endurance, and value, resonate with the plant and nonorganic world. The poem illustrates Hogan's enduring hope that the ancestral world, buried in the red earth of Oklahoma, will one day emerge from its centuries of sleep, like the awakened locusts who shed their hard skin and flew away.

The turtle makes a cameo appearance in several other poems from this collection, which is structured around the recurrence, repetition, and recontextualization of key words and images. As "a pupil in the eye" of the pond, he presides over the world of Hogan's childhood, "watch[ing] us grow dry" (5) in summer, disappearing in time of drought when the pond's empty eye socket exposes "the fine bones of fish / buried in pow-dered silt / beside hooks" (5), and hibernating in the red clay in winter, imperceptibly but steadily "growing / a larger shell, calcium / from inside sleep" (6). Almost god, "old as earth" (6) and just as wise, the turtle is at once a protective presence, a symbol of endurance, and an embodiment of the world Hogan calls her most intimate home. With his slow but stub-born progress over obstacles, and his imperceptible growth even in sleep, he symbolizes Indigenous people's skills of survivance. "We are plodding creatures / like the turtle" (7), observes Hogan. In the title poem of the collection she writes:

> I came back to say goodbye
> to the turtle
> to those bones
> to the shells locked together
> on his back,
> gold atoms dancing underground.

(8)

Destined for extinction by US colonial policy, the ancient world of Native Americans survived thanks to tribal ceremonies held in secret. With the passage of the American Indian Religious Freedom Act of 1978, it could finally emerge from its state of latency into the light of day.

The Oklahoma of the poet's happiest recollections is full of June bugs and locusts, spiders and snakes, coyotes, crows and hawks, fish and turtles. But revisiting the land, she mourns the many disappearances, like that of the trees from her father's farm, stolen for their precious wood one night by "the dark silhouettes of men" (12). They vanished along with the life nesting in their branches, leaving behind an emptiness, a wound that never heals. Hogan misses the noisy quarrels of crows, "speak[ing] like men / to one another" (13), decimated by newcomers who had no reverence for life. The majestic birds, so human-like in their speech, became a sport for the incoming barbarians "with blue guns." Straining her ears to hear the crows "begin to speak, / to hear the dark berries / uncoil through their flesh," the poet waits in vain "for a breath / to escape the warm feathers" (13).

Killing without justification, or hunting for 'sport'—also called 'recreational hunting'—is sheer cruelty, wanton destruction. All creatures want to live. Unfortunately, living also means killing. Hogan has no problem with accepting the idea of the food chain. But taking life for food is the only case of hunting that can be justified. "Coyote" records Hogan's attempt to come to terms with the killing of predators in retaliation for their stealing farm chickens. The poem opens with the image of a cruel-steel jaw trap[4] being set:

> Steel jaws are tense to clamp shut.
> The man is leaving,
> the small coyote comes sniffing
> soft, soft
> feathers from the sky go out quiet like wings.

> (26)

The deadly device, with its open steel jaws, is a parody of justice on a small, soft animal who walks straight into the trap, his cuddliness a ridiculous contrast to the indifferent mechanism of death. In his anthropocentric arrogance, the trap-setter holds god-like power over the animal he self-righteously deems to be a pest. Hogan finds the idea of human supremacy over 'lower' life forms—historically inclusive of non-white humans—sinister. Her choice of words reveals grief and a sense of powerlessness. Before recounting the fate of the ensnared coyote, she muses on the fragility of life. The coyote is now part of a "we" that cuts across the species barrier, each individual a masterpiece of the evolutionary process:

> Such fragile things we all are,
> such bones,
> such silk nests of hair, fine nerves
> touching the smooth beads of vertebrae
> that string us together.
> Coyote with invisible breath
> calling for snow and wind.

> (26)

The bones, which hold all vertebrae together, spill once the string of the backbone is broken. The death of even the tiniest creature tarnishes the whole fabric of life.

Hogan does not turn away from the reality of death. On the contrary, she witnesses the trapped animal's agony with the eye of a documentalist, but one not ashamed of compassion. Her unexpected declaration: "Coyote, you weren't much," redirects the speaker's energy from instinctive rebellion, which would be futile, toward acceptance of the inevitable. It is an attempt to see the larger relevance of the animal's fate:

> Coyote, you weren't much,
> nothing more than a shadow with eyes,
> a wisp of air wanting to leave
> through the thin bones.
>
> (26)

Ultimately, what is "not much" is life in all its fragility. We are all just "a shadow" and a thin "wisp of air" always threatening "to leave." Hogan's meditation brings out the paradox of life, which both is infinitely precious and "isn't much," simultaneously. Even though life is all we have, it is not ours for long; death is part of the bargain of living. To some it comes after a long and eventful life; others, like the little coyote, meet their end early, too early perhaps. To Hogan the tragedy is that he is punished for being who he is—a predator, likely dispossessed of his hunting grounds by the very man who traps him. This is the only injustice in this poem but it is a scandalous one.

To those who see coyotes as thieves stealing chickens and therefore deserving of punishment, the poet soberly points out: "All of us have stolen something / in the night / the long night ending in sweat [...]" (26). The little predator was only trying to survive, as we all are when pressed hard to the wall, in the darkest time of our lives. Hogan speaks here as one familiar with "the blackest sweat / of morning on the ground" (26).

The Oklahoma Hogan celebrates in her first poetry collection also meant poverty, dispossession, hunger. It is here that the little girl learned to be hard as the land itself; to accept death as part of life, even give thanks for it. The poem "Thanksgiving" centers on a dead turkey killed for the family dinner. Unlike the national holiday, which celebrates colonial greed and the theft of Indian lands, the focal point of this verse is Indigenous people's gratitude for the gift of a powerful bird's life. Far from being an absent referent[5], the freshly killed turkey is evoked with realistic precision, his "blue head on the ground / body in a gleaming white tub / with lion claw feet" (20). Almost beautiful in his final repose, with his "bronze, metallic blue and green" feathers, he commands respect. His sacrifice is welcome, received with thanks: "we give thanks for it," says the narrator, "and for the old woman," she adds, "shawl pulled tight around her" (20).

The day marks a double thanksgiving: for the food that will fill empty stomachs and for the woman who took the bird's life. Unlike the trap-setting farmer or the hunters of crows, she killed the turkey with due respect and out of a higher necessity. Like any other predator, the coyote included, she killed for food. Out of gratitude for her respectful taking of life, the woman—too poor to eat meat herself—is invited to share in the rare feast, as is the custom of the people. She is prepared; she has brought her own mismatched spoons, the only ones she has. The host family are too poor to have spoons to spare. The poem ends with the image of Canada geese flying overhead. Ultimately, it is life that the poem is about, and gratitude for its continuance. Life and death balance each other in the superior wisdom of nature.

If a life taken for food is celebrated and thanks are given for it, how much more to be celebrated is every birth. "Celebration: Birth of a Colt" is spoken from the perspective of little girls curiously watching a hugely pregnant mare. They observe water break down her legs and witness the emergence of a new life: "that slick wet colt / like a black tadpole / darts out / beginning at once / to sprout legs" (16). To Hogan, the moment of birth is a potent reminder of our common biological roots. The colt swims out of his mother's birth canal, resembling a tadpole, the larva of its distant evolutionary ancestor. Having touched the ground, he spreads his folded legs, but the image of "sprouting" them suggests affinities with plants. The red land of Oklahoma welcomes the newly born with sunlight and the blessing of corn pollen, sacred to Indigenous people. This land "will always own us" (17), concludes the poet.

The image of tadpoles sprouting legs recurs in the poem "The River Calls Them," which deals with the life cycle of frogs, a topic familiar to every schoolchild. At the time of Hogan's childhood frogs were numerous in Oklahoma. Since the 1950s (cf. Lannoo), however, their worldwide populations have been declining significantly. One of the factors contributing to their decline is environmental damage. As their highly permeable skin easily absorbs bacteria, toxins, and chemicals, frogs are sensitive registers of environmental pollution. Hogan could not have known this in the 1970s, but there are indications in the poem that the change we now associate with the Anthropocene may have already been underway.

The evolutionary origin of frogs goes back at least two to three hundred million years. At around that time proto-amphibians diverged from lobe-finned fishes, and these evolutionary beginnings are reiterated in the early stages of frog ontogenesis. After adults lay eggs in fresh water areas, the eggs hatch to become tadpoles. These have tails and gills like fish, which they lose as they undergo metamorphosis. Adult frogs have legs and lungs, and can no longer breathe under water. It is probably this fluidity, a sort of vacillation on the edge of becoming, being in between distinct life forms, that fascinates Hogan about frogs. As much as it mirrors the Darwinian theory of evolution, frog metamorphosis also lends credence to Indigenous peoples' belief in the shapeshifting potential of living beings.

Hogan's poem starts with "tadpoles in a jar," probably a teaching aid for a lesson in biology. The poet must have been exposed to the life cycle of frogs as a schoolgirl. The opening stanza gives evidence of her sense of wonder at the efficiency of the process, in which nothing is wasted while new formations emerge as if "from nothing." The stanza reads like a hymn to the mystery and mastery of evolutionary adaptation:

> Tadpoles in a jar
> a shock of legs sprouted
> tail swallowed into
> bones growing from nothing,
> dark nipples of
> toes creeping out,
> one at a time.
> And the sudden need for mud.
>
> (31)

In the process of transformation, tadpoles start to sprout legs and absorb their tails into their bodies. The tail is literally "swallowed into the bones" as it contains nutrients which the froglet uses to build its skeleton. It will not eat before the metamorphosis is completed. In contrast to the rapidly sprouting "shock" of hind legs, the front legs form first under skin and literally "creep out, one at a time," only when fully developed. Once this happens, the froglet can no longer swim and must find some foothold for its newly formed legs. It will have lost its gills by this time, too.

Next the poem shifts to fully developed frogs at the time of the mating season. On summer nights, with their "puffed throats," males advertise their presence to females, hoping to attract a breeding partner. With all the noise they make, however, they become easy prey for "young hunters": either schoolchildren ordered to supply a frog for dissection, or kids collecting frogs for fun—although the phrase "bathed in the salt of child hands" may also suggest the frogs' destination as food. An exceptionally dry summer—and the Oklahoma of Hogan's childhood was known for such—will have been dangerous for the amphibian population as well. Their semi-permeable skin is especially sensitive to dehydration. The stanza ends with the image of "moist skin dried in too much sun, / starved beside a heap of dead flies" (31).

The dead frogs' toes, which first "crept out" of the tadpole in the form of "dark nipples," are now brittle, "turned into twigs." In the image of the frogs' gold eyes when "summer [is] gazing at land," Hogan intriguingly plays with perspective to suggest the reversal of death. While the frogs' eyes can no longer see, they are painted gold by the rays of sun shining from above, its eye in the sky "gazing" down, as if to witness the funerals. Clearly, there is agency in the whole world of nature. By the poem's end the frogs are buried, most likely by compassionate children, who drop them "into earth/damp and waiting." Can some of them revive in the damp ground, their skin rehydrated by the moisture? Or is the frogs' return to the universal circulation of matter meant as an equivalent of resurrection? One way or another, their dry bodies will receive a measure of water, most of them turning liquid in the putrefaction of death, reclaimed by the water that gave them life.

Signaling Hogan's growing fascination with biology, "The River Calls Them" also defines the shape of the author's earthly spirituality. Like her tribal ancestors, she embraces death as part of the miracle of life and celebrates immortality in terms of ecological recycling. Occasionally, there is a note of regret at the loss of lives, a wish to reverse the process of entropy, as in "Finding Beads." For a brief moment Hogan imagines the "small bones of birds" found in the dry pond growing back their flesh and flying up to fill the "holes in the sky" (9), but there is no sustained attempt to defy perceived injustices, no activist engagement yet; her focus here is on reconciliation and healing. Leaving Oklahoma, the poet is "like a locust singing goodbye, / feet still clinging / to the black walnut tree" (25), but a healing bath in a hot spring ("Vapor Cave") gives her the strength to let go of the past and move forward with her life.

To sum up, in the politically intense 1970s, when the Indigenous world followed the ups and downs of the American Indian Movement as reported in *Akwasasne Notes*, the "gone animals" of Hogan's ancestral Oklahoma landscape function as correlates of Indigenous America's painful history, as well as of the joyful time of her childhood when the future poet lived in a loving larger-than-human community. The losses she mourns in *Calling Myself Home* are numerous and embrace turtles, frogs, fish, birds, coyotes, and the rich insect world. Dreaming them back, the poet wishes to revive the tribal past along with the animals, to wake her people up from the sleep of colonial brokenness to a life of renewal and resurgence. Drawing on the lessons learned from Oklahoma animals, Hogan receives consolation and hope from the locusts' emergence from their old skin and the toads' hibernation in preparation for the life-giving rain, while crows and coyotes provide her with visions of survivance under conditions of coloniality. All in all, colonization and decolonization are depicted as interspecies endeavors, and the return of the old ways hinges on a renewed awareness of relationality with, and responsibility for, the nonhuman world. In this context thanksgiving—as opposed to the settler colonial celebration blasphemously called Thanksgiving—is a decolonial praxis, an attitude of respect and gratitude for the gift of nonhuman animals' life. As could be expected from a member of the Chickasaw matrilinear culture, Hogan's poetry presents women as bridges between worlds and keepers of tradition ("Turtle").

Notes

1 *Lunch Poems* is a volume of poetry written by Frank O'Hara (City Lights, 1964).
2 *Calling Myself Home*, with stories added, was republished as *Red Clay: Poems and Stories* (Greenfield Review Press, 1991).
3 Indigenous people tend to regard the term "Native American Renaissance" as controversial. Coined by a white academic critic, it belongs to the colonial epistemology that is being contested by anti-colonial movements. The term is often applied to the heightened publishing activity of Indigenous-descendant American writers after the 1960s. The awarding of the Pulitzer Prize to N. Scott Momaday's novel *House Made of Dawn* in 1969 opened the gates of established publishers to (or, as official literary history insists, "inspired") new Native American poets and novelists. The socio-political context, however, played an equally (if not more) important role in the creation of this phenomenon. In the turbulent 1950s and 1960s a whole new consciousness was being forged—widely available university education gave Indigenous students heightened awareness of and the necessary intellectual tools to question the country's colonial mindset and begin to combat it by means of more or less radical activities. One such event was the 19-month long occupation of Alcatraz in 1969. An organization called Indians of All Tribes demanded the return of land to the original inhabitants of the continent. Equally important were conscience-raising campaigns, inclusive of the publication of the pan-tribal magazine *Akwesane Notes*, which advanced the cause of native sovereignty (1969–1992).
4 The steel-jaw traps are now banned in over 100 countries.
5 The absent referent is the actual animal which disappears in the consumption of 'meat' and other animal-derived products. The concept was first introduced by Carol Adams in her *The Sexual Politics of Meat* (1990).

2 1980s
Birth of an Ecofeminist

The 1980s were a busy and difficult decade. Hogan was a single mother now, raising two Lakota girls she and her husband Pat had adopted after the passage of the Indian Children Welfare Act of 1978. When the marriage ended, she tried to provide the children with the safety of a home while struggling with the traumas of the girls' past. Her university position was an added burden. As the only Indigenous professor in a Native American Studies program at the University of Minnesota, Hogan experienced the academic community's resentment toward her and decided to leave. "The despair and stress of my job made me sick," she confessed ("Hogan, Linda, 1947–"). Back at the University of Colorado, Hogan started teaching creative writing. The strain of those years contributed to the development of a chronic medical condition known as fibromyalgia, which with varying intensity was to plague her for the rest of her life. But as she later confessed in the memoir *The Woman Who Watches Over the World*, times of darkness can be spiritually enriching. "Darkness, too, I know now, has its resonance," she wrote (134).

Indeed, her writing of that period explores the symbolism of light and darkness, rewriting the easy binary. Two of her three poetry volumes from the 1980s: *Eclipse*[1] (1983), *Seeing through the Sun* (1985), and *Savings* (1988) bear titles referencing the interplay of light and darkness, with *Eclipse* explicitly dedicated to women activists from around the world who struggle against the manifold forces of darkness and oppression, including environmental degradation and the loss of species.

Kenneth Lincoln, editor of the Native American Series of books which includes Linda Hogan's *Eclipse*, writes about that volume:

> The poems here convey a sense of the physical world enveloped in a burning light, emanating from the sun in eclipse, animating and illuminating fragile tissues of flesh through "lucent skin." The poet also knows the light's terrible potential to annihilate all Peoples in a nuclear genocide.
>
> (vii)

DOI: 10.4324/9781003364252-4

In spite of the ominous undertones of the collection's title, Hogan mines the positive and the negative side of obscurity and lack of clear vision. In her world, darkness can and often does refer to safety from detection, to authenticity and renewal. It is at night that nocturnal animals keep watch over the world, their "cramped armies / growing" while "dictators lose power" (*Eclipse*, "Night Watch," 45); it is at night that old ceremonies and healing dances are held for the restoration of life, "[t]he feet of small animals / step out of shadow / and mine touch softly / night soil / like dancers too shy for the grace of light (*Eclipse*, "Night Dance" 55). Grouped into six sections, two of which directly address animal-related themes, the poems in this collection depict Hogan listening with one ear to the voices rising out of her native Oklahoma soil, while her other ear is tuned to the sounds of the mountainous landscapes of Colorado, the home to which she had now returned. "Transplant has taken," she wrote. "I have sent down a long tap root and want to stay here" (qtd. in Lincoln, v).

Succinctly capturing Hogan's signature employment of animal figures in *Eclipse*, Kenneth Lincoln observes:

> The deer, the insects, and the birds lend images of quiet waiting, silent companionship, and winged light to an earth-bound woman grieving the desecration of the land, history's forewarnings of destruction, and the translucent thin skin of humanity: "loving every small thing / every step we take on earth."
>
> (vi–vii)

The collection is rich in animal presence at the same time as it is permeated with grief at the many disappearances. "The animals are leaving," states the poet, mourning the victims of overhunting and other atrocities. Yet she refuses to accept the dead-end logic of what would soon be named the Anthropocene. "Even gunshots," she continues, "fired down the edge of the world / have missed them" (*Eclipse* 13). Like other tribal people, Hogan has faith that the birds are alive in another world, which they enter through a hole in the sky—a topic that returns powerfully in her later writing.

Although references to nonhuman animal life are scattered throughout the volume, it is the book's third section, entitled "Who Will Speak," that deserves a closer look here. It begins with an epigraph from a speech that tribal Faithkeeper Oren Lyons, an Iroquois activist, delivered in Geneva. "I see no seat for the eagles," he said, criticizing humans for elevating themselves above the rest of creation (*Eclipse* 53). This section's title poem takes its cue from Lyons's speech. It is we who must speak for the animals, declares Hogan. In the reciprocity of relations, as a species endowed with the gift of language, our "tongue / [...] belongs to grass and light / and the four-legged creatures" (*Eclipse* 42). The poet's ardent devotion to this obligation illuminates not only this poetry collection, but the whole of her creative and activist life.

While *Eclipse* does not bring many fresh insights into the human-animal relationship, it contains two interesting animal portraits, "Crayfish" and "Saint Coyote," which merit discussion. The former focuses on freshwater crustaceans known for their susceptibility to environmental stressors. Hogan presents the tragedy of their anthropogenic disappearance in the form of an extended metaphor. The story begins with "the warm hands / the soft hands of kind men / set[ting] fire near water / where crayfish lived" (*Eclipse* 10). As usual, the author marvels at the numerous paradoxes besetting our species. Acting out of good intentions, we often end up creating disaster. This is so because we remain ignorant of the larger context in which our activities take place. The accumulation of adverbs associated with innocence (warm, soft, kind) attests to the men's perceived goodness, their deed, however, unleashes a chain of consequences leading to the decimation of the crayfish. We witness the alarmed animals emerging from their muddy shelter and turning red, which would be a natural response to a fire consuming their dwelling place, but the following disappearance of water (l. 7) suggests processes of much larger proportions—such as global warming—as the poem's ultimate frame of reference.

The poem next shifts to what looks like a mythical perspective:

> In the beginning
> the people taught crayfish to walk
> on two feet
> and to speak.
> Some remained among men.
> Others stayed behind.
>
> (*Eclipse* 10, ll. 9–13)

This story would be a reversal of the usual tribal worldview, though, according to which animals are our teachers and not the other way around. Teaching animals to be like "us" (to walk on two feet, etc.) resembles in fact the assimilationist policy of colonialism, the phrase "In the beginning" possibly hinting at the origin of the colonial era. The violence of animal training—denying their true nature, forcing them to exhibit unnatural behaviors in order to be more acceptable to dominant humanity, be more like "us"—resonates profoundly with the history of colonial violence toward the human Indigenous populations of the continent. Once assimilated, human and nonhuman animals have the same identity problems; some may welcome the opportunities offered by the new style of life ("Some remained among men"), while others will long for the freedom of their old life ("Others stayed behind"). But even those who reject the colonial society are changed by it forever: "They are the silent ones / who live / in the mud of our footprints." Forgotten, deprived of their territory, condemned to silence, the crayfish still "follow us" (l. 17), their shadow filling the kind men with soft hands with unease bordering on fear. A sense of unnamed threat on which the poem turns is almost a kind of hope.

Once again, we can observe that Hogan makes no qualitative distinction between human and animal people. In the beginning is trust, relationship, an I-Thou perspective. An attempt to convert the other to "our" image breaks the bond of trust, disturbs the harmony, reduces the Thou to an It—abstraction, property. The poem argues that colonialism and speciesism are two faces of the same structural violence, invisible to members of the privileged group. This invisibility leads even kind men with soft hands to commit acts of injustice and cruelty. Latin American philosopher Linda Martín Alcoff perceptively argues that ignorance does not simply result from incomplete knowledge. Admitting the interplay of individual and social or group identities in the development of epistemic practices of ignorance, she demonstrates that it is the third type of ignorance, one actively encouraged by the dominant society, that meets the criterion of *substantive* epistemic practice. In other words, ignorance is not merely a question of a dysfunctional cognitive perspective; it refers primarily to a systemic construction of a faulty worldview, one that upholds the dominant ideology and represses countervailing evidence (Alcoff 48). This, in turn, results in "seeing the world wrongly" (Charles W. Mills, qtd. in Alcoff 47). Hogan frequently stresses the settlers' lack of knowledge about the complex web of interdependencies between all life forms. Not all of the newcomers were evil, but all were ignorant of the tribal people's millennia-old knowledge systems. Wanting short-term results, they ruined the delicate balance of the continent.

"Saint Coyote," the second animal portrait of the volume, is equally anti-colonial in tone, but this time Hogan focuses on a guerrilla warrior who refuses to be dominated. Indeed, the veiled note of hope on which "Crayfish" ends is more apparent here and is tied to the opportunistic predator's elusive world. Adapting easily to human-modified environments, the coyote is also one of the most vocal of North American wild animals. His impressive range of vocalizations has earned him a reputation for singing or even speaking. In Native American lore he has the status of a shapeshifter and trickster who accidentally helps to give the world its final shape. Almost human, most active in the shadowy region between day and night, he is a liminal creature in many senses of this word. "St. Coyote passed over the highway" (14), we read in the poem's opening. He is playing it safe, keeping his distance from the deadly traffic, but by throwing his shadow into headlights, coyote lets people know he is never far away, keeping watch. "Wise to traps," he is constantly plotting tricks, misleading, "always gambling," "always lying"—even to the moon. "That saint"—Hogan cannot conceal her admiration for the skill and ease with which coyote manipulates others, the way his lies mock and ultimately perhaps help to dismantle the official lies that mimic truth. Coyote is her hero, an agent of rebellion in environments marked by indigence and despair, "a luminous savior" in "busy suburbs where children kneel / with lights dark as shut eyes." His world is separate, as if superimposed on the world of man-caused destruction, a shadow world which subverts the dysfunctional logic of diurnal reality. With coyote, "another world crosses the streets." Embodying survival and wisdom, he is a scout sent to keep hope alive.

Hogan's later poems, from her 1985 *Seeing through the Sun* collection, continue to play with the ambiguities of light and darkness, appearances and reality, hiding and revealing. "Porcupine on the Road to the River," a poem which centers on another nocturnal creature, starts with a human couple quarreling in a car as they notice a road-killed animal:

> The porcupine walked
> last night's double vision of car lights.
> Everything disappeared.
> One spine after another,
> light went out the brittle needles.
>
> (*Dark* 67)

The slow moving, nocturnal rodents are frequent road casualties in Maryland, where the poet was then living with her husband. With her signature compassion, she tries to recreate the moment of the tragedy from the point of view of the animal, imagining how he sleepwalks into the dark space between two moving points of light, seemingly a safe passage. The car that hits him drives on. Unless their car is damaged, drivers who run over small animals rarely stop, leaving the casualties to die often slow and painful deaths. The "double vision of car lights" disappears as suddenly as it came. Hogan evokes the car's whizzing, breakneck speed with a quick, two-word sentence. Such linguistic minimalism echoes the driver's no-nonsense attitude to roadkill—an increasingly common 'side effect' of the growing mobility of our species. Animal suffering happens off-screen, in the darkness left behind by the car speeding on to its destination. The porcupine disappears into the darkness of death gradually, "one spine after another." The narrator of Hogan's poem honors the dead porcupine, retrieving him from the realm of the absent referent, to which so-called 'roadkill' is routinely confined by being divorced from both the actual animal and the violence of automobile collisions.

Roadkill is a largely overlooked problem within animal studies, although in the US alone automobile collisions with animals cause over a million deaths per day (Seiler 166).[2] These statistics, according to researcher Dennis Soron, demonstrate that the car has become "an apex predator" (109). Not only are car collisions responsible for greater animal loss than hunting, but as "a symbolically potent 'totem' of postwar capitalism," the automobile provides a direct link to anthropogenic environmental destruction (Soron 121). And it must also be considered that extensive road networks fragment animal habitats and migration routes, creating "one of the leading weapons in human society's large-scale assault on biodiversity" (Soron 122). Ruthless capitalism has been linked with death and destruction since the publication of *Das Kapital*, but it needs a careful observer to penetrate behind its many benevolent guises. On the one hand, Ford's assembly line, a cost-effective mode of production, fostered an unbridled capitalist expansion and facilitated aggressive exploitation of mineral resources, habitat pollution, and conscienceless land development; on the other, as Charles Patterson demonstrates in his *Eternal Treblinka*, it provided a model for both the industrialized slaughter of animals and the 'processing' of animalized humans in the Nazi death camps. In both cases the violence is carefully hidden, almost banal.[3]

Although the couple in the poem drive past the dead animal, they do take notice. They stop quarreling, as if embarrassed by the futility of their argument in the face of unmourned life. Only a solitary red-winged blackbird "keeps vigil" at the side of the river, which remains forever inaccessible to the porcupine. In the absence of other mourners, the poem's narrator performs a mental rite. "I take it in / my own eyes to the river" (*Dark* 67). She both "takes in," or understands the implications of the scene in front of her eyes, and takes the dead body, in her mind's eye, to the porcupine's last destination, which is the river. Having performed the ritual and given respect to the dead porcupine, she looks into the rearview mirror, observing how "[e]verything reverses" (67):

> the blackbird grows smaller,
> becomes a speck of singing dust.
> The road lumbers and clatters
> beneath the porcupine's red and black
> diminishing world of salt.

(68)

The receding scene in the rearview mirror brings to mind a film played backward, in which death is reversed, a mutilated body put together again. Although this is not the case—the porcupine's blood is not miraculously soaked up into the body—the speaker wishes for this to happen, as she imagines the road "lumbering and clattering" in imitation of the animal's characteristic noisy, wobbly gait. The porcupine's notorious craving for salt, which may have brought him onto the road in search of salt residue in the first place, serves as a premonition for the couple's future, as, with their "salty love" (67)—irritated and full of recriminations—they too are on a collision course. The woman understands the message (having "taken it in"). She invites the man to the riverbank to enjoy the time together "before [death] stops us in our tracks" (68).

"The Other Side" is another poem of mourning. The title refers to death, which Hogan perceives as "the other side of creation" (79). As the sun begins to set, a white horse visible on the horizon seems to be falling off the western edge of the land, "like the sun running from the teeth of darkness" (78). The opening image establishes the poem's controlling metaphor—of death lying in wait everywhere, like an enormous, greedy predator. The poet imagines the horse fleeing from its jaws:

> Fleeing past men who clean weapons
> in sudden light, women
> breaking eggs in faith
> that new ones will grow
> radiant in feather cribs
> the coyotes watch over.
>
> (78)

But predation is inscribed into all forms of life, sometimes in ways as obvious as humans hunting for food with guns, sometimes in a more veiled form, when a life-bearing, home-making woman takes the unborn babies of hens from their nests to feed her own family. (Although this is not the place to dwell on this image, the way Hogan skillfully navigates the troubled waters of gendering violence deserves at least a mention.) Sometimes the life we raise for food roams free and is able to express its natural behavior, at other times it is raised in restricted environments with little or no respect for its wellbeing. Even the infant eggs' "feather cribs" are little solace for mother hens who lose their children, and if humans overlook an egg or two, these are sure to be noticed by animal predators who "watch over" their food resources as eagerly as humans do. Hogan knows that life means eating and eating means killing.[4] When the grazing cows return home from the pasture, they "turn away / from the world / wearing a death mask" (78). The world appears to be a never-ending carnival of death. Masked as care, animal husbandry is in essence "violence that claims to care" (Wadiwel 112).

"All the innocent predators!" exclaims Hogan, as if overwhelmed by this revelation. As she struggles to accept death as a possibility of life for others, there is a sense of confusion at the realization that even the best intentioned, most innocent creatures—like mothers, usually associated with care and safety, or the beautiful coyote, who always seems to be smiling—kill and eat other living organisms. Her mind knows but her heart refuses to become reconciled to this paradox, which is a natural consequence of our common embodiment. In the face of ubiquitous death, the poet wants at least the white horse to be an exception to the rule, to return "like morning / from the underworld / kicking in its teeth" (78)—to outwit death, like mythical heroes, like the sun-god premodern people believed rose from the dead every morning. She listens for the sound of his hooves, "a testimony of good luck" (78). While there is no open rebellion against the reality of predation in this poem, Hogan has yet to re-position herself within the worldview of her tribal ancestors and identify fully with their ecological animalism.[5]

Whether the horse returns alive or not will not make much difference in the overall pattern, when even the moon is on the run from the jaws of death, unable to stop for a moment in the temporary refuge of "the tree's broken arm." The branch, likewise, although sprouting new leaves and apparently returning to life, "is innocent of its own death" (79) as the air it must absorb for photosynthesis to occur is toxic with pollution. In all probability, the red-winged blackbird from the previous poem, "Porcupine on the Road to the River," did not keep watch over the rodent's body disinterestedly, either.

But darkness need not be sinister. It does not have to be a "mask of death" or a cover for crime. Darkness is just as much the territory of mystery and authenticity. This is where the collection's title—*Seeing through the Sun*—reveals its deeper meaning. It is mostly in full light that we pretend to be somebody different, better than we really are. The night lets us be ourselves, it reveals to us our deepest selves. Additionally, in English the sun has masculine connotations, and many premodern peoples, like the Aztecs, believed the sun to be a war-like, aggressive deity. In this context, the phrase "seeing through the sun" may refer to a feminist critique of the dominant, patriarchal culture of the West. "The Territory of the Night" is a poem resonant with ecofeminist philosophy. The poem's female speaker is attracted to a black horse in the road. She can hear him "breathing in / the solitude of empty space, / breathing out through men's initials, / the world branded on ragged sides" (86). Free range horses are often branded with their owners' initials for easy identification. If they change hands, they will get a new brand next to the old one. The black horse "has been owned and owned again," his scarred sides telling the story of his multiple commodification.

In the course of history branding has been used not only on animals, but on animalized people as well. Slaves on plantations would be branded to make them retrievable if they tried to run away to freedom. The practice of enslaving and owning of human beings and their offspring was called chattel slavery, because slaves, like objects, were considered moveable property. Chattel—property—had no rights; they were born to bring profit to their owners. Etymologically, chattel is related to cattle and capital. The fact that all the three words come from the same Latin root, *capitālis*, helps to reestablish the original connection between property and profit. Again and again, animals and animalized people have suffered commodification as exploitable resources and means to their masters' ends. Even beyond the turn of the 20th century, white American women shared this fate, too, being legally considered the chattel of their husbands.[6] Although male initials were not visibly imprinted on female skin, they were just as effective in confining women to their masters' households, the women's fertility directly related to national and family prosperity.

"Our bodies speak / across illegal borders / of woman and horse," the poem continues. Far from being natural, the borders have been artificially erected by the male guardians of order, the train-encased "diplomats [who] rush forward on metal tracks / that will never touch" (86). Out of touch with one another as much as with the parallel world of the m/other, the patriarchs of this world have exiled humanity to a ghetto of hyperseparation, any longing to cross the border raising the specter of dehumanization. The term "hyperseparation" was introduced by Val Plumwood, an Australian ecofeminist philosopher, to conceptualize the Western construction of human identity as outside nature. In her *Feminism and the Mastery of Nature* (1993), Plumwood holds Cartesian reason responsible for erecting the "illegal borders" Hogan speaks of. Far from being 'natural,' nature is and must be seen as a political category, the 'other' of privileged modern binaries, she argues. Since the politicization of nature allows for the construction of elaborate oppressive hierarchies, liberation from exploitative structures must start with the questioning of the standpoint of mastery and a corollary reconnecting with the natural world. In other words Plumwood, as a spokesperson for critical ecological feminism,[7] urges the liberation of humanity through a collective crossing of the illegitimate, "illegal borders" of hyperseparation toward the older, wiser, more ancient realm of nature, which is our true home. Needless to say, this vision resonates with the decolonial agendas of Indigenous peoples.

The woman in Hogan's poem refuses to be constrained by prescriptive norms. She crosses over to the other side of the modern / colonial binary in obedience to a deeper call, more ancient and true. Recognizing a shared history of colonization and chattel slavery, her "hands touch the black alphabet" imprinted on the horse's sides, overriding the sterile fears of the diplomats who "rush forward on metallic tracks" with machine-like efficiency, escaping from the animal they are, the parallel rows of rails "that will never touch" (86) symbolizing their existential alienation from their deepest identity.

Humanity is embedded in nature; animality—not rationality—is our primordial, primeval, existential experience. Not words, not language understood as an abstract system of arbitrary signs, but the body is our prime instrument of communication. "There is another language in the dark," the poem's speaker discovers, as her hands touch the "alphabet" of the horse's body. Amidst alarming declarations of the breakdown of communication, the advent of the alienated individual, and the death of religion, the woman finds divinity, communication, and communion in realigning herself with the animal, animistic world. Her discovery of "our animal bodies divine" is a manifesto of spiritual ecofeminism and a healing experience. "The solitude of empty space" of the poem's beginning is transmuted into communion energized by the touch. Having reestablished contact with the sacred, her perception is transformed too. Now she sees the whole world as a living, breathing entity; even "the potatoes are alive in the cellar," watching her through the eye-like sprouts on their bodies, and the "dark chickens from South America" that converge on a "warm bulb" seem to suggest that there is some secret "heart of light" (86) beating in the animal bodies we all inhabit.

With "The Territory of the Night" Hogan strongly allies herself with a position Plumwood calls ecological animalism. Challenging the dominant ideology of hu/man mastery over the supposedly inferior sphere of nature, Plumwood affirms connections between the human and nonhuman worlds. According to her, "ecological animalism supports and celebrates animals and encourages a dialogical ethics of sharing and negotiation between humans and animals, while undertaking a re-evaluation of human identity that affirms inclusion in animal and ecological spheres" (*The Eye*, 48).

The frayed problematics of inclusion, as well as the unsettling questioning of human identity, dominate Hogan's animal-centered poems from *Savings*, her last poetry collection published in the 1980s. The greedy expanses of snow in winter, which can easily "swallow" the suddenly absent animals, remind the poet "that I am in every creature / and they are in me" (*Dark* 91). But it is Hogan's struggle with the phenomenon of universal predation that stands out as perhaps the most intriguing development of this volume. Although she touched upon it in her earlier poetry, she now faces unblinkingly the fact that we all live off one another: humans, animals, plants, even minerals.

"Elk Song" begins with thanks to the animal and plant life that provide humans with food, clothing, and shelter. This is followed by the realization that even our most innocent pets are part of the chain of predation and will follow their inbred instincts whenever an opportunity arises. "Even the yelping dog at our heels / is a hungry crow" and would not despise the remains of some bigger animal's feast. At this point Hogan is ready to celebrate nature's bounty regardless of its problematic dark side:

> The earth
> is a rich table
> and a slaughterhouse,
> for humans as well.
>
> (*Dark* 105)

Re-situating humans in ecological terms—the essence of Plumwood's ecological animalism—implies that humans and nonhumans are "mutually available for respectful use in conditions of equality" (*The Eye* 78). After a near-death encounter with a crocodile in 1985, Plumwood was forced to rethink the Western narrative of human exceptionalism. "It was a shocking reduction, from a complex human being to a mere piece of meat," she wrote later ("Prey"). In a direct confrontation with a predator, the ideology of human sovereignty collapses, and with it the artificially constructed hyperseparation between the human and the other-than-human. Unless we accept the fundamental fact of our edibility, she warns, we will never be ready "to coexist with the otherness of the earth, and to recognize ourselves in mutual, ecological terms" ("Prey"). Hogan's celebration of "our animal bodies divine" was an important step toward embracing our common membership in the ecological community, complete with the acceptance of "our essential foodiness" (Plumwood, *The Eye* 91). In accordance with traditional tribal knowledges, life is a gift from and to ecological others, and death signifies a reunion with the earth, our ancestors, and the earth's others.

In her ecofeminist explorations Val Plumwood was largely inspired by Aboriginal wisdom. This helped her to avoid replicating the exclusionary logic plaguing Western re-conceptualizations of human-nonhuman relationships. In her unfinished essay "The Wisdom of the Balanced Rock: The Parallel Universe and the Prey," she suggests that we live in two separate universes. First, there is the "individual justice universe" (*The Eye* 35) where the human body is self-enclosed and needs to be rigidly defended against any assault on its potential foodiness. Then, there is the ecological universe governed by the idea of the food chain, in which "everything flows" and where bodies belong to all. Although generally impermeable to each other, these two converge at the point of death and when food is considered. On account of her immersion in Indigenous cosmologies, Plumwood had a critical approach to what she called "alienated vegetarianism," believing it to be an unsustainable ethical position, one which remains within the binary logic of the West. "All our food is souls," she declared (*The Eye* 45). "Justice in the ecological sphere has tough rules that we have shown great resistance to accepting," she concludes. "It consists of a very radical egalitarian framework in which you have your little piece of life force for just so long as it's not wanted by another" (*The Eye* 45).

In "Elk Song" Hogan imagines such an ecological universe of mutual use. The earth provides nourishment for all its children, but its richly laid table needs to be continually replenished with new food and thus cannot exist without the slaughterhouse, the table's "other." In other words, in order to receive, we all have to give; reciprocity is the cornerstone of mutual respectful use, a standpoint Hogan comes to identify with. When she finally zeroes in on the elk of the poem's title, she remembers a warm night when she slept in the open and an elk ran across her, "every hoof miss[ing] my shaking bones" (*Dark* 106). With his bulk and powerful legs, the animal could have easily trampled her to death, why did he not? Surely, the poet "was an enemy / from the other side of the forest" (106). In essence, she owes her life to what can only be explained as the elk's purposeful avoidance of harming her—a member of the human species notorious for its destructive potential to the elk's own people[8] as well as to the entire natural world. "Didn't I say the earth is a slaughterhouse, / for humans as well?" asks Hogan, touched by the elk's generosity, apparently reconciled to the idea that, potentially, she could be food too. In gratitude for the animal's compassionate attitude, she now pays her tribute to the majestic elk:

> This is for the elk,
> the red running one
> like thunder over hills,
> a saint with its holy hoof dance
> an old woman whose night song
> we try not to hear.
>
> (105)

Again, the poet foregrounds her signature art of close observation, focusing on the animal's characteristic thundering gallop, his mating dance—with its display of strength and physical dominance—and the unusual bugling sound that can be heard at rutting time in Colorado and other Rocky Mountain states. Beginning as a high-pitched squeal and ending with a guttural low rumble, the elk's eerie call sounds like a lament of accursed spirits, some urgent message "we try not to hear." Did Hogan hear in it the tragic history of Turtle Island's once powerful people, robbed of their land by newcomers from across the great sea, a story common to all Indigenous inhabitants of the Americas? If this were the case, it would be better to plug one's ears against such a story, for it opens the still fresh wounds. At the poem's close Hogan imagines "the gone elk" gathering in the darkness of the forest and pulling "the hide of earth tight" to drum "back the woodlands, / tall grass and days we were equal / and strong" (106).

Perhaps that elk who spared her life once still remembered the old treaties with humans and respected the ties of kinship binding him to his non-elk relatives. Sharing the same fate, the elk and Indigenous humans share the same dream as well—the dream of restoring the old ways through traditions and ancient ceremonies. Like the poet's human ancestors, the "gone elk" also contribute to this common cause of repair and restoration. "I know the old ones are here," declares Hogan in another poem,

> And every morning I remember the song
> about how buffalo left through a hole in the sky
> and how the grandmothers look out from those holes
> watching over us
> from there and from there.

(99)

The Indigenous people of North America believe that the animals that once roamed the continent did not simply become extinct. Offended by the disrespectful attitudes of the newcomers, they left in the same way as they had emerged onto this world. To some tribes, this would be a hole in the sky. Although they are in another world now, they watch over their descendants and when the time is ripe they may come back, like the "gone elk" who return for a healing ceremony, or the buffalo "still living / across the drifting face of the moon" (91) and making a promising comeback on the Great Prairies at the turn of the 21st century.[9]

Even today, when native people reach back "to the old world in canyons," they will still see "blood women dancing on walls / to the earth's drum / and the mother of deer and corn" will appear to them. Their invisible presence is constant, Hogan asserts; they are "all around us" (90) at all times. When urban Indians start "drumming and singing," the inessential city will disappear for them too, and they will be able to greet their relatives like they did in the old world: "Hello aunt, hello brother, hello trees / and deer walking quietly on the soft red earth" (97). In her Minneapolis[10] apartment, far from the wild world she loved, the poet was able to keep her inner harmony only when reconnected to this invisible world. "In the first light," she writes, "I remember who rewards me for living, / not bosses / but singing birds and blue sky" (98).

Savings is rich in references to drumming, a ritual expressive of protest and mounting anger. "Those Who Thunder" focuses on people of Native descent who reject the ways of the white man, refuse to work at demeaning, low paid jobs any longer, and who drum and dance at night. These people are sending warning signals which read:

> Take shelter you,
> because we are thundering and beating on floors
> and this is how walls have fallen in other cities.

(129)

Evidently their outrage is shared by America's nonhuman inhabitants, like the elk, who join in the drumming, who gather at night, in the benevolent dark, to drum the old world back. When everyone is asleep, the drumming and the old songs painstakingly piece the world together again. Invisibly "bones are filling up the arms / with new life, / gourds are climbing fences" (104); evolution is still in progress, restoration is taking place everywhere. But it might stop if not for the ritual.

The price for the continuity of life is "breaking"—the seed must break for the seedling to evolve, and to feed new life another one must break open. The nonhuman world "lives like we do," ventures Hogan, "off those before us" (103). In the poem entitled "Pillow" the speaker muses on the feathers which stuff the pillow-slip, imagining they were a bird once who roosted on birch trees. This is followed by the poet's apologies to the pillow:

> Pillow, forgive us the bird's lost life.
> I smell it still,
> my face against the singed dark,
> and forgive us our other trespasses,
> the mice within our poisoned walls,
> the infirm in our beds,
> and refugees driven in snow like rabbits
> chased by a circle of beaters.

(101)

Addressing her feather-stuffed comforter on lonely, sleepless nights, the woman makes a confession of humanity's sins against the holiness of life. The bird who lost her life for the pillow to be made was probably killed by a gunshot.[11] The "singed dark" the speaker can still smell metaphorically collapses the bird marked by gunpowder with the innocent lives burned in the atomic explosions in Hiroshima and Nagasaki, an image which haunts Hogan's poetry of the 1980s. The memory of such atrocities keeps her awake at night. In her nonhierarchical universe, human and nonhuman lives are placed side by side, like the relatives they are, and violence against one, even the most insignificant, creature is violence against the whole network of mutuality. Referencing the extermination of mice, commonly regarded as vermin, the poem reinforces the unsettling connection between human and nonhuman animal holocaust. The death of mice "within our poisoned walls" alludes both to our criminal denial of hospitality to those who seek refuge under our roof, and to the use of Zyklon B, a cyanide-based pesticide, in the gas chambers of Nazi death camps—that ultimate emanation of modernity's dark side.

"In this narrowing life, let us come apart, and float off / light like feathers" (101), concludes Hogan. In accordance with the collection's positive valuation of "breaking," understood as necessary for life to continue, I read this statement as an invitation to face our complicity in humanity's innumerable "trespasses," to open ourselves to devastating grief, without which healing cannot come. Within Christianity, whose principles Hogan assimilated as a schoolgirl, confession of sins must be accompanied by penitence. Only then can forgiveness (feeling "light as feathers") be granted. "This narrowing life" that the poem depicts is the opposite of the biblical fullness we, humans and nonhumans, were created to enjoy. Like her many other poems, "Pillow" is rich in biblical resonances. The way Hogan reads the Bible, however, is counterhegemonic, anarchic, anti-capitalist, and decolonial. In "Those Who Thunder," for instance, she uses the Beatitudes (Matt. 5, 3–10) to rebel against wage slavery: "those poor who will inherit the earth / already work it" (*Dark* 129). The concluding section of "Pillow" points at hardened trespassers who have made death efficient and clean and whose greed has driven the world to the brink of destruction. Mistaking spiritual riches for precious mineral deposits, "businessmen lean forward" over an opening in the mountain, the light from the stone "touching all the perfect creases / of their coats and great-coats" (102).

Although the poor and oppressed seem to be powerless against the mighty of the world, the crow offers a model of resistance within any-body's reach. In "Gamble" Hogan pays tribute to crow the trickster, much as she did to coyote in "Saint Coyote":

Those men with dollars on the mind
are pushed around by Monday
and tricked by Crow,
tricked by the broken look of Crow's thin legs.
That hungry Crow.
But its wings, oh!
Oh! And its laughter
the theft of radishes
from the big men's fingers
like a hand game
where dark women

deceive white men, singing,
You're crazy,
bad luck,
these words sounding like love songs
until the men pay up
with big grins on their faces [...].

(116)

Variously hated and admired, crows are sometimes said to be among the most intelligent animals on earth, their cognitive abilities equaling those of the great apes. Among the most sophisticated skills of these social opportunists are the use of imagination and the ability to anticipate the future. Yet when considered to be pests, crows have been the targets of organized extermination campaigns. Throughout Hogan's poetry the fate of the crow is closely associated with the fate of Indigenous Americans, the former and the latter both surviving due to their resilience, wit, and adaptability. "Gamble" presents the crow as an icon of survivance. Her[12] manipulative skills, coupled with a deceitful appearance, help her to trick even the strongest and the cleverest. It is the crow that has the final laugh. The two choked lines that follow the poem's expository sentence, with their strong end-rhyme: "That hungry Crow. / But its wings, oh!", express the poet's delight, her breathless admiration for the consummate trickster. The next line starts with another exclamation, an echo of the previous one, and this accumulation of "ohs" reinforces the poet's surprised, ecstatic realization that the weak can win against the powers that be. Lost for words at the bird's inventiveness, she is filled with empowering wonder. Taking their cue from the crow, "dark women," victims of patriarchal and colonial violence, use the only power they have—their seductive appeal—in their struggle for dignity and survival. "Those women, oh!" (116), exclaims the poet in an echo of her delighted discovery of the crow's winning strategy. It is these women that have the final laugh. Laughter and deceit are powerful weapons in the face of systemic injustices.

"Gamble" belongs to a substantial group of poems that focus on "animal lessons," or the teachings of the animal elders. Originating in close observation of nonhuman animals' behavior, they draw parallels between nonhuman and human worlds, and apply to human lives the wisdom that animals convey to their observers. In terms of ecological feminism, the animal lessons of Hogan's poetry supply powerful arguments to re-think the assumed uniqueness of our own species.

In conclusion, Hogan's animal-centered poetry of the 1980s shows a significant correlation with ecofeminism, and more specifically with the position Plumwood called critical ecological feminism. Focusing on the intersecting oppressions of colonialism / capitalism, speciesism, and sexism, Hogan becomes an important voice for the voiceless, an outspoken critic of modernity's intertwined structural violences. In the pages of her poetry such animal opportunists and trickster figures as crow and coyote become teachers of decolonial resistance and embodiments of humanimal survivance. In the modern / colonial context reclaiming the bond with non-human animals is an act of resurgence, a dismantling of "illegal borders," and an inscription of the human within the world of universal foodiness, a world which is and has always been irredeemably kin-centric. In a patri-archal culture woman and animal become natural allies in anti-colonial resurgence: the struggle to depose the "human" and restore the ancient culture of the gift. Additionally, the three poetry collections published in the 1980s start to inquire into the ontological mystery of human destruc-tiveness, which will come to be an obsessive motif in Hogan's most mature writings.

Notes

1 The volume's first section contains poems published as *Daughters, I Love You* in 1981. In my analysis of Hogan's poetry from *Eclipse*, I will refer directly to this volume, and not to *Dark. Sweet*, which is referenced in the discussion of other poems (with the exception of the most recent poetry, collected in *A History of Kindness*, which is analyzed in Chapter 7).

2 It is estimated that with the 73% drop in traffic due to the coronavirus pan-demic, roadkill fell by more than 50% (Katz).

3 Philosopher Hannah Arendt introduced the term "the banality of evil" in her book *Eichmann in Jerusalem: A Report on the Banality of Evil* (Viking Press, 1963).

4 Parenthetically speaking, the predator category also includes vegans, who must kill a plant before it can be eaten and who are in many complex ways impli-cated in the capitalist market economy.

5 Ecological animalism is a concept discussed by Val Plumwood in her essay "Animals and Ecology: Towards a Better Integration." It will be theorized later in this chapter.

6 Andrea Dworkin and Catherine MacKinnon write in *Pornography and Civil Rights: A New Day for Women's Equality*: "Put in the simplest terms: women were the chattel property of men under law until the early part of the twenti-eth century. Married women could not own property because they were prop-erty. A woman's body, her children, and the clothes on her back belonged to her husband. When the husband died, another male, not the mother, became the legal guardian of the children. The body of a married woman belonged to her husband just as a slave's body belonged to the white master. A single woman was under the legally formidable authority of her father or other male relatives. Married women were what nineteenth-century feminists called 'civilly dead.' Single women sometimes paid taxes. No women had rights of citizen-ship. Women did not have a constitutionally protected right to vote until 1920" (p. 12).

7 Dissatisfied with environmental philosophy on account of its veiled mascu-linist agenda, and equally critical of ecofeminism for advancing the notion of "the angel in the ecosystem" (*Feminism* 10) and rearticulating the exclusionary

logic it sought to overcome, Plumwood develops a critical ecological feminism as a liberationist framework capable of integrating environmental theory and praxis with the politics of mutuality. Rejecting our species' hyperseparation from nature, as well as postmodern theories (like deep ecology) which dissolve human-nonhuman differences, her third way proposal attempts to preserve both difference and continuity.

8 In 2017 38,555 elk were "harvested" in the state of Colorado alone, as one can read in an internet blog *Backcountry Chronicles*.

9 Oglala Sioux leader Alex White Plum has been instrumental in bringing back herds of wild buffalo to the Great Prairies (Hogan, *Radiant* 50–51).

10 Hogan lived in Minneapolis between 1982 and 1984, teaching American Indian Studies and American Studies at the University of Minnesota.

11 The image of "the singed dark" may also allude to the fact that housewives raising geese for feather would scald the dead bird with hot water before the bird's feathers could be removed.

12 The feminine gender is suggested by the crow's association with the dark women.

3　1990s
Wildness

Linda Hogan ended the 1980s with the publication of her first novel, *Mean Spirit* (1990), which became a finalist for the Pulitzer Prize for Literature in 1991. This success was followed by the release of two more works of fiction in the 1990s: *Solar Storms* (1995) and *Power* (1998), as well as a new volume of poetry, *The Book of Medicines* (1993), finalist for the National Book Critics Circle Award. Apart from fiction and poetry, Hogan coedited a collection of essays on the bond between women and animals under the title *Intimate Nature* (1998), published a book of personal meditations on the natural world entitled *Dwellings: A Spiritual History of the Living World* (1995), and a Native American memoir, *The Woman Who Watches Over the World* (2000). At the age of 52, at the height of her career, she suffered a serious brain and spine injury as a consequence of a dramatic riding accident. Repeated hospitalizations, memory loss, and a long period of convalescence forced her to stop working for the university and slowed down her creative work, but having inherited her tribal ancestors' resilient spirit, she was soon back at her writing, finishing projects begun before the accident and making plans for the future.

"Hogan's natural world in *The Book of Medicines* is beautiful, wild, and also very dangerous," writes environmental critic Donelle Dreese in her article "The Terrestrial and Aquatic Intelligence of Linda Hogan" (17). In comparison with the earlier poetry, this volume, which by critical agreement marks Hogan's poetic maturity, takes a more decisive turn toward the untamed wildness of nature and of drives and instincts. It also marks the poet's passionate involvement with "aquatic intelligence," especially with ocean mammals such as dolphins and whales. Naturally, the danger mentioned by Dreese does not so much reside in nature herself, but originates with humans that have colonized natural resources and are driving the nonhuman world to extinction. In this regard *The Book of Medicines* continues the ecofeminist and decolonial critique which dominated the poet's earlier work. The volume's title brings to mind associations with healing and the Indigenous concept of the medicine wheel—an expression of radical interconnectivity of everything that exists. On the collection's thematic and organizational level, this concept is echoed by recourse to

DOI: 10.4324/9781003364252-5

recurring imagery and the repetition of key words, "hunger" being one of them.

The collection's opening poem, "The History of Red," sets the tone for those to follow. As one of the colors in the medicine wheel, the red of this verse is linked to blood, earth, birth, cave paintings, bleeding and medical experiments, and to fear, hunting and death, but also to fire, love, and life itself. Hogan writes:

> Red is the fear
> that turns a knife back
> against men, holds it at their throats,
> and they cannot see the claw on the handle,
> the animal hand
> that haunts them
> from some place inside their blood.
>
> (*Dark* 136)

Wildness with its primal instincts is the deepest, most ancient place within us. The repository of citified peoples' fears, our repressed evolutionary beginnings come back to haunt us,[1] our forbidden animality threatening to dismantle the myth of human difference, with the entire system of dominance that is built on it. War, one of the most fundamental experiences of mankind, is also one of the most evident throwbacks to human evolution's most primitive stages, when we were simply one animal species among others, competing for food and territory. But we have not changed that much since, Hogan is saying. Hunger remains the primal drive behind so-called progress, which the poet demystifies as all-devouring greed. She personifies hunger as "the fisherman / who said dolphins are like women" (141). Acting on this analogy, men treat both with the same contempt, raping "the sea [...] pregnant / with clear fish" in the same way as they violate the lives of human females. "Hungry, we are hungry for the whole world," she notes in another verse (150).

On the other hand, by infringing on the self-other boundary and pushing us to merge with the outside world, hunger is not unlike love; it is an instinctual, albeit misguided response to the call of the other, a recognition of our interconnectedness within a larger whole. "The body [...] wants to live beyond itself / like the destitute men / who took the shining dolphins from the sea" (142), Hogan writes. These men are "destitute" because they lack the cultural script to translate this primal drive, this "wanting to be inside," into relevant action. Without it, they are bound to destroy the object of their obsessive desire. The men's destitution is spiritual as much as material, the result of centuries of cultivated ignorance.

Hogan locates physiological hunger at the intersection of our ex-static desires—desires which rupture the outer limits of the self in obedience to a call to grow; hunger corresponds to our "wanting to be inside, / to drink / and be held in / the thin, clear milk of the gods" (142). Welcoming the other into oneself and being welcomed back is the only guarantor of immortality. Satisfying physiological hunger by digesting food literally means becoming the other; it is resurrection and radical re-connection to everything that exists. The only thing that matters in this process is conditions of *respectful* use. These and similar insights inform the bulk of *The Book of Medicines*.

In "Bear Fat" the speaker describes how, after a tribal ceremony in which her eyes were rubbed with bear fat, she reconnected with the bear, with her own hunger, and that of the hunters who had killed the hibernating animal. The men and their dogs "grew fat / with the swallowed grease" (143), the satiated dogs possibly dreaming about the wildness they had been part of before domestication. The poem's speaker travels back to that wildness, becoming the bear whose fat, rubbed onto her eyelids, was "the light / I saw through":

> I am afraid of the future
> as if I am the bear
> turned in the stomach
> of needy men
> or the wolf become a dog
> that will turn against itself
> remembering what wildness was
> before the crack of gun [...].

> (144)

The world of hunger is the world of our potential foodiness, a world where food is a sacrament of communion, incorporating everyone and everything in an endless becoming, as much as it is a necessity of life.

Above all, however, it is a world governed by fear and ingenious prey-predator alliances which enhance mutual chances of survival—humanimal survivance—like the case of "the wolf become a dog." We now know that the domestication of wolves involved a two-way relationship. Out of the three pathways to domestication available, wolves, according to archeologist Melinda Zeder, took the commensal one,[2] based on sharing food resources. The dog's wolf ancestors scavenged for food around human settlements and gradually entered into a partnership with humans (Zeder 249). Do they still remember the lost wildness? Hogan wonders, evidently equally concerned by the lost wildness of humans. The image of the dog turning against his wild ancestor the wolf—probably in defense of the human who feeds him—is a veiled reference to those assimilated members of tribal communities who serve the colonial agenda and betray their own people. The commensal pathway attracts humans and nonhumans alike.

"Return: Buffalo" elaborates on the unconscious death wish behind the destructive actions of people who have lost touch with their inner wildness, the sacred place within. The poem starts as follows:

> One man made a ladder
> of stacked-up yellow bones
> to climb the dead
> toward his own salvation.
> He wanted
> light and fire, wanted
> to reach and be close to his god.
>
> (145)

For Hogan the massacre of the buffalo was a desperate attempt by the white man to sate his metaphysical hunger, to fill the gnawing void inside him. Blind to the sacredness around him, he longed for a connection with a god created in his own image, as destructive as that god was. In the eyes of Indigenous people, the cold-blooded extermination of the mountainous animals of the prairie was an act of deicide. The unfortunate man eventually discovers that "his god was the one / who opened his shirt / and revealed the scar of mortal wounding" (145). The new Americans, as Hogan sometimes calls them, lost their chance for salvation when they imagined they were attaining it, while the true god they had slain continued to speak to tribal people in dreams and ceremonies, promising a renewal of the old world.

The return of the buffalo promised by the poem's title can be understood—literally as well as metaphorically—within the decolonial interpretive frame. From inside a mountain of rotting carcasses "a terrible moan" could be heard. It turns out that:

> [...] one was not dead
> or it had come back from there
> [...]
> like a prophet
> coming out of the hills
> with a vision
> too unholy to tell.
>
> (146)

Either buried alive under the bulky bodies of his companions or literally returning from "there," as the Ghost Dancers believed they would, the buffalo comes back from the dead, the sacred comes back, but he remains forever changed by the harrowing experience. Like an Indigenous quester coming back with a vision, the buffalo's is, however, "too unholy to tell." Hogan imagines the animal traveling "the endless journey / of fear" and returning "from the far reaches" (146) without the means to communicate the terror he had lived through. Why do humans do this to sentient, intelligent, nonhuman people?—Hogan cannot stop asking. Why do they have no reverence for life, for the sacredness of it? Again, the role of cultural scripts cannot be underestimated. Those who believe in a patriarchal, unmovable god safely positioned outside the natural world will continue to 'subdue' nature in the name of the abstractions they live by: "they must have thought / how life came together / was a casual thing / war a righteous sin," the poem continues. They would soon find out, however, that their "betrayal [...] would come back to them / one day" (146). It already has, in the shape of the Anthropocene. On the other hand, those who see themselves as part of the natural world and find all life sacred respect untamed nature as the only divinity there is. Having reverence for life, they try to live in harmony with themselves, with others, and with the entire universe. They are the true caretakers of the world.[3]

"Harvesters of Night and Water" returns to the destitute men first introduced in "Hunger." The image of a violated ocean, whose waters have just been broken by a fishing boat, is juxtaposed with that of "tiny men / with impotent nets" searching for food and ending up gathering more than they need, their hunger never abating: "a blue crab, tender inside its shell, / a star from another night of darkness than ours, / a glass eyed halibut" (147) that is so huge she has to be shot dead. All the beauty and the suffering of their 'catch' is lost on the pillaging men. The most desirable yield—an octopus—is pulled up at daybreak. The following exchanges, short and elemental in their structure, enact the excited calculations of the fishermen: "It will be used as bait. / It will sell for two hundred dollars. / It will be cut into pieces [...]" (148). All they can see is the animal's utilitarian value. Meanwhile, the octopus has a mind of her[4] own and her own vision of the future. She fights against the screaming men, never looking them in the eye, never acknowledging their world. An accidental witness to the struggle, the poem's speaker wants to intervene, to defend the animal that "collects coins / like they do" (148), but the men are not likely to be moved by stories of a different intelligence. Luckily, the creature manages to escape into the ocean, "floating / like a man's dream of falling / into worlds he will never know" (149).

Oceanic depths are a world unknown to men, claims Hogan in her autobiographical *The Woman Who Watches Over the World*. It is a woman's world; it guards its mysteries and wants to be left alone, unexplored. Ruled by Sea Mother, called Sedna in the far north (Hogan, *A Woman* 38), it is a healing realm. There, in the "bending dark weeds" where the octopus disappears, "broken waters heal themselves" (*Dark* 149). There the men's destructive potential has no access. The poem's female speaker looks into the deep waters, remembering how the octopus:

> [...] turned red with fear, then paled
> before climbing down the boat.
> It was naked,
> it was beautiful
> like an angel
> with other wings,
> its arms were those of four mothers
> desperate for life.
>
> (149)

The short lines, especially the two that start with the pronoun "it," which mimic the form of the male speculations upon catching the octopus, are a counterresponse to the fishermen's greed. The woman finds beauty where they only saw profit and sympathizes with the sea creature's struggle for life. Hogan closes the poem on a confessional note: "I want the world to be kinder. I am a woman. I am afraid" (150).

The violence she has witnessed is part of the History of Red, the human and nonhuman world's fear caused by exploitative structures of domination and the violence enacted by all the impotent "tiny men" obsessed with the cry of Hunger. Acting out of a metaphysical void, they "have their way" with the weaker and grab more than they need. A woman fears for her children in such a world. Above all, however, she fears that her children may no longer have a world to live in. In essence, the poem's female speaker is afraid of the insatiable appetite of greedy men. Next to that, carnivorous animals pose little threat. "We are safe from the bear," asserts the speaker of another poem, "and we have each other, / we have each other to fear" (*Dark* 152).

These two lines come from "Bear," a poem devoted to an animal most Indigenous Americans consider sacred on account of his similarity to humans. Hogan writes: "The bear is a dark continent / that walks upright / like a man" (151). The speaker lives in bear country and knows how dangerous the predator can be:

> [...] Last night
> it left a mark at my door
> that said winter
> was a long and hungry night of sleep.
> But I am not afraid; I have collected

other nights of fear,
knowing what things walked
the edges of my sleep.

(151)

Being of tribal descent, she has established a respectful relationship with her nonhuman neighbors. She has learned the art of coexistence with predators and is no longer afraid. But others are and they shoot at animals out of fear. The poem shifts to one such story. The mortally wounded bear cried like a human, in the human voice of his hunter. When the latter finally tracked him down, "the bear lay weeping [...] / its black hands / covering its face from sky" (151). The bear's human expression of pain and the human-like character of his death haunt the hunter until he loses his mind and imagines changing places with the dying bear in expiation for the sin of murder. The man wants "to get down on his knees / and lay his own hands / across his face and turn away / from sky where god lives" (152). Fear of our own destructive instincts, over which we have little control, is what makes us more dangerous than nonhuman predators. Truly, "we have each other to fear" (152).

From the physiological point of view, however, fear is a survival mechanism enabling living organisms to minimize aggressive conflict and maintain a safe distance from sources of perceived danger. Fear so conceived is validated in a poem recounting Hogan's encounter with a mountain lion who lives "on the dangerous side / of the clearing" (*Dark*, "Mountain Lion" 153). Strict carnivores, these territorial animals require an extensive habitat to survive and are critically dependent on wilderness preservation. Once thriving, their population has been radically curtailed because they frequently pose a threat to livestock. The mountain lion the poet encounters "in the mortal dusk"—the time many predators come out to hunt—knows that humans are the enemy: "I was the wild thing she had learned to fear" (153). When two apex predators face each other anything can happen. Will the nonhuman animal choose the fight option or will she withdraw to avoid a high-risk conflict? Which defense mechanism will be activated by fear this time?

Standing there in front of each other, both recollect the long history of interspecies violence. There is alertness and a wariness of the opponent in the moment their eyes meet. "What passed between us," writes Hogan, hinting at the fragile connection established between two predators when both defer action to appraise the situation, and seek the best way to move forward. In this instant life is hanging in the balance, the two holding each other's gaze, linked in an unsought-for mutuality:

Red spirits of hunters
walked between us
from the place where blood

goes back to its wound
before fire
before weapons.
Nothing was hidden in our eyes.

(153)

In the intensity of this moment they become transparent to each other,
getting to the source of their fear, understanding the complicated entan-
glement of both worlds. Two sophisticated intelligences, one equal to the
other, are locked in a common vision. Abruptly, the perspective reverses
and the poet looks at herself through the mountain lion's eyes. She realizes
that "[h]er power lived / in the dream of my leaving" (153). Like Hogan's
Indigenous ancestors dreaming of the disappearance of the white people
and the return of the buffalo, the animal longed for the reestablishment of
her primal world, wildness being her original habitat. Paradoxically, both
the woman and the mountain lion had the same dream—of being left alone
by the colonizing forces of modernity. The speaker recognizes this similar-
ity; in the animal's gaze she sees herself looking at non-Indigenous intrud-
ers, "before lowering my eyes / and turning away / from what lives inside
those / who have found / two worlds cannot live / inside a single vision"
(152–153). By lowering her eyes, she avoids falling into the commodify-
ing master-slave dialectic. The encounter ends peacefully, the woman and
the animal respecting each other's otherness, laying no claim upon each
other. They live in parallel worlds, the poet realizes. This time, this human
allows wildness to remain untamed. She keeps her side of the treaty her
people once made with animals. Stacy Alaimo finds the speaker's deci-
sion to lower her eyes expressive of her willingness to "know less" when
nature's independence and her right to remain uncolonized are at stake
(Alaimo 131).

But red is also the color of love, as the volume's introductory poem sug-
gests. "Crossings" begins with the image of a "place at the center of earth"
(155) where two oceans meet like lovers, one "dissolving" in the other.
The idea of the world being in an endless process of becoming has been
a constant in Hogan's writing since the publication of her first volume of
poetry, *Calling Myself Home*, but now this ongoing creative process, the
dissolution of individual boundaries in infinite cycles of transformation
and rearrangement, is called love. It would only be logical to conclude
that for the author everything that exists, everything that has been called
into being—out of love—has to be good. No wonder she is in love with
the world.[5]

Matter and energy constantly circulate, atoms migrate from body to
body, carrying with them ancient memories. Everything and everyone is
constantly exposed to influences from beyond themselves, incorporating

the world, learning, responding. Out of love. "It's why the whales of one sea / know songs of the other" (155), asserts Hogan. This observation is based on scientific data. Research has proved that whales learn new songs as they migrate and that they exchange tunes with the other pods they encounter in their travels. Hogan discovered this and other fascinating facts about those highly intelligent sea mammals when she joined naturalist writer Brenda Peterson on the more than 5,000-mile-long gray whale migration route from the animals' nursery off Baja California to their Arctic feeding grounds. The women observed the migrating whales for seven consecutive years and ended their project in the joint authorship of *Sightings: The Gray Whales' Mysterious Journey*, published by National Geographic in 2002. Hogan became fascinated by whales, partly because they seemed to hold an insight into the mystery of the human. The whales' distant ancestors lived on land but about 50 million years ago they returned to the water from which life had emerged. Traces of this evolutionary history are preserved in whale anatomy. In *Sightings* Hogan comments: "They are, according to science, something like our ancestors, and some think that with their hidden human hands and leg bones, the parts they no longer need, they are what we will become in the future" (*Sightings* 282). The poem's title, "Crossings," refers to such "crossed beginnings" (*Dark* 155) between whales and humans.

After the introductory section, the poem zeroes in on a whale fetus the poet discovered on a block of ice:

> Not yet whale, it still wore the shadow
> of a human face, and fingers
> that had grown before the taking
> back and turning to fin.
>
> (155)

Embryology provides records of transitional forms that blur the distinctions between humans and other mammals, but the embryo of cetacean mammals like whales is exceptional in that it displays advanced evolutionary adaptations—like four limbs and budding fingers—which disappear in the process of fetal development, as if the specimen were reverting to an earlier, less developed evolutionary form. Hogan, however, interprets this process in terms of progress, not regress, believing whales show us the future, not the past, of evolution. For her, whales are literally our future.

The whale fetus with "the shadow of a human face" causes the myth of human exceptionality to crumble. What better evidence of our misguidedly arrogant, and blatantly ignorant, pretense to be "the crown of creation"! The fetal whale "did not want to live in air" (156), he did not want the pseudo-perfect life of humans—a preference evident even on the level of ontogenesis, his fingers about to turn to fin. The poem destabilizes commonly held beliefs about human-animal difference; it levels hierarchies, dismantles binaries. A long time ago, in "the terrain of crossed beginnings" (155), our human ancestors emerged from water to find proto-whales already inhabiting the land. At the time of contact, it was the whale ancestors that had a prior claim to the land and the newcomers were invading a territory already occupied. This is how consistently coloniality replays itself on the crossed paths of human and nonhuman animals' history.

The concept of Indigeneity possibly comes into play, when Hogan admits a longing for that "terrain of crossed beginnings." Gamal Muhammad Elgezeery additionally finds in her longing a "wish to cross her human terrain in order to get healed through water" (20), since throughout Hogan's poetry water is invested with healing power. I would add that the healing Elgezeery[6] talks about transcends the individual perspective and applies, at least in this particular poem, to the entire human race. Had humans lived in water, like whales do, had humans remained "member[s] of the clan of crossings" (*Dark* 156), situated between fixed taxonomic positions, history may have been very different. Somewhere on the edges of the poem, there emerges a ghost of a hope that a human child may one day evolve "out of the human fold" back into "the curving world of water" (155) to become a member of the same clan.[7] And since the poem starts with a hymn to love, Indigenous myths come to mind which speak of humans falling in love with sea animals and joining their beloveds in the watery element. Perhaps these myths stake the path of the future, not the past, of the human race, as Hogan frequently speculates in her novels.

Hogan's meditation on the evolutionary contact zone between whales and humans is followed by "Crow Law," a poem which returns to the Indigenous model of anti-colonial resistance. The poem's title already suggests that conventional law does not apply to the trickster bird. Crow sets her own rules; she uses her brains for a living and lives in a world very different from ours. Yet we tend to apply our own epistemological categories to our nonhuman others, continuing to 'subdue' them in the process of epistemological colonialism. Hogan's poem is an invitation to decolonize our perceptions. The opening line, "[t]he temple where crow worships" (157), starts with our human conceptualization of the sacred (temple, worship). In the parallel world of nonhuman animals, however, analogies can be misleading. Crow's temple does not resemble our artificial places where we pay tribute to an abstract deity dwelling in distant heavens. Crow is much more literal; her worship consists in establishing a most intimate connection with a life-giving, sustaining presence, like that of the moose, whose body is actually crow's temple. Remaining within the human imaginary of the sacred, Hogan further disrupts it when she calls "betrayal [...] crow's way of saying grace":

> Betrayal is crow's way of saying grace
> to the wolf
> so it can eat
> what is left
> when blood is on the ground,
> until what remains of moose
> is crow
> walking out
> the sacred temple of ribs
> in a dance of leaving
> the red tracks of scarce and private gods.
>
> (157)

Still playing on the colonized imaginary of the sacred, the poem collapses the iconic Last Supper with the animals' sharing of the body of the moose god. At the former occasion, Judas Iscariot, about to betray the Son of God, is excluded from the circle of salvation.[8] In the latter feast, however, trickster Crow, who has brought the banqueters together, is included as an agent of salvation and a legitimate commensal. The densely packed poetic aphorism of the first two lines refers to a specific hunting arrangement whereby crows (and ravens), upon locating an injured or dead animal and unable to rip through his or her tough skin, will caw loudly to attract the attention of wolves or other canines to an easy kill. Wolves, in turn, will share their meal, out of gratitude, with their hunting partners. Thus, "crow law" works for both sides of this partnership, and crow's loud calls, which literally betray the whereabouts of a pack of wolves' would-be prey, is the bird's prayer, her thanksgiving to the larger predator for her share of a life-sustaining meal. When the food-sharing ceremony is over, crow stages a sort of sacred dance in the now cleaned-out temple of her inhuman, primeval god,[9] a god too wild for the puny notions of civilized humans. Hogan celebrates here the primal ritual of transformation, the sacred metamorphosis of moose into "wolf and crow." The wild god of the world resides where all roads end, "where crow is calling / where we are all afraid" (157). In wildness one retrieves a religion of the holy beginnings, common to all untamed nature.

Hogan calls this transformation of the eaten into the eater "the oldest war" (157), possibly in recognition of the survival strategies, of all the alliances and "betrayals" life needs to decide on to continue. "Skin" picks up on this idea, calling war "the perfect disguise" for the constant flow of material and energetic exchange. Even human skin is a camouflage, one among many assumed by matter. When it is "removed at night," humans "f[a]ll to the bottom of darkness" (158) and return to the process of cease-less re-formation. Circulation is the only form of immortality and even a deer knows "it could pass / through the bodies of men and return" (158). As in modern physics, a deer can be "a hide of light" and a "hunting song," as much as he can be an animal. He is all of these and much more in the different stages of his coming-to-be. The arrow that kills him "belong[s] to the bow" (158) and hunters are merely "walking into the fire" (159) of eternal becoming. "That's why," concludes Hogan, "war is only another skin" (159).

Another important problem raised in *The Book of Medicines* can be found in "Naming the Animals." In Indigenous cultures words have power, they do things, naming has consequences. There is an intimate connection between the name and the thing named, and a change of one affects the transformation of the other. Much damage was done to traditional societies in the process of imposing European names on tribal people in an attempt to assimilate them to the dominant culture. Indigenous children sent to residential schools received English names along with a new, American identity. Much earlier, European travelers claimed possession of newly discovered lands by giving them new names, names which rewrote their histories and geographies. Naming is thus an imperial gesture of subjugation. The one who has power over language, sets the rules. As Hogan's poem demonstrates, by giving names to animals humans impose identities on them. The question arises, how does one know the identity of nonhuman beings? Does the namer consult the named?

Human languages have words for everything that exists, but as a matter of fact these words imprison the world within cognitive maps which reflect human perspectives, prejudices, and misperceptions, taming the natural world and structuring it in a way which serves our interests. In her rendition of the adamic myth, Hogan imagines man,[10] barely emerged from the "clay of his beginnings," naming animals "as if they had not been there / before his words" (162). This reads like an accusation. From the dawn of history the white man—Adam—has flaunted his arrogance and lack of concern for anything and anyone beside himself. Coming into the world as a younger brother, he lacked the manners to introduce himself to his non-human kin (as Indigenous people would do) and, like the tyrant he turned out to be, proceeded with bending the world to his will. Hogan's ancestors believed animals "spoke an older tongue" (160) and that they had their own names. In the poem entitled "Maps" she claims: "the first language is not our own" (161). Yet the archetypal namer paid no attention to pre-existing languages, convinced of his own overriding claim to importance. Taking the original, unspoken names away by replacing them with his own, he broke the bond of kinship and expelled "wolf, bear, other"

[...] crawling into wilderness
he could not enter,
swimming into untamed water.
He could hear their voices at night
and tracks and breathing
at the fierce edge of forest
where all things know the names for themselves
and no man speaks them
or takes away their tongue.

(162)

Hogan's poem presents the naming of animals as an equivalent of the fall in Christian mythology. Although the narratives—the biblical story of the fall and Hogan's account of naming—are different, the consequences of both are comparable: disintegration of primal unity, loss of balance and holiness, the institution of binaries. In the decolonial perspective adopted by Hogan, naming is the founding moment of division; it separates us (humans) from them (nonhumans). It is at this point that wildness starts to be feared rather than revered. Expelled from a man-made paradise to "the fierce edge of forest" which "he could not enter," "ethnoclass Man" (Wynter, 261) begins to be haunted by wildness because it is that part of himself he has rejected in the act of self-constitution.

The poem's second section shifts its focus from animals to animalized people: "His children would call us pigs" (*Dark* 162), the Chickasaw poet remarks. To ethnoclass Man, Native Americans did not pass the test of full humanity. Considered less than human, they shared the fate of animals: they were spoken for but never listened to, re-named without regard for their original names, robbed of their lands, resettled, and abandoned "at the edge of a savage country / of law and order" (163). From the perspective of the poem's speaker, it is the white man's civilized world that is the true wilderness and Western-style "law and order" is merely an excuse for satisfying modern man's greed. But the speaker, who has not lost her connection with wildness, proudly boasts of the animality ascribed to her people:

I am naked, I am old
before the speaking,
before any Adam's forgotten dream,
and there are no edges to the names,
no beginning, no end.

(163)

She belongs to the primal, undifferentiated world from "before the speaking," where humans and animals are transparent to one another ("naked") and speak the ancient, non-binary tongue. This vision of paradisial harmony is set against the founding narrative of Western culture, which leaves the nonhuman world out of the dream. The biblical Adam—a human master who, by naming, takes possession of the animals—belongs to the fallen, differentiated world. Within Adam's "dream"—characteristically, this dream has always already belonged to him, never to other earth beings—the Anthropocene was bound to happen.

"The Ritual Life of Animals" is staged in the realm of crossings that Hogan explores so well. The human and the animal, waking life and dreaming, interpenetrate and fuse until all become entangled in "the house of pelvic truth" (165) in which biology meets tribal knowledge and poetic sensitivity. At the poem's outset we are exposed to what seems like an animal double or a human-animal split within the speaking self:

> The animal walks beside me,
> long-toothed partner
> in a sacrificial dance.
> It lies down on the land
> as I walk upright.
>
> (164)

The human and the animal live in symmetrical worlds ("beside"), dependent on each other and bound together in a "sacrificial dance" of fear, universal predation, and re-circulation of matter and energy. As coming "from the swampy beginnings," the animal represents wildness, the primal wellspring and sacred source of life. Like crow from "Crow Law," it[11] says grace "before its every meal" (164) by killing its food. The predator from the parallel world goes hunting at night when its human other is asleep. Hogan uses the phrase "dark nocturnal waking" to refer to the animal's beginning to live its own life, no longer walking in an orderly manner but "falling to all fours," and sharpening its animal senses before a kill.

When the controlling consciousness of the sleeper weakens its hold on the brain's subliminal content, an "older order" is stirring underneath (Dark, "Map" 161); the world as it was "before the speaking" surfaces. While Hogan is critical of Western psychology for its narrowly individualistic, culture-specific focus, she believes Jung was much closer than Freud was to capturing the larger world of tribal thought. What modern psychology calls the unconscious, she writes in her tribal memoir, "implies another mind at work inside us [...] that reveals itself in dreams" (The Woman 134). In traditional cultures dreamers are believed to be connected to the larger world, receiving instruction from plants, animals, and spirits. In the "geography of the holy" opened up in dreaming, "[w]e are the dreamed, as well as the dreamers" (The Woman 136).

Hogan's poem explores this zone of "nocturnal waking" where the human meets the primal wildness of nature, complete with its own dreaming. The animal that walked beside her at the poem's beginning is now immersed in the "solemn rite of sleep / that crosses into dream" (*Dark* 164). Dreaming, it "holds / council with foreign tongues / and common thoughts," knowing, remembering, merging with the world, reenacting annual migrations and ritual mating dances, re-living fear. "I am the enemy," declares the poet, "dreamed in the restless sleep" (164) of animals who have developed "desperate gifts" of camouflage and other defense mechanisms to enhance their chances of survival. The poem's final lines shift back to "the warmth of human bodies," connected to the natural world through their "nocturnal wakings":

> Something inside gets down on its haunches.
> At the borders of our beds
> are the strange voices,
> the slow shifting of eyes, turning of ears.
> They hear us, smell us, dream us.
> We lie down
> in the long nights of their waking,
> the world of animal law,
> the house of pelvic truth.

(165)

The poem, which opens with the speaker's sense of unease caused by a shadowy animal presence at her side, ends by troubling the anthropocentric illusion. If they "dream us," perhaps we, humans, are mere projections of the animal dream visions and not the other way around. If this is so, who is speaking, and who is dreaming? Possibly, though, this is no longer relevant, but what counts is that we are together in this geography of the holy, connected to the whole world, inseparable, co-constituting each other. In this world of mutual entanglements, animals have as much agency as humans do; their powers, their intelligence not only equal ours, but can transcend it. "Dreaming is the point at which we begin to know," wrote Hogan (*The Woman* 136). Descendants of Indigenous dreamers know that the animal is the other "me" which wakes up when the human self goes to sleep, haunting "the borders of our beds" (165). As humans "lie down," they seem to abdicate their power, hand it over to "the world of animal law." At night the world restores its wildness and its balance.[12]

Among *The Book of Medicines'* meditations on the many faces of hunger and the fear that accompanies it, one poem refers to the cattle brought to America with European settlers. Their presence greatly facilitated the process of colonization. The lands of the Indigenous inhabitants, human and nonhuman, had been stolen and much of it converted into grazing lands. In her novels Hogan frequently links cattle farming with colonization. In "Milk," however, she casts a kinder look at farm animals, taking pity on their suffering and exploitation. Beginning with the image of the bond milk creates between mother and child—"sharers of the same body" (168), as well as her childhood memories of milk as food, the poet thinks of the journey milk must travel to reach the table. She is reminded of the "cattle brought in the dark / holds of ships" on the long and exhausting journey across the ocean. "They were hungry," she ascertains as she reviews their pitiful condition upon arrival, in the dark hold

> where they stood
> ate, weakened,
> coupled and gave birth afraid
> their kind would not go on.
>
> (169)

The wording evokes the tragic condition of enslaved Africans brought as live cargo to the American shores, as much as it alludes to Hogan's own people when they were forced to travel on the Trail of Tears, in hunger, despair, humiliation, and uncertainty about the future. With this analogy in mind, the poet softens toward the cattle. Even if they furthered their owners' colonial agenda, they had no choice in this matter, having been enslaved, broken, and commodified first. She is especially moved by the cruelty of milk sellers who have a dying cow milked. "Too weak to stand," she had to be hoisted up, the men bothered only about the loss of profit and not in the least about the suffering animal. "They were hungry," Hogan repeats, but this time it is not the natural, physiological hunger she sympathized with earlier. The men who milked death, who drank "its watery milk," were hungry for land that was not theirs. They were ready to steal, kill, lie, and commit any crime to satisfy their hunger.

Reducing nature—human and other-than-human—to an abstraction and commodifying it, capitalism was born in "the long sixteenth century"[13] in the American colonies of Europe. Driven by an insatiable desire for the maximization of profit at all costs (a desire Hogan calls "hunger") and a disregard for the side effects of unlimited economic expansion, capitalism has become a "world ecology," claims environmental historian and historical geographer Jason W. Moore, who proposes to call the new geological epoch in Earth's geology the Capitalocene, rather than the Anthropocene. As he argues in *Capitalism and the Web of Life* (2015), it is not so much human dominance over the natural world during the last two centuries of Western industrial development (the anthropocentric argument), but the totality of economic relations within capitalism as world-ecology that are to blame for the exponential increase of our ecological footprint and the resulting irreversible environmental damage. In her poetic meditations, framed by a decolonial lens, Hogan can be seen arguing a similar position.

Of the remaining animal-centered poems in *The Book of Medicines*, two more deserve a closer examination. The first, "Tracking," remains in the realm of undecidability that is so close to the poet's heart, as a wild pig seems to vanish "into the dark center of things" (*Dark* 166), along that place's first, prehistoric inhabitants, who left without a trace, abandoning their stone houses in perfect condition. Hunters who want to "borrow" the pig's "sharp-backed life [...] inside [their] own" follow her hoofprints over a potato field and into a cave, but the cave is empty, save for wall paintings of ancient birds. Caves, like depths, are "a feminine world," writes Hogan in *Dwellings*. They are "a womb of earth" (*Dwellings* 31), places of emergence and mystery. "There is a different way of knowing" (*Dwellings*, 32) there. To Hogan, the ability to respect the mystery—of the pig's or the tribal people's disappearance—without dissecting it for hints of the ever elusive nature of reality, which seems to want to remain hidden, marks human maturity.

The second poem is "Chambered Nautilus." Here Hogan concentrates on a shelled deep-sea invertebrate, sometimes considered to be a living fossil because it has survived in almost unchanged form for over 400 million years. The poem consists of one long, winding sentence, which reflects the animal's line of ancestry. Attempting to illustrate the chambered nautilus's long and ancient lineage, the poem uses six different images and six times repeats the word "before" to begin a clause:

> It's from before the spin of human fire,
> before the dreaming that grew out of itself,
> before there were people who ate the brains
> of the dead,
> before wind was leaving through a hole in the sky,
> before zero and the powers of ten,
> before empty nets drifting the empty miles of water,
> from when moon was the only tyrant that ruled the sea
> and was the god shells rose to at night [...].
>
> (175)

The ancient sea mollusk has retained this power to respond to the moon to this day, the chambers of its shell controlling its buoyancy, but it is the "before" rather than the actual creature that constitutes the poem's point of gravity. The body of the poem recounts in fact a long list of disasters which started "after," when Europeans reached the shores of America. The time "before," when there was no tyrant, when the water-pulling moon was god, and when "everything that lived had a radiance" (176), seems utopian by comparison. Throughout its long evolution, the chambered nautilus has kept its signature balance in the depths of the sea, always "seeking a new kind of light to live inside" (175), in both its achievements—the balance and the search for light—providing guidance for the poet as she meditates on the powers of humanimal survivance.

The fact that the creature was a witness to the golden days of Indigenous cultures thrills the poet, and she dives with it into the deepest water of memories, to recollect the times when shells, not gold, "were barter" for the many goods necessary for survival, when ancestral Puebloans "built dwellings of stone" and her own people "were strong" and "full" (175). This was when humans were still a species admired by the whole world, before the denials, divisions, and crimes, which Hogan sometimes suggests must have been the deeds of another human subspecies. In her many texts she can be seen struggling to understand the duality of human nature— how a criminal can be a loving husband and father, and how seemingly kind people could become "bear-slayers / and slayers of women and land / and belief" (176). But the chambered nautilus allows her to travel back in time to when good life consisted in living in harmony with all creation and "earth was a turtle / swimming between stars" (176).

By way of conclusion, it can be said that *The Book of Medicines* begins a series of poems on aquatic intelligence, to use Dreese's phrase. Whales, octopuses, and other deep sea animals make a permanent entry into Hogan's life and writing, and are embraced as ancestors and teachers of ancient wisdom, along with the more frequently depicted terrestrial animals living in the wild. While the volume's ecofeminist focus is still clearly visible—specifically in the association of rape with male violence against sea creatures or the ruthless exploitation of a dying cow for the last drop of milk—Hogan is now more devoted to exploring the world of primal instincts, like fear and hunger, but also the more female-associated instincts of love and compassion. The destructive but also regenerative potential of every person, she claims, seems to depend on how we tap into our primordial animality. Repressing this results in destructiveness, but embracing it and allowing ourselves to be guided by its evolutionary wisdom is how we become mature human beings, satisfied with knowing and having less, rather than grasping for all in cannibalistic paroxisms of Windigo monstrosity.[14] It is in our entangled, cross-species beginnings that Hogan locates the realm of the holy, the sanctuary of the wild god of the world who is common to all that exists. From the poet's perspective, the originary moment of our human fallenness was the act of naming the animals and separating our supposedly more evolved selves from them. Names are conceptual maps of legal and punishable violence. By fragmenting the pre-verbal unity of life, expelling primordial wildness beyond the pale of familiarity, and reducing unique, inconceivably complex nonhuman animals to exploitable commodities, humans removed food from the realm of the ensouled and turned wildness into a threat. Still, there exist members of an ancient clan of crossings who remind us of our shared, interspecies history and our human status as the less evolved, younger siblings. To Hogan, the future of the human is bound up with them.

Notes

1 Although this image suggests affinities with the Freudian "uncanny," Hogan deemed Freud's psychoanalysis too narrow to accommodate Indigenous concepts of the "unseen" (*The Woman* 134–136).
2 The other two are the prey pathway and the directed pathway.
3 The Kogi Mamas, Elders of a pre-modern tribe from the Sierra Nevada mountains of Colombia, are keepers of a vast tribal ecological knowledge and call themselves the guardians of the earth. They have contacted their Younger Brothers twice to warn us about the dramatic consequences of our destructive lifestyles. See: *The Heart of the World: Elder Brother's Warning*, directed by Alan Ereira, the BBC, 1992 and *Aluna*, directed and produced by Alan Ereira, 2012.
4 The feminine pronoun seems appropriate in the context of the gendered violence referenced in the poem.
5 "To write poetry, I have to be in love with the world" – this quotation, attributed to Ron Hauschiu, opens *Dark. Sweet* (page immediately preceding the dedication page, n.p.).
6 A similar point is made by Dreese, p. 7.
7 Hogan's novels, especially *Solar Storms*, which focuses on whales, introduce such human "members of the clan of crossings."
8 Judas, explicitly called "the son of perdition" in John 17:12, is believed to have rejected the gift of salvation and chosen eternal damnation instead.
9 Hogan's imagery is suggestive of Robinson Jeffers' "wild God of the world." Cf.: "The wild God of the world is sometimes merciful to those / That ask mercy, not often to the arrogant" (Jeffers, p. 49).
10 In the biblical myth Adam, the first man, names all that exists.
11 Since the animal of this poem is a concept rather than an individual being (which is best seen in "something inside gets down on its haunches"), in my discussion I have decided to preserve the pronoun 'it,' rather than use 'he' or 'she.'
12 The animal double is also potentially connected to the animal ally of a member of a tribal society, a concept Hogan evokes in her novel *Power*.
13 Immanuel Wallerstein uses the term "the long sixteenth century" in his analysis of world-systems theory. Beginning with the discovery of the Americas and ending with the English Revolution (1640 CE), "the long sixteenth century" led to the development of global capitalism.
14 For an explanation see Preface.

4   2000s

Rounding The Human Corners

Out of hospitals and rehabilitation, settling back into the life of a person she hardly knew, Hogan adopted two horses and moved into a little cabin on tribal lands in a wildlife corridor near Denver, in the state of Colorado. She calls the cabin a "house of words" because it was the prototype of the house of Bush from *Solar Storms* and she could afford to buy it after that novel came out (*The Radiant* 18–19). In the 2000s Hogan published one book of poetry, *Rounding the Human Corners* (2008), edited an anthology of essays, *The Inner Journey: Views from Native Traditions* (2009), and brought out her fourth novel, *People of the Whale* (2008), which is set among a fictional tribe modeled on the Makah of the Pacific Northwest. The writer had spent time with Makah tribal elders, who consulted with her about the tribe's planned return to whaling. She was part of the Native Working Group for reauthorization of the Endangered Species Act at that time and followed a pod of gray whales with Brenda Peterson for a project which ended with the publication of *Sightings: The Grey Whale's Mysterious Journey* (2002). Wanting to be of service to the Chickasaw Nation, Hogan also accepted the invitation to be its inaugural writer-in-residence and moved to Tishomingo, Oklahoma, where she lived for a few years, before returning home to Colorado. In 2007 she was inducted into the Chickasaw Nation Hall of Fame.

The dominant mood in *Rounding the Human Corners* is joy. The poet celebrates the beauty of the world, at times almost losing herself in the nonhuman other. After her close encounter with death, she rejoices in life and the privilege of embodiment. In a review of the book, Janet McAdams wrote: "There are three ways in the world, the poet tells us: dangerous, wounding, and beauty. She has written about the dangerous, the wounding. This is her book about beauty" (234). This is true, for even prosaic details, even the process of decay and decomposition, are here somehow beautiful, transformed by Hogan's vision into a mystery of life and light. Without denying the existence of darkness, she nonetheless exults in light, in the radiance of all living things, because "it is light, after all, / first and last, we live for, / die for" (*Dark* 205). Light enters the collection under many guises; it can be a touch of sunlight on the skin, a physical

DOI: 10.4324/9781003364252-6

phenomenon, bioluminescence, or a symbol of spiritual enlightenment. In all its shapes and guises, it blesses life and speaks of a caring, loving, sensuous universe. The poet absorbs this universe on an almost preverbal level, with all her animal senses. "My senses are all awake," she says in a poem that captures the transformational moment of becoming the other which recurs throughout the volume, "and like the tree I can lose myself / layer after layer / all the way down to infinity / and that's when the world has eyes and sees" ("Eucalyptus," *Dark* 193).

In comparison with her previous poetry collections, *Rounding the Human Corners* is, as McAdams puts it, "the work of an elder, gentle in its vision and formally the most expansive of Hogan's poetry" (227). Fittingly, in contrast to *The Book of Medicines*, we find fewer references to fear and predation, the poet's focus having shifted to joy and smaller, less conspicuous, sometimes even altogether invisible life forms. Moreover, while her interest in aquatic life is still prominent, another great love of Hogan's life, her companion horses, appears in touchingly personal vignettes.

The poet's fascination with the phenomenon of life's emergence and its unpredictable evolutionary adaptations is visible in such verses as "In Time," "Anatomy," or "Emergence." Contemplating her ankle bones, she marvels at their long history, their anatomy unchanged from that of primitive amphibians. Sharing three million years of common history, ankle bones are a living proof of human-animal entanglements since the time

> when God's arm, once wing,
> once fin,
> swam through an ocean of creation
> and reached out
> to climb the shores of a world
> without a knowing care for what we would become.
>
> (206)

In contrast to the dominant religions and worldviews, Hogan's tribal wisdom denies the teleological understanding of life, which supposedly reaches its goal with the emergence of humans. In her poetry, evolution is creative, almost whimsical in its moment-by-moment turns and re-turns, its various crossings and ever new "betrayals" of "the elegant, tender bones" (206), which can evolve into fingers that pull the trigger or help life flourish. Nature is Hogan's only approximation of the God of the Christian Bible—experimenting with possibilities since life's evolution "from a single cell," its emergence from the waters of beginning "without a knowing care," with no other purpose than its own enhancement. This ongoing creation is a beautiful risk and life is its "love" and its "misery" ("In Time," *Dark* 206).

"Anatomy" teaches a similarly humbling lesson to those humans who hold to the erroneous belief in their unique position within the great chain of being. We are merely ephemeral creatures, transitional life forms "soon to disappear into the future, neither one of us the original human, as evidenced by the navel" (217). The poet finds it fascinating that anatomy should bear witness to our animal beginnings. Although the spine develops first, before any other organs, within the human mother's womb, it is the fetus's tailbone that disappears last, "as if the body remembers the fine animal / that was lost / someplace in time" (218). It is this "fine animal" that Hogan identifies with, at times even more intimately than with her human kind, whose children's blue eyes "will darken in time" ("Emergence," *Dark* 235), the grace of birth out of and among animals becoming lost in adulthood. Comparing the small toe of the human foot to "the blind wasp infants / in the nest of darkness," Hogan suggests: "You could almost believe / there is no evolution / but that we are returning / to a state of grace / in this life" ("On the Small Toe," *Dark* 221).

This state of grace is revealed especially in nature's small and insignificant creatures, which humans often find repulsive. In "Enigma" the poet asks, "on which day of creation did the insects appear" (213), lost in wonder at the creative beauty, the dazzling diversity of colors, shapes, and forms of tiny winged creatures, the breathless long sentence of the poem's first stanza mimicking her sense of abandon. "I wasn't at any of their births," she regrets, "and know I missed the fashioning of angels / who have learned to hide their great lives" (213). The hidden dimension of their existence haunts her. She feels unworthy of "their lace, their silken powers, / their praise of sun [...]," inadequate to their beauty, and happy to be able to rest in their company as she contemplates two green dragonflies that have been attracted by the light of her desk lamp. In their company she feels wealthy, contented, emptied of restless desires, at peace in the now:

> There is no searching, no wanting,
> and I don't know on which day of creation
> such happiness was made
> and signed by thin feet.
>
> (213)

In the face of this happiness the question with which the poem starts loses its meaning, as do all questions. Life is simple and beautiful again.

Insects, unlike humans, do not pursue—or create—unsolvable existential dilemmas. Questions of identity, fidelity, or betrayed promises do not enter into their vibrant, purpose-directed, present-concentrated lives. In their presence, Hogan's own dilemmas dissolve, as when she sees the intricate beauty of a wasps' nest, with its inner riches, like "silk cocoons"

("Moving the Woodpile," *Dark* 231) and the splendid carvings in the woodflesh underneath. Inside the nest are the most innocent of all creatures, wasp infants so like the small toes of human feet: "only pale fingers searching, without eyes" (231). Such a sight would be happiness itself, were it not for the poet's unintended destruction of their lives. Unaware of their existence, she has lifted a piece of wood and exposed the nest hidden underneath, so that the mature wasps abandon the site, rejecting her offer to take the nest back. Haunted by a sense of guilt, replaying the scene in her memory for years to come, she reflects sadly on the paradox of the human, "generous and thieving / at one and the same time" (232). It is as if we could not help, even in our most heartfelt efforts, "to break by degrees" what we want to protect. As if a betrayal lies in wait between the intention and the deed. Is there a faultline in our ontological setup?—one might ask, considering the tragic history of humanity's endless warfare and destruction. Or is it, more specifically, the curse of the white settler, whose blood, mixed with Chickasaw blood, flows in Hogan's veins? What is a human?—the poet cannot stop asking herself, searching for an answer by writing and by learning from nonhuman, more innocent creatures. "Maybe our sin," she speculates, is our blindness to, and lack of concern for, "everything small and nearly gone" (231), a disregard for such miracles as "the paper wasp nest" (232), created with infinite love and with love maintained in existence.

Trying to make up for our human neglect of the little creatures who are great miracles of nature, she traces "the signature of creation [...] written on the small, / the unloved," finding it shine "with unpraised light" ("Shine," *Dark* 248). This woman who watches over the world rejoices in the blind "shining earthworms" who crawl in the mud, the beetles—"shining"—on a heap of dung, slugs leaving moist trails in the wake of their journeys, and "the satin blue backs of flies." Together with the often despised spiders—spinning silk nets in which a drop of dew may quiver like a diamond—the skunk and the rat whose eyes shine in darkness, these are "not vermin but all the beginning of the great" (249). Nothing is distasteful or ugly, nothing deserves to be eradicated as a pest. A person in love with the world sees only shine and beauty. How strangely reminiscent this is of the poetry of Mary Oliver, who claimed, "My work is loving the world" (Oliver 1).

The depths of the oceans also shine. The autogenic "animal light" (*Dark* 222) of marine organisms, known as bioluminescence, "was created before us / from blood of flesh and sea" (222), writes Hogan in "The Radiant," a poem which follows a manta ray in the animal's descent to the bottomless darkness of the ocean. First "falling on plankton, / bringing food and fish toward it," the animal's self-generated light reveals the depth of anthropogenic destruction—fished-out places and bleached coral reef—before he reaches "the blindness of fish who need no sight" and the depths "where the larger creatures live" (223). Humans who are surprised by a luminous giant manta ray will remain forever "haunted by everything [...] larger than they [are], more beautiful and bearing its own light" (223). Again, in this implicit comparison between human and nonhuman worlds, the latter overwhelms with its beauty, radiance, and environmental adaptability, to the disadvantage of the former. In the poem's concluding lines Hogan expresses her longing "for no other power, / no other light" (223) than that of the open sea. A similar wish is expressed in another poem, where she confides to a fish that she wants to follow it "to the wide, wide waters" ("At the Water," 250).

But it is in "Whale Rising" that the writer's admiration for marine life shines most clearly. The poem was conceived during Hogan's stay at the whale birthing lagoons off Baja California, Mexico. Females in that region are known for seeking contact with humans. They swim up to boats, often with their newborns, and socialize. Known as the Friendly Whale Syndrome, this phenomenon, writes Brenda Peterson, "seemed to be defying the logic of self-preservation" (*Sightings* 19). The poem starts with a whale rising behind the boat. Hogan introduces her as a "milk creature" and "an ancient mother" who "has navigated the world by whale map" (*Dark* 219). Here she hints at a signature development in whale brains—a sort of built-in compass in the form of magnetite which responds to the earth's magnetic pull and thus acts like a map, guiding the huge mammals on their lengthy migration routes. When the women look into the "ancient mother's" eye and see themselves reflected therein, the normative perspective becomes inverted. It is no longer the humans who observe, it is the whale who does the watching and appraising, taking the women's "human measure" (219). Being taken in by this ancient mammal, the women in the boat feel naked and vulnerable, with "nothing to hide behind" (219). In a reminder of our species' ridiculous incompetence and inexperience in the face of our much wiser nonhuman elders, Hogan mines the humbling potential of being the object of a gaze, "fixed" by it, held, and measured— all suggestive of the whale's active agency and human passive receptivity, a reversal of roles ascribed to "us" and "them" by dominant discourses.

David Abram, a close student of the world's Indigenous traditions, in his prize-winning book *The Spell of the Sensuous* shows that perceptual reciprocity with the more than human world is a natural experience for tribal people. Premodern cultures lived in a profoundly carnal world, in which everything was alive. The perceiving, sensuous body was literally immersed in a living, breathing world, sensitive and sentient. In such a world, to look at an animal, plant, rock formation, etc., was "to feel oneself exposed and visible, to feel oneself watched" (*The Spell* 90). Every act of perception was experienced as a meeting, an interchange and a communion between beings (269). Also deeply attuned to the living world, Hogan responds to it with her profoundest, animal self, in which the other is recognized as a different intelligence and perception is reciprocal.

The whale's incomprehensible otherness is made manifest by her apparently counterintuitive friendliness toward "the daughters of her enemies" (*Dark* 219). Considering the long and bloody history of whaling, which brought these animals to the brink of extinction, such trust seems reckless. Yet there she was, seeking contact regardless of the risk involved. The poet confesses defeat in the face of this mystery, one more among a multitude that humans are incapable of penetrating, even with their sophisticated technology. "Like all mystery," this too "could sink or drown us" (219). Through this paradoxically framed alternative, the poet defends the right of the hidden to remain so. Either we "sink" with the unknown, into the unknown, without violating its secrets, or we drown in our all-too-human attempts to dissect it, to decipher nature's secrets, since, being human, we cannot help but destroy what we master. In *Sightings* the poet-activist declares that a human being is compelled "to search [the secret], not to love it, not to care for it, but to see what is there for the taking, intruding on a mystery" (276).

The mystery that resides in the deep is vital for the survival of the world; it keeps reminding us of our limitations, dispelling illusions of our omnipotence. "No one returns from there unchanged / by everything larger" (*Dark* 219), Hogan reiterates. She knows this from first-hand experience, having been

> forever changed by the eye of the whale in which I saw the whole world. Peace is here, in accepting that smallness of our place in the world, in being as humble as the birds around us. This humble place is where we belong, according to the tribal view.
>
> (*Sightings* 79)

Sitting in the boat, fixed by the whale's gaze, Hogan wants her readers to know that the whale "songs from beneath this world" ("Whale Rising," 219), from the realm of mystery inaccessible to humans, are beautiful. She is moved by their beauty, by the beauty of the clouds, "the wind breath of the stormy world," and "the exquisite smell of fish and krill from inside a great life" (219). In short, Hogan is sending us another urgent plea on behalf of the untamed world.

In the Arctic, at the other end of the journey, she returns to the motif of "crossings" (*Dark* 155–156) in a poem entitled "Alone." Having invoked a legend about a sea hunter on a floating piece of ice—who was so lost in thought, possibly contemplating the beauty of nature while waiting for

the seal to reappear, that the ice carried him out to the open sea—the poet
moves her focus to whales:

> In this place they say
> that whales are children who died
> and didn't want to return as humans.
>
> (215)

Crediting whales with child-like innocence and trust and contrasting this
with the corruption rife in the world of human adults they have rejected,
Hogan puts her finger on the friendlies' mystery. Like little children, they
seem to be unacquainted with evil. "That is why they smile so beautifully
[...] before floating back into the unknown" (215). She wonders whether
whales remember their former existence, as human children, "when they
dwelt / in the dark uncharted waters of human life" (215). In contrast
to the darkness of land, ocean waters shine, at night, with phosphores-
cent light, and whales seem so peaceful, so happy, it seems impossible that
they should recall human darkness or "the moments of human loneliness"
(215). Loneliness, the poet claims in another verse, results from holding
back, from a refusal to merge with the larger world; it is a purely human
predicament ("Loneliness," *Dark* 209). The poem's title, "Alone," is a
comment on the human condition, on our irredeemable separation from
"the white floating immensity" (215) where whales feel at home but which
is deadly for the human. The poet's wish "to disappear / back to the birth-
ing sea / and glide away / with the whales I have seen" (215) can come true
only in the realm of imagination.

In "Turtle Watchers" Hogan takes us to a sea turtle breeding site. Every
breeding season turtles come out of the water to lay eggs, sometimes on
the same beach where they hatched. The regularity and predictability of
this little understood ritual, in which the sea creatures drag their heavy
bodies across a beach to deposit eggs in holes dug up in the sand, attracts
poachers and impoverished members of coastal communities, for whom
egg harvesting is the major source of income.[1] The eggs are often dug up
even before the females disappear back into the sea. Having witnessed a
turtle breeding event, Hogan cannot help feeling sympathy with the moth-
ers, "their eyes streaming water like tears" (226) upon emergence from
the ocean, but she also understands and sympathizes with the hunger that
drives people to the beach: "the hungry watchers standing at the edge of
trees / hoping for food when darkness gathers" (226). A solitary elder pays
respect to the incoming females, bowing to them in gratitude for the food
they bring, honoring the ancient pact with a prayer.

Herself a member of the Turtle Clan, Hogan much later chances to
swim alongside a sea turtle:

both of us watching as if clasped together
in the lineage of the same world
the sweep of the same current,
even rising for a breath of air at the same time
still watching.

(226)

The synchronicity of their movements, the ease with which both fall into the same rhythm, their eyes locked, testify to an ancient kinship. The poet is fascinated by the closeness of this relative whom tribal people call "the keeper of doors" (226). Turtles are guardians of the shore, the liminal place where land and water meet and alter each other's contours. In their life cycles they travel between both elements as "water moves the deep shift of life / back to birth and before / as if there is a path where beings truly meet, / as if I am rounding the human corners" (226). Hogan is constantly on the lookout for this path, always hoping to "truly meet" the animal, and herself to truly become a new being, possibly no longer even called human.

Among the animals Hogan watches regularly, rather than seeking them on far-away journeys, are residents of her Colorado homeland, such as one great blue heron she always sees in the same place, "one leg lifted / or wading without seeming to move" ("The Heron," *Dark* 211). Characteristically, she watches this "mystery" (211) from a safe distance, resisting the temptation to come closer or touch the bird, until the morning she finds him lying on one side, needing help:

I know the beak that could attack,
that unwavering golden eye
seeing me, my own saying I am harmless,
but if I had that eye, nothing would be safe.

(211)

Rushing to the bird's aid, the poet exposes herself to real danger. Failing to convince the needy heron of her good intentions could have serious consequences. The bird's beak is powerful and so are the claws that "hold tight" (211) the hand of his would-be rescuer. In the exchange of glances, the poet is transfixed, again, by an "unwavering" eye of something larger than human. The bird is taxing her, taking her human measure, not sure if he can trust the daughter of the enemy. "If I had that eye"—Hogan is acutely aware of the importance of the eye for the carnivorous bird's hunting routine. Sitting still on the edge or standing motionless in shallow water, herons spear their prey with their long bill once they have calculated the prey's position in the water. Nonetheless, she accepts the risk head-on, moved by the perfection she is holding in her hands. "The bird is more beautiful / than my hand," she thinks, even as she realizes her vulnerability vis-á-vis the frightened heron, whose quickened heartbeat bespeaks agitation. "You could kill me or help me" (211), she interprets the heron saying. Again, far from anthropomorphizing the animal, as the daughter of Indigenous people who lived in kinship relations with their nonhuman elders and even spoke the same language once, she is embedded in a larger world and hears the voices of nonhuman animals in a way descendants of modern Europeans cannot, will not, on account of their alienated ontologies. Anthropomorphism becomes a problem once the bonds of kinship are broken. The bird continues:

> I know you and I have no choice
> but to give myself up
> and in whatever supremacy of this moment,
> hold your human hand
> with my bent claws.
>
> (211–212)

The heron recognizes his human rescuer, he knows she is the one who is "always watching" (211) him. Hogan often claims that we are watched by animals, that they recognize our faces and our intentions, even if we merely see generic features in the nonhuman life we encounter. Animal agency is equal to ours, if not greater.

The word "supremacy" notoriously correlates with non-Indigenous constructions of the human-animal difference, but Hogan turns it on its head by relegating it to the realm of factors beyond anyone's control, let alone conscious privilege or subconscious construction. "In whatever supremacy of this moment": the heron has "no choice" but to accept help from whoever offers it. Yet there may come a time in the future in which "supremacy" will reverse the present alignment of power, forcing the human to accept the bird's help. The final image of the hand clasped by claws is a potent reminder of the ancient kinship, of relationship based on cooperation and mutual trust. On the whole, the poem reenacts for us the terms of an ancient and still binding treaty entered into at the beginning of time by Hogan's human and nonhuman ancestors.

A fox is another daily presence and reports regularly at the poet's observation post. There is the same instinctive desire to touch him, the same feeling of being enchanted by his bushy tail, sweet face, and the lightness and purposefulness of his movements as the fox approaches "to watch me, / as if it is easy and not just fear and hunger" (246). Rather than painting a pastoral scene, though, the poet unpacks her fraught emotional relationship to the beautiful animal, whose "body is my cat, / my neighbor's cat."

Yet, loving and hating him simultaneously, she holds no grudge because "[t]his is god swallowing what it must" (246). As she writes in a short poem entitled "The Way In," embodiment necessarily means foodiness: "[t]o enter life, be food" (194).

At night the poet's premises are haunted by the shadowy presence of a mountain lion ("Night Constant"). Sometimes walking in the darkness "just before me," unseen but felt "with the naked eye of skin" (242), the mountain lion seems to have accepted Hogan as a familiar stranger who poses no danger to her world. Accepting but wary of the human, she is attracted to the place by the poet's companion animals. Loving them as she does, Hogan must feel alarmed by the predator prowling around, but cannot help responding to the mountain lion's presence on some primal, physiological level—a testimony of deep ontological kinship with this animal elder:

> I feel it with the naked eye of skin,
> the fine hair, the animal trappings of my body
> begin to rise, a beast remaining [...].
>
> (242)

The mountain lion evokes a sense of awe and respect combined with remorse for our human lack of curiosity about and disregard of the parallel world of animals. Exploring space with our sophisticated technology, reaching for the stars, we "don't even know / the animals that walk outside our sleep." Hogan is puzzled by the fact that the rapid advance of human learning is accompanied by an equally spectacular weight of ignorance. Instead of trying to understand those who share planet earth with us and learning to live with them in peace, we act as if the world were not enough for us, searching the far-away stars and losing the chance to get acquainted with rapidly disappearing nonhuman species. "We call a world that's small / because we've matched it to ourselves" (242), she quips, taking issue with the founding belief of Western modernity that the human is the measure of all things. Accusing humanity of bad faith and unwillingness to face the truth about the havoc we wreak with the planet, she warns that when the world ends "it is not from what is known / but from what is never seen" (243). This is one more urgent wakeup call, published eight years after Crutzen and Stoermer advanced the Anthropocene hypothesis (17–18), and largely unnoticed, like the famous first dramatic appeal of the Kogi Mamas from 1990.[2]

In "Winter Solstice" we are offered a snapshot of Hogan's daily life at the onset of winter. There are "simple chores" to perform, like feeding the horses and raking "frozen manure" (225). There is a sense of peace and contentment as she goes about her duties, and her love for her companion animals is clear in her attention to "frost on their manes, / breath visible in air, / the deep lung of their breath." And then, unexpectedly, she notices a newly shed snake skin, an unusual sight in December: "All night I wonder / how a snake left its den / from its companions woven together in a ball" (225). In the solitary life she has chosen, finding a snake skin out of season is a major event, a mystery worth puzzling over "all night." Her reaction shows her deep intimacy with the life cycles of her untamed neighbors, as well as a concern for their wellbeing. In her sleepless night she wonders whether the day's warmth was sufficient to wake up the snake, but realizes she will never find out, "unless from the split red tongue" of the snake herself. The lighthearted tone of this conclusion suggests that Hogan is at peace with mystery, as long as no harm has been done and nobody needs her help. The poem closes with an image of the snake safely "back home / with its body curled into a three-foot secret / ten thousand years old" (225).

Mystery is the name of a wild mustang mare that Hogan adopted from the Bureau of Land Management after her riding accident.[3] "Affinity: Mustang" is a tribute to this beloved companion horse. In the quiet of the evening the mare almost blends in with the landscape. She is "a gray rock shining. She matches the land / belonging" (233). The mustang's "dark calm face" and "her hooves like black stone" speak of her indigenous origin. She is from the land, one with it, indigenous, her body formed of its dust and from the body of her ancestors born on the same land. In winter,

> her hair changes and becomes snow
> or her belly hair turns the color of red water willows
> at the creek,
> her legs black as trees.
>
> (233)

The imagery and the concept of "belonging" make the mustang an originary manifestation of the land, bound with it in an ancient and sacred relationship.

Hogan's poem subverts the dominant scientific theory concerning the horses' presence in North America, which holds that, having originally evolved on that continent, they became extinct in the Pleistocene, only to be reintroduced to the Americas at the time of European contact. Seventeen years before the publication of *Rounding the Human Corners*, Claire Henderson of Laval University, Quebec challenged the academic world to reconsider the extinction-reintroduction story in the light of oral evidence available from tribal knowledge keepers. In her *The Aboriginal North American Horse* (1991), Henderson lists origin stories and healing ceremonies featuring the horse, or the existence of pre-contact animal husbandry techniques surrounding the horse, as testimony to the flourishing of pre-contact horse cultures in North America. According to the Dakota/Lakota and many other tribal nations, she argues, the aboriginal horse, sometimes called the Indian pony, survived well into the 19th century, when the US government decided to round up and exterminate the aboriginal horses to minimize the risk of tribal peoples' attempts to escape from reservations. As Henderson discovers, the existence of a Dakota horse culture is corroborated by evidence from early French manuscripts (3–5).

More recently Yvette Running Horse Collins, a scholar and enrolled member of the Oglala Lakota Nation, utilized Critical Indigenous Research Methodologies to further deconstruct "the Eurocentric myth" concerning the absence of horses in pre-contact North America. In her 2017 doctoral dissertation *The Relationship Between the Indigenous Peoples of the Americas and the Horse*, Collins argues that white explorers were motivated by cultural prejudices in their failure to accept markers of Native Americans' cultural sophistication—the possession of the horse being one of them—and accurately report on some tribal peoples' advanced horsemanship skills and that these biases continue into the 21st century.[4]

In Hogan's poem "Affinity: Mustang" the fact that the mare belongs to the same land where her pre-contact ancestors once roamed free disrupts the colonial narrative. Her life recalls the bond between wild mustangs and the poet's tribal people, both of whom shared lives and land before settler colonialism broke the ties of kinship, leading to the tragic entanglements of genocide and ecocide. In her memoir Hogan speculates that Mystery may have come from the famous breed of horses known as the Chickasaw Pony (*The Woman* 153). Remnants of the breed were stolen by thieves accompanying the tribe on the Trail of Tears. Even though interbred with other horse races, they mysteriously survived, as evidenced by Hogan's mare. The poem's next line shifts to the plural as if to make this claim stronger: "These horses / almost a shadow, / broken" (*Dark* 233). As a descendant of the virtually extinct Chickasaw Pony, the mare is a shadow of a once powerful horse people native to Turtle Island, her brokenness reflecting the condition of her human relatives, the Chickasaws, and other Indigenous inhabitants of the land. In *The Woman Who Watches Over the World*, Hogan reflects on how much she and Mystery have in common: "a shared history, a world we once knew, the ache of being rounded up, being branded, owned, and being battered" (157–158).

"When we walk together," the poem continues, "in the tall grasses, I feel her / as if I am walking with mystery" (*Dark* 233). Hogan "feels" rather than "knows," or to put it differently, feeling / experiencing is her way of knowing and to knowing. This is why she knows what is beyond the reach of Cartesian reason. "We are never not Indians" (*The Woman* 59), she once observed, commenting on the weight of history, but this comment applies as well to the Indigenous people's signature attentiveness to the whole range of embodied, sensuous life experience. Walking with the mustang, Hogan is walking with the mystery of their shared history and the equally mysterious way they found each other: "I've come such a long way / through time / to find her" (*Dark* 234). Instinctively falling into the same rhythm, "for a while we are the same animal / and remember each other from before" (233). Such a deep bond leads her to the humbling realization that she belongs to the mustang, as much as the mustang belongs to the earth (234).

Hogan's experiencing body is an open, incomplete entity engaging the whole of the sensuous world. In this particular poem she describes her intimate, reciprocal relationship with the horse. Through her attunement to Mystery's bodily rhythms and her expressive preconceptual speech, Hogan achieves a sense of unity and completeness. Adopting the language used by David Abraham in his discussion of such attunement, it can be claimed that Hogan is "[b]ecoming earth. Becoming animal. Becoming, in this manner, fully human" (*Becoming* 3). The fullness of humanity that she has been trying to grasp in much of her writing is achievable only in and through an intimate relationship to the more than human world.

On some occasions the poet sings to her mare the songs she knows from her sleep, and this is another mystery coalescing around the horse's name.

> Some days I sing to her
> remembering the Kiowa man
> who sang to cover the screams
> of their ponies killed by Americans,
> songs I know in my sleep.
>
> (Dark 234)

Historically, many Indigenous Americans had a special relationship with horses. Trusted friends and beloved companions at the time of the colonial wars, horses fought and suffered the same fate as their riders. The Kiowa man Hogan references performed the only act of mercy available to him as he witnessed the slaughter of his four-legged companions—drowning their screams with his singing, he offered a makeshift of peace and company to those still waiting their turn, sharing their pain. Now it is Hogan who sings to Mystery to soothe the mare's despair after the loss of her foal. Upon seeing the horse cry, she "cleans her face" and obeys an inner voice which tells her to "sing" (234).

Once again, Hogan feels how deeply Indigenous identity is kinship-based: the people, the animals, the plants, and the land are one, as beautifully shown in this poem. While "Affinity: Mustang" explores this intimate relationship on the example of a particular horse, "Wild" celebrates—through this same mare—all the mustangs of America. "This is not the horse. It is the poem" (230), declares the opening line, almost immediately raising the problem of translation. The mustang, being an earthly "poem," speaks "in ways the human mind / can't hear / so another part of the human / translates this animal in America" (230). Poetry appeals to the heart rather than the mind; it speaks to our animal bodies and to the carnal, preverbal self that survives within, still connected to the larger world. The horse, like poetry, appeals to us on a bodily level, speaking about her embodied knowledge of loss and pain. She is:

> [...] knowing the herds of buffalo,
> the loss of creation, the missing ones
> who cannot be returned,
> and so it longs to be this translation
> of life in the first light of morning [...].

(230)

Translating the absence of her erstwhile companions into her very being, into the poem she is, the wild horse realizes they have been betrayed by the country, in which "there is no freedom [...], not anymore / in the mustang's changed history." But by maintaining her presence on the land which used to belong to the Indigenous peoples, human and nonhuman, of America, the wild horse questions the narrative of colonial difference, revealing the attempted erasure of Indigenous America as the colonial settlers' delusion. The mustang's epistemological challenge: "What do you know / about this world, do you remember / the forgotten language wild, / can you still call it?" (230), is an accusation and a sobering dismissal of colonial settler claims to the land and to domination.

Hogan's repeated references to an ancient language once shared by all living beings, a language whose echoes she occasionally hears, deserves a short digression. This language should not be understood as a system of highly conventional signs, oral, written or manual, whose function is to represent reality. The representative function of language is a relatively new development. Rather, this common speech of sacred beginnings is connected to premodern humans' perception of the surrounding world as made up of living entities, each of them endowed with an expressive, communicative power, each of them having sung itself into existence. "At the most primordial level of sensuous, bodily experience," writes Abram, "we find ourselves in an expressive, gesturing landscape, in a world that speaks" (*The Spell* 58). Expressions like the "howling" of the wind or the "roaring" of thunder retain this ancient awareness that speech is not the exclusive property of humans. Today the sensuous world continues to provide what Ferdinand de Saussure called a language's deep structure, and it is this deep structure that Indigenous people refer to in their stories of creation. In other words, it is this somatic, expressive function of language that is the origin of all languages, the original speech common to all. To participate in the world's ongoing conversation in "the forgotten language wild" one must be able to enter into the state of participatory awareness, as Hogan repeatedly claims in her poetry.

Given Hogan's delight in wild nature and her affinity with animals, it comes as no surprise that she would willingly "leave off being human / and become what it was slept outside my door last night" (*Dark* 237). This declaration appears in "Deer Dance," a meditation on deer, their ritual shedding of antlers, the famous traditional Yaqui and Mayo ceremony which gives the poem its title, and more generally, the privilege of shapeshifting. In Indigenous worldviews song and dance are associated with creative powers. Through singing and dancing the sacred deer dance, the traditional people of the Sonora Desert participate in the reenactment of the struggle between good and evil, re-creating the original harmony between human and nonhuman worlds. In so doing, they re-presence the time of ancient origins, when boundaries were fluid and shapeshifting was a natural occurrence. In Hogan's poem the young man chosen to dance the deer part danced "beautiful and tireless, / until he was more than human / until he too was deer" (236).

In *Becoming Animal* Abram unpacks the phenomenon of shapeshifting in the context of an animate, constantly metamorphosing world of deeply oral cultures. Such cultures live within a world felt to be "a vast, ever unfolding story" (270) in which all participate, the porous body encountering and being open to the more than human world, and the self "a tangible yet shifting identity that expresses itself in narrative and song" (275). Once a community enacts a sacred ceremony, singing and dancing themselves into contact with the more than human world, they become active participants in the metamorphic nature of reality. In consequence, as Abram puts it, "reality shapeshifts," the world becomes "tranced, animate and trickster-struck" (288). A man can become a deer, an animal can assume human form, a story comes alive, the deep structure of the world makes itself manifest. Is not the dance of the actual animals, in which the deer shed their antlers, an equally sacred ceremony? Do they not dance themselves into contact with the human, do they not shapeshift? Hogan does not exclude this possibility, because their "fur is never quite straight, / as if they'd just stepped into it" (*Dark* 237).

Transformational beings—as evidenced by the proliferation of hybrid creatures or the "crossings" of humans and whales in Hogan's poetic world—have been and will always be with us. It is telling, however, that

Of all those who were transformed into animals,
the travelers Circe turned into pigs,

the woman who became the bear,
the girl who always remained the child of wolves,
none of them wanted to go back
to being human.

(236–237)

The poet finds it noteworthy that, given a choice, those who have tasted
the fullness of embeddedness in the more than human world (like the
alleged feral children Kamala and Amala[5] she dwells on in her memoir
(*The Woman* 83)), find human civilization repulsive and long for their
former life in the wild. Will we ever really become awake to the privilege
of "becoming animal" before it is too late?—Hogan seems to be won-
dering. Her concern is shared by Abram. Commenting on the cost of
consolidating humanity around the idea of a common, printed culture,
he warns:

> If we do not soon remember ourselves to our sensuous surroundings, if
> we do not reclaim solidarity with the other sensibilities that inhabit and
> constitute those surroundings, then the cost of human commonality
> [consequence of the printed culture] may be our common extinction.
> (*The Spell* 161)

In another revealing passage, Abrams notes: "In genuinely oral cultures,
the sensuous world remains the dwelling place of the gods, the numinous
powers that can either sustain or extinguish human life" (*The Spell* 16). In
her poem entitled "Call," Hogan comments on just such enigmatic solici-
tations which are mysteriously obeyed by all participants in the metamor-
phic lives of the more than human world. Hungry or wounded predators
call forward their prey, and they, "with their healthy coats and paws,"
obey: "they go as if death knows their language" (*Dark* 255). This is the
same deep, sensuous matrix, the origin of speech, the primal language
of the carnate world, also spoken by humans before alphabetic writing
and abstract reason tore us away from our natural embeddedness in the
preconceptual, animal dimension of life. This call, heard and obeyed by
all sensuous life, is the closest equivalent to divinity, perhaps it is divinity
itself—the numinous powers capable of sustaining or extinguishing life:

> This is how some hear their god
> and wander off toward it or him
> and then are taken in
> while the god walks on mighty and full,
> passing others, generous at last.
>
> (Hogan, *Dark* 255)

It does seem that with this volume of poetry Hogan has rounded the human corners.

It is evident that Hogan's close encounter with death and her renewed awareness of life's fragility reoriented her writing toward joy in the 2000s. Attunement to the animal body divine and celebration of participatory awareness characterize the bulk of her poems from the first decade of the new millennium. Living in her cabin in the Colorado mountains, the poet rejoices in the small and unseen as well as the large and dangerous; she ecstatically loses herself in the nonhuman animal Other, identifying herself with earth's animals. Her attunement to animals is fully sensuous, instinctive, 'animalistic.' Watching others, she is increasingly conscious of being watched in return, of being caught in the mutuality of perceptual awareness, realizing that she has been forever changed by seeing herself measured by another, nonhuman intelligence. Forging a strong bond with a wild mustang, she experiences the reversal of anthropocentric notions of mastery and control. Hogan feels herself belonging to the mare, being claimed by her, not the other way around. Reality constantly shapeshifts. By harmonizing herself with this ever changing reality, she shapeshifts herself, becoming the animal she loves, becoming animal—any and every animal. But by becoming animal she also becomes more fully human, re-united with the land and its rich network of relationality.

Notes

1 Turtle egg harvesting has been legalized only in Costa Rica's town of Ostional, where once or twice a month sea turtles arrive in tens or hundreds of thousands in what is called *arribada* (mass arrival).
2 For details see Chapter 3, ft. 3.
3 The history of Mystery's adoption is described in Hogan's memoir *The Woman Who Watches Over the World*, pp. 152–158.
4 Evoking Paolo Freire's concept of "cultural invasion" to justify Western scientists' blatant neglect of evidence of pre-contact horse culture in North America, Collins asks: "How [else] would it be possible that the presence of ancient petroglyphs, pictographs, geoglyphs, effigies, and figurines of horses would not compel archeologists to begin a serious movement to scientifically test for dates in order to reevaluate the dominant Western cultural claim? How is it that consistent evidence of the genetic presence of Equus remains outside of the purported extinction time period accepted by the Western Academic establishment has not stimulated a flurry of new research in the area? Are each of these factors not considered substantial enough to debunk the current—and very unscientific—dating methodology utilized, which automatically categorizes petroglyphs, pictographs, geoglyphs, effigies, and figurines into the "post-Columbian" timeframe if it contains a depiction of a horse? (Collins 178).
5 Kamala and Amala were two feral girls allegedly discovered in a wolf den in Bengal, India, in the 1920s.

5 2010s

"I Want Mercy In This World"

In the second decade of the 21st century Hogan continued to be in great demand as a speaker, giving poetry and prose readings, offering creative writing workshops, and being invited to international conferences. The outbreak of the COVID-19 pandemic cut these activities short, but, as she said in an interview for *Southern Review of Books*, "it turned out to be a wonderful time of isolation and quiet, long periods of time watching birds" (Baumel).

The decade was also a time of harvesting as she published several new books. A performance piece entitled *Indios* came out in 2012. Loosely based on the Greek story of Medea, it is a long poem told in the voice of a young Indigenous woman who has married a powerful white man. In 2014, *Dark. Sweet* brought together chosen poems spanning Hogan's entire writing career (about two-thirds of the book's contents) combined with a brand new collection which gave the whole volume its title. Finally, in 2020 there appeared a book of essays, *The Radiant Lives of Animals*, and a poetry collection, *A History of Kindness*. The author has also announced the completion of her fifth novel, *The Mercy Liars*.

The new poems in *Dark. Sweet* begin with a section entitled "Unseen." Extending her explorations of the most humble and innocent manifestations of life, which played such an important role in *Rounding the Human Corners*, Hogan rejoices in the teeming profusion of barely visible creatures, the nymph stage of the mayfly being an especially telling example. Desiring "to be the same as creek bottom" (*Dark* 313), nymphs are a healing counterweight to the greed-defined modern world, whose snapshots dominate the volume's "History" section. With stones glued to their backs (313), they are a counterpoint to the unbearable lightness of the Western world's narcissistic culture. "What a wonder to be the creek bottom / for almost eternity" (313), the poet marvels. Compared to the mayfly imago's ephemeral life, lasting merely a day, the nymph, a stage which may last several years, does seem immortal. Is the ecstasy of "shimmering in sunlight for a day" worth spending an eternity "carry[ing] stones" (313) on one's back?—asks Hogan in the name of birds and other, much more visible creatures who cherish their freedom. Years of obscurity and imprisonment

DOI: 10.4324/9781003364252-7

spent at the rocky bottom of a creek, waiting to grow wings and fly for a brief spell of time? But if this sounds preposterous, Hogan quickly pulls the rug from under judgmental claws and feet:

> And myself at the creek
> near water and birds,
> walking in this house of bones,
> this muscle house with nothing to move me
> but five toes,
> a heel,
> a sole,
> and hidden wings.
>
> (313)

Who am I to judge?—she seems to be saying—locked as I am within my human perspective, imprisoned in my body not unlike the nymph in its aquatic habitat, carrying my house of flesh like the nymph carries its stone, not much more mobile than the nymph either, at least as compared to birds, and not a single chance to unfurl my hidden wings even for one brief day! Moreover, is a human not a sort of nymph herself—merely a stage in the ongoing transformation of life? What we, in our present stage of evolutionary development, consider to be assets, may one day, when we do learn to grow wings, turn out to be liabilities, our current life as drab as the nymph's. All in all, "Mayflies" is an exciting experiment with point of view. Hogan not only unmasks the evaluative nature of perceptions—after all, we do not really know what it is like to be a nymph—but argues that the humble and the invisible are good to think with.

They are also good to bless with. "May the unseen world bless your heart" (327) is the blessing the poet sends to her readers in another poem. Sadly, the once exuberant life—"the many, the untold, the unknown"—so self-evident we take it for granted, is the same life "we have been losing / piece by piece / bone by bone, feather by feather" (327) in what has come to be called the sixth great extinction. Evoking the story of the animals climbing Noah's ark "two by two" (327) to escape from the destructive waters of the Flood, Hogan is by no means expecting another divine intervention to reverse the current destruction. On the contrary, remembering how Christian colonists robbed Indigenous lands of ancient trees, the phrase "two by two" will forever sound "like the present measurement for lumber" (327) to her. In fact, the biblical reference in the poem serves to locate the roots of the ongoing ecological catastrophe in the Judeo–Christian exploitative attitude toward nature. The poem's dense three-line reference to Noah and wood clearances reads like a *précis* of Lynn White's famous thesis.

The consciousness of loss accompanies the poet in her daily activities, and the land reminds her of the many absences, of lives lost seemingly "not so very long ago" ("Not So Very Long Ago," *Dark* 317), a category vast enough to include wolves as well as humans indigenous to the land. As white settlers needed indigenous land for cattle and for newly arriving settlers, one extermination campaign followed another in quick succession. Sitting at a table and drinking coffee, Hogan broods on the wolves that used to live in the valley, "they with first title to this land / of many titles" (317)—which clause implicitly recognizes the ongoing extermination of all the subsequent title holders, perceived as obstacles to Manifest Destiny. Hogan is unable to come to terms with this wanton destruction of life. She dwells on it obsessively, shifting mentally from the coffee or wine on the table to the wolves that used to live in the very place where she lives. The poem's repetitive pattern is in itself a form of mourning: drinking coffee, the poet enjoys the beauty of her surroundings, but apart from conveying beauty, the landscape also speaks of those who are no longer there, their absence being part of the place. The second stanza is typical of the way the whole poem is organized:

> I was with my friends
> drinking coffee and we ate some bread
> in this place where blue birds nest,
> the place where wolves lived
> not so very long ago.
>
> (317)

It is a storied land, its past still alive and blending with the present. But native memories are storied as well, the wolves blending with Hogan's other ancestors, who "Left Not a Great While Ago"—the name given to the Chickasaws after they split from the Choctaws in 1856 (Hogan, *The Woman* 66). The Chickasaws had a title to this land as well. And they, too, stood in the way.

Unable to rouse herself from her sad brooding, she suddenly discovers it is early morning "and I am still sitting and find myself / in a place so suddenly different / in all its animal silence" (318). Such silences are many in the modern world. Whether in the valley of wolves or "the haunted valley of the now-gone / running and thundering horses" ("Valley of the Horses," *Dark* 319), the loss, the absence, the forced silence always originate from "a human lack of vision" (320).

One of the more devastating consequences of this lack of vision was the 2010 Deepwater Horizon oil spill, the largest environmental disaster in US history, which began on April 20, 2010 with an explosion on the BP-operated rig Deepwater Horizon, situated at the Macondo prospect

in the Gulf of Mexico. The oil flowed into the Gulf for 87 days, caus-
ing widespread damage to marine life and the entire ecosystem. "Song for
the Turtles of the Gulf" is Hogan's poetic response to the catastrophe.
Addressed to a turtle she had swum with just a month before—possibly
the same old mother that appears in "Turtle Watchers"—now dead, her
body "torched and pained" (348), it is a song of mourning and an apol-
ogy for a pact broken on the human side, an apology for the politically
and socially marginalized harm against animals. Seeing the dead turtle
handled by a smiling BP representative, Hogan states: "All I can think is
that I loved your life" (348), the death so irreversible and meaningless, no
words seem adequate. Besides, eloquence is neither sought nor desired in
the face of corporate indifference vis-à-vis innocent suffering. But this lost
life was precious in the eyes of Hogan, who dwells in loving detail on her
memories of the "beautiful swimmer," the masterwork that was her life,
mourning the loss of an ancient intelligence, "maybe greater" than human,
and noting bitterly that our advanced technology has a limitless potential
for destruction. "Forgive us for being thrown off true," she pleads to the
turtle, recognizing humanity's transgression in our failure to care for the
world. Asking the turtle's forgiveness for the collective sins of the human
race, the poet reaffirms the normative bonds of kinship originating in our
evolutionary beginnings:

> forgive our trespasses,
> in the eddies of water
> where we first walked.
>
> (348)

In this poem mourning is directly related to the loss caused by a disastrous
anthropogenic catastrophe. In "Dark. Sweet" such catastrophes feature
frequently. In addition to the violence already referenced in Hogan's pre-
vious volumes of poetry, here there are explicit allusions to such devel-
opments as the already mentioned Deepwater Horizon oil spill, to lands
flooded for dams to be built, the violence of fracking, and the poet's
renewed concern over the ongoing American military operations in Iraq
and Afghanistan. Puzzling about the human (self)destructive potential, she
is helpless to know how to account for it. Killing in wars is unlike "the
animal stalking food" (341).[1] While "that is need" and happens only in
response to hunger, human greed and desire for power appear to be com-
pletely un-natural, i.e., not anchored in life's natural drives. In "Justice"
Hogan speculates that the one thing "that makes a man" (343) is the
power to say "No" to destruction. In a dangerous world the poet's little
"home in the woods" offers her the only refuge she can find. It is here that
she "unharms" herself (352).

Missing the marine animals and the trees that continue to be felled, she suddenly rebels: "I want mercy in this world" ("Mercy, the Word," *Dark* 353). Rather than blaming soldiers "who follow orders / sworn to a nation / instead of the spirit of compassion," she would much rather write "a love poem / to ocean, tree, bird, a lover" (353). This tension between the poet's natural inclinations and her sense of responsibility for the world has been a constant since Hogan's earliest poetic publications. A born lover of the world, she has often been forced to act as a warrior, an activist taking a stand in defense of the fragile world she loves. At the heart of this paradox is her signature compassion. This is how she accounts for it:

> There is something wrong with me
> because seeing the suffering
> makes me weep and then I write these words.
>
> (353)

This discovery brings to mind J. M. Coetzee's *The Lives of Animals*. Its heroine, the elderly writer Elizabeth Costello, lectures on animal rights. In the course of her lectures she demonstrates the failure of reason in dealing with animal cruelty. Instead of relying on reason alone, she seems to argue, we need to reclaim the cognitive value of insight and empathy. Costello's passionate criticism of the human-engineered animal Holocaust results in her being mocked by academics and shunned by her family, but she persists in her quixotic activism. With the full knowledge of what humans do to animals, she is unable to live as others do. Her strategy of choice is the use of compassionate imagination in an effort to make a difference in human attitudes to animals.

Hogan's desperate plea for mercy originates in the same sensitivity to the suffering of all the world's sentient creatures. Empathy helps us understand that we are all interconnected, that all suffering is also always 'my' suffering. This is where ethics begins. So, Hogan imagines a world responsible for, and responsive to, the cry of the weaker and the oppressed, a world ruled by mercy. Mercy, she argues in "Mercy, the Word," prevents us from hardening our edges (*Dark* 354); it opens the already porous barrier between me and the other, leaving us implicated in the lives around us. Those who, upon hearing this word, react with kindness, are the new soldiers, sworn to "the spirit of compassion" (353). One can imagine what battles an army of such soldiers would wage and win! Mercy, kindness, and compassion are key terms in Hogan's poetry of the 2010s.

"Season of Butterflies" returns us to the shimmering paradise of insects at a time when adult butterflies emerge from the chrysalis stage and flood the world with "many thousand wings, all colors" (377). Admiring their perfection, the poet regrets she cannot "step out of [her] body of silk flesh" and move with the "winged lives / flower to flower, / pollen to pollen" (377). In her signature fashion, however, enraptured by the sights and sounds of the living world, she does eventually "step outside" (378), as she confesses in "Language of the Frogs," and loses herself in the other.

The stepping out can, on occasion, be followed by a sort of moving in, as in "Allegiance: The Sandhill Cranes," a poem spoken by the birds them-selves, the poet disappearing into the massive numbers she watches with ecstatic attentiveness. The whirl and flutter of wings, the characteristic unison calls, the crash of bodies landing on water, all this sounds like one thunderous voice saying to the waters and the sandbars: "Without regard for our fellow creatures, we will land on you" (383). No doubt Hogan is watching a sandhill crane staging area, where the birds gather on their biannual migrations to nesting and wintering grounds. The magnificent birds peremptorily fill the landscape with "wings, beaks, legs," reciting a pledge of allegiance (the poem is written in italics as if to suggest a shift to a collective, nonhuman speaker):

I pledge my heart, my allegiance,
to the united cranes of the continent
under one sky
indivisible
in one water
and to the republic of crane,
for which we stand,
one nation for which we come,
under cloud, under sky,
even the once ragged and poor,
for which we rise up
with the power and glory
of our union with all the majestic others.

(383)

The sandhill cranes, who have been on the North American continent for at least 2.5 million years, rank with wolves among those with "first title to this land," as Hogan phrased it in "Not So Very Long Ago" (*Dark* 317). Consequently, their oath of allegiance to "the united cranes of the con-tinent" predates the much more famous controversial pledge, still some-times recited at the beginning of every school day by descendants of both those who stole the land from its Indigenous populations and victims of settler colonial politics. Reciting the pledge of allegiance to the US flag effectively means sanctioning the logic of conquest and extermination, and embracing an ideologically sanitized nationalism. Its short text bristles with patriotic propaganda. First, the US has rarely been what it aspires to be, "one nation indivisible," as was recently made manifest on the final day of Donald Trump's presidency.[2] Second, the ambition of extending "liberty and justice" to all has never been achieved, nor was it intended by the republic's Founding Fathers. The incorporation of the words "under God" in 1954 testifies to an unfortunate conflation of Christianity and capitalism, historically co-responsible for the settler colonial project, and in more recent times emblematic of a militant opposition to plans of combating climate change. Above all, the influence of Christian fundamentalist groups on the social and political life of the country betrays the democratic principles on which it was built. In comparison, the sandhill cranes' pledge is a decolonial manifesto of solidarity and unity. Under an undivided sky, respecting no state and country borders, these migrating birds are at home on the entire continent, the one nation for which they stand inclusive of the "once ragged and poor." The commotion and joy of their coordinated descent on the nearby waters has lifted Hogan's spirits.

It has made her re-minded, too. In another poem, "First Language: Sandhill Cranes," she claims that these birds, arriving from the four directions of the world, "were here on the first day of creation / when one of our many gods said or thought, / Let there be infinite sky and creatures with wings" (408). This verse is part of the "Remedies" section, which offers antidotes to the poison of modern history, the memory of ancient lifeways being the most potent of these. Fittingly, the section is dominated by images of transformation and becoming. "First Language: Sandhill Cranes" begins with the idea of change, as the oncoming cranes modify the place beyond easy recognition. "Even the sounds" are different, the poet notes, and this observation leads to the recollection that "[s]ome call these birds the changers of language, / the tellers of stories" (408). They keep talking long into the night as they roost in shallow water and dance their mating dance. As new arrivals continue to appear on the horizon, the poet's eye is tricked into believing that the horizon "is coming up from the ground / and not down from the sky." The masses of birds look like "an island of crane" to Hogan, "all one mind" (409), a nation which is truly one, indivisible. "They are the ancient beginnings," she offers, believing their unity reflects the normative harmony of all creation. The cranes speak "our first language" (409), the preverbal language of ancient beginnings when all reality was one, indivisible and shapeshifting.

The enigmatic "Transformations: Winter Count" focuses on a similar concept:

This winter was a cave we climbed through
like a circle of dark birds entering the light,
becoming lighter by the moment [...]

(391)

Upon seeing the blue sky, the collective speaker becomes ecstatic and emerges out of darkness. After a lapse of time, an old mother intends to explain the story painted on a hide, but gets distracted by the hide's reverse side,

> and through that circle of birds
> we have been changed into,
> the story became a song
> and we flew off into the blue stretch [...].

(391)

On a most basic level, this is a story of emergence. The darkness of winter merges with the darkness of the womb as well as the darkness of the primal cave of the Chickasaw emergence myth, which gets reenacted in the kiva ceremony. Time is layered and inclusive of its three ecstasies, as Heidegger would put it (see: Abram, *The Spell* 127), and so is the speaker. This time the speaker does fly, even if only as a shapeshifting, transformational "we," an ancient arrangement of the atoms that now make up her human body.

Transformation is also the leading motif of "The Deer Mothers," Hogan's different take on the Deer Dance ceremony. After emerging from the kiva into the light of day and seeing the "dancers come out of the darkness, from mystery" (393), she wishes she could stand together with the mothers in the ceremonial center. "We are back," she realizes. Having survived centuries of extermination and cultural genocide, people indigenous to the land are back: "we are the people," she claims, "we are the animals, / this is eternity" (394).

Still, they are embedded in the genocidal culture of "this America" and the progress of re-minding hangs in the balance. "Fields not ours," begins the poem entitled "This America." Here trees on both sides of the roads hide an absence behind them and rabbits are "penned with a lock":

> I am walking in the world of insects
> and the America of the caged,
> all encircled, the gnats in streetlights all brightened,
> and the June bugs at the sewn screens,
> the dogs in cages
> waiting to fight.

(411)

"The America of the caged" distrusts freedom, builds walls, sets up divisions, and keeps four-legged beasts behind bars while allowing numerous human beasts to walk free; it delights in violence while pretending to work for peace. This America offends the sacredness of life, not least when it cages rabbits, which Indigenous hunters believed to be their kin to whom respect was due, to say nothing of 'harvesting meat' as if animals killed for food were objects of purely instrumental value. In this world turned upside-down even religion has been hijacked to serve the political agenda, the Good News militarized against the poor to whom it should be preached. "Jesus washed the feet of the poor / and tired and sick," reflects Hogan. "I call this love," she continues: "he would / not have swerved a car to kill that dog, / that turtle, that cat" (411), and he would not have allowed the clearing of old-growth forests to make room for cattle, either.

"This America's" unwarranted destructiveness fills Hogan with anger, particularly when helpless creatures are at the receiving end of violence. It is toward the poem's conclusion that we learn what triggered her outburst:

> And the old turtle I saw yesterday
> walking across the hot road
> over what must have looked by day like water,
> a mirage, and the man who tried to run over it.
> How I hate it. How it makes me violent
> as him, to him.
>
> (412)

This is a very rare instance when Hogan, who loves all life and wants mercy in this world, can no longer contain her anger, when she actually uses the word "hate" and gets in touch with her own destructive impulses, which are energized by a sense of powerlessness and despair. Violent America infects everyone with the virus of its own sickness. Hogan feels humiliated by becoming as violent "as him," she hates the person she is becoming—a mirror image of the colonizer, ready to harm the person who is harming another life. Realizing what is happening, she checks herself: "But, oh," and rejoices in that man's failure. "The turtle survived" and her joy at seeing the animal safe purges her of the incipient violence. She carries the frightened survivor, "big, heavy, peeing / to the other side of the road / of this America" (412), no doubt wishing she could carry the turtle to the other side of violence just as easily.

Mainstream America's attitude to nonhuman animals, as this poem suggests, is largely built on cruelty and abjection: abused in the entertainment industry and violent spectator sports like dog fighting, kept in tiny cages, killed for fun and food, the actual animal is frequently denied ethical consideration. All this looks familiar to a daughter of the continent's Indigenous people who feels that "the dirty feet of [her] past / still walks on these roads" (411), the structure of settler colonialism resistant to the flow of time. But she knows that sooner or later it will collapse, because it is built on deicide: the killing of Life. Hogan's most accurate definition of god is this: "god is not who or what / or anything at all, but this, Life" (414).

It is this god she addresses in "The Eyes of Animals," one of the most poignant poems in the volume. Looking into the eyes of the elephant, the tortoise, the mountain gorilla infant, the tree frog, the orangutan, the whale, or the wolf, one sees behind the animal mask the animals' disturbing similarity to—or better still, their exact identity with—humans. They have the same desire to live, to be free to raise their children, and to care for them "just as we do" (414). The eyes of the land tortoise and the elephant speak of the animals' desperate search for clean water on a planet undergoing desertification. Both are "on the way to any water, / across a changed world / where nothing is familiar" (413). The mountain gorilla infant has the look of guileless innocence; his eyes say "I am light, kind. / I am the same as you" (413). The orangutan is a precious jewel, a "red ruby of a child" (414) who needs protection against ruthless poachers and palm oil barons. All these lives threatened by extinction speak of the overlapping nexus of speciesism, global capitalism, and settler violence, of exploitation rooted in colonial ontologies. In their eyes the poet reads a plea for kindness, for compassion; the animals pose no threat, they do not hate, their eyes speak only of ancient wisdom and gentleness. "Life," prays Hogan, asking this god to read the prayer in the eyes of the whale, as "there are no words / a man can speak so great as theirs" (414); even poetry seems mute in comparison. The god of life is moved. It returns the gaze and speaks:

> [...] the eyes of the universe
> look back at you
> with a true knowledge of what you are,
> saying, *Human, woman, man, child*
> *this world, even your self*
> *you must learn to love.*
>
> (414)

Because, ultimately, hatred of life comes from our externalized hatred of ourselves. Projecting our own darkness onto the world, we hate this darkness and try to destroy its projected image, leaving its source, however, untouched. Life's answer to the prayer is in effect a commandment of love: love this world—your kin—as you love yourself, Life says. The beguiling simplicity of this answer masks a real challenge, because how can one learn to love if one has been taught to hate oneself? The culture of modernity / coloniality is built on self-destructive drives and is incapable of overcoming its built-in death-wish without opening itself to what has been theorized as decolonial love. In its broadest sense decolonial love is "the principle of receptive generosity" (Maldonado-Torres, "On the Coloniality of Being" 260). In the words of Nelson Maldonado-Torres, decolonial love helps to construct "a world in which genuine ethical relations become the norm and not the exception" (244).

Hogan's last poem in the "Dark. Sweet" section of the *Dark. Sweet* volume, "After Silence: Return," speaks to this hope. Taking issue with the religious exercise of retreating from the world into silence to hear the voice of truth, she argues that it is the opposite that is needed:

> Unless we venture into the world
> where we may find some cure for the present,
> we will not know how far we have to go back
> to speak once again with the animals [...].
>
> (418)

It is in returning to the world from the exile of separation that we can hear the voice of our elders, our teachers, and Life our god. Their voice, not that of our inner darkness, is the voice of truth. Listening to it, turning back from the path of ideological abstractions, we will return to the source, which Hogan identifies with "compassion for all" (418). Only then can the work of recovery begin.

It comes as no surprise that Hogan's next volume of poetry received the title *A History of Kindness*. Placed in the book's middle, the title poem identifies kindness with what "a real human" does (72). Kindness means worrying that a small animal might have got caught in freshly baled hay; it means offering your last withered apple to a horse, speaking gently, treading softly, being protective, generous, and compassionate. Kindness means helping an old woman get safely home and leaving your own coat behind because she needs it more than you do. "What else would a real human do?" (72)—asks Hogan. Relationality and kindness are marks of mature humanity. And it is kindness that will be our passport "on the spirit's journey / to the world of all souls" (10). Alluding to her ancestors' belief that the Milky Way is the path that spirits travel, she refers to the constellation Canis Minor, or the Little Dog, visible just above the horizon of the winter sky. The dog will not let you even start the journey unless he is satisfied with your answer to his one question: "did you ever harm an animal, hurt any creature / or take a life you didn't eat?" (10).

Generosity has always been encouraged among Indigenous people, the most radical act of generosity being what Hogan ironically calls "our giving up the taken land and forest / to those who wanted it so" (*A History*, "The Red Part" 4). Although the settlers took everything they could, they still wanted more, and tribal people continue to give, even today, out of a generous concern for the Whole. At present they give "knowledge you don't hear, / the new mind you can't accept" (*A History, "What We Kept"* 13). Sadly, these offerings that could save the world are among the least appreciated. But the poet will persist in offering them nonetheless, because she is "a warrior / wanting this world to survive"[3] (26). As a "soldier sworn to the spirit of compassion" (*Dark*, "Mercy, the Word" 353) she acts out of concern and wants all people to:

> always remember those birds, the bison,
> their grief, too, and how the land hurts
> in more chambers than one small heart
> may ever hold.
>
> (*A History* 27)

The majority of the poems in *A History of Kindness* rehearse familiar themes, approached from new angles and perspectives. Grief mingles with hope, mourning with joy as the poet "think[s] the gone animals back" (35), the buffalo[4] being a reference point for a whole group of poems. But there are also touching vignettes of Hogan's everyday life with animals, be they her pet companions, the lovely shy deer of the forest, or the beautiful predators that pass by her cabin. Another common theme is the ongoing reflection on the sources of evil.

"Eagle Feather Prayer" is a good entry point to all these concerns. The golden eagle is revered in many Indigenous cultures of North America for her strength, agility, and hunting prowess. Birds in general, and golden eagles in particular, are believed to link the physical world to the spiritual one. In traditional cultures feathers represent the spirit of the bird and eagle feathers are among the most cherished, serving as sacred objects used in many healing ceremonies. There is a special protocol which specifies which Elders are allowed to assemble eagle feather prayer fans or even give eagle feathers to individuals. In *Dwellings* Hogan describes how a golden eagle dropped a feather close to her cabin in what she can only explain as a response to her life-long prayers to have one (15–6920). Commenting on the sacredness of the eagle feather, she writes:

> There is something alive in a feather. The power of it is perhaps in its dream of sky, currents of air, and the silence of its creation. It knows the insides of clouds. It carries our needs and desires, the stories of our brokenness. It rises and falls down elemental space, one part of the elaborate world of life where fish swim against gravity, where eels turn silver as moon to breed.
>
> (*Dwellings* 20)

The poem entitled "Eagle Feather Prayer" shows Hogan enacting a sacred ceremony with a prayer fan given to her by a person identified as Old

Mother. In the first words she thanks the old woman and the eagle for the gift of the fan and for teaching her "to pray with no words" (*A History* 39). In what seems like the first common language, that "part of [her] that is unnamed by anatomy books" faces the creation, "also with secret names," to pray for the water protectors at Standing Rock and elsewhere around the world, and the mention of water makes her think of her "brother and sister animals" on their "paths to needed waters," as she puts it in an essay written in 2016 ("Why We are Singing for Water"). The buffalo were among them, and their extermination has caused the prairies to go dry.[5] Praying for the healing of all creation, the poet finds herself struggling to include their killers in her prayerful thoughts. Coming from people who love—"our horses," "the dogs who helped us," "the wilderness of buffalo herds"—she is perplexed by the identity of "the shooters." "I don't know what they are (...) or their purpose for being" (*A History* 39), she writes, apparently helpless in the face of the mystery of pure evil. In another poem she speculates that the soul of people who hate life "came from some other place" ("Tulsa" 91). They definitely are not human in the normative sense of this word, as it is defined in the pages of *A History of Kindness*.

Hogan's home in the wildlife corridor lies close to Lookout Mountain,[6] which houses the grave and museum of Buffalo Bill Cody (1846–1917), the most infamous buffalo shooter, who holds the notorious record of shooting 4,282 bison in 18 months.[7] As if this was not enough, down the main road from her house lies Bear Creek, where—as Hogan reminisces in *The Radiant Lives of Animals*—"Col. Chivington planned the massacre of human beings at Sand Creek, while promising them peace and safety" (13). On November 29, 1864 an entire camp of Cheyenne and Arapaho people at Sand Creek was wiped out by the US Army. Her home's geographical location fosters recollections, making the past vividly alive. Many poems included in *A History of Kindness* speak to a storied time; they touch the wounds of the past and raise hopes for the future.

This is most explicit in the "Old Mother" section of poems, which revolve around the iconic figure of the buffalo. In "We Have Walked Down Past," the poet rejoices in the unexpected presence of a buffalo calf, who must have become separated from a larger herd of animals. Discovering her not far from the remnants of a mountain lion's last night's feast, she speculates: "I think the mountain lion left the buffalo calf alone / knowing she was holy" (40). The predator and the tribal people may have been equally happy about the reappearance of the one-time god of the prairie, and the tribe left prayer flags and tobacco ties attached to trees in an act of thanksgiving. Slowly but surely, Hogan is suggesting, the return of old ceremonies brings back the life lost, and the animals that have been killed off are coming back. The remedies she prescribed in "Dark. Sweet" (*Dark*, "Remedies" section 391–418) seem to be effective, the butterfly effect works. The enigmatic Elder, simply called Old Mother, continues to heal the land with her sacred pollen prayers (*A History* 40).

"Buffalo Road: Leaving South Dakota" offers a closer look at the traumatized land of the Great Plains, once roamed by bands of free Indians and herds of bulky animals. In the poem's first lines, the thing that arrests the poet's attention is signs of ancient buffalo presence etched into the landscape in the form of deep hillside ridges, and the startling absence of the actual animals. The land remembers and speaks of a loss. Hogan reads in it the story of

> [...] the snow-filled hoof,
> the horns,
> the chins with dark tufts,
> matted wool forced to the forest
> to stand with the minus,
> the many horses lying
> with red shadows of dusk
> and blood.
>
> (42)

In the ruthless military campaigns that were waged against the Great Plains Indians and their way of life, humans and nonhumans suffered the same fate at the hands of soldiers commanded by the likes of Colonel George Armstrong Custer and Nelson A. Miles, who scoured the Dakota territory after the Battle of Little Big Horn to win the final victory over the Lakota and their allies by driving them onto reservations (and to confine the remaining bison to parks and preserves). Hogan is reminded of the violence of "Miles and Custer," whose souls clearly "came from some other place," (*A History* 91). Their crime is that they tried

> to subtract this world,
> to take any living thing,
> even the newly born,
> from the numbers of human and creature life,
> to the food, body, hoof, claw,
> the ghost animals,
> driving them away from earth,
> the killing of horses,
> massacre of bison,
> and that was never enough.
>
> (42–43)

The clinical, impersonal wording, reflective of the agents of coloniality's technical approach to the elimination of undesirables, deserves to be quoted at length. The coldly calculating logic of death already reduces (before the actual "subtraction") animal and animalized lives, the lives deemed non- and sub-human, to the status of *zoe*: killable life, endowed with merely instrumental value and subservient to the needs and desired of the fully "human." The actual life, obscured by the jargon of "food, body, hoof, claw," is no longer visible—it is merely an absent referent in the bodies to be processed and utilized. In Algonquian lore, insatiability is the mark of Windigo, the ever-hungry monster with a heart of ice. Originally a warning against greed, the monster myth is an apt metaphor for settler colonialism, as well as the excesses of capitalism and corporate consumerism (Kimmerer 305–309). Hogan makes extensive use of Windigo in her novel *Solar Storms*.

To the greedy settlers, no matter how much they took, it "was never enough." This terrifies Hogan, who prays:

> God, let us be those
> who create, give, make,
> and do not ever take
> more than we offer.

> (*A History* 43)

The land remembers all the life taken, "each pounding run, / each spill of blood" (43). And the young calf remembers it all in her blood, too. She has come to tell the poet and Old Mother about the "absence" and "the silence" (46). "The Buffalo Again" is Hogan's only poem to make extensive use of the empty page. Placing these two discreet words—"absence" and "the silence"—at the distance of several lines of blank space from one another, Hogan visually evokes the reality they name, mimicking the erasure of life and the emptiness of the land.

Buffalo Bill's presence haunts the land as well, as his fame rested on buffalo genocide[8] and on reducing "the broken, beautiful warriors" (51) of the Great Plains Indians to puppets in his traveling circus. These two strands of the story interweave in "A Need for Happiness," a poem which affirms the triumph of life over death even in tragic circumstances. The grief-stricken Lakota chiefs who performed in Buffalo Bill's Wild West Show "laughed together at night / when the light-bearded man left" (52), and the buffalo calf, breaking off from her herd on the far side of Highway 70, where Buffalo Bill lies buried, returns to claim the land once stolen from her ancestors. The need for happiness is constant and transcends species lines.

If it is difficult to trust this natural instinct, this salutary need for happiness, it is because history repeats itself. "The day the buffalo appeared / where I live with wild horses," Hogan confesses, "I thought, They are clearing the land again / for ranches" (*A History*, "Outside My Cabin"

53). As an Indigenous woman, she is haunted by the past: the removal of people from their tribal lands and the killing of wolves and wild horses to make room for the farm animals that accompanied it. Significantly but unsurprisingly, Hogan uses the expression "clear away" to refer to what happened to both humans and nonhumans, as if they were things that stood in the way, which in the eyes of the settlers they were.

Before returning to the buffalo, who, to her delight, has taken up residence in the vicinity of her cabin, Hogan picks up on the theme of wolves, reminded of the "five ghostly presences / floating across the snow" (53) after a Yellowstone fire, who killed a deer and attacked an elk close to her house. Allowing the wounded elk to stay around and heal, she found it lucky that people disbelieved stories of the wolves' appearance, "because no shooters saw them here" (53). For the same reason, she keeps the presence of the buffalo secret. "Because I know what they would do," she says, remembering the trail of destruction the settlers leave wherever they go, "as if they [...] can't help themselves" (54).

Hogan's poems that center the buffalo poignantly demonstrate the multispecies character of settler colonial violence, as well as the multispecies nature of decolonization. The buffalo calf who has broken off from her herd to reclaim the prairies of her ancestors is a potent agent of decoloniality. Her unexpected appearance raises hopes that whole herds will eventually return, bringing back the constellation of social, cultural, and spiritual practices that once supported the ancient lifeways. In the old times buffalo, being a keystone species, influenced all aspects of life in the Great Plains, supporting an intricate web of interspecies relations. Efforts to reintroduce free-ranging bison herds have shown that the animals can "bring other species back from the brink of extinction" (Taschereau Mamers 29). As depicted by Danielle Taschereau Mamers in her article "Human-Bison Relations as Sites of Settler Colonial Violence and Decolonial Resurgence," bison-restoration endeavors grounded in Indigenous knowledge "shift the emphasis of restoration work [...] to the complete and meaningful restoration of relation," thereby making conservation "a multispecies endeavor with decolonial possibilities" (26).

Recollections and memory play a key role in the "Old Mother" section of *A History of Kindness*. Old Mother remembers "when the near city was a buffalo wallow" (55), and the buffalo calf, too, must have vivid recollections of her ancestral past, considering

> how much memory is in that body,
> how much memory resides in every cell,
> some of it happiness to run with the others through the grass,
> some of it seeing what happened before
> and so miserable that it carries that memory.

(55)

The poet remembers while she is conversing with Old Mother, or is sifting through humanity's collective memories for lessons about the present while patiently waiting for an ancient turtle to cross the road. The turtle, in turn, carries her rich baggage of recollections in her "amazing design of shell" (*A History*, "Memory" 57). In Indigenous eyes, memories, like the need for happiness, are a shared quality among human and nonhuman animals. In a valley where "the fault lines of history broke" (58), the past is never dead. But the opposite is also true: the future comes alive there, signs of resurgence dotting the landscape. The buffalo return, "the old world leaks through" (*A History*, "Holy Springs, Mississippi" 61) in visions, and the poet, who is always watching over the land, knows she is in turn watched by the solitary bison, by the wolves, the hawk, or the fox who comes each morning "to watch how I live, / to make sure it is / the right way" (*A History*, "Watching Over" 59). All the relatives are coming back, celebrating the good life, keeping a sense of neighborliness alive. The old world is coming back, at least from the perspective of "this little cabin made of happiness" (58), where "no one of us is superior / to the minions of insects" (*A History*, "God of the Prairies" 67).

Having staked out the parameters of the land where she lives, Hogan offers glimpses of the simplicity of her daily life with her companion animals: a cat, a dog, two horses and, in time, a burro. All of them are rescue animals and they share her most intimate space, as can be seen in "Isn't It Love." Rising early in the morning to feed and provide for them is the best definition of love the poet can give. There is no monetary value in keeping these animals. They do not work and do not earn their living. On the contrary, the only reason for their existence is love—the love they receive and the love they give in return. Hogan's "little cabin made of happiness" is a place where an interspecies community has come into existence, with love circulating abundantly among all its members. The poem suggests that—far from being its alpha individual—Hogan is in fact a servant of the community, "carrying grain, hay, cleaning the water," even when, on occasion, she would much prefer "to sit with the trees and a book / or paper and ink, / or look down to the field where deer and turkey roam" (83). But she does not complain, because all this is the work of love. At the day's end, after a simple and solitary meal, "I caress the cat, brush the dog, take night hay to the horses / along with their sweet for the night" (84).

This, too, is the work of recovery, a re-minding, or returning to normative kinship relationships with all of creation. Although pets in the contemporary sense of the word were not common among pre-contact American peoples, as all had to work for a living, in the changed world of today, where abandoned and feral animals are heavily dependent on humans, incapable of earning their keep in a way commensurate with their natural interests (a concern crucial to animal justice), Hogan's inter-species family inscribes itself into the Indigenous ethos of relationality. On the Trail of Tears, her ancestors were observed carrying puppies in a basket, unable to leave the helpless creatures behind. A great-great-grand-daughter of "such loving people," as Hogan calls them in *The Woman Who Watches Over the World* (55), she continues on her ancestors' path of generosity and kindness, offering the best she has to those who are the most needy. "What else would a real human do?" (*A History* 72), she muses.

A real human would not walk indifferently by a blind kitten infested with fleas. "I saw her / feral face," writes Hogan, "and said, / Good morning, Sunshine. / Here is a song for you" (*A History*, "Sunshine" 79). From the perspective of people who believe a cat should catch mice for a living, the blind Sunshine is 'useless.' But she is much loved just the way she is, perhaps even more so because of her greater need for protection. So, she is given a loving home, a happy name, and a song in the old language as welcoming gifts, as well as the right to sleep on the poet's heart "now that you no longer sleep in the alley" (79). The poet encourages her:

> Oh beautiful, come to me, with your soft fervent
> rumble, your little paws, still small, not like the others
> who use them to reach out for food
> steal from the table.
>
> (79)

This touching conversation between the poet and the cat, one speaking terms of endearment, the other purring with happiness in response, is reminiscent of a different world, where mutual care is the norm and not the exception, and of a different time, when people and animals spoke the same language. Hogan and Sunshine do this, they communicate beyond words, and when the poet sings, the blind cat follows: "and you come to me, / Sunshine, / like the warm ray in the window you love" (80).

Ultimately, Hogan believes that love and a life-long commitment to those who open themselves to accepting it, human and nonhuman, are the measure of real humanity. The poem "Burying the Horse" deals with the pain of losing one of her beloved horses. Her name was Kelli and Hogan adopted her from Colorado Horse Rescue after her recovery from her near-fatal riding accident (Hogan, *The Woman* 173–175). A horse who had been abandoned by her owners, malnourished and with a history of abuse, Kelli had "blood in hooves" and was "barely able / to move or eat / without help" (*A History*, "Burying the Horse" 112). Yet as the poem evolves and the recovered Kelli shows "such gratitude / and care returning" (113), one wonders who was more indebted to whom. Not that it matters, though.

Initially the mare "was the one not to ride / because she'd been so abused," but she thrived under Hogan's loving eye and started to run again. "Grateful for every morsel / of food and for grass," her eyes spoke of "happy fragility and kindness," while her canine brother, "pretending to be a horse / out in the field bent over / as if eating beside her" (113). Such a loving family it was. Hogan recollects the same look of fragility and kindness in the dying horse's eyes as she was holding her head in her lap, waiting for the doctor to arrive to put Kelli down. Before burying her, Hogan allowed "her sister" (114), the mustang Mystery, to sniff Kelli's body to realize that the mare was dead. Then they both kept vigil beside the horse's body, until the backhoe arrived.

Hogan's moving description of her interspecies family mourning the death of one of its members goes against the grain of what Chloë Taylor calls an "ethical apartheid between humans and nonhuman animals" with respect to death. As Taylor argues, iconographies of death matter; whether a being's death is considered grievable or not has political and ethical implications. "So long as we do not grieve nonhuman animals, the instrumentalisation of their lives, and not only of their corpses, will continue," she claims in the article "Respect for the (Animal) Dead" (99). Experiencing, through mourning, "our commonality with others who have been set outside the sphere of the human" (Taylor, "Respect" 100) is an essential step toward preventing the violence of industrial animal farming, animal experimentation, and other instances of institutional animal abuse.

Companion species occupy a boundary position in the deontological-utilitarian distribution of ethics across the species line. Although we do not generally instrumentalize their corpses, grieving their death is a contested issue. Taylor notes that

> dead pets and those who loved them are left in limbo since it is neither socially acceptable to mourn them nor to eat or otherwise use them. We are expected to do and feel nothing, to get a new pet and be back at work the next day.
>
> ("Respect" 99)

With her testimony of grief and a touching description of the mourning ritual she organized for the horse, Hogan makes a much-needed ethical statement, breaking the unwritten rule described by Taylor. Before burying Kelli's body, she "wrapped her / in more than [her] arms" (*A History* 114), as Hogan puts it. The farewell embrace follows the wrapping of the corpse in an Indian blanket as a mark of respect and love. Hogan then grieves and sings a horse song to her friend:

Oh my love,
how it hurt my body so
but even more my heart
to get you down there
with so little help
you'd always given me
[...]
and part of me
is beneath that ground
in the blanket
wrapped and singing
a good horse song.

(116)

"Burying the Horse" is one of the longest poems in Hogan's *oeuvre*, which tells much about Kelli's importance in her life as well as the depth of her grief.

If part of her was buried with the horse, the opposite is also true. Being so loved, Kelli remains part of Hogan's daily life, her spirit lingering in the place. In clear opposition to the Western separation narrative but consonant with Indigenous worldviews, she claims to have seen "the spirit of my horse" (123) undead, grazing in the field. She rejoices in this vision, which only confirms what she has experienced on many other occasions, namely, that absence is merely "the missing presence" whose continued reality is confirmed by the "phantom pain" (122) we still feel. Whether her uncle's missing toe or "the majestic endangered missing / the beautiful gone" part of creation she cannot stop mourning, the disappeared and the unseen remain with us, much as the body of a snake imprinted in his perfectly shed skin (122).

Outside her little cabin, life continues to thrive, the big and the small. On her daily walks Hogan comes across life's many miracles, one of them being the birth of a fawn. "I stop my own life," she relates, watching "the infant moving" inside a doe, reminded of another fawn that had to be helped to emerge from the exhausted mother's womb. "But this time I merely watch this creation, / beautiful, even with ticks and insects, wounds and scrapes / that humans don't envision because our sight is not large / enough" (126). The trope of our human lack of vision is a characteristic of Hogan's mature poetry. Speaking as an Elder, protector of life, and as a woman who watches over the world, she sends out messages of warning and prescribes curative treatment, but will we listen to words of ancient wisdom?

The larger vision advocated by Hogan demands an extension, perhaps even explosion, of Western ethics in regard to the recognition of our dependence on the nonhuman world, as well as a radical commonality of experience across the species line. In "Fawn," the poem just referred to, one mother watches over another, the birth of the fawn bringing to Hogan's mind the birth of her own grandchild as part of the larger vision she experiences. We are all the same, she argues, depicting the doe speaking to her child, their love being "as great as ours" (*A History*, "This Morning" 128). We are all the same, claims the poet as she envisages doe mothers "praying to the god of deer" to protect their young while they are busy chasing off coyotes (128), or delighting in the grace and elegance of two does dancing and bowing "to one another in respect," the insects dancing in air, affirming life (*A History*, "I Saw Them Dancing" 129). "Each life says to the other, Yes," Hogan interprets their words and she continues: "you are an animal, you are a song, / you are a runner, a flyer, you are so alive" (129). All want to live and Hogan wants us to know it and to love the life that wants to live so. "We were all created together," she reminds her readers later in the poem, even though we live in different worlds now, the "twilight dancers" making their home in "the tangle of thickets" where she disappointingly "can never follow" (129).

Ever a follower, never a guide, she stays attuned to the animals' intentions and expectations, following where *they* wish to take her. This attitude of obedience is highlighted in "White Deer, Your Direction I Will Follow." Somewhere on the border of the real and the visionary, or perhaps on the verge of life and death, a white deer leads her "beyond men with rifles or bows," not unlike "the white dog / my people followed [...] / to the next world after this creation" (131). Hogan knows their destination is far away, but feels surprisingly fit even when crossing a river her guide has just leaped over. When the vision dissolves, she merely re-affirms her commitment to obey and follow, rather than disregard a potential revelation, distrust a messenger, perhaps offend her nonhuman elders. "You have to ask," she writes,

> how often do you see it,
> how often does it come to you,
> how often, really,
> do you follow?

(132)

Apart from animals that are already familiar from Hogan's earlier poetry, *A History of Kindness* offers rare snapshots of one that she encountered while traveling outside of North America. The collection's Book Four, entitled "The Other Country," testifies to Hogan's fascination with camels, animals indigenous to desert countries. First, she delights in the surprising grace of this huge, awkward animal—"not the most loved creature of them

all"—as he lays himself down in the dust and puts his head on her leg, sur-
prising her with "such a sudden act of kindness" ("The Camel" 99). Next,
in "The Great Desert," after windswept sand raged over the place and
the poem's speaker rushed inside with "a lamb and then an injured bird,"
brewing tea for friends, a camel gives birth to an infant "gentle as a human
touch" (100). Caressed by the speaker, the infant camel reciprocates the
touch, "caressing me back, nuzzling my hand" (100). Having survived the
sandstorm and witnessed the miracle of life's renewal in life-threatening
circumstances, having touched the gentle new infant and been touched by
it in return, Hogan is moved to reciprocate the gifts. Although she has no
food left save one apple, she offers it to the camel mother. The apple was
"everything I had left" (100). What else would a real human do?—one can
ask, quoting Hogan's earlier poem. In "the world of the you" (Maldonado-
Torres, "Outline" 23) that Hogan tries to build with her life and writing, in
a human-animal community based on respect, reciprocity, and love, giving
yourself and all you have to the other is the norm rather than an exception.

The two poetry collections from the 2010s foreground mercy, kindness,
and compassion as marks of genuine humanity and coordinates of norma-
tive interspecies ethics. There is much darkness and sorrow in this decade,
too, as Hogan mourns the nonhuman victims of anthropogenic environ-
mental disasters, the genocide of American bison, and many other victims
of the "human." Apart from mourning the larger losses, she also grieves
the death of her beloved horse, Kelli. Above all, however, fighting for the
renewal of the nonhuman world, Hogan confesses to being torn between
the lover and the warrior in her: the inborn need to rejoice in the beauty
and goodness of creation often takes second stage to the more urgent activ-
ist task of speaking on behalf of the victims of human oppression and pro-
tecting the original title holders to the American soil: nonhuman animals
and the humans they coevolved with over long millennia of common his-
tory. The puzzling presence of a solitary buffalo calf, however, is a hopeful
sign of the ongoing Indigenous resurgence. Bringing with it the promise of
renewal of ancient lifeways, the animal seems to announce a forthcoming
fulfillment of the dream that launched Hogan's poetic career—of dreaming
the old world back. Restoring awareness of the humanimal bond, recog-
nizing her nonhuman relatives as endowed with the same emotions, needs,
vulnerabilities, and cognitive abilities as humans, Hogan also offers inti-
mate glimpses of the interspecies community she has established with her
animal companions, a community sealed by bonds of love, care, respect,
and gratitude.

Notes

1 Hogan seems to forget about nonhuman animals' fight over territory or the fact
that some animal societies, like the chimpanzees, wage bloody wars.

2 *A History of Kindness* contains some allusions to president Donald Trump's term in office.

3 This quote comes from a poem included in *A History of Kindness* twice, in slightly modified versions, which looks like an editorial oversight: "Creation," pp. 26–27, and "One Creation," pp. 68–69.

4 The American bison is commonly known as the buffalo. The preferred term among Indigenous peoples is buffalo.

5 Hogan mentions this fact e.g. in her *The Radiant Lives with Animals*, p.50.

6 "Not far up the road, Buffalo Bill is buried, a man known only for his abuses," writes Hogan in *The Radiant Lives of Animals* (13).

7 "Buffalo Kills and Genocide," nativephilanthropy.candid.org. Accessed: February 15, 2021. https://nativephilanthropy.candid.org/events/buffalo-kills -and-genocide/. It is estimated that by 1890 not more than a thousand bison remained in North America. Due to concerted conservation efforts, the number has risen to 400,000 (Taschereau Mamers 17).

8 The word 'genocide' rather than the more usual 'slaughter' is used on purpose. Cf. Hubbard.

Part 2

Reclaiming Animality, Revisioning Humanity

The Novels of Linda Hogan

6 *Mean Spirit*
Decolonizing Nonhuman Animals

Already a successful poet, in 1990 Hogan made a breakthrough as a novelist with *Mean Spirit*. The novel was a finalist for the Pulitzer Prize and won an Oklahoma Book Award. In turning to the novel genre Hogan was attracted to the spaciousness of the medium and its activist potential. "Stories have the capacity to make change in ways that other forms of activism don't," she said in a 2013 interview for *Superstition Review* (Regan). Believing in stories' potential to touch hearts and help readers to imagine another way of being in and with the world, in her novels Hogan creates pan-tribal, interracial, interspecies coalitions in an effort to heal the wounds of the past and open the future. All four novels she has published so far are anchored in Indigenous America's traumatic history and its often bleak present; still, Hogan's focus is on healing and survival. Summer Harrison asserts: "For Hogan, writing historical novels [...] is a deeply political act designed to make historical events resonate affectively with readers" (Harrison 5). She explains:

> Hogan creates a multivocal ceremonial form of storytelling modeled on healing and mourning rituals designed to reintegrate the individual into a more-than-human living community and to redistribute responsibility for ethical trauma responses among a wider alliance public.
> (Harrison 1)

Mean Spirit is set in the fictional Oklahoma town of Talbert, previously known as Watona, where rich oil deposits had been discovered, unexpectedly making the Osage Indian community spectacularly rich. In the 1920s a series of unsolved murders shook the community. Panic gripped the town, land mysteriously changed hands, and the FBI came to investigate the case.

The novel opens on a surreal scene. In the darkness before dawn the world looks like "a silent bedchamber," since many Indians have moved their beds to their gardens to avoid sleeping in the oven-like interiors. The ghostly white beds and the surrounding lush vegetation ready to climb up and "overgrow the sleeping bodies of people" (*Mean Spirit* 3) already hint at Hogan's signature art of blurring boundaries—between sleeping and

DOI: 10.4324/9781003364252-9

waking, right and wrong, human and the more-than-human worlds. The first light of dawn reveals a "forest of burned trees" (*Mean Spirit* 4). In the red blur of the rising sun they look as if they are still burning. The fires of the Oklahoma oil boom continue to rage, Hogan suggests by this opening scene—destroying habitats, lifeways, and communities, wreaking havoc with the hearts and minds of those they contaminate with their insatiable hunger.

Among the sleeping persons is Belle Graycloud, the matron and spiritual lynchpin of an emerging community of resistance:

> Belle Graycloud slept in the middle of her herb garden with a stubborn golden chicken roosting at the foot of the bed, a calico cat by the old woman's side, a fat spotted dog snoring on the ground, and a white horse standing as close to Belle as the fence permitted, looking at her with wide, reverent eyes.
>
> (10)

As the scene implies, Belle has never fallen into modern binaries. She is part of the larger-than-human world, a member of a caring, interspecies community with roots in the ancient times when there was no clear boundary between humans and animals.

At the opposite end of the spectrum is John Hale—a rancher, oilman, and self-styled 'King of the Indians,' who rules the town's criminal underworld while officially posing as a friend of the Osage people. Hale is conscienceless and driven by greed. He is the mastermind behind the mysterious deaths in Talbert. With his unmistakable instinct for business, he has devised a plan to seize control of all the oil fields in the area. One of the things we learn about him at the start of the novel is that "Hale was one of the first men to bring cattle to Indian Territory.[1] They were a good investment" (54). As a shrewd agent of coloniality, Hale broke more than the ground—he broke the local Indians, having paid them to transform the land—their own—into grazing pastures. Soon they became "meat-eaters with sharp teeth, devouring their own land and themselves in the process" (54).

As is well known, domesticated cattle played an instrumental role in the global colonization process. Themselves colonized and reduced to a commodity, the heavily exploited—or domesacrated, as sociologist David Nibert (*Animal Oppression*) rightly puts it—farm animals destroyed the local fauna and flora and changed local foodways, which had devastating effects on Indigenous peoples' health and food security, to say nothing of the atrocious suffering of 'meat' animals killed in ever increasing numbers in the emerging industrialized slaughterhouses, with assembly lines to speed up the killing and meatpacking process. In many respects, John Hale is the vanguard of the phenomenon Jeremy Rifkin calls the "cattlization" of the New World (Rifkin 147)—the introduction of cattle capitalism to America as a consequence of importing and raising cattle.

Concerned solely with profit, Hale progressively takes over the 'unimproved' Indian lands and plans to crossbreed cows with buffalo in order to increase the 'beef-producing' capacity of his herds.[2] It bears stressing that 'land improvement' is a Western concept, invented to justify settler colonialism. The modern idea of private property goes back to John Locke and his "narrative of colonial difference" constructed to "open up the land of America to appropriation without consent," asserts Brian Burkhart in *Indigenizing Philosophy through the Land* (34). Serving the interests of Anglo-Saxon expansionism, Locke theorized American tribal peoples' indifference to wealth accumulation as emblematic of the Indians' existence in the state of nature. Living in the state of nature, they could hold no title to the land they dwelled and hunted on yet failed to "mix their labor" with. Burkhart argues that Locke's constructions of Indianness still underpin current legal arguments about tribal sovereignty, making "the insatiable greed that creates the need for laws to protect individual private property as a prerequisite for advancement to civilized society" (40).

Like most of her community, Belle Graycloud has failed to mix her labor with her allotment. Instead of 'improving' the land, she loves it as it is, but this is exactly what enables Hale to lease more and more of her land as grazing pasture, without even informing her. Soon a stockade encircles part of Belle's land and "a herd of the large wooly buffalo" is brought to the newly created pasture. "The ragged animals were docile and slow and they walked without resistance through the gate," Hogan writes. "It was as if they, too, had given up" (*Mean Spirit* 213). The animals' resigned acceptance of the inevitable resonates with their coevolved human partners' attitude to their own fate. Both have suffered severance from the land, understood as a community of relations; both have lost their kinship-based identity and been offered, in exchange, the alienated individualism of modernity—in the case of humans—and the status of chattel in the case of the animals.

Reduced to cash possessions, Hale's herds cannot even choose their mating partners. Breeding must be regulated by strict biopolitical calculations to bring the desired financial reward. Belle's compassionate heart bleeds as she watches the solitary bull Hale has locked out to let a male buffalo impregnate the bull's cows:

> She saw the exiled Angus bull from across the way unlock his gate and walk down the road to stand at the fence where he cried and watched his cow women that were locked in with the buffalo bull Hale was trying to mate them with.
>
> (*Mean Spirit* 242)

This description speaks of the bull's human-like behavior and intelligence. For Belle, from whose point of view the scene is narrated, there is no 'ontological difference.' She has sympathy for the solitary male, who longs to be reconnected with his cow family as a human would. In her eyes the animal is innocent. Not only does she not blame the bull for the loss of her land, but has respect for his suffering, so similar to the unending suffering of tribal people, torn away from their human and more-than-human relatives. In the meantime, the buffalo cows long for their own man, who has been locked in with the cow women. One day the buffalo bull is found dead—to the surprise of the veterinarian, but not of Belle: "she knew the bull had died of sorrow. He died longing for his life on the land, for his freedom, for his buffalo women" (*Mean Spirit* 251–252).

Definable as deep distress, sadness, or regret, especially for the loss of someone or something loved, sorrow is the novel's dominant mood and much of it comes from watching animals—especially clan animals as sacred as golden eagles or bats—killed for sport or out of ignorance. While Belle is the chief spokesperson for, and defender of, the violated animal people, Hale is instrumental in their victimization. He sponsors an event which is the very essence of evil for the traditional people of the novel: an eagle hunt. Well-preserved eagle carcasses are in demand among snobbish wealthy settlers and can fetch good money. In a world turned upside down, the powerful bird, king of the open sky, regarded with mystic reverence in many ancient cultures, has become a collector's item, worth more dead than alive. In this new world everything comes with a price tag.

But ambassadors of the ancient world, defeated and distraught as they may be, will not stand by in silence. Upon seeing a truckful of dead eagles looking "like a tribe of small, gone people" (*Mean Spirit* 110), the usually composed Belle is devastated by an outpouring of grief. She attacks the hunters with her bare hands, kicking, crying, trying to unload the eagle bodies, and speaking to them in the ancient language. The surprised men react with the words which, in their various shapes and guises, have always justified most atrocious crimes: "They are just birds" (*Mean Spirit* 110). After the Jewish genocide of the 20th century, Theodor Adorno is believed to have said: "Auschwitz begins whenever someone looks at a slaughterhouse and thinks: they're only animals" (qtd. in Patterson, 51). As Hogan demonstrates, there have never been 'just birds' or 'only animals.' Once in the grip of dualistic thinking, the most considerate and respected person is capable of committing the most hideous crimes. In fact one of the hunters "was considerate" (*Mean Spirit* 110). He picked up the spilled contents of Belle's discarded bags and deposited them with the sheriff. Still, with the two other hunters they had just turned the 317 eagles in the truck into profit by mixing their labor with the birds' previously 'unimproved' lives. The eagles' reckless slaughter is emblematic of the larger fate of Indigenous

America. Whenever profit is at stake, the 'considerate' colonists will just as recklessly kill humans as nonhuman animals. It is noteworthy that the same John Hale who sponsors the eagle hunt is the mysterious assassin responsible for hunting down and killing Grace Graycloud, the richest Indian in Watona, whom he had even considered sufficiently beautiful to be a love interest.

Most devastatingly, however, the Indian children who study at residential schools are so damaged by that experience that they unwittingly follow the reckless ways of the settlers even when trying to find their way back to tradition. Two young people, Belle's grandson Ben and his shantytown friend Cal, shoot a golden eagle, wanting to pray with his feathers. When caught by Belle, Ben apologizes and begins to cry. All Belle can do is ask in disbelief: "You took a life in order to pray?" (*Mean Spirit* 276).

Knowing that "the law is on their [the settlers'] side because it's their law" (*Mean Spirit* 113), Moses Graycloud, Belle's husband, decides to inform President Harding of the crimes committed in Talbert/Watona. A character named Michael Horse writes two letters at the dictation of Moses, who is illiterate, and significantly, one of them concerns the eagle massacre, which in fact is a telling illustration of the traditional people's nondualist worldview. "The eagles are our brothers," reads the letter. "Their loss hurts us." Moses justifies his plea for presidential intervention by claiming,

> We do not have a desire to see our fellow creatures gone from the world. We are small and surrounded by your people, but for all our lives we lived here and none of the animals were wasted this way by our Indian people.
>
> (*Mean Spirit* 117)

The other letter informs the president of the Indians who died in mysterious circumstances. Obviously, neither letter ever reaches the president. When Michael Horse, who is the last Indian to live in a tepee, says, "I live here in Sorrow" (*Mean Spirit* 232)—meaning Sorrow Cave, located halfway between the town and the place where the Hill Indians live—his words are understood literally. There was enough sorrow in the place to drown in.

Sorrow Cave becomes the scene of a spectacular act of resistance to colonial violence, a place where a spontaneous anti-colonial coalition is galvanized into existence in defense of a bat population. After a young girl dies of rabies, the town declares a war on bats. Typically for the modern world, the response to a threat—merely theoretical, since the girl caught the disease from a drooling dog—is out of all proportion to the inciting event. And typically, willful misconstructions and financial incentives are employed to guarantee an all-out win in the extermination campaign: "There was a one-dollar bounty per 'flying rat,' as the newspaper called them" (*Mean Spirit* 277).

When Belle arrives at Sorrow Cave, she notices a party of well-dressed citizens shooting excitedly and randomly into the cave, wounding, killing, and scaring the animals, while unemployed oil workers wait their turn to gas the interior. The atmosphere is almost festive—until the shocked Belle pulls out a pistol and threatens to kill anyone who enters the cave. In response she hears the familiar commonsensical reasoning: "You can't go losing your head over every bird and snake" (*Mean Spirit* 278–279). While sheriff Jess Gold uses the "bats are pests" (279) argument, Belle is taking in the extent of the carnage inside the cave, a place "alive with fear" (278). In her eyes, bats are "beautiful creatures," a race of people inhabiting the world of darkness and "hated by those who lived in what they called the light" (279).

The local community has a long history of connections with bats. A Cree healer, Sam Billy, was a practitioner of bat medicine, "one of the strongest traditions of healing," as Belle recalls (*Mean Spirit* 136). Now his son Joe, trained as a Baptist preacher in a Boston seminary, is returning to the traditional ways and feels his father's medicine bundle stir under his touch. He believes the bundle is "speaking to him. It was urgent, he knew, even though he didn't understand what was being said from inside the bag" (137). The urgency of the message is confirmed when a live bat flies out of the medicine bag when Michael Horse chances upon it in Sorrow Cave. "The medicines were coming alive" (241).

In *Dwellings* Hogan comments on the bat medicine bundles sacred to some southern tribes. They typically contained an intact skeleton "found naturally." Had the animals been killed for the bundles, "they would have withdrawn their assistance from people" (*Dwellings* 27). Bats have been revered by some tribes because of their liminal status. "They live in double worlds of many kinds," Hogan writes:

> They are two animals merged into one, a milk producing rodent that bears live young, and a flying bird. They are creatures of the dusk, which is the time between times, people of the threshold, dwelling at the open mouth of inner earth like guardians at the womb of creation.
>
> The bat people are said to live in the first circle of holiness. Thus, they are intermediaries between our world and the next.
>
> (*Dwellings* 27)

Using echolocation to navigate and forage, bats are believed to be great listeners, "hearing the chants of life all around them" and passing them on to those who need guidance and healing (*Dwellings* 27). They are guides, teachers, intermediaries. If offended, they may withdraw their assistance from humans who desperately need it. They are also a people, vulnerable and under attack from ignorant settlers. So Belle, who learned healing from Sam Billy, cannot allow the shootout at Sorrow Cave to continue.

The woman holds up the shooting party at the mouth of Sorrow Cave while her companion rushes uphill to bring reinforcements from the traditional Indians' settlement. Before long most of the compassionate characters in the novel, regardless of their racial or tribal affiliations, have joined Belle in an act of anti-colonial resurgence. Her courage in defending the animals sacred to her people is a liberating force for all. The ranks of the bat defenders include an intergenerational group of Hill Indians; Belle's husband Moses; the tribal firekeeper, water diviner, and diarist Michael Horse; Joe Billy and his Caucasian wife Martha; the Catholic priest Father Dunne, also known as the hog priest; an FBI agent of Lakota Sioux descent named Stace Red Hawk; a wealthy Indian with an interest in gardening named Jim Josh; and the mixed-blood sheriff deputy Willis. While the sheriff and his posse leave for the night, the bat defenders occupy the cave to be sure the animals are safe, and they find joy and empowerment in the newly created community. Some try to help the wounded bats, others place the dead animals outside the cave, and all feel rejuvenated by the temporary victory.

"They have created their own survival rites and have felt the magic of the ancient bat medicine coming alive," writes Andrea Musher in her article, "Showdown at Sorrow Cave" (34). The community has been brought together by bats and by the old world "wanting out" of the medicine bags; it came alive to protect the bats and the old world. In the morning, having acted on a clue provided by the sacred intermediaries, the conspirators discover a hidden way out of the series of interconnected caves, which helps them avoid being captured by the sheriff. Musher comments: "Within the incident at Sorrow Cave, Hogan establishes a protection racket that operates between the bats and the Indian community. First the Indians save the bats' lives, and then the bats save the Indians' lives" (30). When ancient bonds are respected, animal assistance is extended to humans and humans reach out to animals. The gift circulates. At a funeral staged much later to confirm Belle's would-be killers in the conviction that she is dead and thus to protect her life, a delegation of seven eagles is seen circling above her supposed grave.

A number of the characters gathered at Sorrow Cave have strong bonds with animals other than bats. Most men bond with horses, Father Dunne blesses all animals, Michael Horse is learning the language of owls, but none is as deeply attuned to the animal world as Belle. Apart from her beloved chickens, the dog and the cat, she also keeps bees. As it turns out, in return for Belle's caretaking the bees not only provide her with honey, but literally take revenge on her would-be murderer.

Belle's beehives used to stand in close proximity to the land Hale had fenced out for his cattle. The increasing numbers of cows and buffalo disturbed them. One morning they were so distraught that Belle had to move them to a new location. She loaded the still light beehives and rode with them to a creek with wildflowers ready to burst into blossom. This meadow would soon be rich with sweet pollen and nectar. When the bees had settled down, she uncovered the hives, "watching the mysterious, intelligent worlds contained in the white boxes" (*Mean Spirit* 223). Obviously, Belle, who is Hogan's *porte parole* in the novel, loves and holds in high regard the humble insects that act together as one body with a collective mind. We are learning that they have emotions and preferences surprisingly like humans; we know that bees communicate by means of their waggle dance, and find their way back to their hive by means of a mental map they create on the basis of natural landmarks; that they recognize human faces and can build trust with their caretakers (Avargues-Weber et al.). To Belle, they are a people strikingly similar to tribal humans. "Bees were like Indians, Belle thought to herself, with a circular dance, working together for the survival of the next generation" (*Mean Spirit* 312), unlike the white settlers in the novel, who think only about today and ignore the long-term consequences of their actions.

Sadly, Belle's bees continued to be disturbed even in their new location. The Indian agency was leasing more and more of her land for Hale's cattle. When the wildflowers were in bloom, she went down to the creek to check on her bees, worrying that their honey would be spoiled if they continued to be disturbed, and that the bees themselves would become vulnerable to disease. She heard their loud droning sound. "The bees were honest, at least, hollering out their anger, and for that, she respected them" (*Mean Spirit* 313). Her respect and solicitous care are not only appreciated by the intelligent insects. The bees reciprocate them. When Belle is shot at from a clump of trees, they raise a horrible buzz and swarm toward the would-be assassin, chasing and stinging him to death. Without their assistance the assassin would never have been identified and justice would not have been done, as can be assumed from the fact that there have been so many unsolved murder cases in Watona. The bees, however, have no fear of the human crime network, and they target one of its pillars, the sheriff Jess Gold. The discovery that law enforcement agents were involved in the chain of mysterious deaths ravaging the town launches an investigation that leads to the sentencing of the heretofore untouchable John Hale. There is much healthy irony in the fact that evil incarnate is toppled from the pinnacle of his power by the humble bee. There is much hope in it for the Indigenous world too, a world that loves and respects the bee as a full member of the land community, a world, like the bee, struggling with settler expansionism. The swarm—or another one, Belle could not be sure—eventually comes back, "flying in thorough the ruins of burned trees" (*Mean Spirit* 364). She is jubilant:

> Belle couldn't tell for sure if this was the outlaw swarm that had killed the sheriff. They were bees who, like everything else, wanted only to live. That was all they wanted, to live and to continue. Belle loved them. She understood them.
>
> (*Mean Spirit* 365)

The earth, burned and ravaged by the ceaseless oil derricks and endless gas explosions, is a symbolic background for the unexpected return of hope. Even in the most dire circumstances, Hogan believes—and the history of Indigenous America confirms it—there is a way out of sorrow. Life returns, life continues.

Most farmers around Watona keep and breed horses. Although the oil-rich Indians (who nevertheless find it hard to take their wealth seriously) own expensive cars, not all know how to drive, and sometimes their vehicles serve purely stationary purposes. Jim Josh, for example, plants a tomato garden in one car. Thus horses remain the main means of transportation for the novel's characters, especially on the rugged terrain in the hills. When Michael Horse decides to move his tepee to the banks of the Coffee River, higher up in the mountains, he exchanges his flashy car for a prime stallion named Redshirt, a horse believed to be faster than the legendary Man O'War.[3] Not being an expert rider—despite his surname—Michael Horse is unprepared for the stallion's willful intelligence. He cannot even mount the tall animal without assistance or support and is forced to walk part of the way alongside the steed, which is a funny sight. His struggles with Redshirt provide much of the comic relief in this otherwise bleak and serious novel.

Soon, the semi-wild stallion frees himself from the harness and starts to play a specific hide-and-seek game with Michael. Keeping close by but hidden from view, he drives him crazy by demonstrating who is in control. When finally—"miraculously and awkwardly" (*Mean Spirit* 195)—Horse succeeds in catching and mounting the rebellious animal to ride back to town for a wedding, Redshirt puts up such a fight that the rider wishes he had never laid eyes on the horse. Both of them know that Michael will never again manage to corner Redshirt.

Almost a year later we see the horse in the company of a red mare and a colt—evidently a love child of the two. Michael tries to capture the animal again, but not even a bucketful of oats can do the trick. Stace Red Hawk, who chances upon the scene, is enchanted by the "glistening red stallion with a tail and mane so long and beautiful that even Stace, who knew horses, wanted to see it up close, wanted to touch its lean red muscles. He'd never seen a horse like that before" (*Mean Spirit* 230). For a while Stace watches from a clump of trees how the older man steals up to the horse, trying to catch him unawares, "[b]ut the horse was on to him and while Redshirt moved sideways and escaped the rope, the red mare stepped out and ate from the bucket of oats" (*Mean Spirit* 231). Stace burst out laughing. Clearly Michaels' intelligence was not equal to the combined intelligences of both animals who were having fun at his expense. When the temperamental Redshirt kicked at Michael, the unlucky man "ran off like a rodeo clown" (*Mean Spirit* 321).

The antics continue for quite a while. Every time Michael gets closer to the stallion and seems about to catch him, Redshirt puts him wrong. "Stace knew the horse. Already. It was a crazy horse and it needed a crazy man to catch it. The old man wasn't crazy enough to slow the stallion down" (*Mean Spirit* 231). Finally, when the animal charges at him, Michael first runs away and then sits down, closing his eyes and covering his face with his hands, as if waiting for the crazy beast to trample him. It is at this point that Stace decides to reveal his presence, but Michael pretends to be in control of the situation by claiming that Redshirt was being trained how to charge at people and that, when he covered his face, he was just meditating, trying to think like a horse. To which Stace responds: "You'll never think like that one" (*Mean Spirit* 231). Being descended from Lakota Sioux, Stace understands Redshirt's playful and resistant spirit, his desire for freedom, and, above all, his intelligence. He soon discovers that his dark mare is equally impressed. Having volunteered to help in cornering the stallion, Stace gives Michael instructions on how to catch him, "[b]ut Redshirt understood English." He neighed at Stace's mare and she would not budge for a while, allowing the indomitable horse to escape the trap. The men realize they have lost the battle. Both remain in Sorrow Cave for the night and the following morning neither Redshirt nor Stace's mare are to be found. All that remains is the mare's

> halter hanging empty on the branch, attached to the lead rope. Redshirt had unbuckled it. There was even a toothmark in the leather. When [Stace] found Redshirt's narrow tracks, they went in circles and lines and crossed over one another as if the horse had deliberately tried to outwit the men. But Stace could feel the horse watching. He knew he was there, like an outlaw, just outside his line of vision.
>
> (*Mean Spirit* 235)

Hogan's love for, and bond with, horses is unmistakable in this beautiful homage to horse agency, intelligence, and sense of humor. Using the word "outlaw" with respect to the horse, Hogan points to Redshirt's non-conformity and authority. The wise horse knows the (human-made) rules, but consciously disregards them because they do not conform to his own notions of the good life. There is not the slightest doubt that for Hogan, Redshirt knows what he is doing and fully realizes the consequences of his actions. Furthermore, we understand that he asserts his sovereignty over the men trying to catch him and that the men accept this fact. That neither Stace nor Michael force their will on the horse at all costs, that they try to 'think like the horse' and eventually allow him to have his way, testifies to their respect for the animal's choices, their recognition of Redshirt's counter-sovereignty. Both men regard Redshirt as an equal, a person who has his own plans for the future. In the end the men and the horse engage in intriguing, fully reciprocal negotiations.

In the middle of July, Michael Horse makes another, half-hearted attempt to coax the stallion into a trap, while secretly wishing Redshirt success. "The horse kept up his part of the show" (*Mean Spirit* 304). By this time there are three mares with him—including Stace's black one—and two young colts. Redshirt has a veritable harem of adoring females. But in the fall, when colder days announce the change of season, the stallion surprisingly allows Stace to slip a rope over his neck without struggling. It is obvious he has allowed himself to be caught. But instead of celebrating victory, Michael tells Stace to release the stallion. The continuous struggles with Redshirt have made Michael more sure of himself, and he admires the indomitable will of his friend-opponent. After being set free, "Redshirt nuzzled the old man, then turned slowly and walked away" (*Mean Spirit* 363). He wanted to thank Michael for the gift of freedom and say goodbye to him.

Stace's mare, however, was more practical. "She knew it was going to be a hard, cold winter in the Osage hills. It would be more convenient for her to be caught, to have food and a warm blanket." So after saving her honor by staging a fight, she finally let Stace lasso her. Ultimately, as in the case of Redshirt, "it was the mare [...] that made the decision to be caught" (*Mean Spirit* 370). For some time afterward Redshirt, "loving the black mare" (*Mean Spirit* 371), would follow them, and Stace greeted him as one greets a friend. One more time, as in her best poems, Hogan succeeds in showing horses as complex individuals, with different needs and temperaments, but lasting commitments.

Another notable character who bonds strongly with animals is Father Dunne, the Roman Catholic priest. When a cataclysmic tornado destroys his church, he moves into the woods where the winds had deposited the intact figure of St. Francis, the patron saint of animals and the natural environment. Believing God wants to be worshipped among the trees, where he has moved the figure, Father Dunne starts a conversion experience not unlike that of the medieval saint represented by the statue. Even though it is winter, he sleeps on the naked ground in the same spirit of poverty as St. Francis, and feeds the birds that the saint used to preach to. One night, after a powerful explosion in the oil fields, followed by a spectacular gas burnout, Father Dunne is struck by a revelation. Waking up on the thawing earth, he sees a fire behind the trees and is reminded of the story of the burning bush, from which God spoke to Moses. He hears the deep rumbling sound coming from the land and realizes God is speaking to him. "It was as if he had wakened for the first time, as if his eyes were at last opened" (*Mean Spirit* 188). From that night Father Dunne understands that the spirit lives in every creature, no matter how humble or small. For the Indians the day he starts blessing chickens and hogs is the day "the priest went sane" (*Mean Spirit* 189).

This is a rare moment in Hogan's novels when a representative of the colonizers' religion, instrumental in destroying Indigenous worldviews and traditions, recovers Christianity's pre-colonial roots and finds it fully compatible with so-called 'Indian animism.' Like his patron saint, Francis of Assisi, Father Dunne becomes attuned to the voice of the natural world, hears the lament of the wounded earth, and starts to minister to all the earth's creatures. Sleeping on the ground is itself a decolonizing act, a symbolic reconnection with the sacred which permeates the whole world and is not limited to churches or cathedrals. His congregation, like that of St. Francis, is composed of birds and animals, and saying the last rites for the trout shot by Michael Horse seems natural. There is common ground between the West and the tribal world, Hogan suggests; respectful cooperation in the healing of the natural world—which is seen as originally good in both belief traditions—is possible. Christianity and Indigenous spirituality are not incompatible, they have merely been constructed to look like enemies, but when the scales of prejudice fall from Westernized eyes, it becomes obvious that both seek the same goal—salvation from evil, not merely in the afterlife, but in the here and the now. Reclaiming this repressed legacy of Christianity[4] is like recovering from madness. Becoming sane means being reminded of the ties of kinship linking all God's creatures. The indigenized Father Dunne is welcome in the Hill Indians' settlement, which is carefully hidden from the white world. He joins Hogan's pan-tribal, interracial, and interspecies community of survival.

The final stage of Father Dunne's conversion to kinship with the more-than-human world is facilitated by a near-fatal encounter with a rattlesnake. The creature bit the priest and he suddenly realized the fragility and preciousness of earthly existence, which his faith often denigrated. Rather than rejoice in his reward in heaven, he was gripped by the fear of death. The otherworldly illusions of his religion fell away in his existential confrontation with mortality. The man of the cloth felt himself to be a hypocrite; his body and his mind desperately wanted to live. So, trying to think like a snake in order to find an antidote to the poison that could kill him, Father Dunne imaginatively merged with that animal:

> I felt my own snaking spine and double tongue, my own searching for warmth and food, my slabs of muscle and shedding of old skin turned inside out and abandoned. I knew this: the snake is my sister. And when I knew that, the sting and burn of venom went away from my leg.
>
> (*Mean Spirit* 262)

In short, the priest avoided death by 'becoming animal.' Reinserting himself into the animal world he had always already belonged to was a healing act. The animal in him—his physical body, the life of instincts, the history of evolution encoded in every one of his cells—and the animal outside were related to each other; the snake was his sister. The priest failed to impress the Hill Indians with the story, however, because they had always known that.

One Indian character not present at Sorrow Cave, but notable for his love of animals, is John Stink. He is one of the growing number of wealthy Osages of Watona who have been assigned legal guardians on charges on 'incompetency.' He was born mute, which was enough to declare him incompetent in financial matters and to entrust his money to corrupt lawyers who were to 'represent' him. Government agents renamed this man, whose tribal name was Ho-Tah-Moie, or Roaring Thunder, John Stink after he contracted a childhood disease called scrofula. This settler-introduced disease is accompanied by a foul smell. Roaring Thunder's transformation into the demeaned, anglicized John Stink is an apt metaphor of coloniality.

With time John Stink, who is believed to be a millionaire, became "a dog-loving hermit" (*Mean Spirit* 99), living a simple life away from the town, with a number of mongrel dogs who adored him and whom he spoiled with treats. He was a hermit because of fate, not by choice. His disability and pockmarked face discouraged men from befriending him and women from marrying him, but animals were not tricked by such superficialities. They saw right into Stink's loving, caring soul and this was all they cared for. His dogs loved him as he was, unconditionally. Stink, likewise, was not deceived by the appearance of his dogs. Rather than smelly, scrawny, mangy mongrels, they were to him loveworthy and loving creatures in need of food, protection from harm, and a place to stay.

When Stink suddenly collapsed in the street, the dogs were distraught. They would not let the doctor examine his body until "they realized he meant well" (*Mean Spirit* 95). They attended the funeral, "sitting like sentinels" on "their bony haunches in the church," being "attentive" (*Mean Spirit* 99). They followed the coffin to an old Indian cemetery where Stink was buried according to an old tradition—with a little opening in the coffin for the eyes to allow the dead man to see the road he was to travel. They refused to leave the gravesite. Finally, these most faithful of friends became the agents of John Stink's resurrection. Declared dead prematurely and buried too quickly on account of the oppressive heat, he regained consciousness, licked back to life by his dogs' warm tongues. The resurrected Stink was believed to be a ghost and shunned by the Indians but his mongrels were always at his side, providing him with much needed company.

This story of friendship between dogs and a human, a story of animal fidelity and of loving commitments that transcend appearances, resonates deeply with the novel's decolonial perspective. Re-minding implies redefining the human in terms of relationships, interspecies relationships being of crucial importance. If some people seem incapable of being re-minded, of recognizing their place within a larger-than-human community of beings, then perhaps their souls came to them "from some other place," as Hogan puts it in her poem "Tulsa" (*A History* 91). But the broken human-animal bonds predate a John Hale's or a Jess Gold's arrival in Talbert/Watona. They go back to the time of Zebulon Pike's geographical explorations of the Louisiana Territory and its subsequent opening for settlement. Having shot "770 wildcats, 300 female bears, and 3000 deer," Pike published an account of his expeditions, inviting "people to come to the place where game was in abundance" (*Mean Spirit* 267). 'Game' is a technical word; it renders sentient, intelligent animals—with their complex lifeways, emotions, communication systems, and kinship networks—killable and sellable, fixing a price on their body parts. If animals are 'game,' a dime can buy three shots at live ducks and pigeons at a shooting gallery in Talbert, despite Indians' complaints about this cruel practice (*Mean Spirit* 69). If animals are possessions, exotic parrots and monkeys can be taken out of their habitats and kept in cages for the amusement of humans. Sometimes people love these caged creatures with a love that, nevertheless, restricts, limits, denies the fullness of life. Nola, Grace Graycloud's daughter and heiress, understands that much before she herself breaks out of her golden cage, shattering the life constructed for her by her legal guardian. But first she releases the monkey she has adored and the colorful parrot who has always looked to the south, in the direction of the jungle she was taken out from. "The parrot flew away south" (*Mean Spirit* 359).

To Michael Horse, kinship with the more-than-human world is the missing part of the Bible. His own Gospel According to Horse addresses this gap by extending the notion of those Christianity calls "the least of these, my brothers" (Matt. 25:40) to "all people in creation," including insects, plants, and stones, "for every creature and plant wants to live without pain, so do them no harm" (*Mean Spirit* 361). This self-evident truth has been forgotten in the white man's sacrilegious conquest of the earth and its creatures. "The least of these"—the human and nonhuman kin who were to be Christianity's chief means of grace, who brought blessings and provided others with the opportunity to grow in love—have been excluded from moral consideration, removed from legal protection, actively oppressed, and exploited for gain. In the novel, John Hale, sheriff Jess Gold, and the whole criminal racket they operated—which reached all the way up to the top echelons of US administrative offices—repressed and perverted what Michael Horse was trying to draw from the Bible. Without his correction the Word of God is incomplete and God's creation is destroyed rather than loved as it should be. Father Dunne's conversion to sisterhood and brotherhood with nonhuman animals is the best illustration of the normative Christian ethos and normative humanity, both of which are compatible with Indigenous kinship-based identity. When Michael Horse is reading his Gospel to the Indians, one of them asks: "Say, isn't that what Peacemaker of the Iroquois Nation used to say?" To which Horse replies: "The creator probably spoke the same words to him. It wouldn't surprise me at all" (362). One commentator, highlighting the work of caretaking in the novel, notes the redeeming function of such characters as Belle and Michael Horse—who, parenthetically speaking, are the most diligent students of nonhuman animals: "their acts of humanness offset, to some degree, the relentless violence and oil-hungry greed that dominate much of the novel" (Carew-Miller 42).

Hogan's message-driven first novel, imaginatively engaging the traumas of human and nonhuman peoples indigenous to North America, draws on insights gained in the course of the writer's poetic contemplation, restaging scenes and reintroducing motifs used in her poems—which only confirms the status of poetry as Hogan's exploratory tool and her first language. Land theft, cattlization, disrespectful taking of life for snobbish needs and material gain, systemic violence—all these are closely interlocked, as demonstrated in *Mean Spirit*. The novel conveys, in the more accessible language of prose, Hogan's plea for compassion toward all earth beings, and focuses on animals as teachers of wisdom and as Indigenous humans' allies in anti-colonial resurgence. From the majestic (horses), through the despised (bats, stray dogs), to the humble and nearly invisible (bees), the animals in *Mean Spirit* are depicted as dependable companions, models of intelligence, of cooperative spirit and companionship, endowed with a sense of humor (horses), an instinct for justice (bees), and feelings of responsibility for, and gratitude to, their human friends (dogs).

Looking for answers to questions concerning the ending of violence and the possibility of multispecies thriving, Hogan advances the idea that violence is the work of immature humanity. A self-standing individual, alienated from the more-than-human context, is bound to turn (self-) destructive because he or she is merely a stage in the movement of the species toward humanity-in-relation: a complete humanimal being. Re-minding us of the ontological primacy of relationships and keeping alive hope in sustainable futures are central to Hogan's activist agenda.

Notes

1 Indian Territory was originally an area of land west of the Mississippi set aside by the US government for the relocation of Indigenous tribes after the signing of the Indian Removal Act in 1830. Hogan writes in her memoir, "The federal government's plans in those days were to put all American Indian tribes in Oklahoma and build a wall around it, to keep us contained in the country which came to be called Indian Territory. It was then a place they didn't want" (*The Woman* 55).

2 It is not without relevance that due to people like Hale, most current bison herds are genetically polluted or partly crossbred with cattle.

3 Man O'War was an American thoroughbred, regarded as one of the greatest racehorses of all time. Inducted into the National Museum of Racing and Hall of Fame in 1957, Man O'War won 21 races between 1919 and 1920.

4 Early Christianity was an egalitarian, outlaw religion built on such anarchic principles as nonviolence, mercy, unconditional love, and respect for life. The followers of the crucified Christ were persecuted by political and religious authorities for teachings subversive of the existing power structures. By converting to Christianity and integrating the Christian Church with the imperial government, 4th-century Roman emperor Constantine I founded hierarchical Christendom, a political entity with a global colonizing mission. Christendom's ambition to wield global power is sometimes seen as a betrayal of the Good News, especially as proclaimed in the Sermon on the Mount (Matthew 5:3–12). The post-Constantinian Church was built on the consolidation of its doctrine around the concept of obedience and the repression of dissenting voices. Warfare became its way to advance a spiritual (rather than factual) Kingdom of God built on the concepts of privilege (of the saved) and exclusion (of difference). The egalitarian, incarnational spirituality of the early Church has been kept alive within the mystical tradition, anarchic Christianity, and some sectarian movements.

7 *Solar Storms*

Reclaiming Wild, Becoming Human

Hogan's second novel is set in the harsh north country between Minnesota and Ontario "where water was broken apart by land, land split open by water" (*Solar Storms* 21), on labyrinthine waterways whose borders are unstable, shifting under the impact of beaver dams, ice, spring thaws, and—as of 1972 when the novel starts—as a result of large-scale engineering projects. Unlike in *Mean Spirit*, the nonhuman world in *Solar Storms* is almost entirely wild and the human inhabitants live in rhythm with the changing seasons, winterbound for several long months, battling cold, hunger, and solitude, before they are forced to battle the encroaching forces of industrial civilization.

The novel's 17-year-old narrator, Angel, returns to Adam's Rib, the place of her birth, trying to find her mother, Hannah Wing, who had tortured and abandoned her in early childhood. The search for her mother turns out to be Angel's journey back to her stolen Indigenous identity, a journey of re-minding. "My beginning was Hannah's beginning, one of broken lives, gone animals, trees felled and kindled" (*Solar Storms* 96), the girl realizes. As she struggles to leave the destructive legacy of colonialism behind, she becomes a plant dreamer, an activist for tribal rights, and eventually "a girl who turned into a human" (295).

At the outset of the narrative, when Angel revisits the tribal territory on the border of the US and Canada, she comments:

> The waterways on which I arrived had a history. They had been crossed by many before me. When they were frozen, moose crossed over, pursued by wolves. There were French trappers and traders who emptied the land of beaver and fox. Their boats carried precious tons of fur to the trading post at old LeDoux. There were iceboats, cutters and fishers, and the boat that carried the pipe organ for the never built church.
>
> (*Solar Storms* 21)

This water-based community still lives in the shadow of that first, trapping frontier. Adam's Rib was "born of the fur trade" (*Solar Storms* 28), the

DOI: 10.4324/9781003364252-10

tribal women who had accompanied the French trappers being left behind when the fur-bearing animals had been hunted out and the white men moved on, "as if [their women and children] too were used up animals" (*Solar Storms* 28). In due time pigs and cattle arrived and poison was laid out to clear the land of the surviving foxes and wolves. But farm animals were unable to survive Adam's Rib's harsh winters and soon food became scarce. With few wild animals left and no livestock, the local population depended heavily on fish. The construction of a series of gigantic hydroelectric dams in the James Bay area and the flooding of waterscapes that followed, however, resulted in the contamination of fish by mercury, the collapse of the waterfowl populations that subsisted on the poisoned fish, and worries about the safety of drinking water.

Anna Brígido-Corachán recognizes *Solar Storms* as "a pioneering TEK-grounded novel" (40), one that "foresees what political geographers today refer to as waterscapes, that is, water-based environments where a multiplicity of human and other-than-human forces interact with each other producing diverse forms of signification" (37). Invalidating human-drawn maps, water "decolonize[s] border history while inscribing Indigenous knowledge and experience," writes Brígido-Corachán (47). Much of the novel's Indigenous resistance to the artificial damming of rivers to produce electricity comes from the conviction that, in the northern waterways, beavers have the monopoly on dam construction. Redrawing geographies of land and water since the beginning of time, the beaver people are ecosystem engineers. They create wetlands, which attract other species, including deer and moose, on whom tribal hunters depend. In the unstable geography of the far north, beaver is the first person and creator of the world.

An elder and tribal judge from the fictitious tribe of the Fat Eaters narrates the local creation story. When the world was covered by water, beaver emerged from the depths near the center of the earth, with pebbles and clay to make land; then he laid sticks across the water for all life to walk on. "There were no other creatures, none, except beaver," says Tulik (*Solar Storms* 238). He pulled trees down from the sky, created life on earth and then

> shaped the humans, who were strangers to the rest of creation. They gave their word. They would help each other, they said. Beaver offered fish and waterfowl and animals. The people, in turn, would take care of the world and speak with the gods and all creation.
>
> (239)

The humans were the youngest and most vulnerable of life forms, "strangers to the rest of creation." They had to be guided and taught how to live in peace with other creatures. Apparently, what comes naturally to all the other earth beings, requires serious application on the part of humans. In the ancient pact made by beavers, the human was the weaker party; without animal instruction he would remain the stranger he was in the beginning. As creator and teacher, beaver turns the tables on Westernized concepts of sovereignty. Having created life, he becomes responsible for, and response-able to, his creation, instead of claiming dominion over it. He binds himself by a treaty to supply humans with food, in exchange for human prayers and care.

Sadly, the weakest link in this chain broke the covenant. Instead of caring and praying for all creation, humans started to 'subdue' it, making beaver one of the first victims of the lucrative fur trade in colonized North America. The expansion of the fur trade in the 17th century, facilitated by the active cooperation of the continent's Indigenous inhabitants, brought a dramatic decline in the fur-bearing animal populations. "The political alliances and economic forces that resulted from this trade proved to have lasting environmental and social impacts on the land and peoples of North America," writes Kelly Feinstein.

In the waterscapes of the north, where *Solar Storms* is set, there were eventually no more beavers. As of 1938, "there wasn't a single beaver," reminisces one of the characters. "They'd killed them all" (*Solar Storms* 37). Now the newcomers started to usurp the beaver's role in the ecosystem—building mega dams, rerouting rivers, flooding forests and villages; violating the bond between land and its human and nonhuman inhabitants in the process. The consequences of denouncing the ancient pact and assuming the place originally occupied by beaver were tragic: "[t]he devastation and ruin that had fallen over the land fell over the people, too" (*Solar Storms* 226). While beaver had sustainably built dams to help other creatures thrive, BEEVCO, the fictional corporation that stands for Hydro-Quebec corporation, builds a series of dams to change the course of the water, to destroy the ecosystem and the creatures that dwell in it. Although settlers boasted of civilizational progress, tribal people, whose bonds with the land had been most intimate and who were on the receiving end of the violence, were not fooled by modern rhetoric.

"False gods said, 'Let there be light,' and there was alchemy in reverse" (*Solar Storms* 268), says Angel, commenting on the arrival of electricity to Holy String Town and the Fat Eaters. "All across the land created by beaver and by the slow dance of glaciers centuries before, streetlights cast a pale circle on the ground" (*Solar Storms* 266). Along with the pale light, what reached the far north was a kind of darkness unknown before, "the darkness of words and ideas, wants and desires" (*Solar Storms* 268). The reverse side of the light created by false gods was "drowned willows and alders, [...] the three dead lynx caught in a reservoir, ten thousand drowned caribou" (*Solar Storms* 268). The trope of "alchemy in reverse" resonates in the novel with the puzzle of "reverse people"—the ones who destroy instead of creating, "the ones who invented hell" believing themselves to be the builders of paradise. Reverse people have "forgotten wild" (*Solar Storms* 86). In *Solar Storms* Hogan imaginatively rehearses the master theme of her poetry of the same decade, anchoring her narrative in the particulars of the land and a water-based community.

Characters who coexist with the wild in respectful relations of reciprocity realize that "a person is only strong when they feel the land. Until then a person is not a human being" (*Solar Storms* 235). Those who have reached the status of a "human being" in the novel include the teenage narrator's three tribal "grandmothers": the matriarch Dora-Rouge, who converses with water; her daughter Agnes, who used to have a special connection with a bear; and a Chickasaw woman named Bush, once married to Agnes's son, who became a grandmother-substitute for his daughter, Angel—the novel's narrator.

The story of Agnes and the bear is told at the novel's beginning. It explains why the elderly woman wears a fur coat even in warm weather and how this coat teaches her ancient songs no longer remembered by her tribe; but its primary function is to establish a paradigm of courageous, compassionate commitment to a friend, human or nonhuman, which puts the good of the suffering other above all else. The story also offers an insight into the radicality of thinking from the I-Thou relationship and serves as a good illustration of Brian Burkhart's theorizing of Indigenous nonanthropocentric ethics, according to which "morality arises from my reflection regarding what are the right things for me to do" (Burkhart 216). In a particular situation, a deed commonly regarded as sinister or criminal may actually be the best, the kindest thing to do.

Back in the old times, Dora-Rouge reminisces, bears were treated with utmost respect on account of their similarity to humans. But white fur trappers were not held back by this similarity and soon there were almost no bears left, save isolated specimens. One of these was a rare glacier she-bear with unusual pelage, trapped by a Frenchman who decided to make money using her in fights and exhibiting her to the public. "The last one. The last glacier bear. The last. They always loved the last of everything," ironizes Dora-Rouge (*Solar Storms* 47), hinting at the immoral connection between the worth of "the last of its kind" and the hunting that drove animals to near-extinction, thus increasing the value of the few surviving specimens.

When the 12-year-old Agnes befriended the bear, the animal was ruined, physically and mentally. She was malnourished, abused, prevented from hibernating in winter, and eventually tormented even by little boys "jealous of what's wild and strong" (*Solar Storms* 46). Agnes loved and cared for her in every way she could. Initially hired by the Frenchman to feed the bear, the girl tried to protect her from abuse, nurtured her back to health, even stole food to feed her well. Still, the bear's heart was broken beyond repair and one day Agnes did what the animal had been mutely begging her to do. Loving the bear, Agnes put her out of her misery in one dramatic move. Unprotected, she entered the cage with a knife and slit the bear's throat. The bear understood and was grateful. While Agnes was stroking the dying animal, "[t]hat bear put a paw on Agnes and stroked her in return." The animal "touched" and "comforted" (*Solar Storms* 47) her savior before her eyes closed forever. This shocking and deeply touching scene turns an act of violence into one of redemption, sealing an unspoken pact between the two persons, one human and one nonhuman. For the enslaved animal, too damaged even for love to fix her, death was the only possible means of salvation. For the compassionate Agnes, who loved the bear, killing was the only—and the hardest—thing she could do to help the once proud creature regain her freedom.

This act of compassion can be theorized in terms of resistance to the necropolitics of coloniality—the non-Indigenous invaders' construction and management of living death. The captured and tortured bear was neither dead nor alive as long as she 'belonged' to her captor. Incapable of living her life, she was not allowed to die, either. By freeing her from this prolonged state of suspension, Agnes restores the animal's dignity; she also attempts to de-commodify her body. Rather than leave the dead bear behind for the Frenchman to turn the meat and coat into profit, Agnes 'steals' his 'property,' violating one of the most sacred tenets of market economy. As a daughter of Indigenous trappers and hunters, she removes the bear's skin in order to wear it as a fur coat and in this way never part with the animal she loved. Assisted by her mother, Dora-Rouge, she quarters the meat and hides it in a safe place for future respectful consumption. This is Hogan's most radical imaginative elaboration on the "to enter life, be food" motif, the conviction that all food is ensouled. Since we all depend on one another in the food chain, the only thing that really makes a difference is *respectful* use.

The teenage Agnes put up resistance to the men who later stormed the women's house searching for the meat and the coat. Eventually, after the Frenchman's death, she was able to retrieve the coat. Every morning she would brush it tenderly, talking and singing to it, before putting it on. Inside the coat, Agnes would hear forgotten songs and see things the bear once saw. Dora-Rouge believed that Agnes remained in touch with the bear, perhaps even found a gap in time to reconnect with her in some way. She says:

Sometimes it happens that, at twilight, I see those eyes and that large paw brushing Agnes' back and I hear her sing and I get a feeling, just a feeling, Agnes is becoming something. Maybe the bear. Maybe she knows her way back to something.

(*Solar Storms* 48)

The motif of 'becoming bear' links Agnes with a gallery of other transformational characters from Hogan's novels.

Several decades later, the last wish of the aging Agnes was that her body be left as food for animals; she wanted "to be eaten by birds and wolves" (*Solar Storms* 209). Withdrawing her body from the food chain she had benefited from all her life would be an offense against normative reciprocal relations with the more-than-human world. After the disappearance of her body from the canoe set adrift in the waters of the far north, her great-granddaughter Angel relates: "on the chance that she had been eaten by wolves, I called every wolf I saw Grandmother" (*Solar Storms* 216). Perhaps the most radical confirmation of kinship comes after death.

The sacredness of the human-animal relationship is also celebrated after Dora-Rouge dies—she dies in the woods she loved so much and is mourned by her nonhuman relatives. Her great-great-granddaughter, Agnes, sings the animal calling song and the animals come:

Wolf, thin and old, stood back away from us in the trees. He kept his distance. Who could blame him? And there was Eagle with watchful eyes. The sound of bear, snuffling, moving through the brush, and another shadow behind him. Wolverine, I thought, come to pay last respects.

(*Solar Storms* 349)

Bush, the third of Angel's three 'grandmothers,' has something deer-like about her. Angel believes Bush feels more at ease with animals than she does with people. "I think," Angel muses, "she had the brilliant soul of an animal, that she lived somewhere between the human world and theirs" (*Solar Storms* 95). Living alone on Fur Island—a small place with a long and dramatic history of trapping—Bush occasionally assembles animal skeletons for a local mixed-blood Dakota named LaRue, who is a taxidermist and a veteran of the war in Vietnam. Forced to increase her meager income by taking in commercial assignments, Bush approaches her work with a sense of mission. "When I put the bones together," she explains, "I help the soul of the animal. [...] When I put them together, I respect them [...]. I feed them and consider their skills. I think of their intelligence" (*Solar Storms* 95).

Painstakingly re-assembling the bones of an animal to recreate its original shape, Bush touches each piece of the skeleton with devotion and offers food to the animal spirit, performing a long overdue mourning ritual for another victim of the fur trade or other forms of settler colonial violence. Fed and reclaimed from anonymity, another animal can finally find rest. To Angel it looks as if Bush's skill could reverse time and resurrect the animal she is working on, as if time could fly backward and infuse life into the reassembled bones. "She was a woman who put things together" (*Solar Storms* 95), the girl says, realizing that she herself was among the creatures her grandmother was making whole again. Observing Bush at work inspires Angel's dream, in which a woman is sewing a human being out of fragments. The dream is prophetic of the girl's healing under Bush's loving care, a promise of being put together out of "fragments and pieces left behind by fur traders, soldiers, priests, and schools" (*Solar Storms* 77). But in the larger framework of ongoing evolutionary development, the dream spells hope for the whole of human kind. With evolution still in progress, a new human, "love-filled, the way we were meant to be" (*Solar Storms* 86), may yet appear, having learned the lessons of the past; wiser and gentler, a human with a new old mind—re-minded of the ancient ways, at peace with the wild. The way to this new human is pointed out by Agnes—"who was becoming something" in that bear coat she was wearing—and by Angel, who gets a new nickname at the novel's end: Maniki, "a girl who turned into a human" (*Solar Storms* 295).

After returning to the place of her birth, Angel is wintering with Bush on Fur Island, healing from her childhood traumas and reclaiming her stolen identity. On another island, called the Navel of the World, frogs were once respected as sacred beings. They are still believed to be "buried and waiting" (*Solar Storms* 66) to emerge again to announce the resurrection of the old world. Instructed by her grandmothers, Angel tunes in to the older world, realizing that she is being watched. Her discovery that "we are seen, our measure taken" (*Solar Storms* 80) is a key moment in her reawakening, while her instinctive recoil from LaRue's disrespectful killing of fish shows that her inner core has not been ruined by years of forced settler colonial assimilationism. One morning, awakened by the combined noise of a storm and flocks of tundra swans flying south, Angel sits up in her room, whose windows are always wide open to the outside world, and knows herself to be "part of the same equation as birds and rain" (*Solar Storms* 79).

Angel is re-minded. While fishing, she begins to see inside water "as if I was a heron, standing in the shallows with a sharp, hungry eye" (*Solar Storms* 85). Fish do not shun her, because she respects them and, unlike LaRue, kills them painlessly and fast. She knows fish are "a kind of people" (*Solar Storms* 118) and that they want to live as human people do. Sometimes she is terrified by winter's "ancient ritual of hunger" (*Solar Storms* 117)—hearing the cry of a moose stranded on ice and surrounded by a pack of wolves—but mostly she merges with the natural world in such an intimate way that the land speaks to her through dreams, the gone animals visiting her at night: "I remembered or dreamed of the animals taken, marten, beaver, wolverine. I saw their skinless corpses. I heard their cries and felt their pain. I saw their shadows cross snow, ice and cloud" (*Solar Storms* 118). She not only dreams their pain, she partakes of it, co-suffering with them. In one dream, she sees the wolves of Fur Island "torn out of their deaths, [...] stirring about and holding counsel, looking for their human children" (*Solar Storms* 119). The children Angel refers to are part of the history of the island. In 1924 a boy and a girl who had been raised by wolves were captured by people. The children "saw through the savagery of civilization" (*Solar Storms* 65) and died grieving their murdered wolf kin. As earth's visions, dreams communicate to Angel the true, decolonized history of the land. She is accepted. Her animal senses are awake.

When the four women: Angel, Bush, Agnes, and Dora-Rouge undertake the long and dangerous journey north to join the protesters at the site of the proposed new dam, they enter the waterscape as one enters a gap in time, traveling backwards in history, "undoing the routes of explorers" (*Solar Storms* 176). "Everything merged and united," Angel narrates.

> There were no sharp distinctions left between darkness and light. Water and air became the same thing, as did water and land in the marshy broth of creation. Inside the clear water we passed over, rocks looked only a few inches away. Birds swam across lakes. It was all one thing. The canoes were our bodies, our skin.
>
> (*Solar Storms* 177)

In this deep immersion in the wildness of nature, Angel feels watched by innumerable eyes. The four women become one organism, communicating with each other without words, as if they were "one animal" (*Solar Storms* 177), not unlike bees or ants. In this vast waterscape Angel experiences one revelation after another, reconnecting to her tribal and evolutionary past. Diving to look at ancient paintings of fish submerged by the rising waters, she suddenly feels as if she had gills again. "At that moment," she claims, "I remembered being fish. I remembered being oxygen and hydrogen, bird and wolverine" (179). In the wildness there was only now and it seemed that humans could still speak with animals in the old language.

Angel begins to understand the world as it was before Europeans removed the spirit from all the nonhuman relatives and allies. Dora-Rouge remarks: "Once we could ask them to do something, to find our way home, to take away pain. [...] And they would help us." According to her "this knowledge was given on the tenth day of creation" (181). This novel's Indigenous people supplement the information missing from the Bible, not unlike Michael Horse in *Mean Spirit*. Rather than having been completed in six days, creation has never ended, they claim, but some humans must have moved on to the newly formed lands and missed what happened beyond the seventh day. Dora-Rouge's story has a strong anti-colonial ring. Those humans never learned, she speculates, that there even was a day "devoted to snails and slugs, night crawlers and silverfish, roaches" (*Solar Storms* 181). Otherwise, they might have been less determined to destroy the humble lives of animals many consider to be pests, but whose presence keeps ecosystems healthy. They might not have turned into reverse people.

As a matter of fact, Angel's grandmothers can find worth even in mosquitoes, which plague them on part of their journey. Ancient life forms, mosquitoes are respected as witnesses of the land's long history. Having drawn blood from all kinds of creatures across millennia, they have incorporated the past within their cells. "They remembered all the letting of blood" after the arrival of the French. "They remembered the animals sinking down into earth" (*Solar Storms* 175). The novel echoes Hogan's appreciation of all the invisible, humble, and unseen life forms that makes itself felt in her poetry.

Among the animals crossing the paths of the novel's protagonists none is as mysterious as the wolverine, with his reputation for stealth, ferocity, and strength. Considered by Dora-Rouge's people, the Fat Eaters, to be a trickster creator, wolverine is depicted as an agent of decoloniality, a transformational being, and a teacher of survivance. To Angel's innocent question what is wolverine, Bush answers laughingly: "That's what everyone wants to know" (*Solar Storms* 77), but when LaRue offends the spirit of fish by skinning them alive, Angel is certain that it was wolverine who punished him by taking away his luck in hunting. "There are consequences to human sins" (*Solar Storms* 84), Bush agrees. Wolverine is believed to be a keeper of the ancient treaty between humans and animals. When humans break the bond, he may drive the fish away from them. Not surprisingly, with his claim that fish do not feel pain, LaRue hardly catches anything, even in his protective clothing, while Angel, who is new to fishing but treats fish well, has all the luck.

The elusive wolverine is difficult to see, with only his tracks and offensive smell marking his passage, which gives rise to the conviction that he can make himself invisible. His invisibility is attributable to him being a human gone wild or perhaps a human disappointed with his kind who returns to his animal shape, despising humans. Having been human once, wolverine knows how to walk undetected in the prints of other humans when he watches how they treat animals. Still others claim he is "an animal inhabiting a strange, two-legged body, wearing human skin" (*Solar Storms* 253). In either case, wolverine knows enough about humans to be wary of them and to try to protect the nonhuman world from human invasion.

When his prints are detected around Hannah's house after her death or around the burned remains of Tulik's house, tribal people believe these prints mark the trail of a spirit and want to follow the path the creator of their world—called Mondi—has left. Some, however, suggest wolverines are actually witches taking the shape of this particular animal to accomplish their work of the moment. As if that is not enough, wolverines are also believed to hear human thoughts, to "have another kind of listening" (*Solar Storms* 84). This is why they seem to know everything.

On a less esoteric ground, the half-mythical wolverine is known to be an intelligent thief.[1] He steals food from humans to satisfy his voracious appetite. But stealing flints rather than food is more difficult to justify, unless one assumes that wolverine consciously takes the very things people depend on for their survival in order to make them leave his territory. When Tulik's house—which has served as the headquarters of resistance against the lawless destruction of Indigenous land and lives—is set on fire and the protesters move to the local post office, Angel makes headway for the pan-tribal community of resistance by thinking like wolverine: "Wolverine wanted the people to leave, he wanted to starve them out of his territory, his world. Just as quickly, like thunder following the lightning, a plan sprang to my mind: I would starve out the soldiers and police" (*Solar Storms* 322). Under cover of darkness, she slips out of bed "pretending to be wolverine, thinking inside myself the way a wolverine might think" (*Solar Storms* 322). She steals into the occupiers' food store, taking some of the dry goods her people most need and destroying the rest, as wolverine would have done:

> I poured out the flour, ripping the bags open with a knife. I poured their bottled water on top of it so it couldn't be scooped up and salvaged, angry all the time that they'd ruined our water and brought in their own. Then I opened the bags of sugar and poured them out, as well, and when I left, with my pockets and backpack full, I made a trail of white footsteps, the path of a ghost. [...] The only thing a Wolverine would have done that I didn't do was to pee on all the food he left behind.
> (*Solar Storms* 323)

Although they did not manage to stop the first phase of the huge engineering project, by protesting against the injustice and violence the Fat Eaters regained their pride and became the Beautiful People they had been in the past.

As the flooding goes on and waters rise in Adam's Rib, Angel knows "there would be no animals escaping two by two" (*Solar Storms* 335), not from this flood. There would be no one to reach out for those who wander gracefully and far on four legs, to take hold of the wading birds with their golden claws at the bottom of water, to carry to safety the yellow-eyed lynx, the swift dark marten.

(*Solar Storms* 335)

This elegy emerges out of the sense of powerlessness and defeat in the girl's attempts to rescue the lives sentenced to a violent end at the flip of a switch in a modern power house. Her words are her substitute mourning ritual for the beautiful animals she loves and co-suffers with. While the men who accompany Bush and Angel desperately try to help the animals who cannot swim to reach the mainland from the flooded Fur Island, the skeleton of the giant turtle assembled by Bush is claimed back by the waters which will soon devour the animals Western engineers consider to be collateral damage.

But amidst this catastrophic darkness there is a light of hope for those who survive. New life may still emerge from the waters of destruction, as it did in the beginning of time; the universe is still unfolding, another day of creation may still be in order. The novel ends on a tentative note of hope in the possibility of the impossible: that humans can change and the world can become a friendlier place for all. Angel-Maniki has survived the violence of her childhood in the best possible way, growing in love and compassion. Her newborn sister, the child of Hannah, is the tribal people's future. And the construction of new dams has been stopped. "That one fracture was healed," Angel thinks, believing there will be "new dreams, new medicines, and one day, once again," the people will "remember the sacredness of every living thing" (*Solar Storms* 344).

LaRue already has. His participation in the protest along with Indigenous activists and the violence he witnessed have broken the hard outer shell of this war veteran, revealing something soft and alive inside. For the first time LaRue cries, and it is over an animal killed by one of his regular customers. It was a beautiful creature, delicate, almost green-furred, with a long tail and—what else—"the last of this kind of creature" (*Solar Storms* 339). After this private epiphany, LaRue gives up taxidermy and returns to tribal lifeways. Having decolonized himself, he has become a human again, and the task of humans, entrusted to them by the Great Spirit, is to be the caretakers of animals. This teaching comes at the close of Dora-Rouge's retelling of the story of Eho, the woman who fell in love with a whale and pleaded with the mother of water on behalf of all life. After her death the care for animals has been transferred to humans.

Solar Storms, set on the waterways of the US–Canadian border, illustrates the entangled histories of genocide, speciecide, and environmental degradation, but it also foregrounds the strength of animal counter-sovereignty.

Beaver's mastery at environmental engineering ridicules misguided and highly destructive human efforts at 'improving' nature. In the water-locked territory of the north, it is beaver, not human, that is the keystone species, the creator and supporter of life. Wolverine, at the same time, is a trickster god and a master of survivance. By taking away luck in hunting, stealing food and other essentials of life, and eluding detection, wolverine is an agent of decoloniality, a guardian of the original pact between humans and animals. Sadly, both have been among the historical victims of the fur trade and may soon join other fur-bearers hunted out of existence, like the animal who made LaRue cry or the glacier bear Agnes befriended. Among the recent nonhuman victims of settler violence are game animals flooded by the artificial dams, fish poisoned by mercury, and waterfowl who depend on the fish.

Solar Storms focuses almost exclusively on untamed nature. In the state of wildness, survival depends on the ability to satisfy hunger and predation is omnipresent. Conditions of respectful mutual use between human and more-than-human persons are regulated by elaborate protocols, respect being the fundament on which the kin-centric world of Indigeneity is built.

The novel's human protagonists are either at peace with wildness or re-discovering their membership in the "democracy of species" (Kimmerer 58).[2] One such character is Angel, "the girl who turned human" (*Solar Storms* 295), who is in the process of relearning the ancient ways and growing in compassion. Becoming mindful of the living, always watching world, she rediscovers her evolutionary memory, and remembers being animal. Angel's epiphanic moment illustrates the transformative potential of reality, the "implicate order" manifesting itself in ever new forms of the "explicate order," as physicist David Bohm would phrase it.[3] Wolverine's shapeshifting, Agnes's "becoming something, maybe the bear" (*Solar Storms* 48), and the abused girl's transformation into the love-filled Angel-Maniki are part of the same process. The unfinished nature of the creative process keeps alive a spark of hope for the eventual emergence of a mature humanity filled with compassion.

Notes

1   Anthropologist Paul Nadasdy relates a story as told to him by a Kluane trapper, "about a wolverine who learned to run [the Kluane's] trapline ahead of him, devouring all the animals in his traps before he could get to them. In retaliation—and in an effort to salvage his trapping reputation—he began setting traps to catch the wolverine. Despite his efforts, the wolverine managed to spring all the traps set for it and continued making easy meals of the furbearers caught in the hunter's traps. The trapper clearly relished describing to me the ingenious setups he had devised to catch the wolverine and the even more ingenious techniques the wolverine had used to avoid them" (Nadasdy, "The Gift" 32).

2 In the chapter "The Grammar of Animacy," Kimmerer explains: "...grammar is just the way we chart relationships in language. Maybe it also reflects our relationships with each other. Maybe a grammar of animacy could lead us to whole new ways of living in the world, other species as sovereign people, a world with a democracy of species, not a tyranny of one—with moral responsibility to water and wolves, and with a legal system that recognizes the standing of other species. It's all in the pronouns" (57–58).

3 "In the enfolded [or implicate] order, space and time are no longer the dominant factors determining the relationships of dependence or independence of different elements. Rather, an entirely different sort of basic connection of elements is possible, from which our ordinary notions of space and time, along with those of separately existent material particles, are abstracted as forms derived from the deeper order. These ordinary notions in fact appear in what is called the 'explicate' or 'unfolded' order, which is a special and distinguished form contained within the general totality of all the implicate orders" (Bohm 1980, p. xv).

8   Of *Power* and Sacrifice
Rethinking Carnivora, Expanding Sociality

"One of my main interests is the gray area between laws that affect sovereign nations and indigenous, religious freedom and the Endangered Species Act," Hogan told John Murray of *The Bloomsbury Review* (Murray). Her last two novels to date, *Power* and *People of the Whale*, were inspired by actual events which involved the killing of an endangered animal by people of tribal origin. *Power*, published in 1998, is set in the swamps of southern Florida, the habitat of a puma subspecies known as the Florida panther. Being a top predator, the panther needs a vast range of wild territory in order to survive. Predictably, with the advent of European colonization and large-scale anthropogenic changes in the environment, this animal, once flourishing throughout the entire Southeast, became nearly extinct. As of the 1980s, the presumable[1] time of the novel's action, the panther population could not have been higher than 30.

The U.S. Fish & Wildlife Service estimates the species' habitat to have shrunk to a mere 5% of the animals' original range, with devastating effects on their survival rate. Even today, when their population has rebounded to 120–230 ("Florida Panther"), the Florida panther continues to face such threats as ongoing loss, degradation and fragmentation of habitat due to urbanization, road construction, and mining; inbreeding, with the resulting lower survival rates, genetic disorders, and greater susceptibility to diseases; and also vehicle collisions, poaching, and exposure to toxic chemicals in the environment. Much of the pollution comes from the Everglades sugar cane plantations that are concentrated around Lake Okeechobee. According to some estimates, "3,000 tons of hazardous pollutants, including a host of carcinogens, are released into the air each year by sugar cane burning in South Florida" (D'Souza) alone. *Power* repeatedly references pollution from farming and sugar cane plantations, which kills fish and harms the environment. Instead of the immortality of the legendary Fountain of Youth, Florida lakes and rivers are running with sickness and death.

The Florida sugar cane industry, which produces 25% of all sugar in the US, has been a mainstay of the state's political and industrial power since the collapse of Cuban sugar imports in 1959. Large parts of the unique

DOI: 10.4324/9781003364252-11

Everglades ecosystem have been clear-cut, the land drained, rivers diverted for sugar cane cultivation, and game animals drowned. Consistently anchoring the ecosystem's degradation in the ante-bellum slave-driven, profit-oriented plantation system, Hogan's novel offers arguments for renaming the new geological epoch the Plantationocene to keep the inter-sectional oppressions of patriarchal capitalism in focus.

Before writing the novel, Hogan "didn't know anything about the Florida panther" (Murray), she confesses, but being a member of a working group of Native people consulting on the reauthorization of the Endangered Species Act, she chanced upon the story of the Seminole Chairperson James Billy, who had killed a Florida panther on tribal terri-tory in 1983 and was acquitted on the grounds of religious freedom. The argument of religious freedom, as she later discovered, was used for strate-gic reasons; Billy not only failed to take the panther's life in a sacred way, but he shot the animal accidentally when under the influence of alcohol. *Power* offers an Indigenous perspective on a story in which a panther is killed for a sacred reason.

Before sitting down to write, however, Hogan had to do some research on the elusive nonhuman animal that assumes the role of a major char-acter in her book. Unlike the two novels discussed so far, *Power* focuses almost exclusively on one nonhuman animal, foregrounding the panther's co-evolution and kinship with the fictional, 30-member Taiga tribe, which is as critically endangered as the cat. Panthers occupy top of the trophic chain; as strict carnivores, they are feared and subject to the same harmful misperceptions that have driven other big predator eradication campaigns. Before discussing Hogan's imaginative handling of the panther story, I want to examine the nature of these misperceptions from the unique van-tage point offered by neuroscience.

In an article published in *Emergence Magazine*, a periodical devoted to spiritual ecology, Hogan refers to having taken a class from an animal ethologist, Gay Bradshaw ("Ancient Root"). Even though she is unlikely to have met Bradshaw before the publication of *Power*, it is evident that the ethologist-cum-psychologist provided her with the newest scientific validation of traditional Indigenous knowledge about nonhuman animals. In 2005, having discovered that young male elephants in Africa suffer from post-traumatic stress disorder, Bradshaw founded transspecies psychology, a new field of science based on species-common neuroanatomy. According to her, neuropsychology heals "the conceptual and disciplinary apartheid" (Bradshaw 5) between human and nonhuman animals, returning us to the founding intuitions of Darwin's evolutionary theory. Bradshaw considers this new scientific field to be a natural "champion of animal rights" (xxi), critical to unlearning pseudo-classifications based on prejudice and fear. Following insights provided by neuropsychology, she believes we may open up an opportunity *to find out who our species can become*. It is an alternative that harks back to the ancient past when the coyote's howl, snake's rattle, and grizzly [*sic!*] growl inspired awe instead of fear and loathing. The grizzly countenance peering from the pines, diamond-shaped visage nested in his coil, and circumspect feline mien are not faces of strangers—*they are kin*.

(17–18, emphasis added)

Ultimately, hard scientific evidence has confirmed what modern humans consistently and ruthlessly ignored—and continue to do so at a dramatic cost to all. It is a truth masterfully rehearsed in Hogan's *Power*, namely, that we are all—humans and nonhumans—members of a co-evolving family of distinctly endowed, feeling and thinking individuals. Anthropodenial[2] has ceased to be ethically or scientifically defensible.

The book which launched Bradshaw's international career, *Elephants on the Edge* (2009), bears a subtitle which has a *déjà vu* effect on readers familiar with Hogan's work: *What Animals Teach Us about Humanity*. More recently, in 2017, Bradshaw published *Carnivore Minds*, a book devoted to refuting harmful stereotypes about big predators, including pumas, which should provide an enlightening point of entry into Hogan's most lyrical and most organic novel, which I consider to be her prose masterpiece.

Admired as they may be for strength, agility, or beauty, carnivorous animals are often feared as mindless killers and hated for alleged livestock depredation. Generally, they are thought to be in need of human 'management,' which includes preemptive 'culling.' While refuting these and other persistent myths about carnivora, Bradshaw illuminates the roots of the "persecution-protection duality" (240) that Hogan's work references on a number of occasions. On account of the danger they allegedly pose to humans and farm animals, top predators in the US—most notably wolves and grizzly bears—have been alternately protected under the Endangered Species Act and persecuted in pursuance of the Animal Damage Control Act. What needs to be stressed, observes Bradshaw, is that government wildlife agencies responsible for listing and delisting endangered species are closely linked with the private hunting sector, which has a vested interest in keeping the lucrative business of hunting carnivora in operation. In effect, rebounding populations are often immediately removed from the protected species list, the persecution starts anew, and the historical trauma of the species in question never ends. "They hold this in common with American Indians" (256), Bradshaw notes, not hesitating to name this shared experience genocide.

Bradshaw, like many other members of the scientific community, warns that the fear- and prejudice-driven carnivore destruction, which has reached the epic proportions of a cleansing (14), has unleashed a chain of catastrophic ecological reactions. Without the regulatory presence of top predators, entire ecosystems are degenerating. Meanwhile, the seductive appeal of the "adrenaline-laced myths" (Bradshaw 15) is so pervasive that it obscures the view of the actual animal. Those who, nonetheless, take the trouble to "discover who lies behind the mask of falsehoods" will see not a beast red in tooth and claw but someone surprisingly similar to humans, possibly even surpassing us in "civility and grace" (Bradshaw 15). "When it comes to judgement," Bradshaw aptly notices, "it is modern humanity, not carnivores, that warrants ethical scrutiny and reinvention" (17).

Pumas are among the most notoriously misrepresented top predators. Looking back at the long history of puma eradication, Bradshaw observes that Jesuit priests already actively promoted the killing of those iconic cats in the 1500s and that conservationist-president Theodore Roosevelt solidified the rhetoric of the killing machine, calling the puma "the lord of stealthy murder" (qtd. in Bradshaw 13). In reality, nothing could be further from the truth. In the world of nature, energy needs to be conserved and big predators, including pumas, adhere to "a philosophy of studied avoidance rather than open aggression" (Bradshaw 199).

Neuroscience has proved that "puma brains and minds are ecologically engaged and in dialogue with nature in its entirety and are reflective of our ancestral, small-band hunter-gatherer society" (Bradshaw 210). More family oriented than previously believed, pumas have been found to be collaborative and capable of sharing food with one another. As Bradshaw comments: "[t]hat pumas share food with other adults argues for an ethic of care that supersedes the selfish gene" (210). As this chapter will demonstrate, transspecies psychology lends credence to the way Linda Hogan portrays the Florida panther in *Power*. Without this brief overview of Bradshaw's pioneering research, uninformed critics may too glibly label the novel's depiction of the Taiga-panther bond 'sentimental.'

The panther, called Sisa in Taiga, is the center of the novel's tribal world. She is believed to have been the first person who helped breathe humans to life. Imitating her art of hiding and disappearing in the swamps without a trace, the tribe managed to survive colonial wars and avoided relocation to Indian Territory (the Seminoles are the prototype for the Taiga). In the old times, as the teenage Omishto narrates, panther claws were used in the tribe's most sacred ceremonies; at present, however, with her existence as endangered as that of her human kin, the panther is thought to be leaving the world she once created. Almost nobody has seen the animal in recent decades, although at least one Taiga woman feels she is still out there, watching. That woman is Ama Eaton of the Panther Clan, a mysterious, strong-willed person who lives alone between the traditional world of tribal elders and the modern life of the city, because she thinks Indigenous survival calls for some engagement with modernity. The critic Jesse Peters sees Ama as a frontier dweller in the literal and metaphorical sense: "for her, tradition is not stagnation, and she realizes that both the land and the tribe that inhabits it are constantly changing as the realities of existence change" (119). There are those who believe she got married to a panther at 12, when she went missing from home for several weeks, possibly even becoming a panther herself. Most probably, though, she was visiting the old people who live above Kili swamp.

Reporting this episode from Ama's life, Omishto refers to a rumor that "now she was an animal come back to observe us to see if our manner of worldly conduct toward them was right and kind" (*Power* 22). Like a shapeshifter, Ama was thought to have been "a spirit that had changed bodies the way they used to do when people could turn into animals and animals could transform themselves into a human shape" (*Power* 22). Reminiscent of the wolverine from *Solar Storms*, Ama Eaton is a protector of animals, closer to their world than to that of humans. Once she defied a group of armed boys to protect the panther they had treed, her closest relative. Yet the same woman takes the life of the cat she loves and has known all her life, fully aware of her deed's criminal nature. As if that was not puzzling enough, Omishto reports that she claims to have done it at the animal's own bidding in order to renew the dying world. The apparent incongruities, however, start to make sense in the context of the ancient Panther Woman story Ama believed herself to have been reenacting. Dissenting from Eurocentric readings of Ama's hunt as a futile sacrifice, I want to argue that she did follow the orders of Sisa and that her act may have tipped the scales in favor of the tribal world's survival.

The novel takes the form of Omishto's interior monologue. Drawn as she is to the older woman and the natural world, the girl is struggling to reconcile traditional worldviews, which sound like superstitions, with the rational knowledge she excels at in school. Her narration documents the painful process of recovering her Indigenous identity from the debris of modernity's lies and comforting illusions. In the course of her quest, Omishto has to navigate between her constantly shifting understandings of the novel's central event, re-telling the story of Ama's hunt differently for her respective audiences and stumbling over the inadequacies of language. At the court trial she limits herself to bare facts, because this is what she is told to do, but for tribal elders she tells it "more true" (*Power* 162), without, however, revealing the killed panther's wretched condition. Ama had explicitly forbidden the girl to reveal how sick the panther was, knowing that this would break the old people's spirit—even though they would look more favorably at Ama's deed as a case of mercy killing. The final, most complete version of the story—as witnessed, understood, and told in Omishto's narrative voice—is still incomplete, however, since the mythical 'whole truth' will probably always elude the grasp of human understanding. Ultimately, as Omishto discovers, the truth is what you believe (*Power* 108). Struggling to tell the story right, she must admit defeat, being left with more questions than answers: "there is a multitude of things, other truths, behind this truth," she muses; "history, belief, even the story of the panther who is the true owner of this place" (*Power* 161). It is the theft of land by European settlers, and the ensuing extermination of the panther, that was the original crime and the beginning of the story of Ama's hunt.

Humbled by the limitations of human knowing, Omishto comes to accept the coexistence of tangible reality with an older world governed by different rules. "There are other worlds beside us all the time and we cross over and enter one, and every so often, one passes and enters ours" (*Power* 55), Omishto remembers Ama saying. In her doctoral dissertation, anthropogeographer Amba J. Sepie notes:

> Prophecy, and numerous related phenomenon [*sic*] that break with conventional notions of time, space, and personal identity, rely on very different ideas of *what* a human being is, *how* a human comes to know, and where, who, and what knowledge might come *from*.
>
> (182)

Omishto—meaning the One Who Watches—is a keen observer of reality. She knows the swamps and forests to be alive with invisible eyes and ears. "The animals have eyes that see us. The birds, the trees, everything knows what we do" (*Power* 59). Even though she has never seen a panther, she knows it is her territory and at times feels watched by the elusive animal from somewhere close by. It is as if the more-than-human world were "trying to figure out what we are. We must mystify them. As animals, I mean" (*Power* 3). The ease with which Omishto shifts between human and nonhuman viewpoints testifies to her organic oneness with the wild, undamaged by her citified education and upbringing. In fact, she is unaware of ontological differences between humans and nonhuman animals. For her, all life is intelligent, sentient, bound together by ties of kinship. And the panther is her personal relative—which she claims under oath in court. In the old times each member of the Panther Clan was believed to have a panther ally, a cat born at the same time they were born, to give them power and strength, and Omishto fantasizes "what animal it might have been that would have walked with me, in my footsteps, me in its paw prints, and slept beside my skin" (*Power* 16).

The panther Ama watches for and some nights claims to see eye to eye is her animal ally. It is the same panther that comes to her in a dream and, standing on two feet as they used to in the ancient times, tells Ama to follow her. "But it looked so thin and skinny it broke my heart to pieces"

(*Power* 24), she tells Omishto. Waking up, she could still smell the animal's presence, as if the panther had just left. Ama takes the dream seriously. She realizes she has been chosen to reenact the Panther Woman story and renew the world.

The Taiga believe that in the old times a woman raised by animals followed a panther to another world through an opening a storm made in the sky. What she saw there was not unlike the world Ama lives in: "rivers on fire, animals dying of sickness, and foreign vines. The world, she saw, was dying" (*Power* 110). But the woman could not return because the opening between the worlds had been blown closed again. To re-open it she would have to kill the panther she had followed, the one she knew best. According to the story, "[a] sacrifice was called for and if it was done well, all the animals and the panther would come back again and they'd be whole" (*Power* 111). In Taiga, the word for sacrifice and sending away is the same; the two concepts are identical. So the woman killed—or sent away—the panther, as she had been told to do, and the world was renewed. Having done this, she transformed herself into a panther and went to live with her animal ally in the swamps—"the place where a person could be lost for years and never find a hint of direction" (*Power* 111).

When she was 12 years old, Ama had been lost for weeks in such a place. This episode from her early life prepared the ground for what would follow. Because Ama is a contemporary incarnation of Panther Woman; she is a secretive shapeshifting creature who, when she reemerged from the forest, looked as if she "was from another time" (*Power* 23). When the mature Ama dreams about the panther and the next day an earthshattering storm breaks out—with deer flying through the air, fish coming down from the sky, a dead Spanish horse from a ranch miles away landing near Ama's house, snakes seeking cover in the hut, and Methuselah, the oldest tree, being uprooted—it is like the world has ended, and Ama feels called to act. The storm has opened a door to the other world, the sky and the earth have changed places. "Old Grandmother, I am coming" (*Power* 49), she calls out to the panther and takes Omishto along on the tracking path. Both women feel compelled to do things they would not normally do, clambering over fallen trees and dead animals, as if entranced. In this reenactment of the old myth, it is not Ama who takes the initiative, but Sisa. The panther seems to be guiding them to a place of her own choosing, drawing them into the depths of the Taiga birthplace. She is in control. Omishto reports that the panther

> doesn't run. In the darkness its eyes shine and that is what I see. Eyes. It seems to look right through us. It sees through us. Then, at ease, as if certain we will follow, it moves slowly away. It is calling us forward. I can see this in the way it looks back at us from time to time,

and in the fact that it is calm. It does not hide itself the way it could. It does not run or take to the bush. It is sure of us and that we will follow.

(64)

Partners in a world-transforming ceremony, the two women and the cat are related to one another by an intimate bond of kinship and by destiny. A sacrifice is called for and all three of them: the panther, Ama Eaton, and Omishto are the sacrificed. To restore the world to balance, they have to be sacrificed—or sent away—together. For Ama, killing the sacred animal without tribal consent is symbolic suicide. It is not only that her heart is breaking with grief at the thought of having to kill the animal she loves; she will be literally 'sent away,' sentenced to four years of exile from tribal lands. For the 16-year-old narrator, the consequences of the hunt will be equally grave; they will entail sacrificing the securities of modern life to live with the old people and shoulder the burden of becoming the tribe's future.

Before the killing can be done, however, respect must be shown to the animal that has offered herself for the renewal of the world:

> The cat looks up and she shows me to the cat, and what she does is, she introduces me to it, it to me. She says my name as she looks at me, as if I am both an offering and a friend.
>
> (*Power* 65)

The choice of words is telling. All the three characters are an offering and a friend to one another, doing what must be done. "This way is God" (*Power* 62), as Ama puts it—a motif well-rehearsed in Hogan's poetry. After all, life is something one borrows for as long as it is not needed by someone else. And this particular life is urgently needed for the life of the Taiga world, and it is taken with utmost respect: Ama allows the hungry cat to eat before the fatal shot is fired, then she offers the animal to the sky and feeds the cat's spirit tobacco, corn, and pollen. The body is bony, broken-toothed, infested with fleas and ticks, sickly, looking like "something that wanted to live and couldn't" (*Power* 66). It is evident that the panther had been dying a slow and painful death and Omishto ponders whether what Ama did was not an act of mercy after all.

This is where some critics will draw the line and argue the futility and criminal nature of Ama's sacrifice.[3] A critically endangered animal was killed in violation of the Endangered Species Act, a life was lost in vain, and the perpetrator, though acquitted by state law, was sentenced to banishment by a tribal court—which was the equivalent of a death sentence for her. Lydia R. Cooper's interpretation is characteristic in this respect. In her article "Woman Chasing Her God," she argues:

the death of a panther is no longer acceptable nor does it provide renewal because the natural world has become too corrupted, too endangered. The panther—sick, frail, dying—accomplishes nothing through becoming yet one more instance [of] suffering and death, just as Ama, already marginalized and half-feral, seeks to heal her world through her exile but in the end fails in her purpose and fails to provide Omishto with a much-needed mother-figure.

(155)

I believe Cooper and other critics writing in this vein do not take Indigenous worldviews seriously and misread or disregard clues provided by the narrative itself. The person so harshly condemned by Cooper acted on the belief that "her faintest move or thought is governed not only by spirits but by the desires and dreams of animals who are people like ourselves, in different skins" (*Power* 189). Reading the novel through the decolonial lens, I find much evidence to argue that Ama may have achieved her goal, and that the panther did return, healthy and strong, bringing at least a temporary renewal to the world. In the mythical time reenacted by the Taiga woman, conventional notions of time, space, and identity are suspended; an older world surfaces, one ruled by different, perhaps yet unknown, laws of physics. On her way to the old people—who will be her parent substitutes from then on—Omishto has an encounter with a golden cat, "healthy, lean-muscled" (*Power* 232). The scene of encounter has a familiar ring to readers of Hogan's poetry:

> I don't move. It could kill me, swallow me. It thinks the same thing of me. We stand motionlessly and look at each other in the near morning and then I say, "Ni shi holo," I mean no harm, Aunt, Grandmother.
>
> (*Power* 232–233)

Two predators meeting face-to-face, looking each other in the eye, fascinated and petrified at the same time. Omishto's words break the spell and the cat withdraws slowly, disappearing into the dense vegetation. Far from "the lord of stealthy murder," the carnivore is "a model of civility and grace" (Bradshaw 15). As Omishto admits, it may even be the same cat Ama killed, only now "fully grown and beautiful" (*Power* 233). She cannot exclude the possibility that the old myth was true.

Ama's self-sacrifice—her insistence on hiding the information that might have saved her from exile—may not have been futile, either. For one thing, she saves the old people's hope—the only thing that had carried them through the dark times—that the panther has a future and that the Taiga will survive. The novel ends on a hopeful note, with Omishto dancing for the world to continue. And while for Ama exile is not unlike death,

Omishto knows she is able to live by animal rules and even fantasizes that instead of dying, she may have buried herself in mud to re-emerge in four years' time. On the level of the myth she is trapped in, however, if Ama the alleged shapeshifter has reenacted the story to the letter, she may have turned herself into a cat after she disappeared. Alternatively, as Omishto speculates, her friend might have found a way to another world and cannot return to "this America" (*Power* 107). Why should this interpretation be more improbable than the Rapture believed in by members of the First Sanctified Church that Omishto's mother attends? After all, what people believe is true for them.

Finally, there is the question of the animal who is at the center of this drama. Did she really offer herself to Ama? If this question is to make sense at all, it too must be approached from the vantage point of tribal beliefs and Indigenous science, since this is the framework Hogan has chosen to work with. In the state court where Ama is tried, among the prosecutors and the many animal-rights activists in attendance there is no real concern for the good of that particular animal whose case they are arguing. Ama's accusers consider, at best, the good of the species and lose sight of the individual. The most vocal activists are descendants of those who stole the panther's land and brought the animal to the brink of extinction in the first place and thus have no moral ground to pass judgment on a woman related to Sisa, a woman who watched and loved the panther all her life. Then there is the hypocrisy of Sisa's self-styled defenders who enjoy the comfort of driving on newly built highways even though vehicle-related mortality is a major cause of the panthers' decline. According to official statistics, in 2020 there were 22 panther deaths in Florida, of which 20 were caused by vehicle collisions.[4] After musing on the increasing numbers of panthers who die on the roads—"a dozen of them since the highway went in"—Omishto points to another disconcerting attitude of city-bred panther-lovers, namely, the inclination to treat the cats as abstractions emptied of content:

> The high school team is named after them. They are mascots, nothing more. No one wants them around, but they like to look to see them just the same. They just don't want them out there by their places [...] And no one wants them to eat cattle or dogs. There is no place human wants will let them be.
>
> (*Power* 123)

All in all, none of the activists present seem interested in hearing the panther's own version of the story. What did the panther want, then? Ultimately, it is Omishto, a member of the Panther Clan, that gives voice to her. Rather than speaking *for* the panther, she speaks *from within* the cat, seeing the world through Sisa's eyes, hearing her thoughts, which are carried by the wind that the Taiga identify with Oni—the creative spirit, the energy of movement, the breath of life which penetrates everything and knows everything. Sisa, as Omishto learns, feels doomed in a world deprived of her former companions by humans who broke the sacred covenant. She misses "the blue-green crocodile, the many silver-sided fish, bear, and the delicate wood stork" and pities the "poor awkward cattle" (*Power* 190) who are nothing but food but cannot be eaten by her without human retaliation. Sisa's once beautiful green world is now crisscrossed by dangerous highways, dotted by towns, while the humans her own people once helped breathe into life are lost and miserable. "And Sisa believes, sees, that the world could end with their human misery, that she must somehow endure to the end, that humans are pitiable and small and broken" (*Power* 192). With these words the panther confirms her determination to honor the terms of the original pact. She still feels responsible for her human "brothers and sisters" (*Power* 192) and wants to help them, even at the cost of her own life. To this end she chooses the woman who still sang to her, and the girl "who went with [Ama] to this death." Sisa's thoughts continue:

> They met with one another, there in a world no longer their own, and they were all, all three of them, the sacrifice in this place that has grown small with rusty nails and oil drums in the shadows of buildings. But she, the cat, hopes that the world still has golden evening light, will have it again [...].
>
> (*Power* 192)

Far from being romantic or merely anthropomorphic, Hogan's imaginative rendering of the panther's thoughts remains in touch with the discoveries of transspecies psychology. There is no reason to believe that pumas should not be able to think (at least non-linguistically), imagine, and plan ahead, as human animals do. This idea—that animals are capable of thinking—is being accepted by a growing number of anthropologists practicing a radical empirical method, also known as 'radical participation.' They describe situations in which animals appear to be communicating with humans and other "experiences that are similarly inexplicable from within a Euro-American view of the world," in the words of Paul Nadasdy, who practiced radical participation among the hunting people of the Yukon. Many stories of this kind are underreported, Nadasdy claims, because anthropologists are reluctant to risk their professional reputation. Rather than dismiss stories that are incompatible with our Western worldviews, he suggests that professionals in the field should be open to treating them as "a potential means for gaining insights into the nature of a world we only partially understand" ("The Gift" 37). Hunting peoples[5] have been engaged in centuries-old relations of reciprocal exchange with animals. The fact that the best hunters still find their prey through dreaming requires us to rethink our assumptions about the world and align them with the hunters.' Diverse conceptions and experiences of human-animal communication force us to "expand our analytic concepts of society to include animals," writes Nadasdy ("The Gift" 29). Since reciprocity is a social act and takes place among persons, he continues, taking Indigenous ideas about animals seriously "poses a radical challenge to social theory itself" ("The Gift" 26). In traditional hunting cultures animals are part of the social world; they are thinking persons who consciously enter into relationships with other persons, human and nonhuman.

Similarly, readers of Hogan's novel must remain open to the possibility that the panther's thoughts were real and, carried by the wind, were heard and transmitted to us by Omishto. The passage demonstrates that the animal is an intelligent, collaborative, caring, ecologically engaged, and family oriented person, as Bradshaw argues in *Carnivore Minds*. The panther's human family would obviously include members of the Taiga Panther Clan, but it must be remembered that her concern is extended to other members of the tribe, because she is part of the larger Taiga society she has coevolved with.

There are 120–230 adult panthers in Florida, in contrast to the 20–30 that lived at the time of the novel's action, when the life of one endangered panther was taken by Ama. Can this be another hint that the character was possibly right? Disregarding the ample textual evidence pointing to the sacred and consensual nature of the sacrifice would imply imprisonment within the colonial worldview, which has been tried in the court scene and found wanting.

As happens in all the novels Hogan has published so far, humans are not 'born'; it takes time and effort to *become* human. In Indigenous cosmologies humanness is not a given; rather, as multispecies anthropologist Maya Ratnam puts it, it "is a task to be achieved in spaces of shared encounter and habitation." Those who do not learn to relate to others—including animal others—in a proper way do not qualify as humans. In Hogan's novels the list of such characters is long and includes white explorers and land thieves, killers of human and animal people, polluters and destroyers of the environment, and also tribal policemen who drive through and slaughter jumping frogs. Some such characters eventually achieve the status of a human person—such as La Rue from *Solar Storms*; others remain in-human or unfinished humans—like Omishto's stepfather, Herm, who abuses his stepdaughter and takes the lives of fish in a cruel way.

According to a Taiga belief, in the beginning all other-than-human persons loved the human people and wanted to be close to them. In our degraded world the ability to attract animals and gain their trust remains a signature of full humanness. Characters deserving this appellation at the beginning of *Power* include, first of all, Ama Eaton, the woman who still "keeps up relations" (*Power* 17) with spirits and other-then-human people, as well as with her neighbors' farm animals—Willard's horse and Mrs Swallow's goat and kids—who are drawn to her place, so much so that they refuse to return to their owners. Then, there are the old people who live above Kili swamp, with the charismatic head of the Panther Clan, Janie Soto, who even offered one of her legs—which she was forced to cut off to liberate herself from a deadly trap—for the lives of the animals. Part of the novel's appeal is that it details the process of *becoming human* as we follow Omishto's struggles with identity.

After Ama's banishment, when Omishto's dissatisfaction with the human species reaches an apex, she rebels against her human nature, wishing for a more honest existence of the kind she associates with animality. "Why am I a human?" she rails. "Why is it I am not on all fours in the forest or swamp?" Omishto is ready to renounce the evolutionary adaptations which gave humans an edge over other creatures and "go backwards, [...] to feel the land, to enter water" (*Power* 176). She has just shed the old skin of a perfect student, a Taiga with promise. Alienated from her former schoolmates by her participation in the killing—which they perceive to be criminal—in class the girl feels studied like a "specimen" (*Power* 106), more akin to the fetus of a pig from the biology classroom than to her colleagues. Rather than to be armed with theories, books, and microscopes, she longs to be empty-handed and open-minded, to unlearn all she has been taught, to feel at one with the wild again—to be accepted. The storm has metaphorically prepared the way by blowing off her dress and stripping her naked. When Ama's hunt ended, Omishto felt as if her world was no longer familiar and she was "not yet born, not really" (*Power* 109). But before she can be born as a 'real human,' she must reintegrate her animality. One vital moment on this road toward reintegration takes place in Ama's chicken coop, where Omishto locks herself in to avoid Herm's violence. She remains among the chickens for the night, sleeping "like an animal, huddled in the corner of the cage" (*Power* 209), occasionally hearing the chickens' cries, which makes her speculate that they may be dreaming of flying—an ability they are losing with enslavement and human colonization—and this may remind her of her own losses. In the crucial chapter "They Come to Me" Omishto looks at the world through the eyes of other persons, human and nonhuman. Then in her dream animals come to her and she is swimming with an old turtle:

> On this side of the uprooted world the animals walk, the turtle woman who swam with us in an earlier world, a universe of worlds, lays her eggs up along the edge of the canal, moves forward, lays more eggs

[…]. I dream and watch. I dream that I, like the turtle, am swimming and I wake up sweating and tired, my arms tight.

(*Power* 228)

Omishto is ready to be born. She dreams of growing a new skin, of the old people brushing corn pollen on her. One morning her body is covered in dried bloodlines, as if she had been scratched with panther claws at night—the sign of a tribal healing ceremony. Omishto has become fully human, a mature person-in-relation. Her panther ally and clan animal acknowledges this by revealing herself to her.

As Hogan repeatedly asserts, reinventing the human is the reverse side of reclaiming the animal, and *vice versa*—decolonizing the animal results in a simultaneous decolonization of the human as a person-in-relation bound to an entire land community and cognizant of the personhood of other-than-human entities. One of the strengths of *Power* is that it articulates this in a radical way by investing a carnivorous animal—the epitome of the 'civilized' world's nightmares associated with wildness—with what the Western world believes sets humans apart from animals, namely language. The panther's thoughts convey the full measure of her "civility" (Bradshaw 5), intelligence, and compassion. Her concern for her human and nonhuman relatives demands a radical expansion of the concept of sociality, as well as the taking of animal agency seriously.

Because of a long history of victimization, the human and nonhuman people in Hogan's *Power* have a strong reverence for the ties of kinship which have bound them together from the earliest days of creation. Respecting those ties allows them all to combine their efforts toward saving the world they share, even at the cost of self-sacrifice. Since the stories we tell make a real difference in the world, Hogan suggests, building our lives on stories of cooperation and compassion makes us more cooperative and compassionate.

Notes

1 The time of "the Billy case," as I explain below.
2 A term introduced by animal ethologist Frans De Waal. According to him, anthropodenial is "the a priori rejection of shared characteristics between humans and animals" and a "willful blindness to the human-like characteristics of animals or the animal-like characteristics of ourselves" (65).
3 Articles written from the decolonial perspective include, for instance, Deborah Miranda's "A Strong Woman Pursuing Her God: Linda Hogan's *Power*" or Jesse Peters's "'Everything the World Turns On': Inclusion and Exclusion in Linda Hogan's *Power*."
4 Including one killed by a train. By early June 2021, as I am writing these words, 16 panthers are reported to have been found dead this year. The leading cause of mortality remains the same, with 11 lives lost to vehicles, plus 2 cases of

starvation, 2 of intraspecies aggression (the result of PTSD), and one unknown. "2020 Panther Pulse."

5 Nadasdy writes about northern hunters, but his insights are consonant with the worldviews of the hunting peoples depicted in Hogan's writings. For the purpose of this book I will generalize from his description to include other Indigenous hunting nations.

9 *People of the Whale*

Transformational Beings and the Future of Humanity

The release of Hogan's second novel to deal with the fraught relationship between the protection of endangered species and tribal rights was stalled by the author's traumatic horse-riding accident. Finally published in 2008, *People of the Whale* is the result of Hogan's immersion in the world of marine biology, which started in 1996, when she joined writer Brenda Peterson and marine conservationist Jacques Cousteau to follow the gray whale's migration route along the Pacific coast. Hogan became fascinated with the gigantic sea mammals, whose intelligence is so much older than the intelligence of our species and who struck her as friendly, peaceful, and caring. In the introduction to their collaborative book, *Sightings*, which they warn is "not a natural history narrative, but a multifaceted portrait of the human-whale bond" (xiv), Hogan and Peterson claim that the sightings of the title combine "insight" with "science"—"as if we are respectfully studying an unknown culture" (xiii). The need of the whales to forge bonds with humans—despite the damage wrought by centuries of cruel commercial whaling—is one of the most surprising aspects of whale culture explored in their book, as well as in the Hogan novel that followed.

Also in 1996, both women visited a group of elders from the Makah tribe from the Pacific Northwest Coast. The elders wanted to consult with Hogan about the tribe's intended resumption of whale hunting. In 1915, three decades before the signing of the international convention for the regulation of whaling, the Makah had voluntarily given up their traditional cultural practice of hunting to help protect the gray whale from extinction. Now, when this species was no longer on the endangered species list,[1] the Makah tribal council decided to revive their traditional pursuit and petitioned the International Whaling Commission to allow them to hunt whales again. Several elders, headed by Alberta Thompson, protested the tribal decision. "As an indigenous woman," Hogan wrote in *Sightings*, "I saw the story of the Makah and their request to whale as a tale bearing all the dimensions of an American tragedy. It became one" (124). It is this drama that lies at the heart of her 2008 novel.

Depicting whales as 'good to live with,' *People of the Whale* was immediately recognized as a flagship example of multispecies poetics, an emerging

DOI: 10.4324/9781003364252-12

field of literature inspired by, among others, the work of Isabelle Stengers, Marisol De la Cadena, Bruno Latour, and Donna Haraway—especially the latter's 2008 book *When Species Meet*. No longer seeing animals merely through the prism of their being 'good to eat' or even 'good to think,' multispecies poetics—like multispecies ethnography, along with which it originated—centers nonhuman animals' agency and is concerned with human entanglements with other-than-human lives. Hsinya Huang, an expert on ecocritical Indigenous writing, situates *People of the Whale* among books[2] that validate "a restored continuum of human and oceanic nonhuman beings and participate in the emergence of multispecies ecopoetics rooted in the indigenous stories and myths of the Pacific" (122). Another leading ecocritical scholar, Joni Adamson, argues that *People of the Whale* offers "interesting characters and scenarios that can be used to illustrate a new mode of research being referred to as 'multi-species ethnography'" (33). Both Huang and Adamson locate *People of the Whale* within the so-called 'cetacean turn' in Indigenous-authored novels. Jonathan Steinwand, who coined this term in his 2011 article "What the Whales Would Tell Us: Cetacean Communication in Novels by Witi Ihimaera, Linda Hogan, Zakes Mda, and Amitav Ghosh," notes an intriguing analogy between whales and Indigenous people. He observes that both are forced to negotiate boundaries between worlds and elements: the former live between water and land, the latter between "the dominant 'civilization' and wild nature" (184). This in-betweenness, which Steinwand calls "liminality,"[3] challenges hierarchical divisions and privileges tropes of entanglement. With the advent of the new millennium, whales—especially in their coevolved bond with Indigenous humans—have become particularly good to think, as evidenced by the emergence of the 'cetacean turn' in literature.

Human-animal entanglement is often theorized in terms of Mary Louise Pratt's 'contact zones.' In their introduction to a 2019 special issue of *Nature and Science*, Jenny Isaacs and Ariel Otruba discuss the usefulness of Pratt's concept to a critical examination of human relations with nonhumans. Where species meet, they write, a contact is established, an encounter takes place, and this has a disruptive potential for the established ways of knowing, for taxonomies and species hierarchies. Then, drawing on Haraway, they trust in "the transformative potential of the contact zone to imagine new forms of multispecies flourishing" (Isaacs and Otruba 701). All of these approaches shed interesting interpretive light on Hogan's 'cetacean' narrative.

The novel is set in Dark River among the fictitious A'atsika people, a paddling nation of the American Northwest modeled on the Makah. According to their emergence story, the A'atsika were birthed by the whale and sea animals carried them to shore from underwater caves. Traditionally, the whale was the heartbeat of the people's spiritual life and provider of all they needed to survive. In the old times whaling was a sacred activity, a way to keep up relations with the ancestor. In everyday life the principal whaler would be set apart from the community by wearing white to show that he was destined to live between worlds and elements. A man called Witka Just was "the last of a line of traditional men who loved and visited the whales to ensure a good whale hunt" (Hogan, *People* 18). His ability to stay underwater without breathing for extended periods of time was a phenomenon studied by scientists. He also astounded them by his vast knowledge of the sea.

Witka was an intermediary between whales and the tribal people, always watching the sea for whales. He "entreated [whales], and asked, singing with his arms extended, if one of them would offer itself to the poor people on land. He beckoned and pleaded when the people were hungry" (*People* 18). The A'atsika were a hunting people and maintained reciprocal relations with their ancestor animal. In exchange for the gift of life, they offered the whale—their Grandmother and Grandfather—prayers, gratitude, and the blessings of living on land. Witka sang:

> If you come here to land we have beautiful leaves and trees. We have warm places. We have babies to feed and we'll let your eyes gaze upon them. We will let your soul become a child again. We will pray it back into a body. It will enter our bodies. You will be part human. We'll be part whale. Within our bodies you will dance in warm rooms, create life, make love.
>
> (*People* 12–13)

This prayer fleshes out the transformational beliefs of people inhabiting the coastline, where water and land incessantly negotiate their borders, where change is constant. As a people of the whale, the A'atsika used to live by the rhythm of the gray whales' migration, greeting them with joy upon their arrival, watching as they rose and dived, the young lifted on the mothers' backs. The hunt was a reciprocal and communal activity in fulfillment of the sacred obligation imposed by the ties of kinship. When Witka went underwater, leaving the human element of land and entering that of his marine relatives in order to talk to whales about the people's hunger, the whole village waited in silence, all activities stopped, only women stood at the edge of the ocean, singing the whales toward shore, grateful for "the great act of a man who sacrificed for them" (*People* 20). While he was underwater, Witka's wife dug a hole in the earth, got in, and covered herself with twigs, lying still, seeing what he was seeing, maybe even breathing for him, as many thought. Once a whale appeared, "the two of them pleaded and spoke. *Look how we are suffering. Take pity on us. Our people are small. We are hungry*" (*People* 21). If a whale offered him- or herself, the men started to prepare the canoes and whaling equipment. On the day they set out to sea, the women were quiet again, waiting, watching. If they were "pure in heart," the whale "would be coming gladly toward the village" (*People* 22).

This complicated ritual bound humans and whales into an intimate, symbiotic relationship, which turned everybody into "members of the clan of crossings," as Hogan phrases it in her poetry (*Dark* 156). Cultures that privilege ontologies based on transformations believe outward appearance to be accidental, a façade, while the inner core of all persons, human and nonhuman, is the same; there is no qualitative difference, no ontological gap, and shapeshifting can and does take place on a daily basis. So, the whale-consuming A'atsika saw themselves as becoming partly whale, the human and the whale being merely accidental forms matter takes amidst its many transformations. Witka's ability to stay underwater without breathing was a feature he shared with whales. His great-grandson Marco's webbed feet, and the gills that Marco's mother, Ruth, was born with, confirmed the A'atsika's assumptions about the shapeshifting nature of reality and the existence of transformational beings able to cross over from one element to another, from the nonhuman to the human and *vice versa*.

The birth of Witka's grandson, Thomas, was marked by a special event. A 15-foot octopus, the family's clan animal, left the ocean and walked across the beach into Seal Cave, looking each person in the eye, "as if each were known in all their past, all their future" (*People* 15). Octopi are natural shapeshifters, able to fit their bodies into almost any space. This one, however, was to literally shift his shape from animal to human and back, as it turned out years later. Thomas's mother, who had been fed in infancy "on whale and seal fat"—a diet that had apparently endowed her with greater attunement to marine life—at once realized that "it was a holy creature" (*People* 16) come to bring blessings to her child. She presented Thomas to the octopus and asked him to watch over the boy. "You knew his grandfather," she said, remembering that Witka had spent some time with a big octopus once. This request for protection had to be sealed with a gift. "Not to have given something they cared about would have been no gift at all" (*People* 16), so the woman left a pearl, her finest possession. Several days later the octopus disappeared with all the gifts he had received from the community. The people knew their requests would be granted.

The contemporary A'atsika, however, are depicted as struggling with the usual reservation problems: unemployment, poverty, alcohol abuse, and violence. The younger men, who fought in Vietnam, are a lost generation; only the older people still honor tradition and keep up relations with the spiritual and nonhuman worlds. Witka is dead and his grandson and successor, Thomas, is a broken man, suffering from PTSD. When the tribal council decides to revive whale hunting after a break of about

70 years, they claim this will help the people heal and become strong again. But the young men have no spiritual training, the old songs are forgotten, traditional equipment is lost, and, as it turns out, Dwight, the tribal leader, has made a lucrative underhand deal with Japanese businessmen to trade the whale meat with them. In short, instead of reconnecting with the Grandfather/Grandmother whale, the proposed hunt risks to further alienate the tribe from the source of their vitality. What is equally telling, the three women who protest against the resumption of the hunt are brutally intimidated by the self-styled defenders of tradition. As usual, Hogan presents violence as the result of interconnected oppressions. Afraid for the animals they love and organized around Ruth, Thomas's estranged wife, the female keepers of tradition sing old songs and ask the sea to keep its creatures away on the day of the hunt. Sadly, the sea does not seem to hear the warning of the few women.

The hunt is a massacre. The wrong whale is killed, his body riddled with bullets from automatic weapons, the men are drunk, quarreling, and violent, and the only spiritually mature whaler—Ruth and Thomas's son Marco—is drowned in the upheaval. With this sacrilegious taking of two innocent lives, the harmony of the A'atsika world is upset even further. The ocean is mourning, the fish are leaving, a disastrous drought commences. But the drought, as pointed out by critic Hanna Straß-Senol, is also symbolic of the community's spiritual condition: "the absence of a way of life that is guided by traditional values and tribal knowledge" (279). The breaking of the sacred pact and violation of reciprocal relations between humans and whales is merely the tip of the iceberg. "The erratic weather event," explains Straß-Senol,

> provides a motif that encapsulates a conglomerate of historical injustices and their cultural and collective as well as individual ramifications. Colonization, neo-colonialist ventures such as the Vietnam War [...], and the exploitation of natural resources—all instances of violence and from an A'atsika perspective signs of a deep hostility against other living beings—hence contribute to the derailment of the world.
>
> (279)

To make amends and restore spiritual balance to the tribal world, a sacrifice proportional to the magnitude of the request would be necessary.

Hogan's previous novel, *Power*, also pivots on the meaning of sacrifice. Ama has to pay the highest price if she wants to heal the dying world—by killing the sacred clan animal she almost literally kills herself. As a person-in-relation who derives her identity from the community she is part of, she sacrifices herself so that her world might thrive. This is what a mature human is expected to do. In *People of the Whale* it is Ruth who represents her community, asking the old people to intercede in her name with spiritual powers capable of bringing down rain. But to save the land[4] from drought, she must be prepared to offer what is most precious to her, and even this may not be enough. In the hunt she has lost her only son, Marco, and now she is asked for the fishing boat, which is her home and her livelihood. Loving the world as she does, Ruth accepts the terms of the deal without much regard for her own future. Unknown to her (as I shall discuss later), Thomas has added the missing part of the sacrifice in order to make up for his own contribution to the spiritual imbalance.

Born with gills and spending much time in and around water, Ruth is a reincarnation of another transformational character—a girl from the sea who came "to make the People into what they were to be" (*People* 56). An old A'atsika story says:

> every morning [the girl] rose from the sea and went to bed where she looked like a normal human coming out of the house. But from the sea she brought knowledge. She came in with the sounds of the ocean and she sang them to the people [...]. She protected the sea and the animals.
>
> (*People* 56)

Ruth is a woman of compassion, a strong and wise person who watches over the sea and its animals and who eventually helps other characters to become mature humans. When Dark River is sinking in despair, she is determined to hold on and help to revive the traditional A'atsika way. Abandoned by her husband, she nonetheless feels bound to him in a spiritual way, continues to care for him, brings him food, fears for his safety, and watches over his secret diving exercises at night. Like her mythical counterpart, Ruth is a woman of the sea who has left her native element because she is needed on earth. She knows who can plead for rain.

With his thin legs, slender hands, shyness, and love for shiny objects, the Rain Priest is surprisingly octopus-like in appearance. And indeed, "not being fully human" (*People* 133), he is the same octopus—now shapeshifted—who had walked out of the sea when Thomas was born. "Everything here is out of balance" (*People* 143), he says about the conditions at Dark River. When he returns to the town after a short absence, he says only: "it's restored" (*People* 149). The long-awaited rain soon comes and with it come shocking revelations of Dwight's criminal double-dealing, complete with punishment—his newly built house collapses in the same mudslide which has returned the past to the people in the form of the ancient shell houses that had lain buried in the ground. When the two finally meet, Ruth has compassion for the Rain Priest, the man who took away—in the form of partial payment for his services—the most valuable thing she had:

She sees that he is an inward kind of man. When she talks to him, she gets the feeling that he might cry easily. His must be a very hard life. She thinks he would like to be ordinary. He would like to work at a gas station or garage or even a 7-Eleven, or as a greeter at the new Wal-Mart near the city. And he is a kind man. He has a calm face. His countenance is special. A normal life has not been chosen for him. Like the rain, he has his job to do. Just like prayers are sometimes only one-sided, so is he. Just as light enters the sky and falls to earth, this is his life. As water falls from the heaviness of pregnant clouds. She suddenly feels as much compassion for him, as he did for her. He thanks her for it, as if reading her thoughts. "Yes, it is my work."

(People 148–149)

In the world of traditional cultures life is scripted in a particular way: persons (human, nonhuman, or not-quite-human) are born with a particular destiny, a job to do, and a sacrifice is inscribed into it. Ama Eaton, Ruth, the Rain Priest, but also Thomas and Marco have been chosen; they live with the burden of responsibility, an obligation to be equal to the task entrusted to them by a creative force that watches over the world. Its accomplishment is directly related to the chosen one's spiritual purity and her or his embeddedness in tradition.

"Want a different ethic? Tell a different story," quips Thomas King (qtd. in Harrison, 6). Disaster need not be a one-way street leading straight to an apocalypse. It can be a space of renewed beginnings, an opportunity to put the world right, to rebalance what has been upset. In Hogan's novels such a new beginning is always the work of compassion, as well as *com-passion*—the ability to suffer with, an openness to the pain inflicted on other beings. More often than not, it is animals who excel at compassion and teach it to those humans who are still attuned to the speech of creation. Mercy and compassion have become the key concepts in Hogan's creative work in recent decades. It is in compassion that healing begins. The power to contain the hatred and destruction resulting from centuries of violence belongs to compassionate beings, human and not (quite) human. By resuming responsibilities for the community of all earthly beings, they rebalance the world. The world can continue because of them.

Ruth's willingness to sacrifice all she had to restore harmony to her world was more important than the actual offering she made, though. Her fishing boat, offered to the Rain Priest in exchange for his job, is found abandoned far out at sea, a giant octopus climbing out of it. A pearl, the gift of the mother of Thomas to the octopus from Seal Cave, is discovered lying on Ruth's bed. The Rain Priest knows Ruth needs the boat more than he does. He has compassion for her. What Hogan is saying through this scene is that the purity of intention can be enough to begin to set the world right. This is also what we all can do right now, in the face of anthropogenic climate change and the sixth great extinction.

If compassion and purity of motive can save the world, the opposite is also true. Characters unable to *feel with* and *suffer with* others—in other words, those who are unable to relate to other beings in the right way—are capable of committing the most atrocious crimes and acts of unmotivated cruelty. Dwight and his followers laugh, joke, and swear while slaughtering the whale with automatic weapons, just as they slaughtered men, women, and children in Vietnam. Himself animalized by white America, Dwight exhibits indifference to other animalized people and to animals alike. Back from the war, when attempting to intimidate Ruth and suppress her protest against the proposed hunt, he kills her dog. Hoist was a stray who followed Ruth and who ultimately became her and her father's "little canine assistant" (*People* 32). He slept in Ruth's bed, dragged the fishing nets with his teeth "as if to help" (*People* 32), and played cheerfully with the waves. Loved by everyone, the dog was part of Ruth's family until one morning she found him bleeding to death, killed by the man who would later kill her son and attempt to kill her husband.

The tragic death of a beloved dog is a constant in Hogan's novels,[5] but in *People of the Whale* the dog becomes a target of deliberate violence, rather than an accidental victim. Hoist, an innocent creature, is killed by a mentally colonized and spiritually dead A'atsika. Imitating the white men whose war he fought in the jungles of Vietnam, Dwight becomes spiritually alienated from his tradition, renouncing kinship with nonhuman animals and betraying his tribal family as a consequence. Lacking compassion, he regards Hoist and whales as *zoe*—killable life—and extends this category to Marco and Thomas. Like Hannah Wing, Dwight becomes a Windigo, a greedy monster with a heart of ice.

Paradoxically, the man who refused to grant value to a dog's life was not unlike a dog himself. The piece of metal he had worn around his wrist as a soldier in Vietnam, containing details of his identity, was called a dog tag for a reason. Having received her missing husband's dog tag, Ruth muses:

> Dog, that was a man in war. Dog. He had to follow orders. He had to sniff for danger, be willing to die for his owner. He had to hate strangers, be wary, be nothing, be kicked and hungry and still obey. [...] Dog, what Thomas and so many others had been.
>
> (35)

By having Dwight kill an actual dog, Hogan seems to be making a statement about the self-destructiveness of violence. The man who wore the dog tag in the prolonged state of exception called war lives in self-hatred and ultimately destroys himself.

Serving their master—the US Army—with their bodies, Dwight, Thomas, and other soldiers were supposed to take orders unquestioningly, like well-trained dogs, whose only value lay in blind obedience. A well-trained dog is a colonized dog, completely estranged from his wolf's nature. Some dogs, however, retain traces of wildness, and Thomas was one of them. Thomas questioned orders. He protested against being air dropped in a place he knew to be too far south, outside the war zone, having to kill peasants and watch his colleagues' wanton cruelty toward women, old men, and babies. Unlike Dwight, Thomas had compassion; under his military uniform he was still alive. He killed his own men, who had become monster killers in the grip of war, to save the rice-growing villagers who only wanted to live, like all earth beings do.

Thomas survived the war because he was an Indian who trusted his animal instinct and took animal lessons seriously. In the face of invisible danger lurking in the jungle, he "became a snake in his movement, a lizard with his eyes, seeing, seeing. He thought like a lynx. [...] His body had eyes. His back had eyes. His fingers had eyes" (*People* 172). The wildness inside him responded to the untamed nature all around. He also grieved at the destruction of the land, the contaminated rice fields, the burned trees. "Thomas, the grandson of Witka, who respected life, grieved" (*People* 173). This man who would get medals for bravery cried just once, when someone mistakenly shot a rabbit, thinking it was the enemy. Thomas grieved for the "softly furred" creature "with dark eyes, and running to hide" (*People* 166). The innocent creature just wanted to live, like everybody else, Thomas included. Given half a chance, he knew he would do exactly what the rabbit did: he would run to hide—which he eventually did, having killed his fellow-soldiers. Looking at the destroyed termite mounds—"which he thought most beautiful, like the land itself" (*People* 167)—he admired the insects' indomitable spirit as they went about rebuilding their lives from scratch, just like the Vietnamese did, over and over again. He saw the tragic history of Indigenous America being repeated in this distant world and threw his lot in with the victims, starting a new life with the people of the land, an Indigenous tribe from the mountains.

By saving the villagers, Thomas had righted his relations with the new land community, and the land accepted him. He worked in the rice paddies now and blended with the people who had adopted him. He was part of a people again. But he knew his destructive potential and the seductive appeal of his inner darkness. He realized that forging relations with the wrong persons—human and not (quite) human—transforms one into a monster, even though there is no visible change in appearance. There is a kind of shapeshifting that takes place in the spiritual dimension only. With "brother M16 and AK and grenades" he was no longer Thomas, he was a monster, like Dwight and so many others. "What a family he and his weapons were together" (*People* 175), Thomas agonizes from a distance of two decades. But he also knows that "the thing he'd done that was dishonorable [killing American soldiers] was the only, most honorable thing he'd done the whole time" (*People* 180). Like Ama Eaton, he was wrong and not wrong simultaneously.

Realization of the darkness within brings humility and awareness of a shared human condition. "It was a world of doubleness," the novel's narrator writes. "There are no clear lines between evil and good. He is both. This is the slow dawn of his knowing" (*People* 136). Thomas is becoming a mature human being. He will no longer be able to condemn anyone for what he himself was guilty of doing. Back in Dark River, he cannot refuse to give Dwight a second chance, even knowing he has killed his son, Marco. After the disastrous whale hunt, in which he himself was the first to pull the trigger, instinctively, as he had done at war, Thomas decides he wants "to be remembered as the man who could kill but doesn't" (*People* 270). His desire to say no to the violence in him illustrates the power to say no that Hogan believes to be the mark of mature humanity (*Dark* 343). After years of hiding, hating himself, and being "sorry to be a human being" (*People* 275), Thomas slowly starts to care again. His sacrifice to rebalance the world consists in telling the truth about his war crime, compensating Ruth for her years of raising Marco without his help, and reconnecting with Lin, his daughter in Vietnam. He also practices diving like Witka did, wanting to relearn the sea and tradition. Thomas wants again to be a part of the people of the whale.

The inner man shapeshifts once more. Freed by truth, Thomas feels as if he is "a cocoon, soft and new, shining. The dead heart falls away and there is a new one, alive and beating" (*People* 268). He fasts and stays with the old people, paddling and learning the old songs. The sea forgives Thomas and opens its secrets to him. And one day, when diving, he hears

> a low rumble of a whale and it comes to him and it looks at him with its wise old eye and he knows everything in that gaze. He knows how small a human is, not in size but in other ways. As he rises to the surface, it helps him, pushes him slowly and it exhales a breath as he surfaces, too, gasping for air.
>
> (*People* 283)

Like the Florida panther, Sisa, in *Power*, the whale holds a human with her gaze and sees his poverty and vulnerability. And also, like Sisa, she takes pity on humans, knowing she has to help them become what they were meant to be. Coming from a people birthed by a whale, Thomas experiences a rebirth, being pushed up out of the water to take a breath that is synchronized with the breath of his whale ancestor. Having been healed and accepted, he becomes an interpreter of the sea, as his grandfather once had been, bringing the elders a message of hope:

> We are going to be a better people. That is our job now. We are going to be good people. The ocean says we are not going to kill the whales until some year when it may be right. They are our mothers. They are our grandmothers. It is our job to care for them. And an old whale song "comes to him out of a hole opened in time."
>
> (*People* 283–284)

Even though some A'atsika men are still torn between their longing for tradition and their loyalty to their former leader Dwight, when the latter shoots Thomas on a paddling trip, they ultimately denounce him for this and his other crimes and send him to prison, healing themselves in the process. Meanwhile Thomas, given up for dead, is washed ashore and possibly brought back to life by an old person who knows the Rain Priest. Hogan is aware how incredible this twist in the story may sound, but she is determined to tell a story which holds hope for the future. This is part of her literary activism. Thomas's surprising survival is neither more nor less improbable than the story of Jonah traveling in the body of a whale—a story from "the book written by many men who heard the voices of their own gods" (*People* 289), which Hogan's characters often find fault with and therefore supplement with stories derived from their own spiritual traditions. So, Thomas is "washed up from the Great Mysterious," naked, like a newborn. He may have been saved by the giant octopus who had watched him when he was a baby, and then carried to land by "the whale who heard his song and recalled it and knew his intentions" (*People* 289). As the novel's narrator asserts, "[i]ntentions are everything to the whale" (*People* 290). After his miraculous rescue, the old people know that Thomas "is equal to it" (*People* 293), which means that he has become a true human, a person ready to take Witka's place and lead his people to spiritual wholeness.

As for Marco, he was a true human already before his death, knowing himself to be related to the whale. His and the whale's blood mixed together on the day of the hunt. To Ruth and the tribal elders, Marco is "the boy who went to live with the whales" (*People* 258). Born with webbed feet, he was a transformational being and he returned to the sea. Ruth's intuition is confirmed by Thomas. When asked why his son did not wash up the way he did, he answers: "He had other places to go" (*People* 292). As argued by Joni Adamson, "[i]n the context of the oral traditions of many North American indigenous cultures, Hogan's description of Marco implies that he is a transformational being about to take the shape of human or whale" (31). Having become a man "for the purpose of interacting with humans" (Adamson 31–32), Marco returns to whale shape when his task among humans is accomplished.

His mother Ruth, however, remains with humans. Unable to breathe air at birth and kept in a water tank until her gills were sewn up, she is another transformational being and her task is to assist at the birth of new humanity which will be compassionate and kind, and will respect their obligations to human and nonhuman lives. As she is shown to be taking care of Dwight's pregnant girlfriend, it is implied that she will help to bring up the girl's child—the tribe's hope for the future—as a new human.

All four novels Hogan has published so far end on the same hopeful note: a newborn child announces the triumph of life over death and spells a new chance for humanity. In *People of the Whale*, however, the future is most radically associated with transformational beings who assist at its birth and a maternal presence who watches over it. Birthed by ancestor whale—a mammal who once walked the earth as humans do now but returned to water to live like a fish—the new humanity must be transformational, humanimal itself. Hopefully, it will be friendly like the gray whales who, despite their traumatic memories, seek contact with their former hunters to show them their newborn babies.

Notes

1 The gray whale was delisted in 1994.
2 The other two novels by trans-Pacific Indigenous authors referred to by Huang are: Maori writer Witi Ihimaera's *Whale Rider* (1987) and Taiwanese writer Syaman Rapongan's *Eyes in the Sky* (2012).
3 Steinwand's observation that Indigenous people and whales are figures of "liminality and ambiguity" causes Huang, justifiably, to object to its colonialist implications (Huang 126).
4 "Land" denotes here the extended concept of the land-and-water-multispecies-community that Ruth is a part of.
5 In *Mean Spirit* Belle's dog dies in the explosion of the Grayclouds' house; in *Solar Storms* Hannah Wing tortures the family dog to death by feeding him needles, as if replaying Hogan's traumatic recollections of her older daughter's abusive deed.

Conclusions

Implications for Interspecies Thriving in the Literary Works of Linda Hogan

It is difficult if not impossible to imagine a permanent end to the war against animals within a worldview organized around the notions of difference and human dominance. Still, a truce—however fragile—in the ongoing hostilities may, as suggested by Wadiwel, open the space for the emergence of alternative, nonhierarchical solutions capable of offering nonhuman animals the right to participate in the public arena on their own merits, as agents rather than objects of 'care.' Whatever emerges in the space of such a truce, however, would have to be called into existence with utmost caution and full consciousness of the risks involved (see Stengers 1003).

The recent ontological turn in the social sciences has already questioned the hegemony of Western thought, postulating a 'flattening out' of ontological hierarchies and an openness to the entanglements of co-evolving, co-emerging agents, human and nonhuman alike. Inspired by Whiteheadian process philosophy and the Deleuzian concept of 'becoming-animal,' the new materialists have declared agency to be an inherent feature of all matter, discovering surprising (for themselves) convergencies with Indigenous ontologies.

That Indigenous ecological knowledges are starting to be considered indispensable to any serious conversation about the Anthropocene and sustainable futures is a hopeful sign. A number of recent academic publications attest to this new opening. Among them are *Humankind: Solidarity with Nonhuman People* by Timothy Morton (2017), *Ecocene Politics* by Mihnea Tănăsescu (2022), and *Animals as Legal Beings: Contesting Anthropocentric Legal Orders* by Maneesha Deckha (2021). In an attempt to transcend the 'tipping point' of the Anthropocene and in conversation with Māori conceptualizations of kinship with nonhumans, Tănăsescu emphasizes the need to find creative solutions to the ongoing anthropogenic disaster. In the Ecocene—or the age of ecology—he finds it crucial to reimagine relationships with creatures and processes that co-constitute the human. The nurturing ethos of traditional land-based societies offers alternatives to the exploitative, extractivist practices of Western colonialism.

DOI: 10.4324/9781003364252-13

To legal scholar Maneesha Deckha, interspecies justice is integral to reconciliation efforts in settler colonial states like Canada. Based as it is on binary oppositions which prioritize humans over nature understood as resources, Western law effaces Indigenous subjecthood, which derives from one's relationship to the entire ecological community. Decolonizing Indigenous subjecthood implies incorporation of pre-colonial legal traditions into the dominant legal system. Already the inclusion of the rights of Indigenous people into the Universal Declaration of Human Rights, Deckha believes, promises the extension of legal protection to nonhuman subjects, bound by kincentric relationships of reciprocity with their Indigenous relatives ("Unsettling ..." 85). To avoid cultural mistranslations, however, she argues for "beingness" rather than personhood as a new, decolonial legal subjectivity for animals—a subjectivity built on Indigenous concepts integrated with the feminist animal care ethic, the concepts of embodiment, and relationality (*Animals as Legal Beings*).

In this monograph, I have tried to offer glimpses of a potential interspecies cosmopolis based on the social imaginaries of inhabitants indigenous to Turtle Island, in which animals are persons in their own right. In the process I hope to have demonstrated that Linda Hogan's creative works exemplify a nonanthropocentric animal ethics that has practical consequences for human-animal wellbeing and collective survivance well beyond first nations contexts.

From her earliest to her most recent publications, Hogan has been constructing a world hospitable to all inhabitants of planet Earth, whether two-, four-, or no-legged. Hailing from a people who have barely survived the genocide of history, she is also related to those who dispossessed her Indigenous ancestors of their lands and who poisoned, slaughtered, and in many other ways diminished the infinitely rich forms of life that had coevolved with humans on the North American continent. Re-membering the past, mourning the damage, and denouncing the evil done, Hogan nonetheless does not draw comforting divisions "about who killed whom." With victim and victimizer "crowded together and knock[ing] at each other at night" in her own body, Hogan knows "amnesty" is what we all need (*Dark*, "The Truth Is" 65). Rather than pointing the accusing finger, she attempts to map a sustainable future for all. When the lessons of the past have been learned and traditional worldviews revived, the anthropogenic destruction can be stopped, she hopes, and perhaps even reversed.

Assuming a radical commonality of experience across the species line, Hogan advances a nonprescriptive ethic of respect, a praxis of constant renegotiation of human-animal obligations that arise from the urgencies of the moment. Rather than abstract moral codes, she insists, human-animal relations should be regulated by a context-sensitive "reflection regarding what are the right things for me to do," as Brian Burkhart phrases it (216).

In the world created in the pages of Hogan's works, morality inheres in response-ability to the pleas of human and nonhuman agents, as much as it does on obeying the lessons and respecting the wisdom of our animal ancestors. In Indigenous imaginaries morality is a two-way street and humans and animals depend on each other for the full actualization of who we all are as social, relational beings enmeshed in networks of reciprocity. The most persistent message Hogan is sending through her activist literary works is probably this: that the achievement of a true human status depends, in the short run, on respect for, and obedience to, our animal ancestors; in the long run, however, the future may be tied to our 'becoming animal.'

With their survival depending on a skillful navigation of the rights of, and their obligations toward, the whole of the nonhuman world, many premodern nations consider animals as peoples in their own right, with their own interests and complex intertribal relationships, which include humans. Co-creators of the world, ancestors, relatives, and law-givers, animals are to be treated with respect and allowed to live according to their own natures, the taking of life reserved to matters of necessity and ceremonial obligations. But even those Indigenous societies whose cultural survival depends on repeating the sacrificial hunt (in fulfillment of the originary pact sealed between their human and animal ancestors at the beginning of time) recognize the equally sacred obligation to renegotiate treaties whenever circumstances change, the extinction of species being one case in point.

Threatened by disappearance, some animals may need active protection, including instituting a moratorium on hunting, even for subsistence purposes. When this happens, new forms of traditional community-building rituals may appear, more consonant with the evolved human sensitivity which centers mercy and compassion. Although Hogan honors Indigenous nations' right to hunt as part of their cultural identity and recognizes the sacred function of tradition for Indigenous survival, her belief in transformation as the only constant and in compassion as the mark of true humanity opens a way to speculation that she would embrace a future in which the cultural and bonding function of hunting might be replaced by other, bloodless ceremonies. This would be consonant with efforts of Indigenous scholars, such as Mi'kmaq Margaret Robinson, who explore the vegan potential of Indigenous teachings[1] and thus credit abstention from the use of animal products with decolonizing capabilities. In the main, however, Hogan recognizes the universality of predation in the natural world. When all food is ensouled, the human/animal difference dissolves further and humans resume their place in the food chain. The fact that all life feeds on other life is an important lesson that Hogan's animal and human ancestors have taught her. Respectful hunting, combined with gratitude for the gift of life for food, seems thus a responsible alternative—at least for the moment—not only to the cruelties of industrial fishing and farming, which frame animals as objects, but also to the often unsustainable methods of production and transportation of fashionable plant-based foods for commercial vegan markets.

Closure is alien to Native philosophy. In a sentient world inhabited by agential, choice-making beings, the unfolding of the world never stops, each experience being a unique moment and a new manifestation of this unfolding. Etymologically considered, conclusions (from the Latin *concludere* meaning "shut up," "enclose") bring an argument to an end; they terminate the case. The concern which lies at the heart of this book, that of human-animal cosmopolis and multispecies thriving at the time of the Anthropocene—a.k.a Capitalocene or Plantationocene—is too complex and context-sensitive to be 'enclosed' by solutions abstracted from particular, experiential relations. The conclusions must, therefore, remain open to the realignments and renegotiations of mutual interspecies duties and obligations that arise in the context of locality.

Note

1 Arguing for Indigenous veganism as a decolonizing practice, Robinson claims: "Hunting was a traditionally male activity connected with the maintenance of virility. The killing of a moose symbolized a boy's entry into manhood. So when you challenge the hunting traditions, you're challenging how Mi'kmaq men understand their masculinity. At the same time, I want to suggest that the context in which Aboriginal gender identity develops has changed significantly since colonization. Meat, as a symbol of patriarchy, actually binds us closer to white colonial culture, than practices such as veganism do." She also asserts that her Mi'kmaq-inspired veganism is "a spiritual practice that reflects the fact that humans and other animals possess a shared personhood." Robinson, n.p.

Bibliography

"2020 Panther Pulse." *Florida Fish and Wildlife Conservation Commission.* https://myfwc.com/wildlifehabitats/wildlife/panther/pulse/.

Abram, David. *Becoming Animal: An Earthly Cosmology.* Vintage, 2011.

Abram, David. *The Spell of the Sensuous: Perception and Language in a More-than-Human World.* Vintage, 1997.

Adams, Carol. *Sexual Politics of Meat: A Feminist-Vegetarian Critical Theory.* Continuum, 1990.

Adamson, Joni. "Whale as Cosmos: Multi-Species Ethnography and Contemporary Indigenous Cosmopolitics." *Revista Canaria de Estudios Ingleses*, vol. 64, April 2012, pp. 29–45.

Adamson, Joni and Michael Davis (eds.). *Humanities for the Environment: Integrating Knowledge, Forging New Constellations of Practice.* Routledge, 2016.

Alaimo, Stacy. "'Skin Dreaming': The Bodily Transgressions of Fielding Burke, Octavia Butler, and Linda Hogan." In *Ecofeminist Literary Criticism: Theory, Interpretation, Pedagogy.* Edited by Greta Gaard and Patrick D. Murphy. University of Illinois Press, 1998, pp. 123–138.

Alcoff, Linda Martín. "Epistemologies of Ignorance: Three Types." In *Race and Epistemologies of Ignorance.* Edited by Shannon Sullivan and Nancy Tuana. State University of New York Press, 2007, pp. 39–58.

Anderson, Eric Gary. "States of Being in the Dark: Removal and Survival in Linda Hogan's *Mean Spirit.*" *Great Plains Quarterly*, vol. 20, Winter 2000, pp. 55–67.

"Animal Feeding Operations." National Resource Conservation Service. U.S. Department of Agriculture. https://www.nrcs.usda.gov/wps/portal/nrcs/main/national/plantsanimals/livestock/afo/.

Avargues-Weber, Aurore, Geoffrey Portelli, Julie Bénard, Adrian Dyer, and Martin Giurfa. "Configural Processing Enables Discrimination And Categorization of Face-Like Stimuli in Honeybees." *Journal of Experimental Biology*, vol. 213, no. 4, 2010, pp. 593–601.

Backcountry Chronicles: DIY Hunting, Fishing and Outdoor Tips. https://www.backcountrychronicles.com/.

Bartlett, Cheryl, Murdena Marshall and Albert Marshall. (2012). "Two-Eyed Seeing and Other Lessons Learned Within a Co-Learning Journey of Bringing Together Indigenous and Mainstream Knowledges and Ways of Knowing." *Journal of Environmental Studies and Sciences*, vol. 2, 2012, pp. 331–340. https://doi.org/10.1007/s13412-012-0086-8.

Baumel, Alan. "Linda Hogan on *A History of Kindness*: 'I Would Call this Book a Tree.'" *Southern Review of Books*, 2013, vol. 12. https://southernreviewofbooks.com/2020/08/17/a-story-of-kindness-linda-hogan-interview/. Accessed: August 17, 2020.

Bekoff, Marc. *Coyotes: Biology, Behavior, and Management*. Academic Press, Inc., 1978.

Belcourt, Billy-Ray. "Animal Bodies, Colonial Subjects: (Re)Locating Animality in Decolonial Thought." *Societies*, vol. 5, no. 1, 2015, pp. 1–11. https://doi.org/10.3390/soc5010001.

Belle, Betty Louise. "Introduction: Linda Hogan's Lessons in Making Do." *Studies in American Indian Literatures*, vol. 6, no. 3, fall 1994, pp. 3–5.

Berkes, Fikret. "Traditional Ecological Knowledge in Perspective." In *Traditional Ecological Knowledge: Concepts and Cases*. Edited by Julian T. Inglis. International Program on Traditional Ecological Knowledge, International Development Research Centre, 1993, pp. 2–10.

Bevis, William. "Native American Novels: Homing In." In *Recovering the Word: Essays on Native American Literature*. Edited by Brian Swann and Arnold Krupat. University of California Press, 1987, pp. 580–620.

Blaser, Mario. "Is Another Cosmopolitics Possible?" *Cultural Anthropology*, vol. 31, no. 4, 2016, pp. 545–570. https://doi.org/10.14506/ca31.4.05.

Bohm, David. *Wholeness and the Implicate Order*. Routledge, 1980.

Bradshaw, Gay. *Carnivore Minds: Who These Fearsome Animals Really Are*. Yale University Press, 2017.

Brígido-Corachán, Anna. "Native Waterscapes in the Northern Borderlands: Restoring Traditional Environmental Knowledge in Linda Hogan's *Solar Storms*." *Revista de Estudios Norteamericanos*, vol. 22, 2018, pp. 37–57.

"Buffalo Kills and Genocide." *Investing in Native Communities*. https://nativephilanthropy.candid.org/events/buffalo-kills-and-genocide/. Accessed: 15 Feb. 2021.

Burkhart, Brian. *Indigenizing Philosophy through the Land: A Trickster Methodology for Decolonizing Environmental Ethics and Indigenous Futures*. Michigan State University Press, 2019.

Cajete, Gregory. *Native Science: Natural Laws of Interdependence*. Clear Light Books, 2000.

Cajete, Gregory. "Philosophy of Native Science." In *American Indian Thought: Philosophical Essays*. Edited by Anne Waters. Blackwell Publishing, 2007, pp. 45–57.

Calarco, Matthew. *Zoographies: The Question of the Animal from Heidegger to Derrida*. Columbia University Press, 2008.

Carew-Miller. "Caretaking and the Work of the Text in Linda Hogan's *Mean Spirit*." *Studies in American Indian Literatures*, vol. 6, no. 3, Fall 1994, pp. 37–48.

Chloë Taylor, "Respect for the (Animal) Dead." In *Animal Death*. Edited by Jay Johnston and Fiona Probyn-Rapsey. Sydney University Press, 2013.

Clausewitz von, Carl. *On War*. Edited and translated by Michael Howard and Peter Paret. Princeton University Press, 1984.

Clausewitz von, Carl. *Security, Territory, Population. Lectures at the Collège de France, 1977–78.* Edited by Michel Senellart, translated by Graham Burchell. Plagrave Macmillian, 2009.

"Co wiemy o BSE - Chorobie szalonych krów" [What we know about the mad cow disease]." *Wwiadomości.wp.pl*, May 4, 2002. https://wiadomosci.wp.pl/co-wiemy-o-bse-chorobie-szalonych-krow-6109001210381441a. Accessed: December 6, 2020.

Coetzee, John Maxwell. *The Lives of Animals.* Princeton University Press, 1999.

Collin, Yvette. "Running Horse." *The Relationship Between the Indigenous Peoples of the Americas and the Horse: Deconstructing a Eurocentric Myth*, Ph.D., University of Alaska Fairbanks, 2017. ProQuest LLC.

Cook, Barbara J. "From the Center of Tradition: An Interview with Linda Hogan." In *From the Center of Tradition: Critical Perspectives on Linda Hogan.* Edited by Barbara J. Cook. University Press of Colorado, 2003: pp. 11–16.

Cooper, Lydia R. "'Woman Chasing Her God': Ritual, Renewal, and Violence in Linda Hogan's Power." *Interdisciplinary Studies in Literature and Environment*, vol. 18, no. 1, winter 2011, pp. 143–159.

Coulthard, Glen. *Red Skins, White Masks: Rejecting the Colonial Politics of Recognition.* University of Minnesota Press, 2014.

Crutzen, Paul J. and Eugene F. Stoermer. The "Anthropocene." *Global Change Newsletter*, vol. 41, 2000, pp. 17–18.

De la Cadena, Marisol. "Indigenous Cosmopolitics in the Andes: Conceptual Reflections Beyond 'Politics.'" *Cultural Anthropology*, vol. 25, no. 2, 2010, pp. 334–370. https://doi.org/10.1111/j.1548-1360.2010.01061.x.

De Waal, Frans. *Primates and Philosophers: How Morality Evolved.* Princeton University Press, 2006.

Deckha, Maneesha. *Animals as Legal Beings: Contesting Anthropocentric Legal Orders.* University of Toronto Press, 2021.

Deckha, Maneesha. "Unsettling Anthropocentric Legal Systems: Reconciliation, Indigenous Laws, and Animal Personhood." *Journal of Intercultural Studies*, vol. 41, no 1, 2020, pp. 77–97.

Deckha, Maneesha. "The Subhuman as a Cultural Agent of Violence." *Journal for Critical Animal Studies*, vol. 8, no. 3, 2010, pp. 28–51.

Domańska, Ewa. "Humanistyka ekologiczna." *Teksty Drugie*, vol. 1–2, 2013, pp. 13–32.

Donaldson, Sue and Will Kymlicka. "Animal Rights and Aboriginal Rights." In *Perspectives on Animals and the Law in Canada.* Edited by Peter Sankoff, Vaughan Black and Katie Sykes. Irwin Law, 2015, pp. 159–86.

Donaldson, Sue and Will Kymlicka. *Zoopolis: A Political Theory of Animal Rights.* Oxford University Press, 2013.

Dreese, Donelle N. "The Terrestrial and Aquatic Intelligence of Linda Hogan." *Studies in American Indian Literatures*, vol. 11, no. 4, 1999, pp. 6–22.

D'Souza, Tony. "Poor, Black, and Sick Floridians Battle Big Sugar in Court." *Miami New Times*, February 2, 2021. https://www.miaminewtimes.com/news/where-to-get-the-pfizer-vaccine-in-miami-florida-12263504.

Dworkin, Andrea and Catherine MacKinnon. *Pornography and Civil Rights: A New Day for Women's Equality.* Organizing Against Pornography, 1988.

Elgezeery, Gamal Muhammad. "'Boundaries Are All Lies': The Fluidity of Boundaries in Linda Hogan's The Book of Medicines." *International Journal of Linguistics and Literature*, vol. 2, no. 2, May 2013, pp. 17–24.

Elżanowski, Andrzej. "Dzika rzeź." *Polityka*, vol. 35, 28.08.2018, p. 26.

Feinstein, Kelly, "A Brief History of the Beaver Trade." *Fashionable Felted Fur: The Beaver Hat in 17th Century English Society*. March 2006, https://humwp .ucsc.edu/cwh/feinstein/A%20brief%20history%20of%20the%20beaver %20trade.html.

Fix, Adam, Hugh Burnam and Ray Gutteriez. "Toward Interspecies Thinking as a Collaborative Concept: Autoethnographies at the Intersection of Traditional Ecological Knowledge and Animal Studies." *Humanimalia: A Journal of Human-Animal Interface Studies*, vol. 10, no. 2, 2019, pp. 128–149.

"Florida Panther." U.S. Fish & Wildlife Service. https://www.fws.gov/refuge/ florida_panther/wah/panther.html.

Frank, Priscilla. "The Inuit Punk Throat Singer Fighting To Protect Indigenous Women." *Huffington Post*. www.huffpost.com. Accessed: 11/02/2016.

Gandhi, Leela. *Affective Communities: Anticolonial Thought, Fin-de-Siècle Radicalism, and the Politics of Friendship*. Duke University Press, 2006.

Gavillon, François. "Magical Realism, Spiritual Realism, And Ecological Awareness in Linda Hogan's *People of the Whale. ELOHI—Indigenous People and the Environment*, vol. 3, Jan–June 2013, pp. 41–56. *Open Edition Journals*. https:// journals.openedition.org/elohi/602.

Geroux, Robert. "Introduction to the Special Issue: Decolonizing Animals." *Humanimalia: A Journal of Human-Animal Interface Studies*, vol. 10, no. 2, spring 2019, pp.1–6.

Harrison, Summer. "'We Need New Stories': Trauma, Storytelling, and the Mapping of Environmental Injustice in Linda Hogan's *Solar Storms and Standing Rock*." *American Indian Quarterly*, vol. 43, no. 1, winter 2019, pp. 1–35.

Harvey, Graham. "Animism and Ecology: Participating in the World Community." *The Ecological Citizen*, no. 3, 2019, pp. 79–84.

Harvey, Graham. Introduction to *The Handbook of Contemporary Animism*. Edited by Graham Harvey, Routledge, 2013, pp. 1–13.

Henderson, Claire. *The Aboriginal North American Horse*. Laval University, 1991.

Hogan, Linda. *A History of Kindness*. Torrey House Press, 2020.

Hogan, Linda. "Ancient Root." *Emergence Magazine: Ecology, Culture, and Spirituality*. 15 April 2019. https://emergencemagazine.org/story/ancient-root/. Accessed: October 2020.

Hogan, Linda. "Backbone: Holding Up Our Future." In *Humanities for the Environment: Integrating Knowledge, Forging New Constellations of Practice*. Edited by Joni Adamson and Michael Davis. Routledge, 2017, pp. 20–32.

Hogan, Linda. *Dark. Sweet: New and Selected Poems*. Coffee House Press, 2014.

Hogan, Linda. *Dwellings: A Spiritual History of the Living World*. W.W. Norton & Company, 1995.

Hogan, Linda. *Eclipse*. American Indian Studies Center: University of California, 1983.

Hogan, Linda. "First People." In *Intimate Nature: The Bond Between Women and Animals*. Edited by Linda Hogan, Deena Metzger, and Brenda Peterson. The Ballantine Publishing Book, 1998, pp. 6–19.

Hogan, Linda. "Foreword: Viola Cordova—Perspectives by Linda Hogan." In *How is It: The Native American Philosophy of V. F. Cordova*. Edited by Kathleen Dean Moore, Kurt Peters, Ted Jojola, and Amber Lacy. University of Arizona Press, 2007, pp. vii–xi.

Hogan, Linda. *Mean Spirit*. Ivy Books, 1990.

Hogan, Linda. *People of the Whale*. W.W Norton & Company, 2008.

Hogan, Linda. *Power*. W.W Norton & Company, 1998.

Hogan, Linda. *Solar Storms*. Scribner, 1995.

Hogan, Linda. *The Radiant Lives of Animals*. Beacon Press, 2020.

Hogan, Linda. *The Woman Who Watches Over the World: A Native Memoir*. W.W Norton & Company, 2001.

Hogan, Linda. "We Call It Tradition." In *The Handbook of Contemporary Animism*. Edited by Graham Harvey, Routledge, 2013, pp. 17–26.

Hogan, Linda. "Why We Are Singing for Water: In Front of Men With Guns and Surveillance Helicopters." *Yes! Magazine*, Oct. 4, 2016. https://www .yesmagazine.org/democracy/2016/10/04/to-the-standing-rock-sioux-who-are -singing-for-water/.

"Hogan, Linda 1947-." *Contemporary Authors. Encyclopedia.com*. 15 Apr. 2021 https://www.encyclopedia.com.

Hogan, Linda and Brenda Peterson. *Sightings: The Gray Whale's Mysterious Journey*. National Geographic, 2002.

Hogan, Linda, Deena Metzger and Brenda Peterson. *Introduction to Intimate Nature: The Bond Between Women and Animals*. Fawcett Columbine, 1998, pp. xi–xvi.

Holy Bible. New International Version, Zondervan Publishing House, 1984.

Huang, Hsinya. "Toward Transpacific Ecopoetics: Three Indigenous Texts." *Comparative Literature Studies*, vol. 50, no. 1. Special Issue: Sustaining Ecocriticism: Comparative Perspectives, 2013, pp. 120–147.

Huang, Peter I-min. *Linda Hogan and Contemporary Taiwanese Writers: An Ecocritical Study of Indigeneities and Environment*. Lexington Books, 2015.

Hubbard, Tasha. "Buffalo Genocide in Nineteenth-Century North America: 'Kill, Skin, and Sell.'" In *Colonial Genocide in Indigenous North America*. Edited by Andrew Woolford, Jeff Benvenuto, and Alexander Laban Hinton. Duke University Press, 2014, pp. 292–305.

Isaacs, Jenny R. and Ariel Otruba. "Guest Introduction: More-Than-Human Contact Zones." *Nature and Science*, vol. 2, no. 4, 2019, pp. 697–711.

Jeffers, Robinson. "Hurt Hawks." In *The Wild God of the World*. Stanford University Press, 2003.

Jurszo, Robert. "Dzik, czyli kozioł (ofiarny)." *Dzikie Życie*, vol. 2, Feb. 2019, p. 32.

Kanji, Azeezah. "Colonial Animality: Canadian Colonialism and the Human-Animal Relationship." *E-International Relations*, Jul. 3, 2017. https://www.e -ir.info/2017/07/03/.

Karz, Richard. *Indigenous Healing Psychology: Honoring the Wisdom of the First Peoples*. Healing Arts, 2017.

Katz, Cheryl. "Roadkill Rates Fall Dramatically As Lockdown Keeps Drivers at Home." *National Geographic*, June 26, 2020. https://www.nationalgeographic.com/animals/2020/06/decline-road-kill-pandemic-lockdown-traffic/.

Kimmerer, Robin Wall. *Braiding Sweetgrass: Indigenous Wisdom, Scientific Knowledge and the Teaching of Plants*. Milkweed Editions, 2013.

Ko, Aph and Syl Ko. *Aphro-ism: Essays on Pop Culture, Feminism, and Black Veganism from Two Sisters*. Lantern Publishing & Media, 2017.

Kohn, Eduardo. "Anthropology of Ontologies." *Annual Review of Anthropology*, Nov. 2015, vol. 44, no. 1, pp. 311–327. https://doi.org/10.1146/annurev-anthro-102214-014127.

Krugman, Paul. "Bernanke, Blower of Bubbles?" *The New York Times*, 9 May 2013. https://www.nytimes.com/2013/05/10/opinion/krugman-bernanke-blower-of-bubbles.html. Retrieved 03 January 2021.

Kuokkanen, Rauna. "The Logic of the Gift: Reclaiming Indigenous People's Philosophies." In *Re-Ethnicizing the Mind? Cultural Revival in Contemporary Thought*. Edited by Thorsten Botz-Bornstein. Rodopi, 2006, pp. 251–71.

Kymlicka, Will and Sue Donaldson. "Animal Rights and Aboriginal Rights." *Canadian Perspectives on Animals and the Law*. Edited by Peter Sankoff, Vaughan Black, Katie Sykes. Irving Law, 2015, pp. 159–186.

Kymlicka, Will and Sue Donaldson. *Zoopolis: A Political Theory of Animal Rights*. Oxford University Press, 2013.

Lannoo, Michael J. (ed.). *Status and Conservation of Midwestern Amphibians*. University of Iowa Press, 1998.

Lincoln, Kenneth. *Foreword to Eclipse*. Edited by Linda Hogan. University of California, 1983, pp. v–vii.

MacNeil, Jason. "Tanya Tagaq Shuts Down "Sealfie" Cyberbully With Police Help." *The Huffington Post Canada*, Dec. 6, 2012. *HuffPost*. https://www.huffingtonpost.ca/2014/06/12/tanya-tagaq-sealfie-cyberbully_n_5488324.html.

Maldonado-Torres, Nelson. "On the Coloniality of Being." *Cultural Studies*, vol. 21, nos. 2–3, 2007, pp. 240–270.

Malgorzata Poks. http://orcid.org/0000-0003-0055-935X

May, Jon D. "Osage Murders." *The Encyclopedia of Oklahoma History and Culture*. https://www.okhistory.org/publications/enc/entry.php?entry=OS005.

McAdams, Janet. "'Ways in the World': Formal Poetics in Linda Hogan's *Rounding the Human Corners*." *The Kenyon Review, New Series*, vol. 32, no. 1, Winter 2010, pp. 226–235.

Mendieta, Eduardo. "Interspecies Cosmopolitanism." In *Routledge Handbook of Cosmopolitanism*. Edited by Gerard Delanty, Routledge, 2012, pp. 276–287.

Mignolo, Walter D. "Delinking: The Rhetoric of Modernity, the Logic of Coloniality and the Grammar of De-coloniality." *Cultural Studies*, March/May 2007, vol. 21, nos. 2–3, pp. 449–514. http://www.tandf.co.uk/journals. https://doi.org/10.1080/09502380601162647.

Miranda, Deborah. "A Strong Woman Pursuing Her God: Linda Hogan's Power." *Sojourner: The Women's Forum*, vol. 26, no. 3, 2000.

Moore, Jason W. *Capitalism and the Web of Life: Ecology and the Accumulation of Capital*. Verso, 2015.

Morton, Timothy. *Humankind: Solidarity with Nonhuman People*. Verso, 2017.

Murray, John A. "Of Panther and People: An Interview with Linda Hogan." *Terrain.org: A Journal of the Built and Natural Environments*, vol. 5. Sept. 22, 1999. https://www.terrain.org/1999/interviews/linda-hogan/.

Musher, Andrea. "Showdown at Sorrow Cave: Bat Medicine and the Spirit of Resistance in *Mean Spirit*." *Studies in American Indian Literatures. Series 2*, vol. 6, no. 3. Fall 1994, pp. 23–36.

Nadasdy, Paul. "First Nations, Citizenship and Animals, or Why Northern Indigenous People Might Not Want to Live in Zoopolis." *Canadian Journal of Political Science / Revue Canadienne de science politique*, vol. 49, no. 1, 2016, pp. 1–20.

Nadasdy, Paul. "The Gift in the Animal: The Ontology of Hunting and Human-Animal Sociality." *American Ethnologist*, vol. 34, no. 1, 2007, pp. 25–43.

Nibert, David A. *Animal Oppression and Human Violence: Domesacration, Capitalism, and Global Conflict*. New York: Columbia University Press, 2013.

Oliver, Mary. *Thirst*. Bloodaxe Books, 2007.

Patterson, Charles. *Eternal Treblinka: Our Treatment of Animals and the Holocaust*. Lantern Books, 2002.

Peters, Jesse. "Everything the World Turns On: Inclusion and Exclusion in Linda Hogan's *Power*." *The American Indian Quarterly*, vol. 37, no. 1–2, winter/spring 2013, pp. 111–125. https://doi.org/10.1353/aiq.2013.0008

Plumwood, Val. *Environmental Culture: The Ecological Crisis of Reason*. Routledge, 2002.

Plumwood, Val. *Feminism and Mastery of Nature*. Routledge, 1993.

Plumwood, Val. "Prey to a Crocodile." *Aisling Magazine*, vol. 30, 2002. Web.

Plumwood, Val. *The Eye of the Crocodile*. Edited by Lorraine Shannon. Australian National University E Press, 2012.

Quijano, Anibal. "Coloniality of Power, Eurocentrism, and Latin America." Translated by Michael Ennis. *Nepantla: Views from South*, vol. 1, no. 3, 2000, pp. 533–580.

Ratnam, Maya. "Animals, Humans, and Forms of Life." *Engagement. A Blog Published by the Anthropology and Environment Society*, Sept. 22, 2015. https://aesengagement.wordpress.com/2015/09/22/animals-humans-and-forms-of-life/.

Regan, Erin. "'The Way Worlds Are Spoken': An Interview with Linda Hogan." *Superstition Review*, vol. 12, 2013. https://superstitionreview.asu.edu/issue12.

Reid, Andrea J., Lauren E. Eckert, John-Francis Lane, Nathan Young, Scott G. Hinch, Chris T. Darimont, Steven J. Cooke, Natalie C. Ban, Albert Marshall, "'Two-Eyed Seeing': An Indigenous Framework to Transform Fisheries Research and Management." *Fish and Fisheries*, vol. 22, no. 2, March 2021, pp. 243–261.

Rifkin, Jeremy. *Beyond Beef: The Rise and Fall of the Cattle Culture*. Plume, 1993.

Robinson, Margaret. "Indigenous Veganism: Feminist Natives Do Eat Tofu." *Earthling Liberation Collective*. Dec. 22, 2014. https://humanrightsareanimalrights.com/2014/12/22/margaret-robinson-indigenous-veganism-feminist-natives-do-eat-tofu/

Romero, Channette, *Activism and the American Novel: Religion and Resistance in Fiction by Women of Color*. University of Virginia Press, 2012.

Schöler, Bo. "A Heart Made out of Crickets: An Interview with Linda Hogan." *The Journal of Ethnic Studies*, vol. 16, no. 1, Spring 1988, pp. 107–117.

Seiler, Andreas and Jan Olof Helldin. "Mortality in Wildlife Due to Transportation." In *The Ecology of Transportation: Managing Mobility for the Environment*. Edited by John Davenport and Julia L. Davenport. Springer, 2006.

Sepie, Amba J. *Tracing the Motherline: Earth Elders, Decolonising Worldview, and Planetary Futurity*. Thesis Submitted in Fulfilment of the Requirements for the Degree of Doctor of Philosophy in Geography, Te Rāngai Pūtaiao, Te Whare Wānanga O Waitaha, Ōtautahi, Aotearoa, College of Science, University of Canterbury, Christchurch, New Zealand, 2018. www.researchgate.net.

Shaffner, Justin and Huon Wardle. "Introduction: Cosmopolitics as a Way of Thinking." *Cosmopolitics: The Collected Papers of the Open Anthropology Cooperative*, vol. 1, 2017, pp. 1–43.

Smallman, Shawn. *Dangerous Spirits: The Windigo in Myth and History*. Heritage House Publishing Co, 2015.

Soron, Dennis. "Road Kill: Commodity Fetishism and Structural Violence." *TOPIA Canadian Journal of Cultural Studies*, vol. 18, Sept. 2008, pp. 107–125.

"Sorrow." *Merriam-Webster.com Dictionary*, Merriam-Webster. https://www.merriam-webster.com/dictionary/sorrow. Accessed: 28 Apr. 2021.

Stein, Rachel, "An Ecology of Mind: A Conversation with Linda Hogan." *Interdisciplinary Studies in Literature and Environment*, vol. 6, no. 1, winter 1999, pp. 113–118.

Steinwand, Jonathan. "What the Whales Would Tell Us: Cetacean Communication in Novels by Witi Ihimaera, Linda Hogan, Zakes Mda, and Amitav Ghosh." In *Postcolonial Ecologies: Literatures of the Environment*. Edited by Elizabeth Deloughrey and George Handley. Oxford University Press, 2011, pp. 128–199.

Stengers, Isabelle. "The Cosmopolitical Proposal." In *Making Things Public: Atmospheres of Democracy*. Edited by Bruno Latour. The MIT Press, 2005, pp. 993–1003.

Straß-Senol, Hanna. "Weather Phenomena in Linda Hogan's *People of the Whale*." *REAL. Yearbook of Research in English and American Literature*, vol. 33, no. 1, Dec. 2017, pp. 273–289.

Tănăsescu, Mihnea. *Ecocene Politics*. Open Book Publishers, 2022.

Taschereau Mamers, Danielle. "Human-Bison Relations as Sites of Settler Colonial Violence and Decolonial Resurgence." *Humanimalia: A Journal of Human-Animal Interface Studies*, vol. 10, no. 2, 2019, pp. 10–41.

Taylor, Chloë. "Respect for the (Animal) Dead." In *Animal Death*. Edited by Jay Johnston and Fiona Probyn-Rapsey. Sydney University Press, 2013, pp. 85–102.

Taylor, Chloë and Kelly Struthers Montford. "Call for Papers for Decolonizing Critical Animal Studies Cripping Critical Animal Studies Conference." University of Alberta. https://www.ualberta.ca/womens-gender-studies/about-us/news/2015/november/callforpapersfordecolonizingcriticalanimalstudiescrippingcriticalanimalstudiesconference.html.

"The Sugarcane Saga." The Florida Historical Society. Myfloridahisory.org. https://myfloridahistory.org/webextras/webextras/8.

The World Commission on Environment and Development. *Our Common Future.* Oxford University Press, 1987.

Todd, Zoe. "An Indigenous Feminist's Take on the Ontological Turn: "Ontology" Is Just Another Word For Colonialism." *Journal of Historical Sociology*, vol. 29, no. 1, 2016, pp. 4–22.

Viveiros de Castro, Eduardo. *Cannibal Metaphysics.* Univocal Publishing, 2014.

Wadiwel, Dinesh. *The War Against Animals.* Brill, 2015.

Wallerstein, Immanuel. *The Modern World-System I: Capitalist Agriculture and the Origins of the European World-Economy in the Sixteenth Century.* Academic Press, 1974.

Warrior, Robert Allen. "Review Essay of *The Deaths of Sybil Bolton.*" *Wicazo Sa Review*, vol. 11, no. 1, spring 1995, p. 52.

White, Lynn Townsend "The Historical Roots of Our Ecological Crisis." *Science*, vol. 155, no. 3767, 10 March 1967, pp. 1203–1207.

Whyte, Kyle Powys. "On the Role of Traditional Ecological Knowledge as a Collaborative Concept: A Philosophical Study." *Ecological Processes*, vol. 2, no. 7, 2013, pp. 2–7.

Whyte, Kyle Powys. "Is it Colonial Déjà Vu? Indigenous Peoples and Climate Injustice." In *Humanities for the Environment: Integrating Knowledges, Forging New Constellations of Practice.* Edited by J. Adamson, M. Davis. Earthscan Publications, 2017, pp. 88–104.

Willet, Cynthia. *Interspecies Ethics.* Columbia University Press, 2014.

Wolf, Cary. "'In the Shadow of Wittgenstein's Lion' Language, Ethics, and the Question of the Animal." In *Zootologies: The Question of the Animal.* Edited by Carry Wolf. Minnesota University Press, 2003, pp. 1–57.

Wynter, Sylvia. "Unsettling the Coloniality of Being/Power/Truth/Freedom: Towards the Human, after Man, Its Overrepresentation: An Argument." *The New Centennial Review*, vol. 3. no. 3, 2003, pp. 257–337.

Zeder, Melinda A. "Pathways to Animal Domestication." In *Biodiversity in Agriculture: Domestication, Evolution, and Sustainability.* Edited by Robert L. Bettinger, Stephen B. Brush, Ardeshir B Damania, Thomas R. Famula, Paul Gepts, Partick E. McGuire, Calvin O. Qualset. Cambridge University Press, 2012, pp. 227–252.

Index

Note: Page numbers in *italics* indicate figures, **bold** indicate tables in the text

Aboriginal knowledge 58
Abraham, D. 97, 100
Abram, D., *The Spell of the Sensuous* 89–90
activism 23, 28, 48, 127, 143; animal rights 3, 9, 106; literary 29, 181, 185; in *Power* 165–166; protest 150, 153
Adams, C. J. 3
Adamson, J. 21, 172, 181–182
Adorno, T. 130
advocacy 13
African swine fever 2
Agamben, G. 4
agency 183
Akwasasne Notes 46
Alaimo, S. 73
"alchemy in reverse" 145
Alcoff, L. M. 51
anatomy 87
ancestral world 40–41
animal/s 24; activism 9; automobile collisions 52–54; bats 132–134; bear 146–148; beaver 144–145, 152–153; birds 61–62; birth 44; branding 55–56; buffalo 69–70, 114–117; camels 122–123; chambered nautilus 82–83; commodification 56; contact zones 172; coyote 42–43, 51–52; crayfish 50–51; crows 75–76; culling 2; deer 77, 99; dogs 178–179; domestication 68–69; eagles 130–131; elk 59–61; farm 81; fish 149–150; Florida panther 156–157, 165, 167; fox 93–94; frogs 44–46, 149; 'game' 140; genocide 3; horses 95–97, 119–120, 135–137;

"hyperseparation" 58; intelligence 25; language 77; lessons 63; mice 62; moose 76; mountain lion 94, 115; naming 78; octopus 71, 174; pets 118–119, 178; porcupine 52–54; puma 159; rights 10, 106, 165; rights activism 3; science 24–25; shapeshifting 99–100; suffering 6; training 50–51; turkey 43–44; turtles 38–41, 91–92, 105; welfare 4; wolverine 151–153; wolves 68, 104, 117; women's bond with 25–26; *see also* human; insects; whales and whaling
animism: Hogan on 21; in *Mean Spirit* 138; new 19–20
ankle bones 86
Anthropocene 8, 21, 22, 28, 44, 49, 70, 94, 183
anthropocentrism 14–15
anthropology 20; ontological turn 8; radical participation 166
aquatic intelligence 66
automobile collisions 52–54; Florida panther 165
avian flu 2
Aztec 55

bats 132–134
Battle of Little Big Horn 115
bear 71–72; in *Solar Storms* 146–148
Bear Creek 114
beaver 144–145, 152–153
bees 134–135
"beingness" 184
Belcourt, B.-R., "Animal Bodies, Colonial Subjects" 9

Bell, B. L. 30
"belonging" 95
Best, S. 3
Bible, The 62, 78–79, 103, 141, 151
Billy, J. 157
biology 46; marine 171
bioluminescence 88–89
biopolitics, concentration camps 5
biopower 3, 4, 7
biosecurity 2
birds 61–62; crows 62–63; eagles
    130–131; golden eagle 113–114;
    heron 92–93, 149; sandhill cranes
    107–108
birth 44, 182
Bloomsbury Review, The 156
boar, culling 2
Bohm, D. 18, 153
Bradshaw, G. 157, 159; *Carnivore
    Minds* 158, 167; *Elephants on the
    Edge* 158
branding 55–56
"breaking" 61–62
Brígido-Corachán, A. 144
buffalo 69–70, 114–117
Burkhart, B. 146; *Indigenizing
    Philosophy through the Land* 15–17,
    27, 129
Burnam, H. 12–13
butterflies 106–107

Cadena, M., *Ecologies of Practice
    Across Andean Worlds* 8
Cajete, G. 17; "Philosophy of Native
    Science" 18
camels 122–123
cane sugar 156–157
capitalism 23, 53, 81, 108, 116; cattle
    129
Capitalocene 81–82
care 3, 55, 183; of livestock 4
carnivores 158–159, 164; *see also*
    predators and predation
Carson, R., *Silent Spring* 25–26
Cartesian dualism 19, 56
catastrophe, Deepwater Horizon oil
    spill 104–105
cattle 80–81, 128; breeding 129–130;
    capitalism 129
caves 82
ceasefire 6–7
cetacean turn 172

chaos theory 18–19
chattel slavery 56
Chicaza 22
Chickasaw 38, 78, 85, 104; emergency
    myth 109; Pony 96
Christianity 108, 138, 141
climate change 21
Cody, B. 114, 116
Coetzee, J. M., *The Lives of Animals*
    106
Collins, Y., *The Relationship Between
    the Indigenous Peoples of the
    Americas and the Horse* 96
colonialism 3–4, 11, 23, 39, 46,
    50–51, 75, 98, 111–112, 115–116;
    cattle 80–81; chattel slavery 56–57;
    resistance 75, 131–133, 147; Trail of
    Tears 38, 81, 96, 118–119
Colorado 85, 92, 101
commercial fishing 70–71
commodification 56; *see also*
    exploitation
communication 57
compassion 106, 147, 153,
    177–178
Concentrated Animal Feeding
    Operations (CAFOs) 4–5
concentration camp 4–5
conceptual tools 8
confinement 4
consciousness 8, 19
consumerism 22–23, 116
contact zones 172
Cooper, R. L., "Woman Chasing Her
    God" 163–164
cosmology 18, 24; indigenous 58–59
cosmopolitanism 7; interspecies 1
cosmopolitics 7–8
counter-sovereignty 12
Cousteau, J. 171
COVID-19 pandemic 102
coyote 42–43, 51–52
crayfish 50
creation 88, 151; narratives 24
creative writing 48
Cree 31
critical theory 6
crossings 90–91, 99–100
crows 62–63, 75–76
Crutzen, P. J. 94
culling 2, 158; boar 2; *see also* killing
Custer, G. A. 115

Dakota 96
dance 99, 109
darkness 49; night 55
death 43, 44, 46, 55, 58, 62, 116;
mourning 54, 105, 120–121;
predation 54–55
Deckha, M. 184
decolonial theory 3, 6, 8, 11, 12, 31,
46, 108, 111–112, 151, 164, 169;
and animal studies 8–9; interspecies
relations 9; return of stolen land 8;
see also Mean Spirit
"Decolonizing Animals" 9
Deep Ecology 15
deep structure 98–99
Deepwater Horizon oil spill 104–105
deer 77, 99
Derrida, J. 3
desire 68
differentiation 5, 15, 130
dogs 178–179
domestication of animals 68–69
Donaldson, S., *Zoopolis* 5–6
dreams and dreaming 38–39, 79–80,
161–162, 168–169; hunting and
167; in *Solar Storms* 149; waking up
40–41
Dreese, D. 83; "The Terrestrial and
Aquatic Intelligence of Linda
Hogan" 66

eagles 130–131
Eastman, C. 38
Ecocene 183
ecofeminism 55–57, 63–64, 83; *The
Book of Medicines* 66–67
ecological animalism 28, 57–58
economic bubble 22
economic/s: bubble 22; "Windigo" 23
ecoposthumanities 15
ecosystem 14
elephant society 25
Elgezeery, G. M. 75
elk 61
Elzanowski, A. 2
embryology 74
emergence 109
Emergence Magazine 157
empathy 25, 106
endangered species 31, 156, 158–159
England, welfare movement 3
environmental justice 21

epistemology 5
ethics 15, 121–122, 146; Indigenous
16; value-based 16
ethno-science 17–18
Everglades 156–157
evil 114
evolution 45, 74, 86, 87, 103, 149;
whales 74–75
experience 18, 97
exploitation 10, 14, 53, 56, 71, 103;
nature 17
extermination: buffalo 69–70, 114,
116; coyote 42–43; crows 63;
wolves 104

farm animals 81, 128–129; *see also*
livestock
fear 72
Feinstein, K. 145
feminism, eco 55–57, 63–64, 83
fibromyalgia 48
fish/ing 39–41, 149–151; commercial
70–71
Fix, A. 12–13
Florida panther 156–157, 165, 167;
see also Power
food: and hunger 67–68; killing for
44, 54
forgiveness 62
Fossey, D. 25
Foucault, M. 3, 4, 6; *see also*
biopower; governmentality; pastoral
power
fox 93–94
Frankfurt School 6
Friendly Whale Syndrome 89–90
frogs 44–46, 149
From the Center of Tradition 27
fur trade 144–146, 148–149

Galdikas, B. 25
'game' 140
Gandhi, L. 3–4
generosity 112–113
genocide, animal 3
Geroux, R. 12
global warming 50
god 111
golden eagle 113–114
good life 7
good shepherd 4
Goodall, J. 25

governmentality 3–4
gray whale 171; *see also* whales and whaling
Great Plains 115, 117
grief 120–121; *see also* mourning
Gulag Archipelago 5
Gutteriez, R. 12–13

Hallowell, I. 20
Handbook of Contemporary Animism, The 19–21
Haraway, D., *When Species Meet* 172
Harrison, S. 30
Harvey, G. 19–21
healing 66–67, 75, 95–96, 113, 114, 121, 138–139, 149, 177; bat medicine 132–134; neuropsychology 157–158; remedies 114–115
Heidegger, M. 109
Henderson, C., *The Aboriginal North American Horse* 95–96
heron 149
Hogan, L. 23, 25, 26, 157, 167, 184; "Affinity: Mustang" 95–98; "After Silence: Return" 112; "Allegiance: The Sandhill Cranes" 107–108; "Alone" 90–91; "Anatomy" 87; on animism 21; "Bear" 71–72; "Bear Fat" 68; *The Book of Medicines* 28, 66–68, 77, 83, 86; "The Buffalo Again" 116; "Buffalo Road: Leaving South Dakota" 115; "Burying the Horse" 119–120; "Call" 100; *Calling Myself Home* 37–39, 46; "Chambered Nautilus" 82–83; "Coyote" 42–43; "Crayfish" 50–51; "Crossings" 73–74; "Crow Law" 75–76; *Dark. Sweet* 29, 102; "Deer Dance" 99; "The Deer Mothers" 109; *Dwellings* 24; *Dwellings: A Spiritual History of the Living World* 66, 113; "Eagle Feather Prayer" 113–114; *Eclipse* 48–50; "Elk Song" 57–60; "Enigma" 87; "The Eyes of Animals" 111; "Fawn" 122; "Finding Beads" 46; "First Language: Sandhill Cranes" 108; "Gamble" 62–63; "Harvesters of Night and Water" 70–71; "The Heron" 92–93; *A History of Kindness* 29, 102, 112–114; "The History of Red" 67–68; *Indios* 102; "Isn't It Love" 118; "Justice" 105; on language 37; "Maps" 77–79; *Mean Spirit* 66, 127; *see also Mean Spirit*; "Mercy, the Word" 106; *Mercy Liars* 102; "Milk" 81; "Mountain Lion" 72–73; "Naming the Animals" 77; "A Need for Happiness" 116–117; "Not So Very Long Ago" 104; "The Other Side" 54–55; *People of the Whale* 85; *see also People of the Whale*; "Pillow" 61; "Porcupine on the Road to the River" 52–54; *Power* 66; *see also Power*; "The Radiant" 88–89; *The Radiant Lives of Animals* 13, 102; "re-minding" 13–14; "Return:Buffalo" 69–70; "The Ritual Life of Animals" 79–80; "The River Calls Them" 44–46; *Rounding the Human Corners* 28, 85, 86; "Saint Coyote" 50–52; *Savings* 48, 57; "Season of Butterflies" 106–107; *Seeing through the Sun* 48, 52, 55; *Sightings* 90; *Sightings: The Gray Whales' Mysterious Journey* 74, 171; *Solar Storms* 66; *see also Solar Storms*; "Song for the Turtles of the Gulf" 105; "Territory of the Night" 55–57; "Thanksgiving" 43–44; "This America" 109–111; "Those Who Thunder" 60–61; "Tracking" 82; "Transformations: Winter Count" 108–109; "Turtle Watchers" 91–92; "Vally of the Horses" 104; "We Have Walked Down Past" 114–115; "Whales Rising" 89; *What Animals Teach Us about Humanity* 158; "Who Will Speak" 49–50; "Winter Solstice" 94–95; *The Woman Who Watches Over the World* 66, 70–71, 96
"homing" 38
horses 95, 119–120; Chickasaw Pony 96–97; Indigenous peoples' relationship with 97–98; in *Mean Spirit* 135–137
hozho 21–22
Huang, H. 172
Huang, P., *Linda Hogan and Comtemporary Taiwanese Writers: An Ecocritical Study of Indigeneities and Environment* 27

human: -animal relations 28, 50,
    86, 148, 172, 184–185; becoming
    167–168; dominance 7; loneliness
    91; nature 83; sovereignty 5; sub- 11
human exceptionalism 15, 58
Humanimalia, "Decolonizing Animal
    Studies" 12
humanities, decolonial turn 8
hunger 67–68, 71, 80–81, 83, 100
hunting 31, 76, 82, 146, 166, 185–
    186; dreaming and 167; eagles
    130–131; frogs 45; 'game' 140;
    -gathering communities 7, 10;
    recreational 42; survival 10–11;
    traps 42–43; whales 31, 85, 171; *see
    also Power*; predators and predation
Husserl, E. 18
"hyperseparation" 56, 58

ignorance 51, 94
inclusion 11, 57
Indigeneity 75
Indigenous ethics 16–17
Indigenous knowledge 7, 12, 13,
    17–18, 157, 183; Climate Change
    Studies 21; hunting 10; medicine
    wheel 66–67; relationality 118–119;
    Traditional Ecological Knowledge
    (TEK) 12–15
Indigenous peoples 60, 63, 97, 172;
    cosmology 58–59; deep structure
    98–99; dreams and dreamers 38–39,
    80; generosity 112–113; and horses
    97–98; rights 184; women 40–41
*Inner Journeys: Views from Native
    Traditions, The* 85
insects 87–88; bees 134–135;
    butterflies 106–107; mosquitoes
    151; nymphs 102–103
instinct 116; fear 72, 83; hunger
    67–68, 71, 80–81, 83; love 73–74,
    83, 118
instrumental value 15–16
intelligence: aquatic 66; crows 63
intersectionality 3
interspecies cosmopolitanism 1
*Intimate Nature: The Bond Between
    Women and Animals* 25, 66
intrinsic value 15
Inuit 31
Iroquois 49
Isaacs, J. 172

joy 85, 86
justice 58–59; environmental 21;
    interspecies 184

Kanji, A. 8
killing 42, 156; for food 44, 54;
    sacrifice 163; in war 105
Kimmerer, R. W., *Braiding Sweetgrass:
    Indigenous Wisdom, Scientific
    Knowledge and the Teaching of
    Plants* 17, 23
kindness 112
kinship 16–17, 105, 140–141, 161,
    169, 183
knowledge 13; Aboriginal 58; and
    ignorance 51; Native 17–19;
    traditional 17–18; Traditional
    Ecological 12–13, 144; *see also*
    Indigenous knowledge
Ko, S. 11
Kohn, E.: "Anthropology of
    Ontologies" 8; *How Forests Think:
    Toward an Anthropology Beyond
    the Human* 8
Kymlicka, W., *Zoopolis* 5–6

Lakota 115, 116
land improvement 129
language/s 49–50, 56–57, 100, 169;
    animal 77; deep structure 98–99;
    Hogan on 37
lifeworld 18
light and darkness 48–49, 52,
    54, 55, 85–86, 91, 111;
    bioluminescence 88–89; in *Solar
    Storms* 153
liminality 172
Lincoln, K. 38; on *Eclipse* 48, 49
literary activism 29, 181, 185
livestock: branding 55–56; care of 4;
    cattle 80–81, 128
Locke, J. 129
loneliness 91
Lookout Mountain 114
love 73–74, 110, 118
Lyons, O. 49

mad cow disease 2
Makah 31, 85, 171
Maldonado-Torres, N. 11, 112
Mamers, D. T., "Human-Bison
    Relations as Sites of Settler

Colonial Violence and Decolonial Resurgence" 117
manta ray 89
Maryland 52
McAdams, J. 85, 86
Mean Spirit 127–129, 135, 141; eagle hunt 130–131; Father Dunne 138–139; horses 135–137; John Stink 139–140; sorrow 130; Sorrow Cave 132–134
medicine: bat 132–134; wheel 66–67; *see also* healing
memories 118
Mendieta, E. 1
mercy 106
metaphor 54
Metzger, D. 25
mice 62
Miles, N. A. 115
"Mississippi Bubble" 22
Montford, K. S. 9
Moore, J. W., *Capitalism and the Web of Life* 81–82
moose 76
morality 146, 185; Indigenous 16–17
mosquitoes 151
Moss, C. 25
"most different difference" 2
mountain lion 72–73, 94, 115
mourning 54, 105, 120–121, 148–149, 153
multispecies poetics 171–172
Murray, J. 156

Nadasdy, P. 166; "First Nations, Citizenship and Animals, or Why Northern Indigenous People Might Not Want to Live in Zoopolis" 9
names and naming 77, 79, 83; animals 78
National Geographic 74
Native American Renaissance 38
Native knowledge 17–19
nature 56, 86, 129; exploitation 17; human 83
Nature and Science 172
negative rights 5
neuropsychology 157–158
new animism 19–21
Nibert, D. 128
night 55
nymphs 102–103

oceans 71, 88, 90; commercial fishing 70–71; Deepwater Horizon oil spill 104–105; marine life 88–89; sea turtles 91–92; *see also* whales and whaling
octopus 71, 174
Oglala Lakota Nation 96
Ohiyesa 38
Ojibwe 20
Oklahoma 38, 41–43, 49; coyote 42–43; frogs 44–46
Oliver, M. 88
ontology 8
Open Anthropology Cooperative 7–8
Osage 31
'Other' 3, 56, 67, 101
other-than-human beings 10, 20
Otruba, A. 172
Our Common Future 14

Paleolithic era 7
pastoral power 4
Patterson, C., *Eternal Treblinka* 53
Payne, K. 25
People of the Whale 171, 174–182; setting 172–173
perception 39, 89–90, 103
persecution-protection duality *see* killing
pesticide 62
Peters, J. 160
Peterson, B. 25, 85, 89; *Sightings: The Gray Whales' Mysterious Journey* 74, 171
pets 118–119; dogs 178
phenomenology 18
Pike, Z. 140
Pledge of Allegiance 107–108
Plumwood, V. 57–58; *Feminism and the Mastery of Nature* 56; "The Wisdom of the Balanced Rock: The Parallel Universe and the Prey" 58
poetry 28, 98
Poland, wild boar culling 2
politics 3, 7; bio 5; cosmo 7–8
pollution 44, 156
porcupine 52–54
Potawatomi Nation 17, 21
power 6, 12; bio 3, 4; pastoral 4; sovereign 4; white 9
Power 156–157, 160–162, 168–169; activism in 165–166; decolonial reading of 164

Pratt, L. 172
predators and predation 45, 54–55,
    57–58, 68, 79, 100, 158, 164, 185–
    186; bear 71–72; control programs
    14, 42; coyote 42–43; crows 76;
    mountain lion 72–73; puma 159; *see
    also* Florida panther
"preventive culling" 2
private property 129
progress 67
property 129; chattel slavery 56;
    women as 56
protest 150, 153, 175
proto-amphibians 44–45
psychology: neuro 157–158;
    transspecies 157, 166
Pueblo 83
puma 159
punyu 21–22

quantum theory 18–19

racism 11
radical participation 166
Ratnam, M. 167
reciprocity 59, 123, 185; in *People
    of the Whale* 175–176; perceptual
    89–90; in *Solar Storms* 146
recreational hunting 42
Reign of Terror 31
relationality 118–119
remedies 114–115
"re-minding" 13–14
resistance 62, 128, 129, 144, 152; anti-
    colonial 75, 131–133, 147
"re-story-ation" 17, 22–23; *see also*
    storytelling
Rexroth, K. 37
Rifkin, J. 129
right/s 6; animal 10, 106, 165;
    Indigenous peoples 184; negative 5
ritual 10, 53, 68, 76, 79–80, 148–149,
    173–174; mourning 120–121, 153
roadkill 52–54
Robinson, M. M. 185
Romero, C., *Activism and the
    American Novel* 29

sacrifice 162, 163, 165; in *People of
    the Whale* 175–177
sandhill cranes 107–108
Saussure, F. 98–99

science 18, 19; animal 24–25;
    ethno- 17–18; Native 18; neuro
    159; neuropsychology 157–158;
    transspecies psychology 157, 166
sea turtles 91–92
Sedna 70–71
Seneca 14
sensuous world 99–100
Sepie, A. J. 161
settler colonialism 9, 107–108, 116,
    149; land improvement 129
Shaffner, J. 7–8
shapeshifting 51, 99–101, 153, 160, 162,
    174, 176, 179–180; in *Power* 165
Sixth Extinction 103
skin 76–77
sleep 79; waking up 40–41; *see also*
    dreams and dreaming
Smallman, S. 23
Society for the Prevention of Cruelty to
    Animals 3
Solar Storms 143, 149–152; Agnes
    and the bear 146–147; "alchemy in
    reverse" 145–146; 'becoming bear'
    motif 148; light and darkness 153;
    Traditional Ecological Knowledge
    (TEK) 144
solidarity 7
Soron, D. 53
sorrow 130; *see also* mourning
Southern Review of Books 102
sovereign/ty 145; counter- 12; human
    5; power 4; tribal 129
speciesism 11
spirits 19–20, 138, 164
Spivak, G. 9
Steinwand, J., "What the Whales
    Would Tell Us: Cetecean
    Communications in Novels by Witi
    Ihimaera, Linda Hogan, Zakes Mda,
    and Amitav Ghosh" 172
Stoermer, E. F. 94
storytelling 12, 17, 22, 28, 30
Straß-Senol, H. 175
suffering 6, 52–54, 106, 130, 150
Superstition Review 127
"supremacy" 93
survival hunting 10–11
sustainability 21

Tagaq, T. 10–11
Tanasescu, M., *Ecocene Politics* 183

tatanka 7
Taylor, C. 9, 120
Taylor, E., *Primitive Culture* 19–20
Thanksgiving 43–44, 46–47
theory of evolution *see* evolution
Thompson, A. 171
tish 21–22
tradition 21
Traditional Ecological Knowledge
   (TEK) 12–15; in *Solar Storms* 144
traditional knowledge 17–18
traditional societies 12; treaties 10
Trail of Tears 38, 81, 96, 118–119
training animals 50–51
transformation 109
transspecies psychology 157, 166
traps and trapping 42–43, 148
treaty/ies 10, 23, 145, 151, 185
trees 41
tribal nations 14
truce 6–7
trust 51
truth 6, 19, 112, 161
turkey 43–44
Turtle Island 40, 59, 96, 184
turtles 38–41, 105; sea 91–92
"two-eyed seeing" 19

unconscious 79
United Kingdom, mad cow disease 2
United Nations: Earth Summit 14; *Our Common Future* 14
United States 109–111; American
   Indian Religious Freedom Act 41;
   Endangered Species Act 85, 157,
   158, 163; Great Plains 115, 117;
   Indian Children Welfare Act 48;
   Pledge of Allegiance 107–108
Universal Declaration of Human
   Rights 184

University of Colorado 48
University of Minnesota 48

value/s: instrumental 15–16; intrinsic
   15–16
veganarchists 3
violence 3, 4, 6, 11, 50, 61–62, 64,
   71, 72, 83, 110, 115, 141–142,
   178–179; automobile collisions
   52–54; *see also* colonialism; hunting;
   war
Viveiros de Castro, E. 8

Wadiwel, D. 4–6; *The War Against Animals* 3
war 3, 6, 67, 88; ceasefire 6–7; killing
   105; "the oldest" 76–77; in *People of the Whale* 179–180; truce 6–7
Wardle 7–8
wasps 87–88
welfare 4, 7; animal 4, 5;
   movement 3
whales and whaling 31, 85, 89–91,
   173; fetal development 74–75;
   hunting 171; *see also People of the Whale*
White, L. 103
Whyte, K., *Humanities for the Environment* 21
wildness 67, 78, 79, 153
Willett, C., *Interspecies Ethics* 7
Windigo 23, 83, 116
wolverine 151–153
wolves 68, 76, 104, 117
women 40–41, 48, 70–71; bond with
   animals 25–26; as property 56;
   see also ecofeminism

zoopolis 9
Zyklon B 62

For Product Safety Concerns and Information please contact our EU
representative GPSR@taylorandfrancis.com
Taylor & Francis Verlag GmbH, Kaufingerstraße 24, 80331 München, Germany

www.ingramcontent.com/pod-product-compliance
Lightning Source LLC
Chambersburg PA
CBHW071109100726
47908CB00008B/2318